Robert Louis Stevenson (13 November 1850 – 3 December 1894) was a Scottish novelist and travel writer, most noted for Treasure Island, Kidnapped, Strange Case of Dr Jekyll and Mr Hyde, and A Child's Garden of Verses. Born and educated in Edinburgh, Stevenson suffered from serious bronchial trouble for much of his life, but continued to write prolifically and travel widely, in defiance of his poor health. As a young man, he mixed in London literary circles, receiving encouragement from Andrew Lang, Edmund Gosse, Leslie Stephen and W. E. Henley, the last of whom may have provided the model for Long John Silver in Treasure Island. His travels took him to France, America and Australia, before he finally settled in Samoa, where he died. A celebrity in his lifetime, Stevenson attracted a more negative critical response for much of the 20th century, though his reputation has been largely restored. He is currently ranked as the 26th most translated author in the world.(Source: Wikipedia)

Literary works:
The Hair Trunk or The Ideal Commonwealth (1877)
Unfinished and unpublished.
Treasure Island (1883)
Prince Otto (1885)
Strange Case of Dr Jekyll and Mr Hyde (1886),
Kidnapped (1886)
The Black Arrow: A Tale of the Two Roses (1888)
The Master of Ballantrae: A Winter's Tale (1889),
The Wrong Box (1889)
The Wrecker (1892); co-written with Lloyd Osbourne.
Catriona (1893)
The Ebb-Tide (1894); co-written with Lloyd Osbourne.
Weir of Hermiston (1896)

THRONE CLASSICS

LAY MORALS
AND OTHER PAPERS
&
THE WEIR OF
HERMISTON
Robert Louis Stevenson

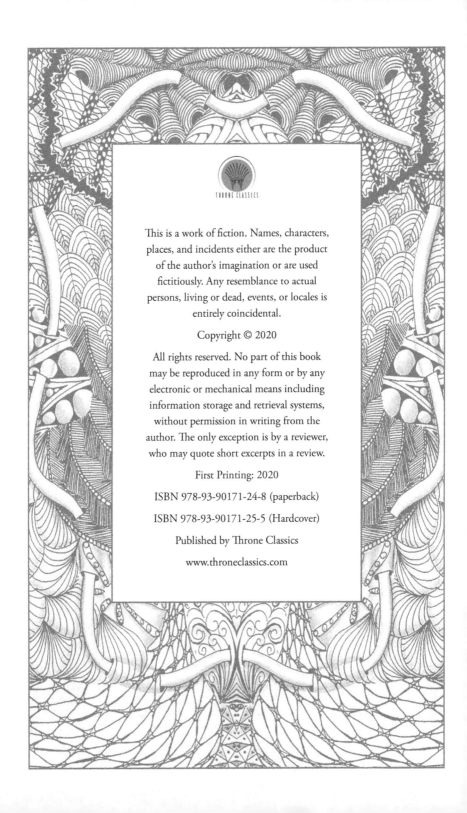

First Printing: 2020

ISBN 978-93-90171-24-8 (paperback)

ISBN 978-93-90171-25-5 (Hardcover)

Published by Throne Classics

www.throneclassics.com

Contents

LAY MORALS
AND OTHER PAPERS
&
THE WEIR OF
HERMISTON

LAY MORALS, AND OTHER PAPERS

PREFACE

BY MRS. ROBERT LOUIS STEVENSON [0]

In our long voyage on the yacht Casco, we visited many islands; I believe on every one we found the scourge of leprosy. In the Marquesas there was a regular leper settlement, though the persons living there seemed free to wander where they wished, fishing on the beach, or visiting friends in the villages. I remember one afternoon, at Anaho, when my husband and I, tired after a long quest for shells, sat down on the sand to rest awhile, a native man stepped out from under some cocoanut trees, regarding us hesitatingly as though fearful of intruding. My husband waved an invitation to the stranger to join us, offering his cigarette to the man in the island fashion. The cigarette was accepted and, after a puff or two, courteously passed back again according to native etiquette. The hand that held it was the maimed hand of a leper. To my consternation my husband took the cigarette and smoked it out. Afterwards when we were alone and I spoke of my horror he said, 'I could not mortify the man. And if you think I liked doing it—that was another reason; because I didn't want to.'

Another day, while we were still anchored in Anaho Bay, a messenger from round a distant headland came in a whale-boat with an urgent request that we go to see a young white girl who was ill with some mysterious malady. We had supposed that, with the beach-comber 'Charley the red,' we were the only white people on our side of the island. Though there was much wind that day and the sea ran high, we started at once, impelled partly by curiosity and partly by the pathetic nature of the message. Fortunately we took our luncheon with us, eating it on the beach before we went up to the house where the sick girl lay. Our hostess, the girl's mother, met us with regrets that we had already lunched, saying, 'I have a most excellent cook; here he is, now.' She turned, as she spoke, to an elderly Chinaman who was plainly in an advanced stage of leprosy. When the man was gone, my husband asked if she had no fear of contagion. 'I don't believe in contagion,' was her reply. But there was little doubt as to what ailed her daughter. She was certainly suffering from leprosy. We could only advise that the girl be taken to the French post at Santa Maria Bay where there was a doctor.

On our return to the Casco we confessed to each other with what alarm and repugnance we touched the miserable girl. We talked long that evening of Father Damien, his sublime heroism, and his martyrdom which was already nearing its sad end. Beyond all noble qualities my husband placed courage. The more he saw of leprosy, and he saw much in the islands, the higher rose his admiration for the simple priest of Molokai. 'I must see Molokai,' he said many times. 'I must somehow manage to see Molokai.'

In January 1889, we arrived in Honolulu, settling in a pleasant cottage by the sea to rest until we were ready to return to England. The Casco we sent back to San Francisco with the captain. But the knowledge that every few days some vessel was leaving Honolulu to cruise among islands we had not seen, and now should never see, was more than we could bear. First we engaged passage on a missionary ship, but changed our minds—my husband would not be allowed to smoke on board, for one reason—and chartered the trading schooner Equator. This was thought too rough a voyage for my mother-in-law, as indeed it would have been; so she was sent, somewhat protesting, back to Scotland.

My husband was still intent on seeing Molokai. After the waste of much time and red tape, he finally received an official permission to visit the leper settlement. It did not occur to him it would be necessary to get a separate official permission to leave Molokai; hence he was nearly left behind when the vessel sailed out. He only saved himself by a prodigious leap which landed him on board the boat, whence nothing but force could dislodge him. By the doctor's orders he took gloves to wear as a precautionary measure against contagion, but they were never worn. At first he avoided shaking hands, but when he played croquet with the young leper girls he would not listen to the Mother Superior's warning that he must wear gloves. He thought it might remind them of their condition. 'What will you do if you find you have contracted leprosy?' I asked. 'Do?' he replied; 'why, you and I would spend the rest of our lives in Molokai and become humble followers of Father Damien.' As Mr. Balfour says in the Life of Stevenson, he was as stern with his family as he was with himself, and as exacting.

He talked very little to us of the tragedy of Molokai, though I could see it lay heavy on his spirits; but of the great work begun by Father Damien and carried on by his successors he spoke fully. He had followed the life of the priest like a detective until there seemed nothing more to learn. Mother Mary Ann, the Mother Superior, he could never mention without deep emotion. One of the first things he did on his return to Honolulu was to send her a grand piano for the use of her girls—the girls with whom he had played croquet. He also sent toys, sewing materials, small tools for the younger children, and other things that I have forgotten. After his death a letter was found among his papers, of which I have only the last few lines. 'I cannot suppose you remember me, but I won't forget you, nor God won't forget you for your kindness to the blind white leper at Molokai.'

During my husband's absence I had made every preparation for our voyage on the Equator, so but little time was lost before we found ourselves on board, our sails set for the south. The Equator, which had easily lived through the great Samoan hurricane, made no such phenomenal runs as the Casco, but we could trust her, and she had no 'tricks and ways' that we did not understand. We liked the sailors, we loved the ship and her captain, so it was with heart-felt regret we said farewell in the harbour of Apia after a long and perfect cruise.

After reading the letters that awaited us in Apia, we looked over the newspapers. Our indignation may be imagined when we read in one item that, owing to the publication of a letter by a well-known Honolulu missionary, depicting Father Damien as a dirty old peasant who had contracted leprosy through his immoral habits, the project to erect a monument to his memory would be abandoned. 'I'll not believe it,' said my husband, 'unless I see it with my own eyes; for it is too damnable for belief!'

But see it he did, in spite of his incredulity, for in Sydney, a month or two later, the very journal containing the letter condemnatory of Father Damien was among the first we chanced to open. I shall never forget my husband's ferocity of indignation, his leaping stride as he paced the room holding the offending paper at arm's-length before his eyes that burned and sparkled with a peculiar flashing light. His cousin Mr. Balfour, in his Life of Robert Louis Stevenson, says: 'his eyes . . . when he was moved to anger or any fierce emotion seemed literally to blaze and glow with a burning light.' In another moment he disappeared through the doorway, and I could hear him, in his own room, pulling his chair to the table, and the sound of his inkstand being dragged towards him.

That afternoon he called us together—my son, my daughter, and myself—saying that he had something serious to lay before us. He went over the circumstances succinctly, and then we three had the incomparable experience of hearing its author read aloud the defence of Father Damien while it was still red-hot from his indignant soul.

As we sat, dazed and overcome by emotion, he pointed out to us that the subject-matter was libellous in the highest degree, and the publication of the article might cause the loss of his entire substance. Without our concurrence he would not take such a risk. There was no dissenting voice; how could there be? The paper was published with almost no change or revision, though afterwards my husband said he considered this a mistake. He thought he should have waited for his anger to cool, when he might have been more impersonal and less egotistic.

The next day he consulted an eminent lawyer, more from curiosity than from any other reason. Mr. Moses—I think that was his name—was at first inclined to be jocular. I remember his smiling question: 'Have you called him a hell-hound or an atheist? Otherwise there is no libel.' But when he looked over the manuscript his countenance changed. 'This is a serious affair,' he said; 'however, no one will publish it for you.' In that Mr. Moses was right; no one dared publish the pamphlet. But that difficulty was soon overcome. My husband hired a printer by the day, and the work was rushed through. We then, my daughter, my son, and myself, were set to work helping address the pamphlets, which were scattered far and wide.

Father Damien was vindicated by a stranger, a man of another country and another religion from his own.

F. V. de G. S.

LAY MORALS

The following chapters of a projected treatise on Ethics were drafted at Edinburgh in the spring of 1879. They are unrevised, and must not be taken as representing, either as to matter or form, their author's final thoughts; but they contain much that is essentially characteristic of his mind.

CHAPTER I

The problem of education is twofold: first to know, and then to utter. Every one who lives any semblance of an inner life thinks more nobly and profoundly than he speaks; and the best of teachers can impart only broken images of the truth which they perceive. Speech which goes from one to another between two natures, and, what is worse, between two experiences, is doubly relative. The speaker buries his meaning; it is for the hearer to dig it up again; and all speech, written or spoken, is in a dead language until it finds a willing and prepared hearer. Such, moreover, is the complexity of life, that when we condescend upon details in our advice, we may be sure we condescend on error; and the best of education is to throw out some magnanimous hints. No man was ever so poor that he could express all he has in him by words, looks, or actions; his true knowledge is eternally incommunicable, for it is a knowledge of himself; and his best wisdom comes to him by no process of the mind, but in a supreme self-dictation, which keeps varying from hour to hour in its dictates with the variation of events and circumstances.

A few men of picked nature, full of faith, courage, and contempt for others, try earnestly to set forth as much as they can grasp of this inner law; but the vast majority, when they come to advise the young, must be content to retail certain doctrines which have been already retailed to them in their own youth. Every generation has to educate another which it has brought upon the stage. People who readily accept the responsibility of parentship, having very different matters in their eye, are apt to feel rueful when that responsibility falls due. What are they to tell the child about life and conduct, subjects on which they have themselves so few and such confused opinions? Indeed, I do not know; the least said, perhaps, the soonest mended; and yet the child keeps asking, and the parent must find some words to say in his own defence. Where does he find them? and what are they when found?

As a matter of experience, and in nine hundred and ninety-nine cases out of a thousand, he will instil into his wide-eyed brat three bad things: the terror of public opinion, and, flowing from that as a fountain, the desire of wealth and applause. Besides these, or what might be deduced as corollaries from these, he will teach not much else of any effective value: some dim notions of divinity, perhaps, and book-keeping, and how to walk through a quadrille.

But, you may tell me, the young people are taught to be Christians. It may be want of penetration, but I have not yet been able to perceive it. As an honest man, whatever we teach, and be it good or evil, it is not the doctrine of Christ. What he taught (and in this he is like all other teachers worthy of the name) was not a code of rules, but a ruling spirit; not truths, but a spirit of truth; not views, but a view. What he showed us was an attitude of mind. Towards the many considerations on which conduct is built, each man stands in a certain relation. He takes life on a certain principle. He has a compass in his spirit which points in a certain direction. It is the attitude, the relation, the point of the compass, that is the whole body and gist of what he has to teach us; in this, the details are comprehended; out of this the specific precepts issue, and by this, and this only, can they be explained and applied. And thus, to learn aright from any teacher, we must first of all, like a historical artist, think ourselves into sympathy with his position and, in the technical phrase, create his character. A historian confronted with some ambiguous politician, or an actor charged with a part, have but one pre-occupation; they must search all round and upon every side, and grope for some central conception which is to explain and justify the most extreme details; until that is found, the politician is an enigma, or perhaps a quack, and the part a tissue of fustian sentiment and big words; but once that is found, all enters into a plan, a human nature appears, the politician or the stage-king is understood from point to point, from end to end. This is a degree of trouble which will be gladly taken by a very humble artist; but not even the terror of eternal fire can teach a business man to bend his imagination to such athletic efforts. Yet without this, all is vain; until we understand the whole, we shall understand none of the parts; and otherwise we have no more than broken images and scattered words; the meaning remains buried; and the language in which our prophet speaks to us is a dead language in our ears.

Take a few of Christ's sayings and compare them with our current doctrines.

'Ye cannot,' he says, 'serve God and Mammon.' Cannot? And our whole system is to teach us how we can!

'The children of this world are wiser in their generation than the children of light.' Are they? I had been led to understand the reverse: that the Christian merchant, for example, prospered exceedingly in his affairs; that honesty was the best policy; that an author of repute had written a conclusive treatise 'How to make the best of both worlds.' Of both worlds indeed! Which am I to believe then—Christ or the author of repute?

'Take no thought for the morrow.' Ask the Successful Merchant; interrogate your own heart; and you will have to admit that this is not only a silly but an immoral position. All we believe, all we hope, all we honour in ourselves or our contemporaries, stands condemned in this one sentence, or, if you take the other view, condemns the sentence as unwise and inhumane. We are not then of the 'same mind that was in Christ.' We disagree with Christ. Either Christ meant nothing, or else he or we must be in the wrong. Well says Thoreau, speaking of some texts from the New Testament, and finding a strange echo of another style which the reader may recognise: 'Let but one of these sentences be rightly read from any pulpit in the land, and there would not be left one stone of that meeting-house upon another.'

It may be objected that these are what are called 'hard sayings'; and that a man, or an education, may be very sufficiently Christian although it leave some of these sayings upon one side. But this is a very gross delusion. Although truth is difficult to state, it is both easy and agreeable to receive, and the mind runs out to meet it ere the phrase be done. The universe, in relation to what any man can say of it, is plain, patent and staringly comprehensible. In itself, it is a great and travailing ocean, unsounded, unvoyageable, an eternal mystery to man; or, let us say, it is a monstrous and impassable mountain, one side of which, and a few near slopes and foothills, we can dimly study with these mortal eyes. But what any man can say of it, even in his highest utterance, must have relation to this little and plain corner, which is no less visible to us than to him. We are looking on the same map; it will go hard if we cannot follow the demonstration. The longest and most abstruse flight of a philosopher becomes clear and shallow, in the flash of a moment, when we suddenly perceive the aspect and drift of his intention. The longest argument is but a finger pointed; once we get our own finger rightly parallel, and we see what the man meant, whether it be a new star or an old street-lamp. And briefly, if a saying is hard to understand, it is because we are thinking of something else.

But to be a true disciple is to think of the same things as our prophet, and to think of different things in the same order. To be of the same mind with another is to see all things in the same perspective; it is not to agree in a few indifferent matters near at hand and not much debated; it is to follow him in his farthest flights, to see the force of his hyperboles, to stand so exactly in the centre of his vision that whatever he may express, your eyes will light at once on the original, that whatever he may see to declare, your mind will at once accept. You do not belong to the school of any philosopher, because you agree with him that theft is, on the whole, objectionable, or that the sun is overhead at noon. It is by the hard sayings that discipleship is tested. We are all agreed about the middling and indifferent parts of knowledge and morality; even the most soaring spirits too often take them tamely upon trust. But the man, the philosopher or the moralist, does not stand upon these chance adhesions; and the purpose of any system looks towards those extreme points where it steps valiantly beyond tradition and returns with some covert hint of things outside. Then only can you be certain that the words are not words of course, nor mere echoes of the past; then only are you sure that if he be indicating anything at all, it is a star and not a street-lamp; then only do you touch the heart of the mystery, since it was for these that the author wrote his book.

Now, every now and then, and indeed surprisingly often, Christ finds a word that transcends all common-place morality; every now and then he quits the beaten track to pioneer the unexpressed, and throws out a pregnant and magnanimous hyperbole; for it is only by some bold poetry of thought that men can be strung up above the level of everyday conceptions to take a broader look upon experience or accept some higher principle of conduct. To a man who is of the same mind that was in Christ, who stands at some centre not too far from his, and looks at the world and conduct from some not dissimilar or, at least, not opposing attitude—or, shortly, to a man who is of Christ's philosophy—every such saying should come home with a thrill of joy and corroboration; he should feel each one below his feet as another sure foundation in the flux of time and chance; each should be another proof that in the torrent of the years and generations, where doctrines and great armaments and empires are swept away and swallowed, he stands immovable, holding by the eternal stars. But alas! at this juncture of the ages it is not so with us; on each and every such occasion our whole fellowship of Christians falls back in disapproving wonder and implicitly denies the saying. Christians! the farce is impudently broad. Let us stand up in the sight of heaven and confess. The ethics that we hold are those of Benjamin Franklin. Honesty is the best policy, is perhaps a hard saying; it is certainly one by which a wise man of these days will not too curiously direct his steps; but I think it shows a glimmer of meaning to even our most dimmed intelligences; I think we perceive a principle behind it; I think, without hyperbole, we are of the same mind that was in Benjamin Franklin.

CHAPTER II

But, I may be told, we teach the ten commandments, where a world of morals lies condensed, the very pith and epitome of all ethics and religion; and a young man with these precepts engraved upon his mind must follow after profit with some conscience and Christianity of method. A man cannot go very far astray who neither dishonours his parents, nor kills, nor commits adultery, nor steals, nor bears false witness; for these things, rightly thought out, cover a vast field of duty.

Alas! what is a precept? It is at best an illustration; it is case law at the best which can be learned by precept. The letter is not only dead, but killing; the spirit which underlies, and cannot be uttered, alone is true and helpful. This is trite to sickness; but familiarity has a cunning disenchantment; in a day or two she can steal all beauty from the mountain tops; and the most startling words begin to fall dead upon the ear after several repetitions. If you see a thing too often, you no longer see it; if you hear a thing too often, you no longer hear it. Our attention requires to be surprised; and to carry a fort by assault, or to gain a thoughtful hearing from the ruck of mankind, are feats of about an equal difficulty and must be tried by not dissimilar means. The whole Bible has thus lost its message for the common run of hearers; it has become mere words of course; and the parson may bawl himself scarlet and beat the pulpit like a thing possessed, but his hearers will continue to nod; they are strangely at peace, they know all he has to say; ring the old bell as you choose, it is still the old bell and it cannot startle their composure. And so with this byword about the letter and the spirit. It is quite true, no doubt; but it has no meaning in the world to any man of us. Alas! it has just this meaning, and neither more nor less: that while the spirit is true, the letter is eternally false.

The shadow of a great oak lies abroad upon the ground at noon, perfect, clear, and stable like the earth. But let a man set himself to mark out the boundary with cords and pegs, and were he never so nimble and never so exact, what with the multiplicity of the leaves and the progression of the shadow as it flees before the travelling sun, long ere he has made the circuit the whole figure will have changed. Life may be compared, not to a single tree, but to a great and complicated forest; circumstance is more swiftly changing than a shadow, language much more inexact than the tools of a surveyor; from day to day the trees fall and are renewed; the very essences are fleeting as we look; and the whole world of leaves is swinging tempest-tossed among the winds of time. Look now for your shadows. O man of formulæ, is this a place for you? Have you fitted the spirit to a single case? Alas, in the cycle of the ages when shall such another be proposed for the judgment of man? Now when the sun shines and the winds blow, the wood is filled with an innumerable multitude of shadows, tumultuously tossed and changing; and at every gust the whole carpet leaps and becomes new. Can you or your heart say more?

Look back now, for a moment, on your own brief experience of life; and although you lived it feelingly in your own person, and had every step of conduct burned in by pains and joys upon your memory, tell me what definite lesson does experience hand on from youth to manhood, or from both to age? The settled tenor which first strikes the eye is but the shadow of a delusion. This is gone; that never truly was; and you yourself are altered beyond recognition. Times and men and circumstances change about your changing character, with a speed of which no earthly hurricane affords an image. What was the best yesterday, is it still the best in this changed theatre of a to-morrow? Will your own Past truly guide you in your own violent and unexpected Future? And if this be questionable, with what humble, with what hopeless eyes, should we not watch other men driving beside us on their unknown careers, seeing with unlike eyes, impelled by different gales, doing and suffering in another sphere of things?

And as the authentic clue to such a labyrinth and change of scene, do you offer me these two score words? these five bald prohibitions? For the moral precepts are no more than five; the first four deal rather with matters of observance than of conduct; the tenth, Thou shalt not covet, stands upon another basis, and shall be spoken of ere long. The Jews, to whom they were first given, in the course of years began to find these precepts insufficient; and made an addition of no less than six hundred and fifty others! They hoped to make a pocket-book of reference on morals, which should stand to life in some such relation, say, as Hoyle stands in to the scientific game of whist. The comparison is just, and condemns the design; for those who play by rule will never be more than tolerable players; and you and I would like to play our game in life to the noblest and the most divine advantage. Yet if the Jews took a petty and huckstering view of conduct, what view do we take ourselves, who callously leave youth to go forth into the enchanted forest, full of spells and dire chimeras, with no guidance more complete than is afforded by these five precepts?

Honour thy father and thy mother. Yes, but does that mean to obey? and if so, how long and how far? Thou shall not kill. Yet the very intention and purport of the prohibition may be best fulfilled by killing. Thou shall not commit adultery. But some of the ugliest adulteries are committed in the bed of marriage and under the sanction of religion and law. Thou shalt not bear false witness. How? by speech or by silence also? or even by a smile? Thou shalt not steal. Ah, that indeed! But what is to steal?

To steal? It is another word to be construed; and who is to be our guide? The police will give us one construction, leaving the word only that least minimum of meaning without which society would fall in pieces; but surely we must take some higher sense than this; surely we hope more than a bare subsistence for mankind; surely we wish mankind to prosper and go on from strength to strength, and ourselves to live rightly in the eye of some more exacting potentate than a policeman. The approval or the disapproval of the police must be eternally indifferent to a man who is both valorous and good. There is extreme discomfort, but no shame, in the condemnation of the law. The law represents that modicum of morality which can be squeezed out of the ruck of mankind; but what is that to me, who aim higher and seek to be my own more stringent judge? I observe with pleasure that no brave man has ever given a rush for such considerations. The Japanese have a nobler and more sentimental feeling for this social bond into which we all are born when we come into the world, and whose comforts and protection we all indifferently share throughout our lives:—but even to them, no more than to our Western saints and heroes, does the law of the state supersede the higher law of duty. Without hesitation and without remorse, they transgress the stiffest enactments rather than abstain from doing right. But the accidental superior duty being thus fulfilled, they at once return in allegiance to the common duty of all citizens; and hasten to denounce themselves; and value at an equal rate their just crime and their equally just submission to its punishment.

The evading of the police will not long satisfy an active conscience or a thoughtful head. But to show you how one or the other may trouble a man, and what a vast extent of frontier is left unridden by this invaluable eighth commandment, let me tell you a few pages out of a young man's life.

He was a friend of mine; a young man like others; generous, flighty, as variable as youth itself, but always with some high motions and on the search for higher thoughts of life. I should tell you at once that he thoroughly agrees with the eighth commandment. But he got hold of some unsettling works, the New Testament among others, and this loosened his views of life and led him into many perplexities. As he was the son of a man in a certain position, and well off, my friend had enjoyed from the first the advantages of education, nay, he had been kept alive through a sickly childhood by constant watchfulness, comforts, and change of air; for all of which he was indebted to his father's wealth.

At college he met other lads more diligent than himself, who followed the plough in summer-time to pay their college fees in winter; and this inequality struck him with some force. He was at that age of a conversible temper, and insatiably curious in the aspects of life; and he spent much of his time scraping acquaintance with all classes of man- and woman-kind. In this way he came upon many depressed ambitions, and many intelligences stunted for want of opportunity; and this also struck him. He began to perceive that life was a handicap upon strange, wrong-sided principles; and not, as he had been told, a fair and equal race. He began to tremble that he himself had been unjustly favoured, when he saw all the avenues of wealth, and power, and comfort closed against so many of his superiors and equals, and held unwearyingly open before so idle, so desultory, and so dissolute a being as himself. There sat a youth beside him on the college benches, who had only one shirt to his back, and, at intervals sufficiently far apart, must stay at home to have it washed. It was my friend's principle to stay away as often as he dared; for I fear he was no friend to learning. But there was something that came home to him sharply, in this fellow who had to give over study till his shirt was washed, and the scores of others who had never an opportunity at all. If one of these could take his place, he thought; and the thought tore away a bandage from his eyes. He was eaten by the shame of his discoveries, and despised himself as an unworthy favourite and a creature of the back-stairs of Fortune. He could no longer see without confusion one of these brave young fellows battling up-hill against adversity. Had he not filched that fellow's birthright? At best was he not coldly profiting by the injustice of society, and greedily devouring stolen goods? The money, indeed, belonged to his father, who had worked, and thought, and given up his liberty to earn it; but by what justice could the money belong to my friend, who had, as yet, done nothing but help to squander it? A more sturdy honesty, joined to a more even and impartial temperament, would have drawn from these considerations a new force of industry, that this equivocal position might be brought as swiftly as possible to an end, and some good services to mankind justify the appropriation of expense. It was not so with my friend, who was only unsettled and discouraged, and filled full of that trumpeting anger with which young men regard injustices in the first blush of youth; although in a few years they will tamely acquiesce in their existence, and knowingly profit by their complications. Yet all this while he suffered many indignant pangs. And once, when he put on his boots, like any other unripe donkey, to run away from home, it was his best consolation that he was now, at a single plunge, to free himself from the responsibility of this wealth that was not his, and do battle equally against his fellows in the warfare of life.

Some time after this, falling into ill-health, he was sent at great expense to a more favourable climate; and then I think his perplexities were thickest. When he thought of all the other young men of singular promise, upright, good, the prop of families, who must remain at home to die, and with all their possibilities be lost to life and mankind; and how he, by one more unmerited favour, was chosen out from all these others to survive; he felt as if there were no life, no labour, no devotion of soul and body, that could repay and justify these partialities. A religious lady, to whom he communicated these reflections, could see no force in them whatever. 'It was God's will,' said she. But he knew it was by God's will that Joan of Arc was burnt at Rouen, which cleared neither Bedford nor Bishop Cauchon; and again, by God's will that Christ was crucified outside Jerusalem, which excused neither the rancour of the priests nor the timidity of Pilate. He knew, moreover, that although the possibility of this favour he was now enjoying issued from his circumstances, its acceptance was the act of his own will; and he had accepted it greedily, longing for rest and sunshine. And hence this allegation of God's providence did little to relieve his scruples. I promise you he had a very troubled mind. And I would not laugh if I were you, though while he was thus making mountains out of what you think molehills, he were still (as perhaps he was) contentedly practising many other things that to you seem black as hell. Every man is his own judge and mountain-guide through life. There is an old story of a mote and a beam, apparently not true, but worthy perhaps of some consideration. I should, if I were you, give some consideration to these scruples of his, and if I were he, I should do the like by yours; for it is not unlikely that there may be something under both. In the meantime you must hear how my friend acted. Like many invalids, he supposed that he would die. Now, should he die, he saw no means of repaying this huge loan which, by the hands of his father, mankind had advanced him for his sickness. In that case it would be lost money. So he determined that the advance should be as small as possible; and, so long as he continued to doubt his recovery, lived in an upper room, and grudged himself all but necessaries. But so soon as he began to perceive a change for the better, he felt justified in spending more freely, to speed and brighten his return to health, and trusted in the future to lend a help to mankind, as mankind, out of its treasury, had lent a help to him.

I do not say but that my friend was a little too curious and partial in his view; nor thought too much of himself and too little of his parents; but I do say that here are some scruples which tormented my friend in his youth, and still, perhaps, at odd times give him a prick in the midst of his enjoyments, and which after all have some foundation in justice, and point, in their confused way, to some more honourable honesty within the reach of man. And at least, is not this an unusual gloss upon the eighth commandment? And what sort of comfort, guidance, or illumination did that precept afford my friend throughout these contentions? 'Thou shalt not steal.' With all my heart! But am I stealing?

The truly quaint materialism of our view of life disables us from pursuing any transaction to an end. You can make no one understand that his bargain is anything more than a bargain, whereas in point of fact it is a link in the policy of mankind, and either a good or an evil to the world. We have a sort of blindness which prevents us from seeing anything but sovereigns. If one man agrees to give another so many shillings for so many hours' work, and then wilfully gives him a certain proportion of the price in bad money and only the remainder in good, we can see with half an eye that this man is a thief. But if the other spends a certain proportion of the hours in smoking a pipe of tobacco, and a certain other proportion in looking at the sky, or the clock, or trying to recall an air, or in meditation on his own past adventures, and only the remainder in downright work such as he is paid to do, is he, because the theft is one of time and not of money,—is he any the less a thief? The one gave a bad shilling, the other an imperfect hour; but both broke the bargain, and each is a thief. In piecework, which is what most of us do, the case is none the less plain for being even less material. If you forge a bad knife, you have wasted some of mankind's iron, and then, with unrivalled cynicism, you pocket some of mankind's money for your trouble. Is there any man so blind who cannot see that this is theft? Again, if you carelessly cultivate a farm, you have been playing fast and loose with mankind's resources against hunger; there will be less bread in consequence, and for lack of that bread somebody will die next winter: a grim consideration. And you must not hope to shuffle out of blame because you got less money for your less quantity of bread; for although a theft be partly punished, it is none the less a theft for that. You took the farm against competitors; there were others ready to shoulder the responsibility and be answerable for the tale of loaves; but it was you who took it. By the act you came under a tacit bargain with mankind to cultivate that farm with your best endeavour; you were under no superintendence, you were on parole; and you have broke your bargain, and to all who look closely, and yourself among the rest if you have moral eyesight, you are a thief. Or take the case of men of letters. Every piece of work which is not as good as you can make it, which you have palmed off imperfect, meagrely thought, niggardly in execution, upon mankind who is your paymaster on parole and in a sense your pupil, every hasty or slovenly or untrue performance, should rise up against you in the court of your own heart and condemn you for a thief. Have you a salary? If you trifle with your health, and so render yourself less capable for duty, and still touch, and still greedily pocket the emolument—what are you but a thief? Have you double accounts? do you by any time-honoured juggle, deceit, or ambiguous process, gain more from those who deal with you than it you were bargaining and dealing face to face in front of God?—What are you but a thief? Lastly, if you fill an office, or produce an article, which, in your heart of hearts, you think a delusion and a fraud upon mankind, and still draw your salary and go through the sham manœuvres of this office, or still book your profits and keep on flooding the world with these injurious goods?—though you were old, and bald, and the first at church, and a baronet, what are you but a thief? These may seem hard words and mere curiosities of the intellect, in an age when the spirit of honesty is so sparingly cultivated that all business is conducted upon lies and so-called customs of the trade, that not a man bestows two thoughts on the utility or honourableness of his pursuit. I would say less if I thought less. But looking to my own reason and the right of things, I can only avow that I am a thief myself, and that I passionately suspect my neighbours of the same guilt.

Where did you hear that it was easy to be honest? Do you find that in your Bible? Easy! It is easy to be an ass and follow the multitude like a blind, besotted bull in a stampede; and that, I am well aware, is what you and Mrs. Grundy mean by being honest. But it will not bear the stress of time nor the scrutiny of conscience. Even before the lowest of all tribunals,— before a court of law, whose business it is, not to keep men right, or within a thousand miles of right, but to withhold them from going so tragically wrong that they will pull down the whole jointed fabric of society by their misdeeds—even before a court of law, as we begin to see in these last days, our easy view of following at each other's tails, alike to good and evil, is beginning to be reproved and punished, and declared no honesty at all, but open theft and swindling; and simpletons who have gone on through life with a quiet conscience may learn suddenly, from the lips of a judge, that the custom of the trade may be a custom of the devil. You thought it was easy to be honest. Did you think it was easy to be just and kind and truthful? Did you think the whole duty of aspiring man was as simple as a horn-pipe? and you could walk through life like a gentleman and a hero, with no more concern than it takes to go to church or to address a circular? And yet all this time you had the eighth commandment! and, what makes it richer, you would not have broken it for the world!

The truth is, that these commandments by themselves are of little use in private judgment. If compression is what you want, you have their whole spirit compressed into the golden rule; and yet there expressed with more significance, since the law is there spiritually and not materially stated. And in truth, four out of these ten commands, from the sixth to the ninth, are rather legal than ethical. The police-court is their proper home. A magistrate cannot tell whether you love your neighbour as yourself, but he can tell more or less whether you have murdered, or stolen, or committed adultery, or held up your hand and testified to that which was not; and these things, for rough practical tests, are as good as can be found. And perhaps, therefore, the best condensation of the Jewish moral law is in the maxims of the priests, 'neminem lædere' and 'suum cuique tribuere.' But all this granted, it becomes only the more plain that they are inadequate in the sphere of personal morality; that while they tell the magistrate roughly when to punish, they can never direct an anxious sinner what to do.

Only Polonius, or the like solemn sort of ass, can offer us a succinct proverb by way of advice, and not burst out blushing in our faces. We grant them one and all and for all that they are worth; it is something above and beyond that we desire. Christ was in general a great enemy to such a way of teaching; we rarely find him meddling with any of these plump commands but it was to open them out, and lift his hearers from the letter to the spirit. For morals are a personal affair; in the war of righteousness every man fights for his own hand; all the six hundred precepts of the Mishna cannot shake my private judgment; my magistracy of myself is an indefeasible charge, and my decisions absolute for the time and case. The moralist is not a judge of appeal, but an advocate who pleads at my tribunal. He has to show not the law, but that the law applies. Can he convince me? then he gains the cause. And thus you find Christ giving various counsels to varying people, and often jealously careful to avoid definite precept. Is he asked, for example, to divide a heritage? He refuses: and the best advice that he will offer is but a paraphrase of that tenth commandment which figures so strangely among the rest. Take heed, and beware of covetousness. If you complain that this is vague, I have failed to carry you along with me in my argument. For no definite precept can be more than an illustration, though its truth were resplendent like the sun, and it was announced from heaven by the voice of God. And life is so intricate and changing, that perhaps not twenty times, or perhaps not twice in the ages, shall we find that nice consent of circumstances to which alone it can apply.

CHAPTER III

Although the world and life have in a sense become commonplace to our experience, it is but in an external torpor; the true sentiment slumbers within us; and we have but to reflect on ourselves or our surroundings to rekindle our astonishment. No length of habit can blunt our first surprise. Of the world I have but little to say in this connection; a few strokes shall suffice. We inhabit a dead ember swimming wide in the blank of space, dizzily spinning as it swims, and lighted up from several million miles away by a more horrible hell-fire than was ever conceived by the theological imagination. Yet the dead ember is a green, commodious dwelling-place; and the reverberation of this hell-fire ripens flower and fruit and mildly warms us on summer eves upon the lawn. Far off on all hands other dead embers, other flaming suns, wheel and race in the apparent void; the nearest is out of call, the farthest so far that the heart sickens in the effort to conceive the distance. Shipwrecked seamen on the deep, though they bestride but the truncheon of a boom, are safe and near at home compared with mankind on its bullet. Even to us who have known no other, it seems a strange, if not an appalling, place of residence.

But far stranger is the resident, man, a creature compact of wonders that, after centuries of custom, is still wonderful to himself. He inhabits a body which he is continually outliving, discarding and renewing. Food and sleep, by an unknown alchemy, restore his spirits and the freshness of his countenance. Hair grows on him like grass; his eyes, his brain, his sinews, thirst for action; he joys to see and touch and hear, to partake the sun and wind, to sit down and intently ponder on his astonishing attributes and situation, to rise up and run, to perform the strange and revolting round of physical functions. The sight of a flower, the note of a bird, will often move him deeply; yet he looks unconcerned on the impassable distances and portentous bonfires of the universe. He comprehends, he designs, he tames nature, rides the sea, ploughs, climbs the air in a balloon, makes vast inquiries, begins interminable labours, joins himself into federations and populous cities, spends his days to deliver the ends of the earth or to benefit unborn posterity; and yet knows himself for a piece of unsurpassed fragility and the creature of a few days. His sight, which conducts him, which takes notice of the farthest stars, which is miraculous in every way and a thing defying explanation or belief, is yet lodged in a piece of jelly, and can be extinguished with a touch. His heart, which all through life so indomitably, so athletically labours, is but a capsule, and may be stopped with a pin. His whole body, for all its savage energies, its leaping and its winged desires, may yet be tamed and conquered by a draught of air or a sprinkling of cold dew. What he calls death, which is the seeming arrest of everything, and the ruin and hateful transformation of the visible body, lies in wait for him outwardly in a thousand accidents, and grows up in secret diseases from within. He is still learning to be a man when his faculties are already beginning to decline; he has not yet understood himself or his position before he inevitably dies. And yet this mad, chimerical creature can take no thought of his last end, lives as though he were eternal, plunges with his vulnerable body into the shock of war, and daily affronts death with unconcern. He cannot take a step without pain or pleasure. His life is a tissue of sensations, which he distinguishes as they seem to come more directly from himself or his surroundings. He is conscious of himself as a joyer or a sufferer, as that which craves, chooses, and is satisfied; conscious of his surroundings as it were of an inexhaustible purveyor, the source of aspects, inspirations, wonders, cruel knocks and transporting caresses. Thus he goes on his way, stumbling among delights and agonies.

Matter is a far-fetched theory, and materialism is without a root in man. To him everything is important in the degree to which it moves him. The telegraph wires and posts, the electricity speeding from clerk to clerk, the clerks, the glad or sorrowful import of the message, and the paper on which it is finally brought to him at home, are all equally facts, all equally exist for man. A word or a thought can wound him as acutely as a knife of steel. If he thinks he is loved, he will rise up and glory to himself, although he be in a distant land and short of necessary bread. Does he think he is not loved?—he may have the woman at his beck, and there is not a joy for him in all the world. Indeed, if we are to make any account of this figment of reason, the distinction between material and immaterial, we shall conclude that the life of each man as an individual is immaterial, although the continuation and prospects of mankind as a race turn upon material conditions. The physical business of each man's body is transacted for him; like a sybarite, he has attentive valets in his own viscera; he breathes, he sweats, he digests without an effort, or so much as a consenting volition; for the most part he even eats, not with a wakeful consciousness, but as it were between two thoughts. His life is centred among other and more important considerations; touch him in his honour or his love, creatures of the imagination which attach him to mankind or to an individual man or woman; cross him in his piety which connects his soul with heaven; and he turns from his food, he loathes his breath, and with a magnanimous emotion cuts the knots of his existence and frees himself at a blow from the web of pains and pleasures.

It follows that man is twofold at least; that he is not a rounded and autonomous empire; but that in the same body with him there dwell other powers tributary but independent. If I now behold one walking in a garden, curiously coloured and illuminated by the sun, digesting his food with elaborate chemistry, breathing, circulating blood, directing himself by the sight of his eyes, accommodating his body by a thousand delicate balancings to the wind and the uneven surface of the path, and all the time, perhaps, with his mind engaged about America, or the dog-star, or the attributes of God—what am I to say, or how am I to describe the thing I see? Is that truly a man, in the rigorous meaning of the word? or is it not a man and something else? What, then, are we to count the centre-bit and axle of a being so variously compounded? It is a question much debated. Some read his history in a certain intricacy of nerve and the success of successive digestions; others find him an exiled piece of heaven blown upon and determined by the breath of God; and both schools of theorists will scream like scalded children at a word of doubt. Yet either of these views, however plausible, is beside the question; either may be right; and I care not; I ask a more particular answer, and to a more immediate point. What is the man? There is Something that was before hunger and that remains behind after a meal. It may or may not be engaged in any given act or passion, but when it is, it changes, heightens, and sanctifies. Thus it is not engaged in lust, where satisfaction ends the chapter; and it is engaged in love, where no satisfaction can blunt the edge of the desire, and where age, sickness, or alienation may deface what was desirable without diminishing the sentiment. This something, which is the man, is a permanence which abides through the vicissitudes of passion, now overwhelmed and now triumphant, now unconscious of itself in the immediate distress of appetite or pain, now rising unclouded above all. So, to the man, his own central self fades and grows clear again amid the tumult of the senses, like a revolving Pharos in the night. It is forgotten; it is hid, it seems, for ever; and yet in the next calm hour he shall behold himself once more, shining and unmoved among changes and storm.

Mankind, in the sense of the creeping mass that is born and eats, that generates and dies, is but the aggregate of the outer and lower sides of man. This inner consciousness, this lantern alternately obscured and shining, to and by which the individual exists and must order his conduct, is something special to himself and not common to the race. His joys delight, his sorrows wound him, according as this is interested or indifferent in the affair; according as they arise in an imperial war or in a broil conducted by the tributary chieftains of the mind. He may lose all, and this not suffer; he may lose what is materially a trifle, and this leap in his bosom with a cruel pang. I do not speak of it to hardened theorists: the living man knows keenly what it is I mean.

'Perceive at last that thou hast in thee something better and more divine than the things which cause the various effects, and, as it were, pull thee by the strings. What is that now in thy mind? is it fear, or suspicion, or desire, or anything of that kind?' Thus far Marcus Aurelius, in one of the most notable passages in any book. Here is a question worthy to be answered. What is in thy mind? What is the utterance of your inmost self when, in a quiet hour, it can be heard intelligibly? It is something beyond the compass of your thinking, inasmuch as it is yourself; but is it not of a higher spirit than you had dreamed betweenwhiles, and erect above all base considerations? This soul seems hardly touched with our infirmities; we can find in it certainly no fear, suspicion, or desire; we are only conscious—and that as though we read it in the eyes of some one else—of a great and unqualified readiness. A readiness to what? to pass over and look beyond the objects of desire and fear, for something else. And this something else? this something which is apart from desire and fear, to which all the kingdoms of the world and the immediate death of the body are alike indifferent and beside the point, and which yet regards conduct—by what name are we to call it? It may be the love of God; or it may be an inherited (and certainly well concealed) instinct to preserve self and propagate the race; I am not, for the moment, averse to either theory; but it will save time to call it righteousness. By so doing I intend no subterfuge to beg a question; I am indeed ready, and more than willing, to accept the rigid consequence, and lay aside, as far as the treachery of the reason will permit, all former meanings attached to the word righteousness. What is right is that for which a man's central self is ever ready to sacrifice immediate or distant interests; what is wrong is what the central self discards or rejects as incompatible with the fixed design of righteousness.

To make this admission is to lay aside all hope of definition. That which is right upon this theory is intimately dictated to each man by himself, but can never be rigorously set forth in language, and never, above all, imposed upon another. The conscience has, then, a vision like that of the eyes, which is incommunicable, and for the most part illuminates none but its possessor. When many people perceive the same or any cognate facts, they agree upon a word as symbol; and hence we have such words as tree, star, love, honour, or death; hence also we have this word right, which, like the others, we all understand, most of us understand differently, and none can express succinctly otherwise. Yet even on the straitest view, we can make some steps towards comprehension of our own superior thoughts. For it is an incredible and most bewildering fact that a man, through life, is on variable terms with himself; he is aware of tiffs and reconciliations; the intimacy is at times almost suspended, at times it is renewed again with joy. As we said before, his inner self or soul appears to him by successive revelations, and is frequently obscured. It is from a study of these alternations that we can alone hope to discover, even dimly, what seems right and what seems wrong to this veiled prophet of ourself.

All that is in the man in the larger sense, what we call impression as well as what we call intuition, so far as my argument looks, we must accept. It is not wrong to desire food, or exercise, or beautiful surroundings, or the love of sex, or interest which is the food of the mind. All these are craved; all these should be craved; to none of these in itself does the soul demur; where there comes an undeniable want, we recognise a demand of nature. Yet we know that these natural demands may be superseded; for the demands which are common to mankind make but a shadowy consideration in comparison to the demands of the individual soul. Food is almost the first prerequisite; and yet a high character will go without food to the ruin and death of the body rather than gain it in a manner which the spirit disavows. Pascal laid aside mathematics; Origen doctored his body with a knife; every day some one is thus mortifying his dearest interests and desires, and, in Christ's words, entering maim into the Kingdom of Heaven. This is to supersede the lesser and less harmonious affections by renunciation; and though by this ascetic path we may get to heaven, we cannot get thither a whole and perfect man. But there is another way, to supersede them by reconciliation, in which the soul and all the faculties and senses pursue a common route and share in one desire. Thus, man is tormented by a very imperious physical desire; it spoils his rest, it is not to be denied; the doctors will tell you, not I, how it is a physical need, like the want of food or slumber. In the satisfaction of this desire, as it first appears, the soul sparingly takes part; nay, it oft unsparingly regrets and disapproves the satisfaction. But let the man learn to love a woman as far as he is capable of love; and for this random affection of the body there is substituted a steady determination, a consent of all his powers and faculties, which supersedes, adopts, and commands the other. The desire survives, strengthened, perhaps, but taught obedience and changed in scope and character. Life is no longer a tale of betrayals and regrets; for the man now lives as a whole; his consciousness now moves on uninterrupted like a river; through all the extremes and ups and downs of passion, he remains approvingly conscious of himself.

Now to me, this seems a type of that rightness which the soul demands.

It demands that we shall not live alternately with our opposing tendencies in continual see-saw of passion and disgust, but seek some path on which the tendencies shall no longer oppose, but serve each other to a common end. It demands that we shall not pursue broken ends, but great and comprehensive purposes, in which soul and body may unite like notes in a harmonious chord. That were indeed a way of peace and pleasure, that were indeed a heaven upon earth. It does not demand, however, or, to speak in measure, it does not demand of me, that I should starve my appetites for no purpose under heaven but as a purpose in itself; or, in a weak despair, pluck out the eye that I have not yet learned to guide and enjoy with wisdom. The soul demands unity of purpose, not the dismemberment of man; it seeks to roll up all his strength and sweetness, all his passion and wisdom, into one, and make of him a perfect man exulting in perfection. To conclude ascetically is to give up, and not to solve, the problem. The ascetic and the creeping hog, although they are at different poles, have equally failed in life. The one has sacrificed his crew; the other brings back his seamen in a cock-boat, and has lost the ship. I believe there are not many sea-captains who would plume themselves on either result as a success.

But if it is righteousness thus to fuse together our divisive impulses and march with one mind through life, there is plainly one thing more unrighteous than all others, and one declension which is irretrievable and draws on the rest. And this is to lose consciousness of oneself. In the best of times, it is but by flashes, when our whole nature is clear, strong and conscious, and events conspire to leave us free, that we enjoy communion with our soul. At the worst, we are so fallen and passive that we may say shortly we have none. An arctic torpor seizes upon men. Although built of nerves, and set adrift in a stimulating world, they develop a tendency to go bodily to sleep; consciousness becomes engrossed among the reflex and mechanical parts of life; and soon loses both the will and power to look higher considerations in the face. This is ruin; this is the last failure in life; this is temporal damnation, damnation on the spot and without the form of judgment. 'What shall it profit a man if he gain the whole world and lose himself?'

It is to keep a man awake, to keep him alive to his own soul and its fixed design of righteousness, that the better part of moral and religious education is directed; not only that of words and doctors, but the sharp ferule of calamity under which we are all God's scholars till we die. If, as teachers, we are to say anything to the purpose, we must say what will remind the pupil of his soul; we must speak that soul's dialect; we must talk of life and conduct as his soul would have him think of them. If, from some conformity between us and the pupil, or perhaps among all men, we do in truth speak in such a dialect and express such views, beyond question we shall touch in him a spring; beyond question he will recognise the dialect as one that he himself has spoken in his better hours; beyond question he will cry, 'I had forgotten, but now I remember; I too have eyes, and I had forgot to use them! I too have a soul of my own, arrogantly upright, and to that I will listen and conform.' In short, say to him anything that he has once thought, or been upon the point of thinking, or show him any view of life that he has once clearly seen, or been upon the point of clearly seeing; and you have done your part and may leave him to complete the education for himself.

Now, the view taught at the present time seems to me to want greatness; and the dialect in which alone it can be intelligibly uttered is not the dialect of my soul. It is a sort of postponement of life; nothing quite is, but something different is to be; we are to keep our eyes upon the indirect from the cradle to the grave. We are to regulate our conduct not by desire, but by a politic eye upon the future; and to value acts as they will bring us money or good opinion; as they will bring us, in one word, profit. We must be what is called respectable, and offend no one by our carriage; it will not do to make oneself conspicuous—who knows? even in virtue? says the Christian parent! And we must be what is called prudent and make money; not only because it is pleasant to have money, but because that also is a part of respectability, and we cannot hope to be received in society without decent possessions. Received in society! as if that were the kingdom of heaven! There is dear Mr. So-and-so;—look at him!—so much respected—so much looked up to—quite the Christian merchant! And we must cut our conduct as strictly as possible after the pattern of Mr. So-and-so; and lay our whole lives to make money and be strictly decent. Besides these holy injunctions, which form by far the greater part of a youth's training in our Christian homes, there are at least two other doctrines. We are to live just now as well as we can, but scrape at last into heaven, where we shall be good. We are to worry through the week in a lay, disreputable way, but, to make matters square, live a different life on Sunday.

The train of thought we have been following gives us a key to all these positions, without stepping aside to justify them on their own ground. It is because we have been disgusted fifty times with physical squalls, and fifty times torn between conflicting impulses, that we teach people this indirect and tactical procedure in life, and to judge by remote consequences instead of the immediate face of things. The very desire to act as our own souls would have us, coupled with a pathetic disbelief in ourselves, moves us to follow the example of others; perhaps, who knows? they may be on the right track; and the more our patterns are in number, the better seems the chance; until, if we be acting in concert with a whole civilised nation, there are surely a majority of chances that we must be acting right. And again, how true it is that we can never behave as we wish in this tormented sphere, and can only aspire to different and more favourable circumstances, in order to stand out and be ourselves wholly and rightly! And yet once more, if in the hurry and pressure of affairs and passions you tend to nod and become drowsy, here are twenty-four hours of Sunday set apart for you to hold counsel with your soul and look around you on the possibilities of life.

This is not, of course, all that is to be, or even should be, said for these doctrines. Only, in the course of this chapter, the reader and I have agreed upon a few catchwords, and been looking at morals on a certain system; it was a pity to lose an opportunity of testing the catchwords, and seeing whether, by this system as well as by others, current doctrines could show any probable justification. If the doctrines had come too badly out of the trial, it would have condemned the system. Our sight of the world is very narrow; the mind but a pedestrian instrument; there's nothing new under the sun, as Solomon says, except the man himself; and though that changes the aspect of everything else, yet he must see the same things as other people, only from a different side.

And now, having admitted so much, let us turn to criticism.

If you teach a man to keep his eyes upon what others think of him, unthinkingly to lead the life and hold the principles of the majority of his contemporaries, you must discredit in his eyes the one authoritative voice of his own soul. He may be a docile citizen; he will never be a man. It is ours, on the other hand, to disregard this babble and chattering of other men better and worse than we are, and to walk straight before us by what light we have. They may be right; but so, before heaven, are we. They may know; but we know also, and by that knowledge we must stand or fall. There is such a thing as loyalty to a man's own better self; and from those who have not that, God help me, how am I to look for loyalty to others? The most dull, the most imbecile, at a certain moment turn round, at a certain point will hear no further argument, but stand unflinching by their own dumb, irrational sense of right. It is not only by steel or fire, but through contempt and blame, that the martyr fulfils the calling of his dear soul. Be glad if you are not tried by such extremities. But although all the world ranged themselves in one line to tell you 'This is wrong,' be you your own faithful vassal and the ambassador of God—throw down the glove and answer 'This is right.' Do you think you are only declaring yourself? Perhaps in some dim way, like a child who delivers a message not fully understood, you are opening wider the straits of prejudice and preparing mankind for some truer and more spiritual grasp of truth; perhaps, as you stand forth for your own judgment, you are covering a thousand weak ones with your body; perhaps, by this declaration alone, you have avoided the guilt of false witness against humanity and the little ones unborn. It is good, I believe, to be respectable, but much nobler to respect oneself and utter the voice of God. God, if there be any God, speaks daily in a new language by the tongues of men; the thoughts and habits of each fresh generation and each new-coined spirit throw another light upon the universe and contain another commentary on the printed Bibles; every scruple, every true dissent, every glimpse of something new, is a letter of God's alphabet; and though there is a grave responsibility for all who speak, is there none for those who unrighteously keep silence and conform? Is not that also to conceal and cloak God's counsel? And how should we regard the man of science who suppressed all facts that would not tally with the orthodoxy of the hour?

Wrong? You are as surely wrong as the sun rose this morning round the revolving shoulder of the world. Not truth, but truthfulness, is the good of your endeavour. For when will men receive that first part and prerequisite of truth, that, by the order of things, by the greatness of the universe, by the darkness and partiality of man's experience, by the inviolate secrecy of God, kept close in His most open revelations, every man is, and to the end of the ages must be, wrong? Wrong to the universe; wrong to mankind; wrong to God. And yet in another sense, and that plainer and nearer, every man of men, who wishes truly, must be right. He is right to himself, and in the measure of his sagacity and candour. That let him do in all sincerity and zeal, not sparing a thought for contrary opinions; that, for what it is worth, let him proclaim. Be not afraid; although he be wrong, so also is the dead, stuffed Dagon he insults. For the voice of God, whatever it is, is not that stammering, inept tradition which the people holds. These truths survive in travesty, swamped in a world of spiritual darkness and confusion; and what a few comprehend and faithfully hold, the many, in their dead jargon, repeat, degrade, and misinterpret.

So far of Respectability; what the Covenanters used to call 'rank conformity': the deadliest gag and wet blanket that can be laid on men. And now of Profit. And this doctrine is perhaps the more redoubtable, because it harms all sorts of men; not only the heroic and self-reliant, but the obedient, cowlike squadrons. A man, by this doctrine, looks to consequences at the second, or third, or fiftieth turn. He chooses his end, and for that, with wily turns and through a great sea of tedium, steers this mortal bark. There may be political wisdom in such a view; but I am persuaded there can spring no great moral zeal. To look thus obliquely upon life is the very recipe for moral slumber. Our intention and endeavour should be directed, not on some vague end of money or applause, which shall come to us by a ricochet in a month or a year, or twenty years, but on the act itself; not on the approval of others, but on the rightness of that act. At every instant, at every step in life, the point has to be decided, our soul has to be saved, heaven has to be gained or lost. At every step our spirits must applaud, at every step we must set down the foot and sound the trumpet. 'This have I done,' we must say; 'right or wrong, this have I done, in unfeigned honour of intention, as to myself and God.' The profit of every act should be this, that it was right for us to do it. Any other profit than that, if it involved a kingdom or the woman I love, ought, if I were God's upright soldier, to leave me untempted.

It is the mark of what we call a righteous decision, that it is made directly and for its own sake. The whole man, mind and body, having come to an agreement, tyrannically dictates conduct. There are two dispositions eternally opposed: that in which we recognise that one thing is wrong and another right, and that in which, not seeing any clear distinction, we fall back on the consideration of consequences. The truth is, by the scope of our present teaching, nothing is thought very wrong and nothing very right, except a few actions which have the disadvantage of being disrespectable when found out; the more serious part of men inclining to think all things rather wrong, the more jovial to suppose them right enough for practical purposes. I will engage my head, they do not find that view in their own hearts; they have taken it up in a dark despair; they are but troubled sleepers talking in their sleep. The soul, or my soul at least, thinks very distinctly upon many points of right and wrong, and often differs flatly with what is held out as the thought of corporate humanity in the code of society or the code of law. Am I to suppose myself a monster? I have only to read books, the Christian Gospels for example, to think myself a monster no longer; and instead I think the mass of people are merely speaking in their sleep.

It is a commonplace, enshrined, if I mistake not, even in school copy-books, that honour is to be sought and not fame. I ask no other admission; we are to seek honour, upright walking with our own conscience every hour of the day, and not fame, the consequence, the far-off reverberation of our footsteps. The walk, not the rumour of the walk, is what concerns righteousness. Better disrespectable honour than dishonourable fame. Better useless or seemingly hurtful honour, than dishonour ruling empires and filling the mouths of thousands. For the man must walk by what he sees, and leave the issue with God who made him and taught him by the fortune of his life. You would not dishonour yourself for money; which is at least tangible; would you do it, then, for a doubtful forecast in politics, or another person's theory in morals?

So intricate is the scheme of our affairs, that no man can calculate the bearing of his own behaviour even on those immediately around him, how much less upon the world at large or on succeeding generations! To walk by external prudence and the rule of consequences would require, not a man, but God. All that we know to guide us in this changing labyrinth is our soul with its fixed design of righteousness, and a few old precepts which commend themselves to that. The precepts are vague when we endeavour to apply them; consequences are more entangled than a wisp of string, and their confusion is unrestingly in change; we must hold to what we know and walk by it. We must walk by faith, indeed, and not by knowledge.

You do not love another because he is wealthy or wise or eminently respectable: you love him because you love him; that is love, and any other only a derision and grimace. It should be the same with all our actions. If we were to conceive a perfect man, it should be one who was never torn between conflicting impulses, but who, on the absolute consent of all his parts and faculties, submitted in every action of his life to a self-dictation as absolute and unreasoned as that which bids him love one woman and be true to her till death. But we should not conceive him as sagacious, ascetical, playing off his appetites against each other, turning the wing of public respectable immorality instead of riding it directly down, or advancing toward his end through a thousand sinister compromises and considerations. The one man might be wily, might be adroit, might be wise, might be respectable, might be gloriously useful; it is the other man who would be good.

The soul asks honour and not fame; to be upright, not to be successful; to be good, not prosperous; to be essentially, not outwardly, respectable. Does your soul ask profit? Does it ask money? Does it ask the approval of the indifferent herd? I believe not. For my own part, I want but little money, I hope; and I do not want to be decent at all, but to be good.

CHAPTER IV

We have spoken of that supreme self-dictation which keeps varying from hour to hour in its dictates with the variation of events and circumstances. Now, for us, that is ultimate. It may be founded on some reasonable process, but it is not a process which we can follow or comprehend. And moreover the dictation is not continuous, or not continuous except in very lively and well-living natures; and between-whiles we must brush along without it. Practice is a more intricate and desperate business than the toughest theorising; life is an affair of cavalry, where rapid judgment and prompt action are alone possible and right. As a matter of fact, there is no one so upright but he is influenced by the world's chatter; and no one so headlong but he requires to consider consequences and to keep an eye on profit. For the soul adopts all affections and appetites without exception, and cares only to combine them for some common purpose which shall interest all. Now, respect for the opinion of others, the study of consequences, and the desire of power and comfort, are all undeniably factors in the nature of man; and the more undeniably since we find that, in our current doctrines, they have swallowed up the others and are thought to conclude in themselves all the worthy parts of man. These, then, must also be suffered to affect conduct in the practical domain, much or little according as they are forcibly or feebly present to the mind of each.

Now, a man's view of the universe is mostly a view of the civilised society in which he lives. Other men and women are so much more grossly and so much more intimately palpable to his perceptions, that they stand between him and all the rest; they are larger to his eye than the sun, he hears them more plainly than thunder, with them, by them, and for them, he must live and die. And hence the laws that affect his intercourse with his fellow-men, although merely customary and the creatures of a generation, are more clearly and continually before his mind than those which bind him into the eternal system of things, support him in his upright progress on this whirling ball, or keep up the fire of his bodily life. And hence it is that money stands in the first rank of considerations and so powerfully affects the choice. For our society is built with money for mortar; money is present in every joint of circumstance; it might be named the social atmosphere, since, in society, it is by that alone that men continue to live, and only through that or chance that they can reach or affect one another. Money gives us food, shelter, and privacy; it permits us to be clean in person, opens for us the doors of the theatre, gains us books for study or pleasure, enables us to help the distresses of others, and puts us above necessity so that we can choose the best in life. If we love, it enables us to meet and live with the loved one, or even to prolong her health and life; if we have scruples, it gives us an opportunity to be honest; if we have any bright designs, here is what will smooth the way to their accomplishment. Penury is the worst slavery, and will soon lead to death.

But money is only a means; it presupposes a man to use it. The rich can go where he pleases, but perhaps please himself nowhere. He can buy a library or visit the whole world, but perhaps has neither patience to read nor intelligence to see. The table may be loaded and the appetite wanting; the purse may be full, and the heart empty. He may have gained the world and lost himself; and with all his wealth around him, in a great house and spacious and beautiful demesne, he may live as blank a life as any tattered ditcher. Without an appetite, without an aspiration, void of appreciation, bankrupt of desire and hope, there, in his great house, let him sit and look upon his fingers. It is perhaps a more fortunate destiny to have a taste for collecting shells than to be born a millionaire. Although neither is to be despised, it is always better policy to learn an interest than to make a thousand pounds; for the money will soon be spent, or perhaps you may feel no joy in spending it; but the interest remains imperishable and ever new. To become a botanist, a geologist, a social philosopher, an antiquary, or an artist, is to enlarge one's possessions in the universe by an incalculably higher degree, and by a far surer sort of property, than to purchase a farm of many acres. You had perhaps two thousand a year before the transaction; perhaps you have two thousand five hundred after it. That represents your gain in the one case. But in the other, you have thrown down a barrier which concealed significance and beauty. The blind man has learned to see. The prisoner has opened up a window in his cell and beholds enchanting prospects; he will never again be a prisoner as he was; he can watch clouds and changing seasons, ships on the river, travellers on the road, and the stars at night; happy prisoner! his eyes have broken jail! And again he who has learned to love an art or science has wisely laid up riches against the day of riches; if prosperity come, he will not enter poor into his inheritance; he will not slumber and forget himself in the lap of money, or spend his hours in counting idle treasures, but be up and briskly doing; he will have the true alchemic touch, which is not that of Midas, but which transmutes dead money into living delight and satisfaction.

Être et pas avoir—to be, not to possess—that is the problem of life. To be wealthy, a rich nature is the first requisite and money but the second. To be of a quick and healthy blood, to share in all honourable curiosities, to be rich in admiration and free from envy, to rejoice greatly in the good of others, to love with such generosity of heart that your love is still a dear possession in absence or unkindness—these are the gifts of fortune which money cannot buy and without which money can buy nothing. For what can a man possess, or what can he enjoy, except himself? If he enlarge his nature, it is then that he enlarges his estates. If his nature be happy and valiant, he will enjoy the universe as if it were his park and orchard.

But money is not only to be spent; it has also to be earned. It is not merely a convenience or a necessary in social life; but it is the coin in which mankind pays his wages to the individual man. And from this side, the question of money has a very different scope and application. For no man can be honest who does not work. Service for service. If the farmer buys corn, and the labourer ploughs and reaps, and the baker sweats in his hot bakery, plainly you who eat must do something in your turn. It is not enough to take off your hat, or to thank God upon your knees for the admirable constitution of society and your own convenient situation in its upper and more ornamental stories. Neither is it enough to buy the loaf with a sixpence; for then you are only changing the point of the inquiry; and you must first have bought the sixpence. Service for service: how have you bought your sixpences? A man of spirit desires certainty in a thing of such a nature; he must see to it that there is some reciprocity between him and mankind; that he pays his expenditure in service; that he has not a lion's share in profit and a drone's in labour; and is not a sleeping partner and mere costly incubus on the great mercantile concern of mankind.

Services differ so widely with different gifts, and some are so inappreciable to external tests, that this is not only a matter for the private conscience, but one which even there must be leniently and trustfully considered. For remember how many serve mankind who do no more than meditate; and how many are precious to their friends for no more than a sweet and joyous temper. To perform the function of a man of letters it is not necessary to write; nay, it is perhaps better to be a living book. So long as we love we serve; so long as we are loved by others, I would almost say that we are indispensable; and no man is useless while he has a friend. The true services of life are inestimable in money, and are never paid. Kind words and caresses, high and wise thoughts, humane designs, tender behaviour to the weak and suffering, and all the charities of man's existence, are neither bought nor sold.

Yet the dearest and readiest, if not the most just, criterion of a man's services, is the wage that mankind pays him or, briefly, what he earns. There at least there can be no ambiguity. St. Paul is fully and freely entitled to his earnings as a tentmaker, and Socrates fully and freely entitled to his earnings as a sculptor, although the true business of each was not only something different, but something which remained unpaid. A man cannot forget that he is not superintended, and serves mankind on parole. He would like, when challenged by his own conscience, to reply: 'I have done so much work, and no less, with my own hands and brain, and taken so much profit, and no more, for my own personal delight.' And though St. Paul, if he had possessed a private fortune, would probably have scorned to waste his time in making tents, yet of all sacrifices to public opinion none can be more easily pardoned than that by which a man, already spiritually useful to the world, should restrict the field of his chief usefulness to perform services more apparent, and possess a livelihood that neither stupidity nor malice could call in question. Like all sacrifices to public opinion and mere external decency, this would certainly be wrong; for the soul should rest contented with its own approval and indissuadably pursue its own calling. Yet, so grave and delicate is the question, that a man may well hesitate before he decides it for himself; he may well fear that he sets too high a valuation on his own endeavours after good; he may well condescend upon a humbler duty, where others than himself shall judge the service and proportion the wage.

And yet it is to this very responsibility that the rich are born. They can shuffle off the duty on no other; they are their own paymasters on parole; and must pay themselves fair wages and no more. For I suppose that in the course of ages, and through reform and civil war and invasion, mankind was pursuing some other and more general design than to set one or two

Englishmen of the nineteenth century beyond the reach of needs and duties. Society was scarce put together, and defended with so much eloquence and blood, for the convenience of two or three millionaires and a few hundred other persons of wealth and position. It is plain that if mankind thus acted and suffered during all these generations, they hoped some benefit, some ease, some wellbeing, for themselves and their descendants; that if they supported law and order, it was to secure fair-play for all; that if they denied themselves in the present, they must have had some designs upon the future. Now, a great hereditary fortune is a miracle of man's wisdom and mankind's forbearance; it has not only been amassed and handed down, it has been suffered to be amassed and handed down; and surely in such a consideration as this, its possessor should find only a new spur to activity and honour, that with all this power of service he should not prove unserviceable, and that this mass of treasure should return in benefits upon the race. If he had twenty, or thirty, or a hundred thousand at his banker's, or if all Yorkshire or all California were his to manage or to sell, he would still be morally penniless, and have the world to begin like Whittington, until he had found some way of serving mankind. His wage is physically in his own hand; but, in honour, that wage must still be earned. He is only steward on parole of what is called his fortune. He must honourably perform his stewardship. He must estimate his own services and allow himself a salary in proportion, for that will be one among his functions. And while he will then be free to spend that salary, great or little, on his own private pleasures, the rest of his fortune he but holds and disposes under trust for mankind; it is not his, because he has not earned it; it cannot be his, because his services have already been paid; but year by year it is his to distribute, whether to help individuals whose birthright and outfit have been swallowed up in his, or to further public works and institutions.

At this rate, short of inspiration, it seems hardly possible to be both rich and honest; and the millionaire is under a far more continuous temptation to thieve than the labourer who gets his shilling daily for despicable toils. Are you surprised? It is even so. And you repeat it every Sunday in your churches. 'It is easier for a camel to pass through the eye of a needle than for a rich man to enter the kingdom of God.' I have heard this and similar texts ingeniously explained away and brushed from the path of the aspiring Christian by the tender Great-heart of the parish. One excellent clergyman told us that the 'eye of a needle' meant a low, Oriental postern through which camels could not pass till they were unloaded—which is very likely just; and then went on, bravely confounding the 'kingdom of God' with heaven, the future paradise, to show that of course no rich person could expect to carry his riches beyond the grave—which, of course, he could not and never did. Various greedy sinners of the congregation drank in the comfortable doctrine with relief. It was worth the while having come to church that Sunday morning! All was plain. The Bible, as usual, meant nothing in particular; it was merely an obscure and figurative school-copybook; and if a man were only respectable, he was a man after God's own heart.

Alas! I fear not. And though this matter of a man's services is one for his own conscience, there are some cases in which it is difficult to restrain the mind from judging. Thus I shall be very easily persuaded that a man has earned his daily bread; and if he has but a friend or two to whom his company is delightful at heart, I am more than persuaded at once. But it will be very hard to persuade me that any one has earned an income of a hundred thousand. What he is to his friends, he still would be if he were made penniless to-morrow; for as to the courtiers of luxury and power, I will neither consider them friends, nor indeed consider them at all. What he does for mankind there are most likely hundreds who would do the same, as effectually for the race and as pleasurably to themselves, for the merest fraction of this monstrous wage. Why it is paid, I am, therefore, unable to conceive, and as the man pays it himself, out of funds in his detention, I have a certain backwardness to think him honest.

At least, we have gained a very obvious point: that what a man spends upon himself, he shall have earned by services to the race. Thence flows a principle for the outset of life, which is a little different from that taught in the present day. I am addressing the middle and the upper classes; those who have already been fostered and prepared for life at some expense; those who have some choice before them, and can pick professions; and above all, those who are what is called independent, and need do nothing unless pushed by honour or ambition. In this particular the poor are happy; among them, when a lad comes to his strength, he must take the work that offers, and can take it with an easy conscience. But in the richer classes the question is complicated by the number of opportunities and a variety of considerations. Here, then, this principle of ours comes in helpfully. The young man has to seek, not a road to wealth, but an opportunity of service; not money, but honest work. If he has some strong propensity, some calling of nature, some over-weening interest in any special field of industry, inquiry, or art, he will do right to obey the impulse; and that for two reasons: the first external, because there he will render the best services; the second personal, because a demand of his own nature is to him without appeal whenever it can be satisfied with the consent of his other faculties and appetites. If he has no such elective taste, by the very principle on which he chooses any pursuit at all he must choose the most honest and serviceable, and not the most highly remunerated. We have here an external problem, not from or to ourself, but flowing from the constitution of society; and we have our own soul with its fixed design of righteousness. All that can be done is to present the problem in proper terms, and leave it to the soul of the individual. Now, the problem to the poor is one of necessity: to earn wherewithal to live, they must find remunerative labour. But the problem to the rich is one of honour: having the wherewithal, they must find serviceable labour. Each has to earn his daily bread: the one, because he has not yet got it to eat; the other, who has already eaten it, because he has not yet earned it.

Of course, what is true of bread is true of luxuries and comforts, whether for the body or the mind. But the consideration of luxuries leads us to a new aspect of the whole question, and to a second proposition no less true, and maybe no less startling, than the last.

At the present day, we, of the easier classes, are in a state of surfeit and disgrace after meat. Plethora has filled us with indifference; and we are covered from head to foot with the callosities of habitual opulence. Born into what is called a certain rank, we live, as the saying is, up to our station. We squander without enjoyment, because our fathers squandered. We eat of the best, not from delicacy, but from brazen habit. We do not keenly enjoy or eagerly desire the presence of a luxury; we are unaccustomed to its absence.

And not only do we squander money from habit, but still more pitifully waste it in ostentation. I can think of no more melancholy disgrace for a creature who professes either reason or pleasure for his guide, than to spend the smallest fraction of his income upon that which he does not desire; and to keep a carriage in which you do not wish to drive, or a butler of whom you are afraid, is a pathetic kind of folly. Money, being a means of happiness, should make both parties happy when it changes hands; rightly disposed, it should be twice blessed in its employment; and buyer and seller should alike have their twenty shillings worth of profit out of every pound. Benjamin Franklin went through life an altered man, because he once paid too dearly for a penny whistle. My concern springs usually from a deeper source, to wit, from having bought a whistle when I did not want one. I find I regret this, or would regret it if I gave myself the time, not only on personal but on moral and philanthropical considerations. For, first, in a world where money is wanting to buy books for eager students and food and medicine for pining children, and where a large majority are starved in their most immediate desires, it is surely base, stupid, and cruel to squander money when I am pushed by no appetite and enjoy no return of genuine satisfaction. My philanthropy is wide enough in scope to include myself; and when I have made myself happy, I have at least one good argument that I have acted rightly; but where that is not so, and I have bought and not enjoyed, my mouth is closed, and I conceive that I have robbed the poor. And, second, anything I buy or use which I do not sincerely want or cannot vividly enjoy, disturbs the balance of supply and demand, and contributes to remove industrious hands from the production of what is useful or pleasurable and to keep them busy upon ropes of sand and things that are a weariness to the flesh. That extravagance is truly sinful, and a very silly sin to boot, in which we impoverish mankind and ourselves. It is another question for each man's heart. He knows if he can enjoy what he buys and uses; if he cannot, he is a dog in the manger; nay, it he cannot, I contend he is a thief, for nothing really belongs to a man which he cannot use. Proprietor is connected with propriety; and that only is the man's which is proper to his wants and faculties.

A youth, in choosing a career, must not be alarmed by poverty. Want is a sore thing, but poverty does not imply want. It remains to be seen whether with half his present income, or a third, he cannot, in the most generous sense, live as fully as at present. He is a fool who objects to luxuries; but he is also a fool who does not protest against the waste of luxuries on those who do not desire and cannot enjoy them. It remains to be seen, by each man who would live a true life to himself and not a merely specious life to society, how many luxuries he truly wants and to how many he merely submits as to a social propriety; and all these last he will immediately forswear. Let him do this, and he will be surprised to find how little money it requires to keep him in complete contentment and activity of mind and senses. Life at any level among the easy classes is conceived upon a principle of rivalry, where each man and each household must ape the tastes and emulate the display of others. One is delicate in eating, another in wine, a third in furniture or works of art or dress; and I, who care nothing for any of these refinements, who am perhaps a plain athletic creature and love exercise, beef, beer, flannel shirts and a camp bed, am yet called upon to assimilate all these other tastes and make these foreign occasions of expenditure my own. It may be cynical: I am sure I shall be told it is selfish; but I will spend my money as I please and for my own intimate personal gratification, and should count myself a nincompoop indeed to lay out the colour of a halfpenny on any fancied social decency or duty. I shall not wear gloves unless my hands are cold, or unless I am born with a delight in them. Dress is my own affair, and that of one other in the world; that, in fact and for an obvious reason, of any woman who shall chance to be in love with me. I shall lodge where I have a mind. If I do not ask society to live with me, they must be silent; and even if I do, they have no further right but to refuse the invitation! There is a kind of idea abroad that a man must live up to his station, that his house, his table, and his toilette, shall be in a ratio of equivalence, and equally imposing to the world. If this is in the Bible, the passage has eluded my inquiries. If it is not in the Bible, it is nowhere but in the heart of the fool. Throw aside this fancy. See what you want, and spend upon that; distinguish what you do not care about, and spend nothing upon that. There are not many people who can differentiate wines above a certain and that not at all a high price. Are you sure you are one of these? Are you sure you prefer cigars at sixpence each to pipes at some fraction of a farthing? Are you sure you wish to keep a gig? Do you care about where you sleep, or are you not as much at your ease in a cheap lodging as in an Elizabethan manor-house? Do you enjoy fine clothes? It is not possible to answer these questions without a trial; and there is nothing more obvious to my mind, than that a man who has not experienced some ups and downs, and been forced to live more cheaply than in his father's house, has still his education to begin. Let the experiment be made, and he will find to his surprise that he has been eating beyond his appetite up to that hour; that the cheap lodging, the cheap tobacco, the rough country clothes, the plain table, have not only no power to damp his spirits, but perhaps give him as keen pleasure in the using as the dainties that he took, betwixt sleep and waking, in his former callous and somnambulous submission to wealth.

The true Bohemian, a creature lost to view under the imaginary Bohemians of literature, is exactly described by such a principle of life. The Bohemian of the novel, who drinks more than is good for him and prefers anything to work, and wears strange clothes, is for the most part a respectable Bohemian, respectable in disrespectability, living for the outside, and an adventurer. But the man I mean lives wholly to himself, does what he wishes, and not what is thought proper, buys what he wants for himself, and not what is thought proper, works at what he believes he can do well and not what will bring him in money or favour. You may be the most respectable of men, and yet a true Bohemian. And the test is this: a Bohemian, for as poor as he may be, is always open-handed to his friends; he knows what he can do with money and how he can do without it, a far rarer and more useful knowledge; he has had less, and continued to live in some contentment; and hence he cares not to keep more, and shares his sovereign or his shilling with a friend. The poor, if they are generous, are Bohemian in virtue of their birth. Do you know where beggars go? Not to the great houses where people sit dazed among their thousands, but to the doors of poor men who have seen the world; and it was the widow who had only two mites, who cast half her fortune into the treasury.

But a young man who elects to save on dress or on lodging, or who in any way falls out of the level of expenditure which is common to his level in society, falls out of society altogether. I suppose the young man to have chosen his career on honourable principles; he finds his talents and instincts can be best contented in a certain pursuit; in a certain industry, he is sure that he is serving mankind with a healthy and becoming service; and he is not sure that he would be doing so, or doing so equally well, in any other industry within his reach. Then that is his true sphere in life; not the one in which he was born to his father, but the one which is proper to his talents and instincts. And suppose he does fall out of society, is that a cause of sorrow? Is your heart so dead that you prefer the recognition of many to the love of a few? Do you think society loves you? Put it to the proof. Decline in material expenditure, and you will find they care no more for you than for the Khan of Tartary. You will lose no friends. If you had any, you will keep them. Only those who were friends to your coat and equipage will disappear; the smiling faces will disappear as by enchantment; but the kind hearts will remain steadfastly kind. Are you so lost, are you so dead, are you so little sure of your own soul and your own footing upon solid fact, that you prefer before goodness and happiness the countenance of sundry diners-out, who will flee from you at a report of ruin, who will drop you with insult at a shadow of disgrace, who do not know you and do not care to know you but by sight, and whom you in your turn neither know nor care to know in a more human manner? Is it not the principle of society, openly avowed, that friendship must not interfere with business; which being paraphrased, means simply that a consideration of money goes before any consideration of affection known to this cold-blooded gang, that they have not even the honour of thieves, and will rook their nearest and dearest as readily as a stranger? I hope I would go as far as most to serve a friend; but I declare openly I would not put on my hat to do a pleasure to society. I may starve my appetites and control my temper for the sake of those I love; but society shall take me as I choose to be, or go without me. Neither they nor I will lose; for where there is no love, it is both laborious and unprofitable to associate.

But it is obvious that if it is only right for a man to spend money on that which he can truly and thoroughly enjoy, the doctrine applies with equal force to the rich and to the poor, to the man who has amassed many thousands as well as to the youth precariously beginning life. And it may be asked, Is not this merely preparing misers, who are not the best of company? But the principle was this: that which a man has not fairly earned, and, further, that which he cannot fully enjoy, does not belong to him, but is a part of mankind's treasure which he holds as steward on parole. To mankind, then, it must be made profitable; and how this should be done is, once more, a problem which each man must solve for himself, and about which none has a right to judge him. Yet there are a few considerations which are very obvious and may here be stated. Mankind is not only the whole in general, but every one in particular. Every man or woman is one of mankind's dear possessions; to his or her just brain, and kind heart, and active hands, mankind intrusts some of its hopes for the future; he or she is a possible well-spring of good acts and source of blessings to the race. This money which you do not need, which, in a rigid sense, you do not want, may therefore be returned not only in public benefactions to the race, but in private kindnesses. Your wife, your children, your friends stand nearest to you, and should be helped the first. There at least there can be little imposture, for you know their necessities of your own knowledge. And consider, if all the world did as you did, and according to their means extended help in the circle of their affections, there would be no more crying want in times of plenty and no more cold, mechanical charity given with a doubt and received with confusion. Would not this simple rule make a new world out of the old and cruel one which we inhabit?

[After two more sentences the fragment breaks off.]

FATHER DAMIEN

AN OPEN LETTER TO THE REVEREND DR. HYDE OF HONOLULU

SYDNEY,

February 25, 1890.

Sir,—It may probably occur to you that we have met, and visited, and conversed; on my side, with interest. You may remember that you have done me several courtesies, for which I was prepared to be grateful. But there are duties which come before gratitude, and offences which justly divide friends, far more acquaintances. Your letter to the Reverend H. B. Gage is a document which, in my sight, if you had filled me with bread when I was starving, if you had sat up to nurse my father when he lay a-dying, would yet absolve me from the bonds of gratitude. You know enough, doubtless, of the process of canonisation to be aware that, a hundred years after the death of Damien, there will appear a man charged with the painful office of the devil's advocate. After that noble brother of mine, and of all frail clay, shall have lain a century at rest, one shall accuse, one defend him. The circumstance is unusual that the devil's advocate should be a volunteer, should be a member of a sect immediately rival, and should make haste to take upon himself his ugly office ere the bones are cold; unusual, and of a taste which I shall leave my readers free to qualify; unusual, and to me inspiring. If I have at all learned the trade of using words to convey truth and to arouse emotion, you have at last furnished me with a subject. For it is in the interest of all mankind, and the cause of public decency in every quarter of the world, not only that Damien should be righted, but that you and your letter should be displayed at length, in their true colours, to the public eye.

To do this properly, I must begin by quoting you at large: I shall then proceed to criticise your utterance from several points of view, divine and human, in the course of which I shall attempt to draw again, and with more specification, the character of the dead saint whom it has pleased you to vilify:

so much being done, I shall say farewell to you for ever.

'HONOLULU,

'*August* 2, 1889.

'Rev. H. B. Gage.

'Dear Brother,—In answer to your inquiries about Father Damien, I can only reply that we who knew the man are surprised at the extravagant newspaper laudations, as if he was a most saintly philanthropist. The simple truth is, he was a coarse, dirty man, head-strong and bigoted. He was not sent to Molokai, but went there without orders; did not stay at the leper settlement (before he became one himself), but circulated freely over the whole island (less than half the island is devoted to the lepers), and he came often to Honolulu. He had no hand in the reforms and improvements inaugurated, which were the work of our Board of Health, as occasion required and means were provided. He was not a pure man in his relations with women, and the leprosy of which he died should be attributed to his vices and carelessness. Others have done much for the lepers, our own ministers, the government physicians, and so forth, but never with the Catholic idea of meriting eternal life.— Yours, etc.,

'C. M. Hyde.' [65]

To deal fitly with a letter so extraordinary, I must draw at the outset on my private knowledge of the signatory and his sect. It may offend others; scarcely you, who have been so busy to collect, so bold to publish, gossip on your rivals. And this is perhaps the moment when I may best explain to you the character of what you are to read: I conceive you as a man quite beyond and below the reticences of civility: with what measure you mete, with that shall it be measured you again; with you, at last, I rejoice to feel the button off the foil and to plunge home. And if in aught that I shall say I should offend others, your colleagues, whom I respect and remember with affection, I can but offer them my regret; I am not free, I am inspired by the consideration of interests far more large; and such pain as can be inflicted by anything from me must be indeed trifling when compared with the pain with which they read your letter. It is not the hangman, but the criminal, that brings dishonour on the house.

You belong, sir, to a sect—I believe my sect, and that in which my ancestors laboured—which has enjoyed, and partly failed to utilise, an exceptional advantage in the islands of Hawaii. The first missionaries came; they found the land already self-purged of its old and bloody faith; they were embraced, almost on their arrival, with enthusiasm; what troubles they supported came far more from whites than from Hawaiians; and to these last they stood (in a rough figure) in the shoes of God. This is not the place to enter into the degree or causes of their failure, such as it is. One element alone is pertinent, and must here be plainly dealt with. In the course of their evangelical calling, they—or too many of them—grew rich. It may be news to you that the houses of missionaries are a cause of mocking on the streets of Honolulu. It will at least be news to you, that when I returned your civil visit, the driver of my cab commented on the size, the taste, and the comfort of your home. It would have been news certainly to myself, had any one told me that afternoon that I should live to drag such matter into print. But you see, sir, how you degrade better men to your own level; and it is needful that those who are to judge betwixt you and me, betwixt Damien and the devil's advocate, should understand your letter to have been penned in a house which could raise, and that very justly, the envy and the comments of the passers-by. I think (to employ a phrase of yours which I admire) it 'should be attributed' to you that you have never visited the scene of Damien's life and death. If you had, and had recalled it, and looked about your pleasant rooms, even your pen perhaps would have been stayed.

Your sect (and remember, as far as any sect avows me, it is mine) has not done ill in a worldly sense in the Hawaiian Kingdom. When calamity befell their innocent parishioners, when leprosy descended and took root in the Eight Islands, a quid pro quo was to be looked for. To that prosperous mission, and to you, as one of its adornments, God had sent at last an opportunity. I know I am touching here upon a nerve acutely sensitive. I know that others of your colleagues look back on the inertia of your Church, and the intrusive and decisive heroism of Damien, with something almost to be called remorse.

I am sure it is so with yourself; I am persuaded your letter was inspired by a certain envy, not essentially ignoble, and the one human trait to be espied in that performance. You were thinking of the lost chance, the past day; of that which should have been conceived and was not; of the service due and not rendered. Time was, said the voice in your ear, in your pleasant room, as you sat raging and writing; and if the words written were base beyond parallel, the rage, I am happy to repeat—it is the only compliment I shall pay you—the rage was almost virtuous. But, sir, when we have failed, and another has succeeded; when we have stood by, and another has stepped in; when we sit and grow bulky in our charming mansions, and a plain, uncouth peasant steps into the battle, under the eyes of God, and succours the afflicted, and consoles the dying, and is himself afflicted in his turn, and dies upon the field of honour—the battle cannot be retrieved as your unhappy irritation has suggested. It is a lost battle, and lost for ever. One thing remained to you in your defeat—some rags of common honour; and these you have made haste to cast away.

Common honour; not the honour of having done anything right, but the honour of not having done aught conspicuously foul; the honour of the inert: that was what remained to you. We are not all expected to be Damiens; a man may conceive his duty more narrowly, he may love his comforts better; and none will cast a stone at him for that. But will a gentleman of your reverend profession allow me an example from the fields of gallantry? When two gentlemen compete for the favour of a lady, and the one succeeds and the other is rejected, and (as will sometimes happen) matter damaging to the successful rival's credit reaches the ear of the defeated, it is held by plain men of no pretensions that his mouth is, in the circumstance, almost necessarily closed. Your Church and Damien's were in Hawaii upon a rivalry to do well: to help, to edify, to set divine examples. You having (in one huge instance) failed, and Damien succeeded, I marvel it should not have occurred to you that you were doomed to silence; that when you had been outstripped in that high rivalry, and sat inglorious in the midst of your wellbeing, in your pleasant room—and Damien, crowned with glories and horrors, toiled and rotted in that pigsty of his under the cliffs of Kalawao—you, the elect who would not, were the last man on earth to collect and propagate gossip on the volunteer who would and did.

I think I see you—for I try to see you in the flesh as I write these sentences—I think I see you leap at the word pigsty, a hyperbolical expression at the best. 'He had no hand in the reforms,' he was 'a coarse, dirty man'; these were your own words; and you may think it possible that I am come to support you with fresh evidence. In a sense, it is even so. Damien has been too much depicted with a conventional halo and conventional features; so drawn by men who perhaps had not the eye to remark or the pen to express the individual; or who perhaps were only blinded and silenced by generous admiration, such as I partly envy for myself—such as you, if your soul were enlightened, would envy on your bended knees. It is the least defect of such a method of portraiture that it makes the path easy for the devil's advocate, and leaves for the misuse of the slanderer a considerable field of truth. For the truth that is suppressed by friends is the readiest weapon of the enemy. The world, in your despite, may perhaps owe you something, if your letter be the means of substituting once for all a credible likeness for a wax abstraction. For, if that world at all remember you, on the day when Damien of Molokai shall be named Saint, it will be in virtue of one work: your letter to the Reverend H. B. Gage.

You may ask on what authority I speak. It was my inclement destiny to become acquainted, not with Damien, but with Dr. Hyde. When I visited the lazaretto, Damien was already in his resting grave. But such information as I have, I gathered on the spot in conversation with those who knew him well and long: some indeed who revered his memory; but others who had sparred and wrangled with him, who beheld him with no halo, who perhaps regarded him with small respect, and through whose unprepared and scarcely partial communications the plain, human features of the man shone on me convincingly. These gave me what knowledge I possess; and I learnt it in that scene where it could be most completely and sensitively understood— Kalawao, which you have never visited, about which you have never so much as endeavoured to inform yourself; for, brief as your letter is, you have found the means to stumble into that confession. 'Less than one-half of the island,' you say, 'is devoted to the lepers.' Molokai—'Molokai ahina,' the 'grey,' lofty, and most desolate island—along all its northern side plunges a front of precipice into a sea of unusual profundity. This range of cliff is, from east to west, the true end and frontier of the island. Only in one spot there projects into the ocean a certain triangular and rugged down, grassy, stony, windy, and rising in the midst into a hill with a dead crater: the whole bearing to the cliff that overhangs it somewhat the same relation as a bracket to a wall. With this hint you will now be able to pick out the leper station on a map; you will be able to judge how much of Molokai is thus cut off between the surf and precipice, whether less than a half, or less than a quarter, or a fifth, or a tenth—or, say, a twentieth; and the next time you burst into print you will be in a position to share with us the issue of your calculations.

I imagine you to be one of those persons who talk with cheerfulness of that place which oxen and wain-ropes could not drag you to behold. You, who do not even know its situation on the map, probably denounce sensational descriptions, stretching your limbs the while in your pleasant parlour on Beretania Street. When I was pulled ashore there one early morning, there sat with me in the boat two sisters, bidding farewell (in humble imitation of Damien) to the lights and joys of human life. One of these wept silently; I could not withhold myself from joining her. Had you been there, it is my belief that nature would have triumphed even in you; and as the boat drew but a little nearer, and you beheld the stairs crowded with abominable deformations of our common manhood, and saw yourself landing in the midst of such a population as only now and then surrounds us in the horror of a nightmare—what a haggard eye you would have rolled over your reluctant shoulder towards the house on Beretania Street! Had you gone on; had you found every fourth face a blot upon the landscape; had you visited the hospital and seen the butt-ends of human beings lying there almost unrecognisable, but still breathing, still thinking, still remembering; you would have understood that life in the lazaretto is an ordeal from which the nerves of a man's spirit shrink, even as his eye quails under the brightness of the sun; you would have felt it was (even to-day) a pitiful place to visit and a hell to dwell in. It is not the fear of possible infection. That seems a little thing when compared with the pain, the pity, and the disgust of the visitor's surroundings, and the atmosphere of affliction, disease, and physical disgrace in which he breathes. I do not think I am a man more than usually timid; but I never recall the days and nights I spent upon that island promontory (eight days and seven nights), without heartfelt thankfulness that I am somewhere else. I find in my diary that I speak of my stay as a 'grinding experience': I have once jotted in the margin, 'Harrowing is the word'; and when the Mokolii bore me at last towards the outer world, I kept repeating to myself, with a new conception of their pregnancy, those simple words of the song—

''Tis the most distressful country that ever yet was seen.'

And observe: that which I saw and suffered from was a settlement purged, bettered, beautified; the new village built, the hospital and the Bishop-Home excellently arranged; the sisters, the doctor, and the missionaries, all indefatigable in their noble tasks. It was a different place when Damien came there and made his great renunciation, and slept that first night under a tree amidst his rotting brethren: alone with pestilence; and looking forward (with what courage, with what pitiful sinkings of dread, God only knows) to a lifetime of dressing sores and stumps.

You will say, perhaps, I am too sensitive, that sights as painful abound in cancer hospitals and are confronted daily by doctors and nurses. I have long learned to admire and envy the doctors and the nurses. But there is no cancer hospital so large and populous as Kalawao and Kalaupapa; and in such a matter every fresh case, like every inch of length in the pipe of an organ, deepens the note of the impression; for what daunts the onlooker is that monstrous sum of human suffering by which he stands surrounded. Lastly, no doctor or nurse is called upon to enter once for all the doors of that gehenna; they do not say farewell, they need not abandon hope, on its sad threshold; they but go for a time to their high calling, and can look forward as they go to relief, to recreation, and to rest. But Damien shut-to with his own hand the doors of his own sepulchre.

I shall now extract three passages from my diary at Kalawao.

A. 'Damien is dead and already somewhat ungratefully remembered in the field of his labours and sufferings. "He was a good man, but very officious," says one. Another tells me he had fallen (as other priests so easily do) into something of the ways and habits of thought of a Kanaka; but he had the wit to recognise the fact, and the good sense to laugh at' [over] 'it. A plain man it seems he was; I cannot find he was a popular.'

B. 'After Ragsdale's death' [Ragsdale was a famous Luna, or overseer, of the unruly settlement] 'there followed a brief term of office by Father Damien which served only to publish the weakness of that noble man. He was rough in his ways, and he had no control. Authority was relaxed; Damien's life was threatened, and he was soon eager to resign.'

C. 'Of Damien I begin to have an idea. He seems to have been a man of the peasant class, certainly of the peasant type: shrewd, ignorant and bigoted, yet with an open mind, and capable of receiving and digesting a reproof if it were bluntly administered; superbly generous in the least thing as well as in the greatest, and as ready to give his last shirt (although not without human grumbling) as he had been to sacrifice his life; essentially indiscreet and officious, which made him a troublesome colleague; domineering in all his ways, which made him incurably unpopular with the Kanakas, but yet destitute of real authority, so that his boys laughed at him and he must carry out his wishes by the means of bribes. He learned to have a mania for doctoring; and set up the Kanakas against the remedies of his regular rivals: perhaps (if anything matter at all in the treatment of such a disease) the worst thing that he did, and certainly the easiest. The best and worst of the man appear very plainly in his dealings with Mr. Chapman's money; he had originally laid it out' [intended to lay it out] 'entirely for the benefit of Catholics, and even so not wisely; but after a long, plain talk, he admitted his error fully and revised the list. The sad state of the boys' home is in part the result of his lack of control; in part, of his own slovenly ways and false ideas of hygiene. Brother officials used to call it "Damien's Chinatown." "Well," they would say, "your China-town keeps growing." And he would laugh with perfect good-nature, and adhere to his errors with perfect obstinacy. So much I have gathered of truth about this plain, noble human brother and father of ours; his imperfections are the traits of his face, by which we know him for our fellow; his martyrdom and his example nothing can lessen or annul; and only a person here on the spot can properly appreciate their greatness.'

I have set down these private passages, as you perceive, without correction; thanks to you, the public has them in their bluntness. They are almost a list of the man's faults, for it is rather these that I was seeking: with his virtues, with the heroic profile of his life, I and the world were already sufficiently acquainted. I was besides a little suspicious of Catholic testimony; in no ill sense, but merely because Damien's admirers and disciples were the least likely to be critical. I know you will be more suspicious still; and the facts set down above were one and all collected from the lips of Protestants who had opposed the father in his life. Yet I am strangely deceived, or they build up the image of a man, with all his weaknesses, essentially heroic, and alive with rugged honesty, generosity, and mirth.

Take it for what it is, rough private jottings of the worst sides of Damien's character, collected from the lips of those who had laboured with and (in your own phrase) 'knew the man';—though I question whether Damien would have said that he knew you. Take it, and observe with wonder how well you were served by your gossips, how ill by your intelligence and sympathy; in how many points of fact we are at one, and how widely our appreciations vary. There is something wrong here; either with you or me. It is possible, for instance, that you, who seem to have so many ears in Kalawao, had heard of the affair of Mr. Chapman's money, and were singly struck by Damien's intended wrong-doing. I was struck with that also, and set it fairly down; but I was struck much more by the fact that he had the honesty of mind to be convinced. I may here tell you that it was a long business; that one of his colleagues sat with him late into the night, multiplying arguments and accusations; that the father listened as usual with 'perfect good-nature and perfect obstinacy'; but at the last, when he was persuaded—'Yes,' said he, 'I am very much obliged to you; you have done me a service; it would have been a theft.' There are many (not Catholics merely) who require their heroes and saints to be infallible; to these the story will be painful; not to the true lovers, patrons, and servants of mankind.

And I take it, this is a type of our division; that you are one of those who have an eye for faults and failures; that you take a pleasure to find and publish them; and that, having found them, you make haste to forget the overvailing virtues and the real success which had alone introduced them to your knowledge. It is a dangerous frame of mind. That you may understand how dangerous, and into what a situation it has already brought you, we will (if you please) go hand-in-hand through the different phrases of your letter, and candidly examine each from the point of view of its truth, its appositeness, and its charity.

Damien was coarse.

It is very possible. You make us sorry for the lepers, who had only a coarse old peasant for their friend and father. But you, who were so refined, why were you not there, to cheer them with the lights of culture? Or may I remind you that we have some reason to doubt if John the Baptist were genteel; and in the case of Peter, on whose career you doubtless dwell approvingly in the pulpit, no doubt at all he was a 'coarse, headstrong' fisherman! Yet even in our Protestant Bibles Peter is called Saint.

Damien was dirty.

He was. Think of the poor lepers annoyed with this dirty comrade! But the clean Dr. Hyde was at his food in a fine house.

Damien was headstrong.

I believe you are right again; and I thank God for his strong head and heart.

Damien was bigoted.

I am not fond of bigots myself, because they are not fond of me. But what is meant by bigotry, that we should regard it as a blemish in a priest? Damien believed his own religion with the simplicity of a peasant or a child; as I would I could suppose that you do. For this, I wonder at him some way off; and had that been his only character, should have avoided him in life. But the point of interest in Damien, which has caused him to be so much talked about and made him at last the subject of your pen and mine, was that, in him, his bigotry, his intense and narrow faith, wrought potently for good, and strengthened him to be one of the world's heroes and exemplars.

Damien was not sent to Molokai, but went there without orders.

Is this a misreading? or do you really mean the words for blame? I have heard Christ, in the pulpits of our Church, held up for imitation on the ground that His sacrifice was voluntary. Does Dr. Hyde think otherwise?

Damien did not stay at the settlement, etc.

It is true he was allowed many indulgences. Am I to understand that you blame the father for profiting by these, or the officers for granting them? In either case, it is a mighty Spartan standard to issue from the house on Beretania Street; and I am convinced you will find yourself with few supporters.

Damien had no hand in the reforms, etc.

I think even you will admit that I have already been frank in my description of the man I am defending; but before I take you up upon this head, I will be franker still, and tell you that perhaps nowhere in the world can a man taste a more pleasurable sense of contrast than when he passes from Damien's 'Chinatown' at Kalawao to the beautiful Bishop-Home at Kalaupapa. At this point, in my desire to make all fair for you, I will break my rule and adduce Catholic testimony. Here is a passage from my diary about my visit to the Chinatown, from which you will see how it is (even now) regarded by its own officials: 'We went round all the dormitories, refectories, etc.—dark and dingy enough, with a superficial cleanliness, which he' [Mr. Dutton, the lay-brother] 'did not seek to defend. "It is almost decent," said he; "the sisters will make that all right when we get them here."' And yet I gathered it was already better since Damien was dead, and far better than when he was there alone and had his own (not always excellent) way. I have now come far enough to meet you on a common ground of fact; and I tell you that, to a mind not prejudiced by jealousy, all the reforms of the lazaretto, and even those which he most vigorously opposed, are properly the work of Damien. They are the evidence of his success; they are what his heroism provoked from the reluctant and the careless. Many were before him in the field; Mr. Meyer, for instance, of whose faithful work we hear too little: there have been many since; and some had more worldly wisdom, though none had more devotion, than our saint. Before his day, even you will confess, they had effected little. It was his part, by one striking act of martyrdom, to direct all men's eyes on that distressful country. At a blow, and with the price of his life, he made the place illustrious and public. And that, if you will consider largely, was the one reform needful; pregnant of all that should succeed. It brought money; it brought (best individual addition of them all) the sisters; it brought supervision, for public opinion and public interest landed with the man at Kalawao. If ever any man brought reforms, and died to bring them, it was he. There is not a clean cup or towel in the Bishop-Home, but dirty Damien washed it.

Damien was not a pure man in his relations with women, etc.

How do you know that? Is this the nature of the conversation in that house on Beretania Street which the cabman envied, driving past?—racy details of the misconduct of the poor peasant priest, toiling under the cliffs of Molokai?

Many have visited the station before me; they seem not to have heard the rumour. When I was there I heard many shocking tales, for my informants were men speaking with the plainness of the laity; and I heard plenty of complaints of Damien. Why was this never mentioned? and how came it to you in the retirement of your clerical parlour?

But I must not even seem to deceive you. This scandal, when I read it in your letter, was not new to me. I had heard it once before; and I must tell you how. There came to Samoa a man from Honolulu; he, in a public-house on the beach, volunteered the statement that Damien had 'contracted the disease from having connection with the female lepers'; and I find a joy in telling you how the report was welcomed in a public-house. A man sprang to his feet; I am not at liberty to give his name, but from what I heard I doubt if you would care to have him to dinner in Beretania Street. 'You miserable little—' (here is a word I dare not print, it would so shock your ears). 'You miserable little—,' he cried, 'if the story were a thousand times true, can't you see you are a million times a lower—for daring to repeat it?' I wish it could be told of you that when the report reached you in your house, perhaps after family worship, you had found in your soul enough holy anger to receive it with the same expressions; ay, even with that one which I dare not print; it would not need to have been blotted away, like Uncle Toby's oath, by the tears of the recording angel; it would have been counted to you for your brightest righteousness. But you have deliberately chosen the part of the man from Honolulu, and you have played it with improvements of your own. The man from Honolulu—miserable, leering creature—communicated the tale to a rude knot of beach-combing drinkers in a public-house, where (I will so far agree with your temperance opinions) man is not always at his noblest; and the man from Honolulu had himself been drinking—drinking, we may charitably fancy, to excess. It was to your 'Dear Brother, the Reverend H. B. Gage,' that you chose to communicate the sickening story; and the blue ribbon which adorns your portly bosom forbids me to allow you the extenuating plea that you were drunk when it was done. Your 'dear brother'—a brother indeed—made haste to deliver up your letter (as a means of grace, perhaps) to the religious papers; where, after many months, I found and read and wondered at it; and whence I have now reproduced it for the wonder of others. And you and your dear brother have, by this cycle of operations, built up a contrast very edifying to examine in detail. The man whom you would not care to have to dinner, on the one side; on the other, the Reverend Dr. Hyde and the Reverend H. B. Gage: the Apia bar-room, the Honolulu manse.

But I fear you scarce appreciate how you appear to your fellow-men; and to bring it home to you, I will suppose your story to be true. I will suppose—and God forgive me for supposing it—that Damien faltered and stumbled in his narrow path of duty; I will suppose that, in the horror of his isolation, perhaps in the fever of incipient disease, he, who was doing so much more than he had sworn, failed in the letter of his priestly oath—he, who was so much a better man than either you or me, who did what we have never dreamed of daring—he too tasted of our common frailty. 'O, Iago, the pity of it!' The least tender should be moved to tears; the most incredulous to prayer. And all that you could do was to pen your letter to the Reverend H. B. Gage!

Is it growing at all clear to you what a picture you have drawn of your own heart? I will try yet once again to make it clearer. You had a father: suppose this tale were about him, and some informant brought it to you, proof in hand: I am not making too high an estimate of your emotional nature when I suppose you would regret the circumstance? that you would feel the tale of frailty the more keenly since it shamed the author of your days? and that the last thing you would do would be to publish it in the religious press? Well, the man who tried to do what Damien did, is my father, and the father of the man in the Apia bar, and the father of all who love goodness; and he was your father too, if God had given you grace to see it.

THE PENTLAND RISING

A PAGE OF HISTORY

1666

'A cloud of witnesses lyes here,

Who for Christ's interest did appear.'

Inscription on Battlefield at Rullion Green.

CHAPTER I—THE CAUSES OF THE REVOLT

'Halt, passenger; take heed what thou dost see,

This tomb doth show for what some men did die.'

Monument, Greyfriars' Churchyard, Edinburgh,

1661–1668. [85]

Two hundred years ago a tragedy was enacted in Scotland, the memory whereof has been in great measure lost or obscured by the deep tragedies which followed it. It is, as it were, the evening of the night of persecution—a sort of twilight, dark indeed to us, but light as the noonday when compared with the midnight gloom which followed. This fact, of its being the very threshold of persecution, lends it, however, an additional interest.

The prejudices of the people against Episcopacy were 'out of measure increased,' says Bishop Burnet, 'by the new incumbents who were put in the places of the ejected preachers, and were generally very mean and despicable in all respects. They were the worst preachers I ever heard; they were ignorant to a reproach; and many of them were openly vicious. They . . . were indeed the dreg and refuse of the northern parts. Those of them who arose above contempt or scandal were men of such violent tempers that they were as much hated as the others were despised.' [86] It was little to be wondered at, from this account that the country-folk refused to go to the parish church, and chose rather to listen to outed ministers in the fields. But this was not to be allowed, and their persecutors at last fell on the method of calling a roll of the parishioners' names every Sabbath, and marking a fine of twenty shillings Scots to the name of each absenter. In this way very large debts were incurred by persons altogether unable to pay. Besides this, landlords were fined for their tenants' absences, tenants for their landlords', masters for their servants', servants for their masters', even though they themselves were perfectly regular in their attendance. And as the curates were allowed to fine with the sanction of any common soldier, it may be imagined that often the pretexts were neither very sufficient nor well proven.

When the fines could not be paid at once, Bibles, clothes, and household utensils were seized upon, or a number of soldiers, proportionate to his wealth, were quartered on the offender. The coarse and drunken privates filled the houses with woe; snatched the bread from the children to feed their dogs; shocked the principles, scorned the scruples, and blasphemed the religion of their humble hosts; and when they had reduced them to destitution, sold the furniture, and burned down the roof-tree which was consecrated to the peasants by the name of Home. For all this attention each of these soldiers received from his unwilling landlord a certain sum of money per day—three shillings sterling, according to Naphtali. And frequently they were forced to pay quartering money for more men than were in reality 'cessed on them.' At that time it was no strange thing to behold a strong man begging for money to pay his fines, and many others who were deep in arrears, or who had attracted attention in some other way, were forced to flee from their homes, and take refuge from arrest and imprisonment among the wild mosses of the uplands. [87a]

One example in particular we may cite:

John Neilson, the Laird of Corsack, a worthy man, was, unfortunately for himself, a Nonconformist. First he was fined in four hundred pounds Scots, and then through cessing he lost nineteen hundred and ninety-three pounds Scots. He was next obliged to leave his house and flee from place to place, during which wanderings he lost his horse. His wife and children were turned out of doors, and then his tenants were fined till they too were almost

71

ruined. As a final stroke, they drove away all his cattle to Glasgow and sold them. [87b] Surely it was time that something were done to alleviate so much sorrow, to overthrow such tyranny.

About this time too there arrived in Galloway a person calling himself Captain Andrew Gray, and advising the people to revolt. He displayed some documents purporting to be from the northern Covenanters, and stating that they were prepared to join in any enterprise commenced by their southern brethren. The leader of the persecutors was Sir James Turner, an officer afterwards degraded for his share in the matter. 'He was naturally fierce, but was mad when he was drunk, and that was very often,' said Bishop Burnet. 'He was a learned man, but had always been in armies, and knew no other rule but to obey orders. He told me he had no regard to any law, but acted, as he was commanded, in a military way.' [88]

This was the state of matters, when an outrage was committed which gave spirit and determination to the oppressed countrymen, lit the flame of insubordination, and for the time at least recoiled on those who perpetrated it with redoubled force.

CHAPTER II—THE BEGINNING

I love no warres,

I love no jarres,

Nor strife's fire.

May discord cease,

Let's live in peace:

This I desire.

If it must be

Warre we must see

(So fates conspire),

May we not feel

The force of steel:

This I desire.

T. JACKSON, 1651 [89]

Upon Tuesday, November 13th, 1666, Corporal George Deanes and three other soldiers set upon an old man in the clachan of Dalry and demanded the payment of his fines. On the old man's refusing to pay, they forced a large party of his neighbours to go with them and thresh his corn. The field was a certain distance out of the clachan, and four persons, disguised as countrymen, who had been out on the moors all night, met this mournful drove of slaves, compelled by the four soldiers to work for the ruin of their friend. However, chided to the bone by their night on the hills, and worn out by want of food, they proceeded to the village inn to refresh themselves. Suddenly some people rushed into the room where they were sitting, and told them that the soldiers were about to roast the old man, naked, on his own girdle. This was too much for them to stand, and they repaired immediately to the scene of this gross outrage, and at first merely requested that the captive should be released. On the refusal of the two soldiers who were in the front room, high words were given and taken on both sides, and the other two rushed forth from an adjoining chamber and made at the countrymen with drawn swords. One of the latter, John M'Lellan of Barscob, drew a pistol and shot the corporal in the body. The pieces of tobacco-pipe with which it was loaded, to the number of ten at least, entered him, and he was so much disturbed that he never appears to have recovered, for we find long afterwards a petition to the Privy Council requesting a pension for him. The other soldiers then laid down their arms, the old man was rescued, and the rebellion was commenced. [90]

And now we must turn to Sir James Turner's memoirs of himself; for, strange to say, this extraordinary man was remarkably fond of literary composition, and wrote, besides the amusing account of his own adventures just mentioned, a large number of essays and short biographies, and a work on war, entitled Pallas Armata. The following are some of the shorter pieces 'Magick,' 'Friendship,' 'Imprisonment,' 'Anger,' 'Revenge,' 'Duells,' 'Cruelty,'

'A Defence of some of the Ceremonies of the English Liturgie—to wit—Bowing at the Name of Jesus, The frequent repetition of the Lord's Prayer and Good Lord deliver us, Of the Doxologie, Of Surplesses, Rotchets, Canonnicall Coats,' etc. From what we know of his character we should expect 'Anger' and 'Cruelty' to be very full and instructive. But what earthly right he had to meddle with ecclesiastical subjects it is hard to see.

Upon the 12th of the month he had received some information concerning Gray's proceedings, but as it was excessively indefinite in its character, he paid no attention to it. On the evening of the 14th, Corporal Deanes was brought into Dumfries, who affirmed stoutly that he had been shot while refusing to sign the Covenant—a story rendered singularly unlikely by the after conduct of the rebels. Sir James instantly dispatched orders to the cessed soldiers either to come to Dumfries or meet him on the way to Dalry, and commanded the thirteen or fourteen men in the town with him to come at nine next morning to his lodging for supplies.

On the morning of Thursday the rebels arrived at Dumfries with 50 horse and 150 foot. Neilson of Corsack, and Gray, who commanded, with a considerable troop, entered the town, and surrounded Sir James Turner's lodging. Though it was between eight and nine o'clock, that worthy, being unwell, was still in bed, but rose at once and went to the window.

Neilson and some others cried, 'You may have fair quarter.'

'I need no quarter,' replied Sir James; 'nor can I be a prisoner, seeing there is no war declared.' On being told, however, that he must either be a prisoner or die, he came down, and went into the street in his night-shirt. Here Gray showed himself very desirous of killing him, but he was overruled by Corsack. However, he was taken away a prisoner, Captain Gray mounting him on his own horse, though, as Turner naively remarks, 'there was good reason for it, for he mounted himself on a farre better one of mine.' A large coffer containing his clothes and money, together with all his papers, were taken away by the rebels. They robbed Master Chalmers, the Episcopalian minister of Dumfries, of his horse, drank the King's health at the market cross, and then left Dumfries. [92]

CHAPTER III—THE MARCH OF THE REBELS

'Stay, passenger, take notice what thou reads,

At Edinburgh lie our bodies, here our heads;

Our right hands stood at Lanark, these we want,

Because with them we signed the Covenant.'

Epitaph on a Tombstone at Hamilton. [93]

On Friday the 16th, Bailie Irvine of Dumfries came to the Council at Edinburgh, and gave information concerning this 'horrid rebellion.' In the absence of Rothes, Sharpe presided—much to the wrath of some members; and as he imagined his own safety endangered, his measures were most energetic. Dalzell was ordered away to the West, the guards round the city were doubled, officers and soldiers were forced to take the oath of allegiance, and all lodgers were commanded to give in their names. Sharpe, surrounded with all these guards and precautions, trembled—trembled as he trembled when the avengers of blood drew him from his chariot on Magus Muir,—for he knew how he had sold his trust, how he had betrayed his charge, and he felt that against him must their chiefest hatred be directed, against him their direst thunder-bolts be forged. But even in his fear the apostate Presbyterian was unrelenting, unpityingly harsh; he published in his manifesto no promise of pardon, no inducement to submission. He said, 'If you submit not you must die,' but never added, 'If you submit you may live!' [94a]

Meantime the insurgents proceeded on their way. At Carsphairn they were deserted by Captain Gray, who, doubtless in a fit of oblivion, neglected to leave behind him the coffer containing Sir James's money. Who he was is a mystery, unsolved by any historian; his papers were evidently forgeries—that, and his final flight, appear to indicate that he was an agent of the Royalists, for either the King or the Duke of York was heard to say, 'That, if he might have his wish, he would have them all turn rebels and go to arms.' [94b]

Upon the 18th day of the month they left Carsphairn and marched onwards.

Turner was always lodged by his captors at a good inn, frequently at the

75

best of which their halting-place could boast. Here many visits were paid to him by the ministers and officers of the insurgent force. In his description of these interviews he displays a vein of satiric severity, admitting any kindness that was done to him with some qualifying souvenir of former harshness, and gloating over any injury, mistake, or folly, which it was his chance to suffer or to hear. He appears, notwithstanding all this, to have been on pretty good terms with his cruel 'phanaticks,' as the following extract sufficiently proves:

'Most of the foot were lodged about the church or churchyard, and order given to ring bells next morning for a sermon to be preached by Mr. Welch. Maxwell of Morith, and Major M'Cullough invited me to heare "that phanatick sermon" (for soe they merrilie called it). They said that preaching might prove an effectual meane to turne me, which they heartilie wished. I answered to them that I was under guards, and that if they intended to heare that sermon, it was probable I might likewise, for it was not like my guards wold goe to church and leave me alone at my lodgeings. Bot to what they said of my conversion, I said it wold be hard to turne a Turner. Bot because I founde them in a merrie humour, I said, if I did not come to heare Mr. Welch preach, then they might fine me in fortie shillings Scots, which was double the suome of what I had exacted from the phanatics.' [95]

This took place at Ochiltree, on the 22nd day of the month. The following is recounted by this personage with malicious glee, and certainly, if authentic, it is a sad proof of how chaff is mixed with wheat, and how ignorant, almost impious, persons were engaged in this movement; nevertheless we give it, for we wish to present with impartiality all the alleged facts to the reader:

'Towards the evening Mr. Robinsone and Mr. Crukshank gaue me a visite; I called for some ale purposelie to heare one of them blesse it. It fell Mr. Robinsone to seeke the blessing, who said one of the most bombastick graces that ever I heard in my life. He summoned God Allmightie very imperiouslie to be their secondarie (for that was his language). "And if," said he, "thou wilt not be our Secondarie, we will not fight for thee at all, for it is not our cause bot thy cause; and if thou wilt not fight for our cause and thy oune cause, then we are not obliged to fight for it. They say," said he, "that Dukes, Earles, and Lords are coming with the King's General against us, bot they shall be nothing bot a threshing to us." This grace did more fullie satisfie me of the folly and injustice of their cause, then the ale did quench my thirst.' [96a]

Frequently the rebels made a halt near some roadside alehouse, or in some convenient park, where Colonel Wallace, who had now taken the command, would review the horse and foot, during which time Turner was sent either into the alehouse or round the shoulder of the hill, to prevent him from seeing the disorders which were likely to arise. He was, at last, on the 25th day of the month, between Douglas and Lanark, permitted to behold their evolutions. 'I found their horse did consist of four hundreth and fortie, and the foot of five hundreth and upwards. . . . The horsemen were armed for most part with suord and pistoll, some onlie with suord. The foot with musket, pike, sith (scythe), forke, and suord; and some with suords great and long.' He admired much the proficiency of their cavalry, and marvelled how they had attained to it in so short a time. [96b]

At Douglas, which they had just left on the morning of this great wapinshaw, they were charged—awful picture of depravity!—with the theft of a silver spoon and a nightgown. Could it be expected that while the whole country swarmed with robbers of every description, such a rare opportunity for plunder should be lost by rogues—that among a thousand men, even though fighting for religion, there should not be one Achan in the camp? At Lanark a declaration was drawn up and signed by the chief rebels. In it occurs the following:

'The just sense whereof '—the sufferings of the country—'made us choose, rather to betake ourselves to the fields for self-defence, than to stay at home, burdened daily with the calamities of others, and tortured with the fears of our own approaching misery.' [97]

The whole body, too, swore the Covenant, to which ceremony the epitaph at the head of this chapter seems to refer.

A report that Dalzell was approaching drove them from Lanark to Bathgate, where, on the evening of Monday the 26th, the wearied army stopped. But at twelve o'clock the cry, which served them for a trumpet, of 'Horse! horse!' and 'Mount the prisoner!' resounded through the night-shrouded town, and called the peasants from their well-earned rest to toil onwards in their march. The wind howled fiercely over the moorland; a close, thick, wetting rain descended. Chilled to the bone, worn out with long fatigue, sinking to the knees in mire, onward they marched to destruction. One by one the weary peasants fell off from their ranks to sleep, and die in the rain-soaked moor, or to seek some house by the wayside wherein to hide till daybreak. One by one at first, then in gradually increasing numbers, at every shelter that was seen, whole troops left the waning squadrons, and rushed to hide themselves from the ferocity of the tempest. To right and left nought could be descried but the broad expanse of the moor, and the figures of their fellow-rebels, seen dimly through the murky night, plodding onwards through the sinking moss. Those who kept together—a miserable few—often halted to rest themselves, and to allow their lagging comrades to overtake them. Then onward they went again, still hoping for assistance, reinforcement, and supplies; onward again, through the wind, and the rain, and the darkness—onward to their defeat at Pentland, and their scaffold at Edinburgh. It was calculated that they lost one half of their army on that disastrous night-march.

Next night they reached the village of Colinton, four miles from Edinburgh, where they halted for the last time. [98]

CHAPTER IV—RULLION GREEN

'From Covenanters with uplifted hands,

From Remonstrators with associate bands,

Good Lord, deliver us!'

Royalist Rhyme, KIRKTON, p. 127.

Late on the fourth night of November, exactly twenty-four days before Rullion Green, Richard and George Chaplain, merchants in Haddington, beheld four men, clad like West-country Whigamores, standing round some object on the ground. It was at the two-mile cross, and within that distance from their homes. At last, to their horror, they discovered that the recumbent figure was a livid corpse, swathed in a blood-stained winding-sheet. [99] Many thought that this apparition was a portent of the deaths connected with the Pentland Rising.

On the morning of Wednesday, the 28th of November 1666, they left Colinton and marched to Rullion Green. There they arrived about sunset. The position was a strong one. On the summit of a bare, heathery spur of the Pentlands are two hillocks, and between them lies a narrow band of flat marshy ground. On the highest of the two mounds—that nearest the Pentlands, and on the left hand of the main body—was the greater part of the cavalry, under Major Learmont; on the other Barscob and the Galloway gentlemen; and in the centre Colonel Wallace and the weak, half-armed infantry. Their position was further strengthened by the depth of the valley below, and the deep chasm-like course of the Rullion Burn.

The sun, going down behind the Pentlands, cast golden lights and blue shadows on their snow-clad summits, slanted obliquely into the rich plain before them, bathing with rosy splendour the leafless, snow-sprinkled trees, and fading gradually into shadow in the distance. To the south, too, they beheld a deep-shaded amphitheatre of heather and bracken; the course of the Esk, near Penicuik, winding about at the foot of its gorge; the broad, brown expanse of Maw Moss; and, fading into blue indistinctness in the south, the wild heath-clad Peeblesshire hills. In sooth, that scene was fair, and many a yearning glance was cast over that peaceful evening scene from the spot where the rebels awaited their defeat; and when the fight was over, many a noble fellow lifted his head from the blood-stained heather to strive with darkening eyeballs to behold that landscape, over which, as over his life and his cause, the shadows of night and of gloom were falling and thickening.

It was while waiting on this spot that the fear-inspiring cry was raised: 'The enemy! Here come the enemy!'

Unwilling to believe their own doom—for our insurgents still hoped for success in some negotiations for peace which had been carried on at Colinton—they called out, 'They are some of our own.'

'They are too blacke' (i.e. numerous), 'fie! fie! for ground to draw up on,' cried Wallace, fully realising the want of space for his men, and proving that it was not till after this time that his forces were finally arranged. [101a]

First of all the battle was commenced by fifty Royalist horse sent obliquely across the hill to attack the left wing of the rebels. An equal number of Learmont's men met them, and, after a struggle, drove them back. The course of the Rullion Burn prevented almost all pursuit, and Wallace, on perceiving it, dispatched a body of foot to occupy both the burn and some ruined sheep-walls on the farther side.

Dalzell changed his position, and drew up his army at the foot of the hill, on the top of which were his foes. He then dispatched a mingled body of infantry and cavalry to attack Wallace's outpost, but they also were driven back. A third charge produced a still more disastrous effect, for Dalzell had to check the pursuit of his men by a reinforcement.

These repeated checks bred a panic in the Lieutenant-General's ranks, for several of his men flung down their arms. Urged by such fatal symptoms, and by the approaching night, he deployed his men, and closed in overwhelming numbers on the centre and right flank of the insurgent army. In the increasing twilight the burning matches of the firelocks, shimmering on barrel, halbert, and cuirass, lent to the approaching army a picturesque effect, like a huge, many-armed giant breathing flame into the darkness.

Placed on an overhanging hill, Welch and Semple cried aloud, 'The God of Jacob! The God of Jacob!' and prayed with uplifted hands for victory. [101b]

But still the Royalist troops closed in.

Captain John Paton was observed by Dalzell, who determined to capture him with his own hands. Accordingly he charged forward, presenting his pistols. Paton fired, but the balls hopped off Dalzell's buff coat and fell into his boot. With the superstition peculiar to his age, the Nonconformist concluded that his adversary was rendered bullet-proof by enchantment, and, pulling some small silver coins from his pocket, charged his pistol therewith. Dalzell, seeing this, and supposing, it is likely, that Paton was putting in larger balls, hid behind his servant, who was killed. [102]

Meantime the outposts were forced, and the army of Wallace was enveloped in the embrace of a hideous boa-constrictor—tightening, closing, crushing every semblance of life from the victim enclosed in his toils. The flanking parties of horse were forced in upon the centre, and though, as even Turner grants, they fought with desperation, a general flight was the result.

But when they fell there was none to sing their coronach or wail the death-wail over them. Those who sacrificed themselves for the peace, the liberty, and the religion of their fellow-countrymen, lay bleaching in the field of death for long, and when at last they were buried by charity, the peasants dug up their bodies, desecrated their graves, and cast them once more upon the open heath for the sorry value of their winding-sheets!

Inscription on stone at Rullion Green:

HERE

AND NEAR TO

THIS PLACE LYES THE

REVEREND MR JOHN CROOKSHANK

AND MR ANDREW MCCORMICK

MINISTERS OF THE GOSPEL AND

ABOUT FIFTY OTHER TRUE COVENANTED

PRESBYTERIANS WHO WERE

KILLED IN THIS PLACE IN THEIR OWN

INOCENT SELF DEFENCE AND DEFFENCE

OF THE COVENANTED

WORK OF REFORMATION BY

THOMAS DALZEEL OF BINS

UPON THE 28 OF NOVEMBER

1666. REV. 12. 11. ERECTED

SEPT. 28 1738.

Back of stone:

A Cloud of Witnesses lyes here,

Who for Christ's Interest did appear,

For to restore true Liberty,

O'erturnèd then by tyranny.

And by proud Prelats who did Rage

Against the Lord's Own heritage.

They sacrificed were for the laws

Of Christ their king, his noble cause.

These heroes fought with great renown;

By falling got the Martyr's crown. [103]

CHAPTER V—A RECORD OF BLOOD

'They cut his hands ere he was dead,

And after that struck of his head.

His blood under the altar cries

For vengeance on Christ's enemies.'

Epitaph on Tomb at Longcross of Clermont. [104]

Master Andrew Murray, an outed minister, residing in the Potterrow, on the morning after the defeat, heard the sounds of cheering and the march of many feet beneath his window. He gazed out. With colours flying, and with music sounding, Dalzell, victorious, entered Edinburgh. But his banners were dyed in blood, and a band of prisoners were marched within his ranks. The old man knew it all. That martial and triumphant strain was the death-knell of his friends and of their cause, the rust-hued spots upon the flags were the tokens of their courage and their death, and the prisoners were the miserable remnant spared from death in battle to die upon the scaffold. Poor old man! he had outlived all joy. Had he lived longer he would have seen increasing torment and increasing woe; he would have seen the clouds, then but gathering in mist, cast a more than midnight darkness over his native hills, and have fallen a victim to those bloody persecutions which, later, sent their red memorials to the sea by many a burn. By a merciful Providence all this was spared to him—he fell beneath the first blow; and ere four days had passed since Rullion Green, the aged minister of God was gathered to is fathers. [105a]

When Sharpe first heard of the rebellion, he applied to Sir Alexander Ramsay, the Provost, for soldiers to guard his house. Disliking their occupation, the soldiers gave him an ugly time of it. All the night through they kept up a continuous series of 'alarms and incursions,' 'cries of "Stand!" "Give fire!"' etc., which forced the prelate to flee to the Castle in the morning, hoping there to find the rest which was denied him at home. [105b] Now, however, when all danger to himself was past, Sharpe came out in his true colours, and scant was the justice likely to be shown to the foes of Scottish Episcopacy when the Primate was by. The prisoners were lodged in Haddo's Hole, a part of St. Giles' Cathedral, where, by the kindness of Bishop Wishart, to his credit be it spoken, they were amply supplied with food. [105c]

Some people urged, in the Council, that the promise of quarter which had been given on the field of battle should protect the lives of the miserable men. Sir John Gilmoure, the greatest lawyer, gave no opinion—certainly a suggestive circumstance—but Lord Lee declared that this would not interfere with their legal trial, 'so to bloody executions they went.' [105d] To the number of thirty they were condemned and executed; while two of them, Hugh M'Kail, a young minister, and Neilson of Corsack, were tortured with the boots.

The goods of those who perished were confiscated, and their bodies were dismembered and distributed to different parts of the country; 'the heads of Major M'Culloch and the two Gordons,' it was resolved, says Kirkton, 'should be pitched on the gate of Kirkcudbright; the two Hamiltons and Strong's head should be affixed at Hamilton, and Captain Arnot's sett on the Watter Gate at Edinburgh. The armes of all the ten, because they hade with uplifted hands renewed the Covenant at Lanark, were sent to the people of that town to expiate that crime, by placing these arms on the top of the prison.' [106] Among these was John Neilson, the Laird of Corsack, who saved Turner's life at Dumfries; in return for which service Sir James attempted, though without success, to get the poor man reprieved. One of the condemned died of his wounds between the day of condemnation and the day of execution. 'None of them,' says Kirkton, 'would save their life by taking the declaration and renouncing the Covenant, though it was offered to them. . . . But never men died in Scotland so much lamented by the people, not only spectators, but those in the country. When Knockbreck and his brother were turned over, they clasped each other in their armes, and so endured the pangs of death. When Humphrey Colquhoun died, he spoke not like an ordinary citizen, but like a heavenly minister, relating his comfortable Christian experiences, and called for his Bible, and laid it on his wounded arm, and read John iii. 8, and spoke upon it to the admiration of all. But most of all, when Mr. M'Kail died, there was such a lamentation as was never known in Scotland before; not one dry cheek upon all the street, or in all the numberless windows in the mercate place.' [107a]

The following passage from this speech speaks for itself and its author:

'Hereafter I will not talk with flesh and blood, nor think on the world's consolations. Farewell to all my friends, whose company hath been refreshful to me in my pilgrimage. I have done with the light of the sun and the moon; welcome eternal light, eternal life, everlasting love, everlasting praise, everlasting glory. Praise to Him that sits upon the throne, and to the Lamb for ever! Bless the Lord, O my soul, that hath pardoned all my iniquities in the blood of His Son, and healed all my diseases. Bless Him, O all ye His angels that excel in strength, ye ministers of His that do His pleasure. Bless the Lord, O my soul!' [107b]

After having ascended the gallows ladder he again broke forth in the following words of touching eloquence: 'And now I leave off to speak any more to creatures, and begin my intercourse with God, which shall never be broken off. Farewell father and mother, friends and relations! Farewell the world and all delights! Farewell meat and drink! Farewell sun, moon, and stars!—Welcome God and Father! Welcome sweet Jesus Christ, the Mediator of the new covenant! Welcome blessed Spirit of grace and God of all consolation! Welcome glory! Welcome eternal life! Welcome Death!' [107c]

At Glasgow, too, where some were executed, they caused the soldiers to beat the drums and blow the trumpets on their closing ears. Hideous refinement of revenge! Even the last words which drop from the lips of a dying man—words surely the most sincere and the most unbiassed which mortal mouth can utter—even these were looked upon as poisoned and as poisonous. 'Drown their last accents,' was the cry, 'lest they should lead the crowd to take their part, or at the least to mourn their doom!' [108a] But, after all, perhaps it was more merciful than one would think—unintentionally so, of course; perhaps the storm of harsh and fiercely jubilant noises, the clanging of trumpets, the rattling of drums, and the hootings and jeerings of an unfeeling mob, which were the last they heard on earth, might, when the mortal fight was over, when the river of death was passed, add tenfold sweetness to the hymning of the angels, tenfold peacefulness to the shores which they had reached.

Not content with the cruelty of these executions, some even of the peasantry, though these were confined to the shire of Mid-Lothian, pursued, captured, plundered, and murdered the miserable fugitives who fell in their way. One strange story have we of these times of blood and persecution: Kirkton the historian and popular tradition tell us alike of a flame which often would arise from the grave, in a moss near Carnwath, of some of those poor rebels: of how it crept along the ground; of how it covered the house of their murderer; and of how it scared him with its lurid glare.

Hear Daniel Defoe: [108b]

'If the poor people were by these insupportable violences made desperate, and driven to all the extremities of a wild despair, who can justly reflect on them when they read in the Word of God "That oppression makes a wise man mad"? And therefore were there no other original of the insurrection known by the name of the Rising of Pentland, it was nothing but what the intolerable oppressions of those times might have justified to all the world, nature having dictated to all people a right of defence when illegally and arbitrarily attacked in a manner not justifiable either by laws of nature, the laws of God, or the laws of the country.'

Bear this remonstrance of Defoe's in mind, and though it is the fashion of the day to jeer and to mock, to execrate and to contemn, the noble band of Covenanters—though the bitter laugh at their old-world religious views, the curl of the lip at their merits, and the chilling silence on their bravery and their determination, are but too rife through all society—be charitable to what was evil and honest to what was good about the Pentland insurgents, who fought for life and liberty, for country and religion, on the 28th of November 1666, now just two hundred years ago.

Edinburgh, *28th November* 1866.

THE DAY AFTER TO-MORROW

History is much decried; it is a tissue of errors, we are told, no doubt correctly; and rival historians expose each other's blunders with gratification. Yet the worst historian has a clearer view of the period he studies than the best of us can hope to form of that in which we live. The obscurest epoch is to-day; and that for a thousand reasons of inchoate tendency, conflicting report, and sheer mass and multiplicity of experience; but chiefly, perhaps, by reason of an insidious shifting of landmarks. Parties and ideas continually move, but not by measurable marches on a stable course; the political soil itself steals forth by imperceptible degrees, like a travelling glacier, carrying on its bosom not only political parties but their flag-posts and cantonments; so that what appears to be an eternal city founded on hills is but a flying island of Laputa. It is for this reason in particular that we are all becoming Socialists without knowing it; by which I would not in the least refer to the acute case of Mr. Hyndman and his horn-blowing supporters, sounding their trumps of a Sunday within the walls of our individualist Jericho—but to the stealthy change that has come over the spirit of Englishmen and English legislation. A little while ago, and we were still for liberty; 'crowd a few more thousands on the bench of Government,' we seemed to cry; 'keep her head direct on liberty, and we cannot help but come to port.' This is over; laisser faire declines in favour; our legislation grows authoritative, grows philanthropical, bristles with new duties and new penalties, and casts a spawn of inspectors, who now begin, note-book in hand, to darken the face of England. It may be right or wrong, we are not trying that; but one thing it is beyond doubt: it is Socialism in action, and the strange thing is that we scarcely know it.

Liberty has served us a long while, and it may be time to seek new altars. Like all other principles, she has been proved to be self-exclusive in the long run. She has taken wages besides (like all other virtues) and dutifully served Mammon; so that many things we were accustomed to admire as the benefits of freedom and common to all were truly benefits of wealth, and took their value from our neighbours' poverty. A few shocks of logic, a few disclosures (in the journalistic phrase) of what the freedom of manufacturers, landlords, or shipowners may imply for operatives, tenants, or seamen, and we not unnaturally begin to turn to that other pole of hope, beneficent tyranny. Freedom, to be desirable, involves kindness, wisdom, and all the virtues of the free; but the free man as we have seen him in action has been, as of yore, only the master of many helots; and the slaves are still ill-fed, ill-clad, ill-taught, ill-housed, insolently treated, and driven to their mines and workshops by the lash of famine. So much, in other men's affairs, we have begun to see clearly; we have begun to despair of virtue in these other men, and from our seat in Parliament begin to discharge upon them, thick as arrows, the host of our inspectors. The landlord has long shaken his head over the manufacturer; those who do business on land have lost all trust in the virtues of the shipowner; the professions look askance upon the retail traders and have even started their co-operative stores to ruin them; and from out the smoke-wreaths of Birmingham a finger has begun to write upon the wall the condemnation of the landlord. Thus, piece by piece, do we condemn each other, and yet not perceive the conclusion, that our whole estate is somewhat damnable. Thus, piece by piece, each acting against his neighbour, each sawing away the branch on which some other interest is seated, do we apply in detail our Socialistic remedies, and yet not perceive that we are all labouring together to bring in Socialism at large. A tendency so stupid and so selfish is like to prove invincible; and if Socialism be at all a practicable rule of life, there is every chance that our grand-children will see the day and taste the pleasures of existence in something far liker an ant-heap than any previous human polity. And this not in the least because of the voice of Mr. Hyndman or the horns of his followers; but by the mere glacier movement of the political soil, bearing forward on its bosom, apparently undisturbed, the proud camps of Whig and Tory. If Mr. Hyndman were a man of keen humour, which is far from my conception of his character, he might rest from his troubling and look on: the walls of Jericho begin already to crumble and dissolve. That great servile war, the Armageddon of money and numbers, to which we looked forward when young, becomes more and more unlikely; and we may rather look to see a peaceable and blindfold evolution, the work of dull men immersed in political tactics and dead to political results.

The principal scene of this comedy lies, of course, in the House of Commons; it is there, besides, that the details of this new evolution (if it proceed) will fall to be decided; so that the state of Parliament is not only diagnostic of the present but fatefully prophetic of the future. Well, we all know what Parliament is, and we are all ashamed of it. We may pardon it some faults, indeed, on the ground of Irish obstruction—a bitter trial, which it supports with notable good humour. But the excuse is merely local; it cannot apply to similar bodies in America and France; and what are we to say of these? President Cleveland's letter may serve as a picture of the one; a glance at almost any paper will convince us of the weakness of the other. Decay appears to have seized on the organ of popular government in every land; and this just at the moment when we begin to bring to it, as to an oracle of justice, the whole skein of our private affairs to be unravelled, and ask it, like a new Messiah, to take upon itself our frailties and play for us the part that should be played by our own virtues. For that, in few words, is the case. We cannot trust ourselves to behave with decency; we cannot trust our consciences; and the remedy proposed is to elect a round number of our neighbours, pretty much at random, and say to these: 'Be ye our conscience; make laws so wise, and continue from year to year to administer them so wisely, that they shall save us from ourselves and make us righteous and happy, world without end. Amen.' And who can look twice at the British Parliament and then seriously bring it such a task? I am not advancing this as an argument against Socialism: once again, nothing is further from my mind. There are great truths in Socialism, or no one, not even Mr. Hyndman, would be found to hold it; and if it came, and did one-tenth part of what it offers, I for one should make it welcome. But if it is to come, we may as well have some notion of what it will be like; and the first thing to grasp is that our new polity will be designed and administered (to put it courteously) with something short of inspiration. It will be made, or will grow, in a human parliament; and the one thing that will not very hugely change is human nature. The Anarchists think otherwise, from which it is only plain that they have not carried to the study of history the lamp of human sympathy.

Given, then, our new polity, with its new waggon-load of laws, what headmarks must we look for in the life? We chafe a good deal at that excellent thing, the income-tax, because it brings into our affairs the prying fingers, and exposes us to the tart words, of the official. The official, in all degrees, is already something of a terror to many of us. I would not willingly have to do with even a police-constable in any other spirit than that of kindness. I still remember in my dreams the eye-glass of a certain attaché at a certain embassy—an eyeglass that was a standing indignity to all on whom it looked; and my next most disagreeable remembrance is of a bracing, Republican postman in the city of San Francisco. I lived in that city among working folk, and what my neighbours accepted at the postman's hands—nay, what I took from him myself—it is still distasteful to recall. The bourgeois, residing in the upper parts of society, has but few opportunities of tasting this peculiar bowl; but about the income-tax, as I have said, or perhaps about a patent, or in the halls of an embassy at the hands of my friend of the eye-glass, he occasionally sets his lips to it; and he may thus imagine (if he has that faculty of imagination, without which most faculties are void) how it tastes to his poorer neighbours, who must drain it to the dregs. In every contact with authority, with their employer, with the police, with the School Board officer, in the hospital, or in the workhouse, they have equally the occasion to appreciate the light-hearted civility of the man in office; and as an experimentalist in several out-of-the-way provinces of life, I may say it has but to be felt to be appreciated. Well, this golden age of which we are speaking will be the golden age of officials. In all our concerns it will be their beloved duty to meddle, with what tact, with what obliging words, analogy will aid us to imagine. It is likely these gentlemen will be periodically elected; they will therefore have their turn of being underneath, which does not always sweeten men's conditions. The laws they will have to administer will be no clearer than those we know to-day, and the body which is to regulate their administration no wiser than the British Parliament. So that upon all hands we may look for a form of servitude most galling to the blood—servitude to many and changing masters, and for all the slights that accompany the rule of jack-in-office. And if the Socialistic programme be carried out with the least fulness, we shall have lost a thing, in most respects not much to be regretted, but as a moderator of oppression, a thing nearly invaluable—the newspaper. For the independent journal is a creature of capital and competition; it stands and falls with millionaires and railway bonds and all the abuses and glories of to-day; and as soon as the State has fairly taken its bent to authority and philanthropy, and laid the least touch on private property, the days of the independent journal are numbered. State railways may be good things and so may State bakeries; but a State newspaper will never be a very trenchant critic of the State officials.

But again, these officials would have no sinecure. Crime would perhaps be less, for some of the motives of crime we may suppose would pass away. But if Socialism were carried out with any fulness, there would be more contraventions. We see already new sins ringing up like mustard—School Board sins, factory sins, Merchant Shipping Act sins—none of which I would be thought to except against in particular, but all of which, taken together, show us that Socialism can be a hard master even in the beginning. If it go on to such heights as we hear proposed and lauded, if it come actually to its ideal of the ant-heap, ruled with iron justice, the number of new contraventions will be out of all proportion multiplied. Take the case of work alone. Man is an idle animal. He is at least as intelligent as the ant; but generations of advisers have in vain recommended him the ant's example. Of those who are found truly indefatigable in business, some are misers; some are the practisers of delightful industries, like gardening; some are students, artists, inventors, or discoverers, men lured forward by successive hopes; and the rest are those who live by games of skill or hazard—financiers, billiard-players, gamblers, and the like. But in unloved toils, even under the prick of necessity, no man is continually sedulous. Once eliminate the fear of starvation, once eliminate or bound the hope of riches, and we shall see plenty of skulking and malingering. Society will then be something not wholly unlike a cotton plantation in the old days; with cheerful, careless, demoralised slaves, with elected overseers, and, instead of the planter, a chaotic popular assembly. If the blood be purposeful and the soil strong, such a plantation may succeed, and be, indeed, a busy ant-heap, with full granaries and long hours of leisure. But even then I think the whip will be in the overseer's hands, and not in vain. For, when it comes to be a question of each man doing his own share or the rest doing more, prettiness of sentiment will be forgotten. To dock the skulker's food is not enough; many will rather eat haws and starve on petty

91

pilferings than put their shoulder to the wheel for one hour daily. For such as these, then, the whip will be in the overseer's hand; and his own sense of justice and the superintendence of a chaotic popular assembly will be the only checks on its employment. Now, you may be an industrious man and a good citizen, and yet not love, nor yet be loved by, Dr. Fell the inspector. It is admitted by private soldiers that the disfavour of a sergeant is an evil not to be combated; offend the sergeant, they say, and in a brief while you will either be disgraced or have deserted. And the sergeant can no longer appeal to the lash. But if these things go on, we shall see, or our sons shall see, what it is to have offended an inspector.

This for the unfortunate. But with the fortunate also, even those whom the inspector loves, it may not be altogether well. It is concluded that in such a state of society, supposing it to be financially sound, the level of comfort will be high. It does not follow: there are strange depths of idleness in man, a too-easily-got sufficiency, as in the case of the sago-eaters, often quenching the desire for all besides; and it is possible that the men of the richest ant-heaps may sink even into squalor. But suppose they do not; suppose our tricksy instrument of human nature, when we play upon it this new tune, should respond kindly; suppose no one to be damped and none exasperated by the new conditions, the whole enterprise to be financially sound—a vaulting supposition—and all the inhabitants to dwell together in a golden mean of comfort: we have yet to ask ourselves if this be what man desire, or if it be what man will even deign to accept for a continuance. It is certain that man loves to eat, it is not certain that he loves that only or that best. He is supposed to love comfort; it is not a love, at least, that he is faithful to. He is supposed to love happiness; it is my contention that he rather loves excitement. Danger, enterprise, hope, the novel, the aleatory, are dearer to man than regular meals. He does not think so when he is hungry, but he thinks so again as soon as he is fed; and on the hypothesis of a successful ant-heap, he would never go hungry. It would be always after dinner in that society, as, in the land of the Lotos-eaters, it was always afternoon; and food, which, when we have it not, seems all-important, drops in our esteem, as soon as we have it, to a mere prerequisite of living.

That for which man lives is not the same thing for all individuals nor in all ages; yet it has a common base; what he seeks and what he must have is that which will seize and hold his attention. Regular meals and weatherproof lodgings will not do this long. Play in its wide sense, as the artificial induction of sensation, including all games and all arts, will, indeed, go far to keep him conscious of himself; but in the end he wearies for realities. Study or experiment, to some rare natures, is the unbroken pastime of a life. These are enviable natures; people shut in the house by sickness often bitterly envy them; but the commoner man cannot continue to exist upon such altitudes: his feet itch for physical adventure; his blood boils for physical dangers, pleasures, and triumphs; his fancy, the looker after new things, cannot continue to look for them in books and crucibles, but must seek them on the breathing stage of life. Pinches, buffets, the glow of hope, the shock of disappointment, furious contention with obstacles: these are the true elixir for all vital spirits, these are what they seek alike in their romantic enterprises and their unromantic dissipations. When they are taken in some pinch closer than the common, they cry, 'Catch me here again!' and sure enough you catch them there again—perhaps before the week is out. It is as old as Robinson Crusoe; as old as man. Our race has not been strained for all these ages through that sieve of dangers that we call Natural Selection, to sit down with patience in the tedium of safety; the voices of its fathers call it forth. Already in our society as it exists, the bourgeois is too much cottoned about for any zest in living; he sits in his parlour out of reach of any danger, often out of reach of any vicissitude but one of health; and there he yawns. If the people in the next villa took pot-shots at him, he might be killed indeed, but so long as he escaped he would find his blood oxygenated and his views of the world brighter. If Mr. Mallock, on his way to the publishers, should have his skirts pinned to a wall by a javelin, it would not occur to him—at least for several hours—to ask if life were worth living; and if such peril were a daily matter, he would ask it never more; he would have other things to think about, he would be living indeed—not lying in a box with cotton, safe, but immeasurably dull. The aleatory, whether it touch life, or fortune, or renown—whether we explore Africa or only toss for halfpence—that is what I conceive men to love best, and that is what we are seeking to exclude from men's existences. Of all forms of the aleatory, that which most commonly attends our working men—the danger of misery from want of work—is the least inspiriting: it does not whip the blood, it does not evoke the glory of contest; it is tragic, but it is passive; and yet, in so far as it is aleatory, and a peril sensibly touching them, it does truly season the men's lives. Of those who fail, I do not speak—despair should be sacred; but to those who even modestly succeed, the changes of their life bring interest: a job found, a shilling saved, a dainty earned, all these are wells of pleasure springing afresh for the successful poor; and it is not from these but from the villa-dweller that we hear complaints of the unworthiness of life. Much, then, as the average of the proletariat would gain in this new state of life, they would also lose a certain something, which would not be missed in the beginning, but would be missed progressively and progressively lamented. Soon there would be a looking back: there would be tales of the old world humming in young men's ears, tales of the tramp and the pedlar, and the hopeful emigrant. And in the stall-fed life of the successful ant-heap—with its regular meals, regular duties, regular pleasures, an even course of life, and fear excluded—the vicissitudes, delights, and havens of to-day will seem of epic breadth. This may seem a shallow observation; but the springs by which men are moved lie much on the surface. Bread, I believe, has always been considered first, but the circus comes close upon its heels. Bread we suppose to be given amply; the cry for circuses will be the louder, and if the life of our descendants be such as we have conceived, there are two beloved pleasures on which they will be likely to fall back: the pleasures of intrigue and of sedition.

In all this I have supposed the ant-heap to be financially sound. I am no economist, only a writer of fiction; but even as such, I know one thing that bears on the economic question—I know the imperfection of man's faculty for business. The Anarchists, who count some rugged elements of common sense among what seem to me their tragic errors, have said upon this matter all that I could wish to say, and condemned beforehand great economical polities. So far it is obvious that they are right; they may be right also in predicting a period of communal independence, and they may even be right in thinking that desirable. But the rise of communes is none the less the end of economic equality, just when we were told it was beginning. Communes will not be all equal in extent, nor in quality of soil, nor in growth of population; nor will the surplus produce of all be equally marketable. It will be the old story of competing interests, only with a new unit; and, as it appears to me, a new, inevitable danger. For the merchant and the manufacturer, in this new world, will be a sovereign commune; it is a sovereign power that will see its crops undersold, and its manufactures worsted in the market. And all the more dangerous that the sovereign power should be small. Great powers are slow to stir; national affronts, even with the aid of newspapers, filter slowly into popular consciousness; national losses are so unequally shared, that one part of the population will be counting its gains while another sits by a cold hearth. But in the sovereign commune all will be centralised and sensitive. When jealousy springs up, when (let us say) the commune of Poole has overreached the commune of Dorchester, irritation will run like quicksilver throughout the body politic; each man in Dorchester will have to suffer directly in his diet and his dress; even the secretary, who drafts the official correspondence, will sit down to his task embittered, as a man who has dined ill and may expect to dine worse; and thus a business difference between communes will take on much the same colour as a dispute between diggers in the lawless West, and will lead as directly to the arbitrament of blows. So that the establishment of the communal system will not only reintroduce all the injustices and heart-burnings of economic inequality, but will, in all human likelihood, inaugurate a world of hedgerow warfare. Dorchester will march on Poole, Sherborne on Dorchester, Wimborne on both; the waggons will be fired on as they follow the highway, the trains wrecked on the lines, the ploughman will go armed into the field of tillage; and if we have not a return of ballad literature, the local press at least will celebrate in a high vein the victory of Cerne Abbas or the reverse of Toller Porcorum. At least this will not be dull; when I was younger, I could have welcomed such a world with relief; but it is the New-Old with a vengeance, and irresistibly suggests the growth of military powers and the foundation of new empires.

COLLEGE PAPERS

CHAPTER I—EDINBURGH STUDENTS IN 1824

On the 2nd of January 1824 was issued the prospectus of the Lapsus Linguæ; or, the College Tatler; and on the 7th the first number appeared. On Friday the 2nd of April 'Mr. Tatler became speechless.' Its history was not all one success; for the editor (who applies to himself the words of Iago, 'I am nothing if I am not critical') overstepped the bounds of caution, and found himself seriously embroiled with the powers that were. There appeared in No. xvi. a most bitter satire upon Sir John Leslie, in which he was compared to Falstaff, charged with puffing himself, and very prettily censured for publishing only the first volume of a class-book, and making all purchasers pay for both. Sir John Leslie took up the matter angrily, visited Carfrae the publisher, and threatened him with an action, till he was forced to turn the hapless Lapsus out of doors. The maltreated periodical found shelter in the shop of Huie, Infirmary Street; and No. xvii. was duly issued from the new office. No. xvii. beheld Mr. Tatler's humiliation, in which, with fulsome apology and not very credible assurances of respect and admiration, he disclaims the article in question, and advertises a new issue of No. xvi. with all objectionable matter omitted. This, with pleasing euphemism, he terms in a later advertisement, 'a new and improved edition.' This was the only remarkable adventure of Mr. Tatler's brief existence; unless we consider as such a silly Chaldee manuscript in imitation of Blackwood, and a letter of reproof from a divinity student on the impiety of the same dull effusion. He laments the near approach of his end in pathetic terms. 'How shall we summon up sufficient courage,' says he, 'to look for the last time on our beloved little devil and his inestimable proof-sheet? How shall we be able to pass No. 14 Infirmary Street and feel that all its attractions are over? How shall we bid farewell for ever to that excellent man, with the long greatcoat, wooden leg and wooden board, who acts as our representative at the gate of Alma Mater?' But alas! he had no choice: Mr. Tatler, whose career, he says himself, had been successful, passed peacefully away, and has ever since dumbly implored 'the bringing home of bell and burial.'

Alter et idem. A very different affair was the Lapsus Linguæ from the Edinburgh University Magazine. The two prospectuses alone, laid side by side, would indicate the march of luxury and the repeal of the paper duty. The penny bi-weekly broadside of session 1828–4 was almost wholly dedicated to Momus. Epigrams, pointless letters, amorous verses, and University grievances are the continual burthen of the song. But Mr. Tatler was not without a vein of hearty humour; and his pages afford what is much better: to wit, a good picture of student life as it then was. The students of those polite days insisted on retaining their hats in the class-room. There was a cab-stance in front of the College; and 'Carriage Entrance' was posted above the main arch, on what the writer pleases to call 'coarse, unclassic boards.' The benches of the 'Speculative' then, as now, were red; but all other Societies (the 'Dialectic' is the only survivor) met downstairs, in some rooms of which it is pointedly said that 'nothing else could conveniently be made of them.' However horrible these dungeons may have been, it is certain that they were paid for, and that far too heavily for the taste of session 1823–4, which found enough calls upon its purse for porter and toasted cheese at Ambrose's, or cranberry tarts and ginger-wine at Doull's. Duelling was still a possibility; so much so that when two medicals fell to fisticuffs in Adam Square, it was seriously hinted that single combat would be the result. Last and most wonderful of all, Gall and Spurzheim were in every one's mouth; and the Law student, after having exhausted Byron's poetry and Scott's novels, informed the ladies of his belief in phrenology. In the present day he would dilate on 'Red as a rose is she,' and then mention that he attends Old Greyfriars', as a tacit claim to intellectual superiority. I do not know that the advance is much.

But Mr. Tatler's best performances were three short papers in which he hit off pretty smartly the idiosyncrasies of the 'Divinity,' the 'Medical,' and the 'Law' of session 1823–4. The fact that there was no notice of the 'Arts' seems to suggest that they stood in the same intermediate position as they do now—the epitome of student-kind. Mr. Tatler's satire is, on the whole, good-humoured, and has not grown superannuated in all its limbs. His descriptions may limp at some points, but there are certain broad traits that apply equally well to session 1870–1. He shows us the Divinity of the period—tall, pale, and slender—his collar greasy, and his coat bare about the seams—'his white neckcloth serving four days, and regularly turned the third'—'the rim of his hat deficient in wool'—and 'a weighty volume of theology under his arm.' He was the man to buy cheap 'a snuff-box, or a dozen of pencils, or a six-bladed knife, or a quarter of a hundred quills,' at any of the public sale-rooms. He was noted for cheap purchases, and for exceeding the legal tender in halfpence. He haunted 'the darkest and remotest corner of the Theatre Gallery.' He was to be seen issuing from 'aerial lodging-houses.' Withal, says mine author, 'there were many good points about him: he paid his landlady's bill, read his Bible, went twice to church on Sunday, seldom swore, was not often tipsy, and bought the Lapsus Linguæ.'

The Medical, again, 'wore a white greatcoat, and consequently talked loud'—(there is something very delicious in that consequently). He wore his hat on one side. He was active, volatile, and went to the top of Arthur's Seat on the Sunday forenoon. He was as quiet in a debating society as he was loud in the streets. He was reckless and imprudent: yesterday he insisted on your sharing a bottle of claret with him (and claret was claret then, before the cheap-and-nasty treaty), and to-morrow he asks you for the loan of a penny to buy the last number of the Lapsus.

The student of Law, again, was a learned man. 'He had turned over the leaves of Justinian's Institutes, and knew that they were written in Latin. He was well acquainted with the title-page of Blackstone's Commentaries, and argal (as the gravedigger in Hamlet says) he was not a person to be laughed at.' He attended the Parliament House in the character of a critic, and could give you stale sneers at all the celebrated speakers. He was the terror of essayists at the Speculative or the Forensic. In social qualities he seems to have stood unrivalled. Even in the police-office we find him shining with undiminished lustre. 'If a Charlie should find him rather noisy at an untimely hour, and venture to take him into custody, he appears next morning like a Daniel come to judgment. He opens his mouth to speak, and the divine precepts of unchanging justice and Scots law flow from his tongue. The magistrate listens in amazement, and fines him only a couple of guineas.'

Such then were our predecessors and their College Magazine. Barclay, Ambrose, Young Amos, and Fergusson were to them what the Café, the Rainbow, and Rutherford's are to us. An hour's reading in these old pages absolutely confuses us, there is so much that is similar and so much that is different; the follies and amusements are so like our own, and the manner of frolicking and enjoying are so changed, that one pauses and looks about him in philosophic judgment. The muddy quadrangle is thick with living students; but in our eyes it swarms also with the phantasmal white greatcoats and tilted hats of 1824. Two races meet: races alike and diverse. Two performances are played before our eyes; but the change seems merely of impersonators, of scenery, of costume. Plot and passion are the same. It is the fall of the spun shilling whether seventy-one or twenty-four has the best of it.

In a future number we hope to give a glance at the individualities of the present, and see whether the cast shall be head or tail—whether we or the readers of the Lapsus stand higher in the balance.

CHAPTER II—THE MODERN STUDENT CONSIDERED GENERALLY

We have now reached the difficult portion of our task. Mr. Tatler, for all that we care, may have been as virulent as he liked about the students of a former; but for the iron to touch our sacred selves, for a brother of the Guild to betray its most privy infirmities, let such a Judas look to himself as he passes on his way to the Scots Law or the Diagnostic, below the solitary lamp at the corner of the dark quadrangle. We confess that this idea alarms us. We enter a protest. We bind ourselves over verbally to keep the peace. We hope, moreover, that having thus made you secret to our misgivings, you will excuse us if we be dull, and set that down to caution which you might before have charged to the account of stupidity.

The natural tendency of civilisation is to obliterate those distinctions which are the best salt of life. All the fine old professional flavour in language has evaporated. Your very gravedigger has forgotten his avocation in his electorship, and would quibble on the Franchise over Ophelia's grave, instead of more appropriately discussing the duration of bodies under ground. From this tendency, from this gradual attrition of life, in which everything pointed and characteristic is being rubbed down, till the whole world begins to slip between our fingers in smooth undistinguishable sands, from this, we say, it follows that we must not attempt to join Mr. Taller in his simple division of students into Law, Divinity, and Medical. Nowadays the Faculties may shake hands over their follies; and, like Mrs. Frail and Mrs. Foresight (in Love for Love) they may stand in the doors of opposite class-rooms, crying: 'Sister, Sister—Sister everyway!' A few restrictions, indeed, remain to influence the followers of individual branches of study. The Divinity, for example, must be an avowed believer; and as this, in the present day, is unhappily considered by many as a confession of weakness, he is fain to choose one of two ways of gilding the distasteful orthodox bolus. Some swallow it in a thin jelly of metaphysics; for it is even a credit to believe in God on the evidence of some crack-jaw philosopher, although it is a decided slur to believe in Him on His own authority. Others again (and this we think the worst method), finding German grammar a somewhat dry morsel, run their own little heresy as a proof of independence; and deny one of the cardinal doctrines that they may hold the others without being laughed at.

Besides, however, such influences as these, there is little more distinction between the faculties than the traditionary ideal, handed down through a long sequence of students, and getting rounder and more featureless at each successive session. The plague of uniformity has descended on the College. Students (and indeed all sorts and conditions of men) now require their faculty and character hung round their neck on a placard, like the scenes in Shakespeare's theatre. And in the midst of all this weary sameness, not the least common feature is the gravity of every face. No more does the merry medical run eagerly in the clear winter morning up the rugged sides of Arthur's Seat, and hear the church bells begin and thicken and die away below him among the gathered smoke of the city. He will not break Sunday to so little purpose. He no longer finds pleasure in the mere output of his surplus energy. He husbands his strength, and lays out walks, and reading, and amusement with deep consideration, so that he may get as much work and pleasure out of his body as he can, and waste none of his energy on mere impulse, or such flat enjoyment as an excursion in the country.

See the quadrangle in the interregnum of classes, in those two or three minutes when it is full of passing students, and we think you will admit that, if we have not made it 'an habitation of dragons,' we have at least transformed it into 'a court for owls.' Solemnity broods heavily over the enclosure; and wherever you seek it, you will find a dearth of merriment, an absence of real youthful enjoyment. You might as well try

'To move wild laughter in the throat of death'

as to excite any healthy stir among the bulk of this staid company.

The studious congregate about the doors of the different classes, debating the matter of the lecture, or comparing note-books. A reserved rivalry sunders them. Here are some deep in Greek particles: there, others are already inhabitants of that land

'Where entity and quiddity,

'Like ghosts of defunct bodies fly—

Where Truth in person does appear

Like words congealed in northern air.'

But none of them seem to find any relish for their studies—no pedantic love of this subject or that lights up their eyes—science and learning are only means for a livelihood, which they have considerately embraced and which they solemnly pursue. 'Labour's pale priests,' their lips seem incapable of laughter, except in the way of polite recognition of professorial wit. The stains of ink are chronic on their meagre fingers. They walk like Saul among the asses.

The dandies are not less subdued. In 1824 there was a noisy dapper dandyism abroad. Vulgar, as we should now think, but yet genial—a matter of white greatcoats and loud voices—strangely different from the stately frippery that is rife at present. These men are out of their element in the quadrangle. Even the small remains of boisterous humour, which still clings to any collection of young men, jars painfully on their morbid sensibilities; and they beat a hasty retreat to resume their perfunctory march along Princes Street. Flirtation is to them a great social duty, a painful obligation, which they perform on every occasion in the same chill official manner, and with the same commonplace advances, the same dogged observance of traditional behaviour. The shape of their raiment is a burden almost greater than they can bear, and they halt in their walk to preserve the due adjustment of their trouser-knees, till one would fancy he had mixed in a procession of Jacobs. We speak, of course, for ourselves; but we would as soon associate with a herd of sprightly apes as with these gloomy modern beaux. Alas, that our Mirabels, our Valentines, even our Brummels, should have left their mantles upon nothing more amusing!

Nor are the fast men less constrained. Solemnity, even in dissipation, is the order of the day; and they go to the devil with a perverse seriousness, a systematic rationalism of wickedness that would have surprised the simpler sinners of old. Some of these men whom we see gravely conversing on the steps have but a slender acquaintance with each other. Their intercourse consists principally of mutual bulletins of depravity; and, week after week, as they meet they reckon up their items of transgression, and give an abstract of their downward progress for approval and encouragement. These folk form a freemasonry of their own. An oath is the shibboleth of their sinister fellowship. Once they hear a man swear, it is wonderful how their tongues loosen and their bashful spirits take enlargement, under the consciousness of brotherhood. There is no folly, no pardoning warmth of temper about them; they are as steady-going and systematic in their own way as the studious in theirs.

Not that we are without merry men. No. We shall not be ungrateful to those, whose grimaces, whose ironical laughter, whose active feet in the 'College Anthem' have beguiled so many weary hours and added a pleasant variety to the strain of close attention. But even these are too evidently professional in their antics. They go about cogitating puns and inventing tricks. It is their vocation, Hal. They are the gratuitous jesters of the class-room; and, like the clown when he leaves the stage, their merriment too often sinks as the bell rings the hour of liberty, and they pass forth by the Post-Office, grave and sedate, and meditating fresh gambols for the morrow.

This is the impression left on the mind of any observing student by too many of his fellows. They seem all frigid old men; and one pauses to think how such an unnatural state of matters is produced. We feel inclined to blame for it the unfortunate absence of University feeling which is so marked a characteristic of our Edinburgh students. Academical interests are so few and far between—students, as students, have so little in common, except a peevish rivalry—there is such an entire want of broad college sympathies and ordinary college friendships, that we fancy that no University in the kingdom is in so poor a plight. Our system is full of anomalies. A, who cut B whilst he was a shabby student, curries sedulously up to him and cudgels his memory for anecdotes about him when he becomes the great so-and-so. Let there be an end of this shy, proud reserve on the one hand, and this shuddering fine ladyism on the other; and we think we shall find both ourselves and the College bettered. Let it be a sufficient reason for intercourse that two men sit together on the same benches. Let the great A be held excused for nodding to the shabby B in Princes Street, if he can say, 'That fellow is a student.' Once this could be brought about, we think you would find the whole heart of the University beat faster. We think you would find a fusion among the students, a growth of common feelings, an increasing sympathy between class and class, whose influence (in such a heterogeneous company as ours) might be of incalculable value in all branches of politics and social progress. It would do more than this. If we could find some method of making the University a real mother to her sons—something beyond a building of class-rooms, a Senatus and a lottery of somewhat shabby prizes—we should strike a death-blow at the constrained and unnatural attitude of our Society. At present we are not a united body, but a loose gathering of individuals, whose inherent attraction is allowed to condense them into little knots and coteries. Our last snowball riot read us a plain lesson on our condition. There was no party spirit—no unity of interests. A few, who were mischievously inclined, marched off to the College of Surgeons in a pretentious file; but even before they reached their destination the feeble inspiration had died out in many, and their numbers were sadly thinned. Some followed strange gods in the direction of Drummond Street, and others slunk back to meek good-boyism at the feet of the Professors. The same is visible in better things. As you send a man to an English University that he may have his prejudices rubbed off, you might send him to Edinburgh that he may have them ingrained—rendered indelible—fostered by sympathy into living principles of his spirit. And the reason of it is quite plain. From this absence of University feeling it comes that a man's friendships are always the direct and immediate results of these very prejudices. A common weakness is the best master of ceremonies in our quadrangle: a mutual vice is the readiest introduction. The studious associate with the studious alone—the dandies with the dandies. There is nothing to force them to rub shoulders with the others; and so they grow day by day more wedded to their own original opinions and affections. They see through the same spectacles continually. All broad sentiments, all real catholic humanity expires; and the mind gets gradually stiffened into one position—becomes so habituated to a contracted atmosphere, that it shudders and withers under the least draught of the free air that circulates in the general field of mankind.

Specialism in Society then is, we think, one cause of our present state. Specialism in study is another. We doubt whether this has ever been a good thing since the world began; but we are sure it is much worse now than it was. Formerly, when a man became a specialist, it was out of affection for his subject. With a somewhat grand devotion he left all the world of Science to follow his true love; and he contrived to find that strange pedantic interest which inspired the man who

'Settled Hoti's business—let it be—

Properly based Oun—

Gave us the doctrine of the enclitic De,

Dead from the waist down.'

Nowadays it is quite different. Our pedantry wants even the saving clause of Enthusiasm. The election is now matter of necessity and not of choice. Knowledge is now too broad a field for your Jack-of-all-Trades; and, from beautifully utilitarian reasons, he makes his choice, draws his pen through a dozen branches of study, and behold—John the Specialist. That this is the way to be wealthy we shall not deny; but we hold that it is not the way to be healthy or wise. The whole mind becomes narrowed and circumscribed to one 'punctual spot' of knowledge. A rank unhealthy soil breeds a harvest of prejudices. Feeling himself above others in his one little branch—in the classification of toadstools, or Carthaginian history—he waxes great in his own eyes and looks down on others. Having all his sympathies educated in one way, they die out in every other; and he is apt to remain a peevish, narrow, and intolerant bigot. Dilettante is now a term of reproach; but there is a certain form of dilettantism to which no one can object. It is this that we want among our students. We wish them to abandon no subject until they have seen and felt its merit—to act under a general interest in all branches of knowledge, not a commercial eagerness to excel in one.

In both these directions our sympathies are constipated. We are apostles of our own caste and our own subject of study, instead of being, as we should, true men and loving students. Of course both of these could be corrected by the students themselves; but this is nothing to the purpose: it is more important to ask whether the Senatus or the body of alumni could do nothing towards the growth of better feeling and wider sentiments. Perhaps in another paper we may say something upon this head.

One other word, however, before we have done. What shall we be when we grow really old? Of yore, a man was thought to lay on restrictions and acquire new deadweight of mournful experience with every year, till he looked back on his youth as the very summer of impulse and freedom. We please ourselves with thinking that it cannot be so with us. We would fain hope that, as we have begun in one way, we may end in another; and that when we are in fact the octogenarians that we seem at present, there shall be no merrier men on earth. It is pleasant to picture us, sunning ourselves in Princes Street of a morning, or chirping over our evening cups, with all the merriment that we wanted in youth.

CHAPTER III—DEBATING SOCIETIES

A debating society is at first somewhat of a disappointment. You do not often find the youthful Demosthenes chewing his pebbles in the same room with you; or, even if you do, you will probably think the performance little to be admired. As a general rule, the members speak shamefully ill. The subjects of debate are heavy; and so are the fines. The Ballot Question—oldest of dialectic nightmares—is often found astride of a somnolent sederunt. The Greeks and Romans, too, are reserved as sort of general-utility men, to do all the dirty work of illustration; and they fill as many functions as the famous waterfall scene at the 'Princess's,' which I found doing duty on one evening as a gorge in Peru, a haunt of German robbers, and a peaceful vale in the Scottish borders. There is a sad absence of striking argument or real lively discussion. Indeed, you feel a growing contempt for your fellow-members; and it is not until you rise yourself to hawk and hesitate and sit shamefully down again, amid eleemosynary applause, that you begin to find your level and value others rightly. Even then, even when failure has damped your critical ardour, you will see many things to be laughed at in the deportment of your rivals.

Most laughable, perhaps, are your indefatigable strivers after eloquence. They are of those who 'pursue with eagerness the phantoms of hope,' and who, since they expect that 'the deficiencies of last sentence will be supplied by the next,' have been recommended by Dr. Samuel Johnson to 'attend to the History of Rasselas, Prince of Abyssinia.' They are characterised by a hectic hopefulness. Nothing damps them. They rise from the ruins of one abortive sentence, to launch forth into another with unabated vigour. They have all the manner of an orator. From the tone of their voice, you would expect a splendid period—and lo! a string of broken-backed, disjointed clauses, eked out with stammerings and throat-clearings. They possess the art (learned from the pulpit) of rounding an uneuphonious sentence by dwelling on a single syllable—of striking a balance in a top-heavy period by lengthening out a word into a melancholy quaver. Withal, they never cease to hope. Even at last, even when they have exhausted all their ideas, even after the would-be peroration has finally refused to perorate, they remain upon their feet with their mouths open, waiting for some further inspiration, like Chaucer's widow's son in the dung-hole, after

'His throat was kit unto the nekké bone,'

in vain expectation of that seed that was to be laid upon his tongue, and give him renewed and clearer utterance.

These men may have something to say, if they could only say it—indeed they generally have; but the next class are people who, having nothing to say, are cursed with a facility and an unhappy command of words, that makes them the prime nuisances of the society they affect. They try to cover their absence of matter by an unwholesome vitality of delivery. They look triumphantly round the room, as if courting applause, after a torrent of diluted truism. They talk in a circle, harping on the same dull round of argument, and returning again and again to the same remark with the same sprightliness, the same irritating appearance of novelty.

After this set, any one is tolerable; so we shall merely hint at a few other varieties. There is your man who is pre-eminently conscientious, whose face beams with sincerity as he opens on the negative, and who votes on the affirmative at the end, looking round the room with an air of chastened pride. There is also the irrelevant speaker, who rises, emits a joke or two, and then sits down again, without ever attempting to tackle the subject of debate. Again, we have men who ride pick-a-back on their family reputation, or, if their family have none, identify themselves with some well-known statesman, use his opinions, and lend him their patronage on all occasions. This is a dangerous plan, and serves oftener, I am afraid, to point a difference than to adorn a speech.

But alas! a striking failure may be reached without tempting Providence by any of these ambitious tricks. Our own stature will be found high enough for shame. The success of three simple sentences lures us into a fatal parenthesis in the fourth, from whose shut brackets we may never disentangle the thread of our discourse. A momentary flush tempts us into a quotation; and we may be left helpless in the middle of one of Pope's couplets, a white film gathering before our eyes, and our kind friends charitably trying to cover our disgrace by a feeble round of applause. Amis lecteurs, this is a painful topic. It is possible that we too, we, the 'potent, grave, and reverend' editor, may have suffered these things, and drunk as deep as any of the cup of shameful failure. Let us dwell no longer on so delicate a subject.

In spite, however, of these disagreeables, I should recommend any student to suffer them with Spartan courage, as the benefits he receives should repay him an hundredfold for them all. The life of the debating society is a handy antidote to the life of the classroom and quadrangle. Nothing could be conceived more excellent as a weapon against many of those peccant humours that we have been railing against in the jeremiad of our last 'College Paper'— particularly in the field of intellect. It is a sad sight to see our heather-scented students, our boys of seventeen, coming up to College with determined views—roués in speculation—having gauged the vanity of philosophy or learned to shun it as the middle-man of heresy—a company of determined, deliberate opinionists, not to be moved by all the sleights of logic. What have such men to do with study? If their minds are made up irrevocably, why burn the 'studious lamp' in search of further confirmation? Every set opinion I hear a student deliver I feel a certain lowering of my regard. He who studies, he who is yet employed in groping for his premises, should keep his mind fluent and sensitive, keen to mark flaws, and willing to surrender untenable positions. He should keep himself teachable, or cease the expensive farce of being taught. It is to further this docile spirit that we desire to press the claims of debating societies. It is as a means of melting down this museum of premature petrifactions into living and impressionable soul that we insist on their utility. If we could once prevail on our students to feel no shame in avowing an uncertain attitude towards any subject, if we could teach them that it was unnecessary for every lad to have his opinionette on every topic, we should have gone a far way towards bracing the intellectual tone of the coming race of thinkers; and this it is which debating societies are so well fitted to perform.

We there meet people of every shade of opinion, and make friends with them. We are taught to rail against a man the whole session through, and then hob-a-nob with him at the concluding entertainment. We find men of talent far exceeding our own, whose conclusions are widely different from ours; and we are thus taught to distrust ourselves. But the best means of all towards catholicity is that wholesome rule which some folk are most inclined to condemn—I mean the law of obliged speeches. Your senior member commands; and you must take the affirmative or the negative, just as suits his best convenience. This tends to the most perfect liberality. It is no good hearing the arguments of an opponent, for in good verity you rarely follow them; and even if you do take the trouble to listen, it is merely in a captious search for weaknesses. This is proved, I fear, in every debate; when you hear each speaker arguing out his own prepared spécialité (he never intended speaking, of course, until some remarks of, etc.), arguing out, I say, his own coached-up subject without the least attention to what has gone before, as utterly at sea about the drift of his adversary's speech as Panurge when he argued with Thaumaste, and merely linking his own prelection to the last by a few flippant criticisms. Now, as the rule stands, you are saddled with the side you disapprove, and so you are forced, by regard for your own fame, to argue out, to feel with, to elaborate completely, the case as it stands against yourself; and what a fund of wisdom do you not turn up in this idle digging of the vineyard! How many new difficulties take form before your eyes? how many superannuated arguments cripple finally into limbo, under the glance of your enforced eclecticism!

Nor is this the only merit of Debating Societies. They tend also to foster taste, and to promote friendship between University men. This last, as we have had occasion before to say, is the great requirement of our student life; and it will therefore be no waste of time if we devote a paragraph to this subject in its connection with Debating Societies. At present they partake too much of the nature of a clique. Friends propose friends, and mutual friends second them, until the society degenerates into a sort of family party. You may confirm old acquaintances, but you can rarely make new ones. You find yourself in the atmosphere of your own daily intercourse. Now, this is an unfortunate circumstance, which it seems to me might readily be rectified. Our Principal has shown himself so friendly towards all College improvements that I cherish the hope of seeing shortly realised a certain suggestion, which is not a new one with me, and which must often have been proposed and canvassed heretofore—I mean, a real University Debating Society, patronised by the Senatus, presided over by the Professors, to which every one might gain ready admittance on sight of his matriculation ticket, where it would be a favour and not a necessity to speak, and where the obscure student might have another object for attendance besides the mere desire to save his fines: to wit, the chance of drawing on himself the favourable consideration of his teachers. This would be merely following in the good tendency, which has been so noticeable during all this session, to increase and multiply student societies and clubs of every sort. Nor would it be a matter of much difficulty. The united societies would form a nucleus: one of the class-rooms at first, and perhaps afterwards the great hall above the library, might be the place of meeting. There would be no want of attendance or enthusiasm, I am sure; for it is a very different thing to speak under the bushel of a private club on the one hand, and, on the other, in a public place, where a happy period or a subtle argument may do the speaker permanent service in after life. Such a club might end, perhaps, by rivalling the 'Union' at Cambridge or the 'Union' at Oxford.

CHAPTER IV—THE PHILOSOPHY OF UMBRELLAS [151]

It is wonderful to think what a turn has been given to our whole Society by the fact that we live under the sign of Aquarius—that our climate is essentially wet. A mere arbitrary distinction, like the walking-swords of yore, might have remained the symbol of foresight and respectability, had not the raw mists and dropping showers of our island pointed the inclination of Society to another exponent of those virtues. A ribbon of the Legion of Honour or a string of medals may prove a person's courage; a title may prove his birth; a professorial chair his study and acquirement; but it is the habitual carriage of the umbrella that is the stamp of Respectability. The umbrella has become the acknowledged index of social position.

Robinson Crusoe presents us with a touching instance of the hankering after them inherent in the civilised and educated mind. To the superficial, the hot suns of Juan Fernandez may sufficiently account for his quaint choice of a luxury; but surely one who had borne the hard labour of a seaman under the tropics for all these years could have supported an excursion after goats or a peaceful constitutional arm in arm with the nude Friday. No, it was not this: the memory of a vanished respectability called for some outward manifestation, and the result was—an umbrella. A pious castaway might have rigged up a belfry and solaced his Sunday mornings with the mimicry of church-bells; but Crusoe was rather a moralist than a pietist, and his leaf-umbrella is as fine an example of the civilised mind striving to express itself under adverse circumstances as we have ever met with.

It is not for nothing, either, that the umbrella has become the very foremost badge of modern civilisation—the Urim and Thummim of respectability. Its pregnant symbolism has taken its rise in the most natural manner. Consider, for a moment, when umbrellas were first introduced into this country, what manner of men would use them, and what class would adhere to the useless but ornamental cane. The first, without doubt, would be the hypochondriacal, out of solicitude for their health, or the frugal, out of care for their raiment; the second, it is equally plain, would include the fop, the fool, and the Bobadil. Any one acquainted with the growth of Society, and knowing out of what small seeds of cause are produced great revolutions, and wholly new conditions of intercourse, sees from this simple thought how the carriage of an umbrella came to indicate frugality, judicious regard for bodily welfare, and scorn for mere outward adornment, and, in one word, all those homely and solid virtues implied in the term respectability. Not that the umbrella's costliness has nothing to do with its great influence. Its possession, besides symbolising (as we have already indicated) the change from wild Esau to plain Jacob dwelling in tents, implies a certain comfortable provision of fortune. It is not every one that can expose twenty-six shillings' worth of property to so many chances of loss and theft. So strongly do we feel on this point, indeed, that we are almost inclined to consider all who possess really well-conditioned umbrellas as worthy of the Franchise. They have a qualification standing in their lobbies; they carry a sufficient stake in the common-weal below their arm. One who bears with him an umbrella—such a complicated structure of whalebone, of silk, and of cane, that it becomes a very microcosm of modern industry—is necessarily a man of peace. A half-crown cane may be applied to an offender's head on a very moderate provocation; but a six-and-twenty shilling silk is a possession too precious to be adventured in the shock of war.

These are but a few glances at how umbrellas (in the general) came to their present high estate. But the true Umbrella-Philosopher meets with far stranger applications as he goes about the streets.

Umbrellas, like faces, acquire a certain sympathy with the individual who carries them: indeed, they are far more capable of betraying his trust; for whereas a face is given to us so far ready made, and all our power over it is in frowning, and laughing, and grimacing, during the first three or four decades of life, each umbrella is selected from a whole shopful, as being most consonant to the purchaser's disposition. An undoubted power of diagnosis rests with the practised Umbrella-Philosopher. O you who lisp, and amble, and change the fashion of your countenances—you who conceal all these, how little do you think that you left a proof of your weakness in our umbrella-stand—that even now, as you shake out the folds to meet the thickening snow, we read in its ivory handle the outward and visible sign of your snobbery, or from the exposed gingham of its cover detect, through coat and waistcoat, the hidden hypocrisy of the 'dickey'! But alas! even the umbrella is no certain criterion. The falsity and the folly of the human race have degraded that graceful symbol to the ends of dishonesty; and while some umbrellas, from carelessness in selection, are not strikingly characteristic (for it is only in what a man loves that he displays his real nature), others, from certain prudential motives, are chosen directly opposite to the person's disposition. A mendacious umbrella is a sign of great moral degradation. Hypocrisy naturally shelters itself below a silk; while the fast youth goes to visit his religious friends armed with the decent and reputable gingham. May it not be said of the bearers of these inappropriate umbrellas that they go about the streets 'with a lie in their right hand'?

The kings of Siam, as we read, besides having a graduated social scale of umbrellas (which was a good thing), prevented the great bulk of their subjects from having any at all, which was certainly a bad thing. We should be sorry to believe that this Eastern legislator was a fool—the idea of an aristocracy of umbrellas is too philosophic to have originated in a nobody—and we have accordingly taken exceeding pains to find out the reason of this harsh restriction. We think we have succeeded; but, while admiring the principle at which he aimed, and while cordially recognising in the Siamese potentate the only man before ourselves who had taken a real grasp of the umbrella, we must be allowed to point out how unphilosophically the great man acted in this particular. His object, plainly, was to prevent any unworthy persons from bearing the sacred symbol of domestic virtues. We cannot excuse his limiting these virtues to the circle of his court. We must only remember that such was the feeling of the age in which he lived. Liberalism had not yet raised the war-cry of the working classes. But here was his mistake: it was a needless regulation. Except in a very few cases of hypocrisy joined to a powerful intellect, men, not by nature umbrellarians, have tried again and again to become so by art, and yet have failed—have expended their patrimony in the purchase of umbrella after umbrella, and yet have systematically lost them, and have finally, with contrite spirits and shrunken purses, given up their vain struggle, and relied on theft and borrowing for the remainder of their lives. This is the most remarkable fact that we have had occasion to notice; and yet we challenge the candid reader to call it in question. Now, as there cannot be any moral selection in a mere dead piece of furniture— as the umbrella cannot be supposed to have an affinity for individual men equal and reciprocal to that which men certainly feel toward individual umbrellas—we took the trouble of consulting a scientific friend as to whether there was any possible physical explanation of the phenomenon. He was unable to supply a plausible theory, or even hypothesis; but we extract from his letter the following interesting passage relative to the physical peculiarities of umbrellas: 'Not the least important, and by far the most curious property of the umbrella, is the energy which it displays in affecting the atmospheric strata. There is no fact in meteorology better established—indeed, it is almost the only one on which meteorologists are agreed—than that the carriage of an umbrella produces desiccation of the air; while if it be left at home, aqueous vapour is largely produced, and is soon deposited in the form of rain. No theory,' my friend continues, 'competent to explain this hygrometric law has been given (as far as I am aware) by Herschel, Dove, Glaisher, Tait, Buchan, or any other writer; nor do I pretend to supply the defect. I venture, however, to throw out the conjecture that it will be ultimately found to belong to the same class of natural laws as that agreeable to which a slice of toast always descends with the buttered surface downwards.'

But it is time to draw to a close. We could expatiate much longer upon this topic, but want of space constrains us to leave unfinished these few desultory remarks—slender contributions towards a subject which has fallen sadly backward, and which, we grieve to say, was better understood by the king of Siam in 1686 than by all the philosophers of to-day. If, however, we have awakened in any rational mind an interest in the symbolism of umbrellas—in any generous heart a more complete sympathy with the dumb companion of his daily walk—or in any grasping spirit a pure notion of respectability strong enough to make him expend his six-and-twenty shillings—we shall have deserved well of the world, to say nothing of the many industrious persons employed in the manufacture of the article.

CHAPTER V—THE PHILOSOPHY OF NOMENCLATURE

'How many Cæsars and Pompeys, by mere inspirations of the names, have been rendered worthy of them? And how many are there, who might have done exceeding well in the world, had not their characters and spirits been totally depressed and Nicodemus'd into nothing?'—Tristram Shandy, vol. i. chap xix.

Such were the views of the late Walter Shandy, Esq., Turkey merchant. To the best of my belief, Mr. Shandy is the first who fairly pointed out the incalculable influence of nomenclature upon the whole life—who seems first to have recognised the one child, happy in an heroic appellation, soaring upwards on the wings of fortune, and the other, like the dead sailor in his shotted hammock, haled down by sheer weight of name into the abysses of social failure. Solomon possibly had his eye on some such theory when he said that 'a good name is better than precious ointment'; and perhaps we may trace a similar spirit in the compilers of the English Catechism, and the affectionate interest with which they linger round the catechumen's name at the very threshold of their work. But, be these as they may, I think no one can censure me for appending, in pursuance of the expressed wish of his son, the Turkey merchant's name to his system, and pronouncing, without further preface, a short epitome of the 'Shandean Philosophy of Nomenclature.'

To begin, then: the influence of our name makes itself felt from the very cradle. As a schoolboy I remember the pride with which I hailed Robin Hood, Robert Bruce, and Robert le Diable as my name-fellows; and the feeling of sore disappointment that fell on my heart when I found a freebooter or a general who did not share with me a single one of my numerous prænomina. Look at the delight with which two children find they have the same name.

They are friends from that moment forth; they have a bond of union stronger than exchange of nuts and sweetmeats. This feeling, I own, wears off in later life. Our names lose their freshness and interest, become trite and indifferent. But this, dear reader, is merely one of the sad effects of those 'shades of the prison-house' which come gradually betwixt us and nature with advancing years; it affords no weapon against the philosophy of names.

In after life, although we fail to trace its working, that name which careless godfathers lightly applied to your unconscious infancy will have been moulding your character, and influencing with irresistible power the whole course of your earthly fortunes. But the last name, overlooked by Mr. Shandy, is no whit less important as a condition of success. Family names, we must recollect, are but inherited nicknames; and if the sobriquet were applicable to the ancestor, it is most likely applicable to the descendant also. You would not expect to find Mr. M'Phun acting as a mute, or Mr. M'Lumpha excelling as a professor of dancing. Therefore, in what follows, we shall consider names, independent of whether they are first or last. And to begin with, look what a pull Cromwell had over Pym—the one name full of a resonant imperialism, the other, mean, pettifogging, and unheroic to a degree. Who would expect eloquence from Pym—who would read poems by Pym—who would bow to the opinion of Pym? He might have been a dentist, but he should never have aspired to be a statesman. I can only wonder that he succeeded as he did. Pym and Habakkuk stand first upon the roll of men who have triumphed, by sheer force of genius, over the most unfavourable appellations. But even these have suffered; and, had they been more fitly named, the one might have been Lord Protector, and the other have shared the laurels with Isaiah. In this matter we must not forget that all our great poets have borne great names. Chaucer, Spenser, Shakespeare, Milton, Pope, Wordsworth, Shelley—what a constellation of lordly words! Not a single common-place name among them—not a Brown, not a Jones, not a Robinson; they are all names that one would stop and look at on a door-plate. Now, imagine if Pepys had tried to clamber somehow into the enclosure of poetry, what a blot would that word have made upon the list! The thing was impossible. In the first place a certain natural consciousness that men would have held him down to the level of his name, would have prevented him from rising above the Pepsine standard, and so haply withheld him altogether from attempting verse. Next, the booksellers would refuse to publish, and the world to read them, on the mere evidence of the fatal appellation. And now, before I close this section, I must say one word as to punnable names, names that stand alone, that have a significance and life apart from him that bears them. These are the bitterest of all. One friend of mine goes bowed and humbled through life under the weight of this misfortune; for it is an awful thing when a man's name is a joke, when he cannot be mentioned without exciting merriment, and when even the intimation of his death bids fair to carry laughter into many a home.

So much for people who are badly named. Now for people who are too well named, who go top-heavy from the font, who are baptized into a false position, and find themselves beginning life eclipsed under the fame of some of the great ones of the past. A man, for instance, called William Shakespeare could never dare to write plays. He is thrown into too humbling an apposition with the author of Hamlet. Its own name coming after is such an anti-climax. 'The plays of William Shakespeare'? says the reader—'O no! The plays of William Shakespeare Cockerill,' and he throws the book aside. In wise pursuance of such views, Mr. John Milton Hengler, who not long since delighted us in this favoured town, has never attempted to write an epic, but has chosen a new path, and has excelled upon the tight-rope. A marked example of triumph over this is the case of Mr. Dante Gabriel Rossetti. On the face of the matter, I should have advised him to imitate the pleasing modesty of the last-named gentleman, and confine his ambition to the sawdust. But Mr. Rossetti has triumphed. He has even dared to translate from his mighty name-father; and the voice of fame supports him in his boldness.

Dear readers, one might write a year upon this matter. A lifetime of comparison and research could scarce suffice for its elucidation. So here, if it please you, we shall let it rest. Slight as these notes have been, I would that the great founder of the system had been alive to see them. How he had warmed and brightened, how his persuasive eloquence would have fallen on the ears of Toby; and what a letter of praise and sympathy would not the editor have received before the month was out! Alas, the thing was not to be. Walter

Shandy died and was duly buried, while yet his theory lay forgotten and neglected by his fellow-countrymen. But, reader, the day will come, I hope, when a paternal government will stamp out, as seeds of national weakness, all depressing patronymics, and when godfathers and godmothers will soberly and earnestly debate the interest of the nameless one, and not rush blindfold to the christening. In these days there shall be written a 'Godfather's Assistant,' in shape of a dictionary of names, with their concomitant virtues and vices; and this book shall be scattered broadcast through the land, and shall be on the table of every one eligible for godfathership, until such a thing as a vicious or untoward appellation shall have ceased from off the face of the earth.

CRITICISMS

CHAPTER I—LORD LYTTON'S 'FABLES IN SONG'

It seems as if Lord Lytton, in this new book of his, had found the form most natural to his talent. In some ways, indeed, it may be held inferior to Chronicles and Characters; we look in vain for anything like the terrible intensity of the night-scene in Irene, or for any such passages of massive and memorable writing as appeared, here and there, in the earlier work, and made it not altogether unworthy of its model, Hugo's Legend of the Ages. But it becomes evident, on the most hasty retrospect, that this earlier work was a step on the way towards the later. It seems as if the author had been feeling about for his definite medium, and was already, in the language of the child's game, growing hot. There are many pieces in Chronicles and Characters that might be detached from their original setting, and embodied, as they stand, among the Fables in Song.

For the term Fable is not very easy to define rigorously. In the most typical form some moral precept is set forth by means of a conception purely fantastic, and usually somewhat trivial into the bargain; there is something playful about it, that will not support a very exacting criticism, and the lesson must be apprehended by the fancy at half a hint. Such is the great mass of the old stories of wise animals or foolish men that have amused our childhood. But we should expect the fable, in company with other and more important literary forms, to be more and more loosely, or at least largely, comprehended as time went on, and so to degenerate in conception from this original type. That depended for much of its piquancy on the very fact that it was fantastic: the point of the thing lay in a sort of humorous inappropriateness; and it is natural enough that pleasantry of this description should become less common, as men learn to suspect some serious analogy underneath. Thus a comical story of an ape touches us quite differently after the proposition of Mr. Darwin's theory. Moreover, there lay, perhaps, at the bottom of this primitive sort of fable, a humanity, a tenderness of rough truths; so that at the end of some story, in which vice or folly had met with its destined punishment, the fabulist might be able to assure his auditors, as we have often to assure tearful children on the like occasions, that they may dry their eyes, for none of it was true.

But this benefit of fiction becomes lost with more sophisticated hearers and authors: a man is no longer the dupe of his own artifice, and cannot deal playfully with truths that are a matter of bitter concern to him in his life. And hence, in the progressive centralisation of modern thought, we should expect the old form of fable to fall gradually into desuetude, and be gradually succeeded by another, which is a fable in all points except that it is not altogether fabulous. And this new form, such as we should expect, and such as we do indeed find, still presents the essential character of brevity; as in any other fable also, there is, underlying and animating the brief action, a moral idea; and as in any other fable, the object is to bring this home to the reader through the intellect rather than through the feelings; so that, without being very deeply moved or interested by the characters of the piece, we should recognise vividly the hinges on which the little plot revolves. But the fabulist now seeks analogies where before he merely sought humorous situations. There will be now a logical nexus between the moral expressed and the machinery employed to express it. The machinery, in fact, as this change is developed, becomes less and less fabulous. We find ourselves in presence of quite a serious, if quite a miniature division of creative literature; and sometimes we have the lesson embodied in a sober, everyday narration, as in the parables of the New Testament, and sometimes merely the statement or, at most, the collocation of significant facts in life, the reader being left to resolve for himself the vague, troublesome, and not yet definitely moral sentiment which has been thus created. And step by step with the development of this change, yet another is developed: the moral tends to become more indeterminate and large. It ceases to be possible to append it, in a tag, to the bottom of the piece, as one might write the name below a caricature; and the fable begins to take rank with all other forms of creative literature, as something too ambitious, in spite of its miniature dimensions, to be resumed in any succinct formula without the loss of all that is deepest and most suggestive in it.

Now it is in this widest sense that Lord Lytton understands the term; there are examples in his two pleasant volumes of all the forms already mentioned, and even of another which can only be admitted among fables by the utmost possible leniency of construction. 'Composure,' 'Et Cætera,' and several more, are merely similes poetically elaborated. So, too, is the pathetic story of the grandfather and grandchild: the child, having treasured away an icicle and forgotten it for ten minutes, comes back to find it already nearly melted, and no longer beautiful: at the same time, the grandfather has just remembered and taken out a bundle of love-letters, which he too had stored away in years gone by, and then long neglected; and, behold! the letters are as faded and sorrowfully disappointing as the icicle. This is merely a simile poetically worked out; and yet it is in such as these, and some others, to be mentioned further on, that the author seems at his best. Wherever he has really written after the old model, there is something to be deprecated: in spite of all the spirit and freshness, in spite of his happy assumption of that cheerful acceptation of things as they are, which, rightly or wrongly, we come to attribute to the ideal fabulist, there is ever a sense as of something a little out of place. A form of literature so very innocent and primitive looks a little over-written in Lord Lytton's conscious and highly-coloured style. It may be bad taste, but sometimes we should prefer a few sentences of plain prose narration, and a little Bewick by way of tail-piece. So that it is not among those fables that conform most nearly to the old model, but one had nearly said among those that most widely differ from it, that we find the most satisfactory examples of the author's manner.

In the mere matter of ingenuity, the metaphysical fables are the most remarkable; such as that of the windmill who imagined that it was he who raised the wind; or that of the grocer's balance ('Cogito ergo sum') who considered himself endowed with free-will, reason, and an infallible practical judgment; until, one fine day, the police made a descent upon the shop, and find the weights false and the scales unequal; and the whole thing is broken up for old iron. Capital fables, also, in the same ironical spirit, are 'Prometheus

Unbound,' the tale of the vainglorying of a champagne-cork, and 'Teleology,' where a nettle justifies the ways of God to nettles while all goes well with it, and, upon a change of luck, promptly changes its divinity.

In all these there is still plenty of the fabulous if you will, although, even here, there may be two opinions possible; but there is another group, of an order of merit perhaps still higher, where we look in vain for any such playful liberties with Nature. Thus we have 'Conservation of Force'; where a musician, thinking of a certain picture, improvises in the twilight; a poet, hearing the music, goes home inspired, and writes a poem; and then a painter, under the influence of this poem, paints another picture, thus lineally descended from the first. This is fiction, but not what we have been used to call fable. We miss the incredible element, the point of audacity with which the fabulist was wont to mock at his readers. And still more so is this the case with others. 'The Horse and the Fly' states one of the unanswerable problems of life in quite a realistic and straightforward way. A fly startles a cab-horse, the coach is overset; a newly-married pair within and the driver, a man with a wife and family, are all killed. The horse continues to gallop off in the loose traces, and ends the tragedy by running over an only child; and there is some little pathetic detail here introduced in the telling, that makes the reader's indignation very white-hot against some one. It remains to be seen who that some one is to be: the fly? Nay, but on closer inspection, it appears that the fly, actuated by maternal instinct, was only seeking a place for her eggs: is maternal instinct, then, 'sole author of these mischiefs all'? 'Who's in the Right?' one of the best fables in the book, is somewhat in the same vein. After a battle has been won, a group of officers assemble inside a battery, and debate together who should have the honour of the success; the Prince, the general staff, the cavalry, the engineer who posted the battery in which they then stand talking, are successively named: the sergeant, who pointed the guns, sneers to himself at the mention of the engineer; and, close by, the gunner, who had applied the match, passes away with a smile of triumph, since it was through his hand that the victorious blow had been dealt. Meanwhile, the cannon claims the honour over the gunner; the cannon-ball, who actually goes forth on the dread mission, claims it over the cannon, who remains idly behind; the powder reminds the cannon-ball that, but for him, it would still be lying on the arsenal floor; and the match caps the discussion; powder, cannon-ball, and cannon would be all equally vain and ineffectual without fire. Just then there comes on a shower of rain, which wets the powder and puts out the match, and completes this lesson of dependence, by indicating the negative conditions which are as necessary for any effect, in their absence, as is the presence of this great fraternity of positive conditions, not any one of which can claim priority over any other. But the fable does not end here, as perhaps, in all logical strictness, it should. It wanders off into a discussion as to which is the truer greatness, that of the vanquished fire or that of the victorious rain. And the speech of the rain is charming:

'Lo, with my little drops I bless again

And beautify the fields which thou didst blast!

Rend, wither, waste, and ruin, what thou wilt,

But call not Greatness what the Gods call Guilt.

Blossoms and grass from blood in battle spilt,

And poppied corn, I bring.

'Mid mouldering Babels, to oblivion built,

My violets spring.

Little by little my small drops have strength

To deck with green delights the grateful earth.'

And so forth, not quite germane (it seems to me) to the matter in hand, but welcome for its own sake.

Best of all are the fables that deal more immediately with the emotions. There is, for instance, that of 'The Two Travellers,' which is profoundly moving in conception, although by no means as well written as some others. In this, one of the two, fearfully frost-bitten, saves his life out of the snow at the cost of all that was comely in his body; just as, long before, the other, who has now quietly resigned himself to death, had violently freed himself from Love at the cost of all that was finest and fairest in his character. Very graceful and sweet is the fable (if so it should be called) in which the author sings the praises of that 'kindly perspective,' which lets a wheat-stalk near the eye cover twenty leagues of distant country, and makes the humble circle about a man's hearth more to him than all the possibilities of the external world. The companion fable to this is also excellent. It tells us of a man who had, all his life through, entertained a passion for certain blue hills on the far horizon, and had promised himself to travel thither ere he died, and become familiar with these distant friends. At last, in some political trouble, he is banished to the very place of his dreams. He arrives there overnight, and, when he rises and goes forth in the morning, there sure enough are the blue hills, only now they have changed places with him, and smile across to him, distant as ever, from the old home whence he has come. Such a story might have been very cynically treated; but it is not so done, the whole tone is kindly and consolatory, and the disenchanted man submissively takes the lesson, and understands that things far away are to be loved for their own sake, and that the unattainable is not truly unattainable, when we can make the beauty of it our own. Indeed, throughout all these two volumes, though there is much practical scepticism, and much irony on abstract questions, this kindly and consolatory spirit is never absent. There is much that is cheerful and, after a sedate, fireside fashion, hopeful. No one will be discouraged by reading the book; but the ground of all this hopefulness and cheerfulness remains to the end somewhat vague. It does not seem to arise from any practical belief in the future either of the individual or the race, but rather from the profound personal contentment of the writer. This is, I suppose, all we must look for in the case. It is as much as we can expect, if the fabulist shall prove a shrewd and cheerful fellow-wayfarer, one with whom the world does not seem to have gone much amiss, but who has yet laughingly learned something of its evil. It will depend much, of course, upon our own character and circumstances, whether the encounter will be agreeable and bracing to the spirits, or offend us as an ill-timed mockery. But where, as here, there is a little tincture of bitterness along with the good-nature, where it is plainly not the humour of a man cheerfully ignorant, but of one who looks on, tolerant and superior and smilingly attentive, upon the good and bad of our existence, it will go hardly if we do not catch some reflection of the same spirit to help us on our way. There is here no impertinent and lying proclamation of peace—none of the cheap optimism of the well-to-do; what we find here is a view of life that would be even grievous, were it not enlivened with this abiding cheerfulness, and ever and anon redeemed by a stroke of pathos.

It is natural enough, I suppose, that we should find wanting in this book some of the intenser qualities of the author's work; and their absence is made up for by much happy description after a quieter fashion. The burst of jubilation over the departure of the snow, which forms the prelude to 'The Thistle,' is full of spirit and of pleasant images. The speech of the forest in 'Sans Souci' is inspired by a beautiful sentiment for nature of the modern sort, and pleases us more, I think, as poetry should please us, than anything in Chronicles and Characters. There are some admirable felicities of expression here and there; as that of the hill, whose summit

'Did print

The azure air with pines.'

Moreover, I do not recollect in the author's former work any symptom of that sympathetic treatment of still life, which is noticeable now and again in the fables; and perhaps most noticeably, when he sketches the burned letters as they hover along the gusty flue, 'Thin, sable veils, wherein a restless spark Yet trembled.' But the description is at its best when the subjects are unpleasant, or even grisly. There are a few capital lines in this key on the last spasm of the battle before alluded to. Surely nothing could be better, in its own way, than the fish in 'The Last Cruise of the Arrogant,' 'the shadowy, side-faced, silent things,' that come butting and staring with lidless eyes at the sunken steam-engine. And although, in yet another, we are told, pleasantly enough, how the water went down into the valleys, where it set itself gaily to saw wood, and on into the plains, where it would soberly carry grain to town; yet the real strength of the fable is when it dealt with the shut pool in which certain unfortunate raindrops are imprisoned among slugs and snails, and in the company of an old toad. The sodden contentment of the fallen acorn is strangely significant; and it is astonishing how unpleasantly we are startled by the appearance of her horrible lover, the maggot.

And now for a last word, about the style. This is not easy to criticise. It is impossible to deny to it rapidity, spirit, and a full sound; the lines are never lame, and the sense is carried forward with an uninterrupted, impetuous rush. But it is not equal. After passages of really admirable versification, the author falls back upon a sort of loose, cavalry manner, not unlike the style of some of Mr. Browning's minor pieces, and almost inseparable from wordiness, and an easy acceptation of somewhat cheap finish. There is nothing here of that compression which is the note of a really sovereign style. It is unfair, perhaps, to set a not remarkable passage from Lord Lytton side by side with one of the signal masterpieces of another, and a very perfect poet; and yet it is interesting, when we see how the portraiture of a dog, detailed through thirty odd lines, is frittered down and finally almost lost in the mere laxity of the style, to compare it with the clear, simple, vigorous delineation that Burns, in four couplets, has given us of the ploughman's collie. It is interesting, at first, and then it becomes a little irritating; for when we think of other passages so much more finished and adroit, we cannot help feeling, that with a little more ardour after perfection of form, criticism would have found nothing left for her to censure. A similar mark of precipitate work is the number of adjectives tumultuously heaped together, sometimes to help out the sense, and sometimes (as one cannot but suspect) to help out the sound of the verses. I do not believe, for instance, that Lord Lytton himself would defend the lines in which we are told how Laocoön 'Revealed to Roman crowds, now Christian grown, That Pagan anguish which, in Parian stone, The Rhodian artist,' and so on. It is not only that this is bad in itself; but that it is unworthy of the company in which it is found; that such verses should not have appeared with the name of a good versifier like Lord Lytton. We must take exception, also, in conclusion, to the excess of alliteration. Alliteration is so liable to be abused that we can scarcely be too sparing of it; and yet it is a trick that seems to grow upon the author with years. It is a pity to see fine verses, such as some in 'Demos,' absolutely spoiled by the recurrence of one wearisome consonant.

CHAPTER II—SALVINI'S MACBETH

Salvini closed his short visit to Edinburgh by a performance of Macbeth. It was, perhaps, from a sentiment of local colour that he chose to play the Scottish usurper for the first time before Scotsmen; and the audience were not insensible of the privilege. Few things, indeed, can move a stronger interest than to see a great creation taking shape for the first time. If it is not purely artistic, the sentiment is surely human. And the thought that you are before all the world, and have the start of so many others as eager as yourself, at least keeps you in a more unbearable suspense before the curtain rises, if it does not enhance the delight with which you follow the performance and see the actor 'bend up each corporal agent' to realise a masterpiece of a few hours' duration. With a player so variable as Salvini, who trusts to the feelings of the moment for so much detail, and who, night after night, does the same thing differently but always well, it can never be safe to pass judgment after a single hearing. And this is more particularly true of last week's Macbeth; for the whole third act was marred by a grievously humorous misadventure. Several minutes too soon the ghost of Banquo joined the party, and after having sat helpless a while at a table, was ignominiously withdrawn. Twice was this ghostly Jack-in-the-box obtruded on the stage before his time; twice removed again; and yet he showed so little hurry when he was really wanted, that, after an awkward pause, Macbeth had to begin his apostrophe to empty air. The arrival of the belated spectre in the middle, with a jerk that made him nod all over, was the last accident in the chapter, and worthily topped the whole. It may be imagined how lamely matters went throughout these cross purposes.

In spite of this, and some other hitches, Salvini's Macbeth had an emphatic success. The creation is worthy of a place beside the same artist's Othello and Hamlet. It is the simplest and most unsympathetic of the three; but the absence of the finer lineaments of Hamlet is redeemed by gusto, breadth, and a headlong unity. Salvini sees nothing great in Macbeth beyond the royalty of muscle, and that courage which comes of strong and copious circulation. The moral smallness of the man is insisted on from the first, in the shudder of uncontrollable jealousy with which he sees Duncan embracing Banquo. He may have some northern poetry of speech, but he has not much logical understanding. In his dealings with the supernatural powers he is like a savage with his fetich, trusting them beyond bounds while all goes well, and whenever he is crossed, casting his belief aside and calling 'fate into the list.' For his wife, he is little more than an agent, a frame of bone and sinew for her fiery spirit to command. The nature of his feeling towards her is rendered with a most precise and delicate touch. He always yields to the woman's fascination; and yet his caresses (and we know how much meaning Salvini can give to a caress) are singularly hard and unloving. Sometimes he lays his hand on her as he might take hold of any one who happened to be nearest to him at a moment of excitement. Love has fallen out of this marriage by the way, and left a curious friendship. Only once—at the very moment when she is showing herself so little a woman and so much a high-spirited man—only once is he very deeply stirred towards her; and that finds expression in the strange and horrible transport of admiration, doubly strange and horrible on Salvini's lips—'Bring forth men-children only!'

The murder scene, as was to be expected, pleased the audience best. Macbeth's voice, in the talk with his wife, was a thing not to be forgotten; and when he spoke of his hangman's hands he seemed to have blood in his utterance. Never for a moment, even in the very article of the murder, does he possess his own soul. He is a man on wires. From first to last it is an exhibition of hideous cowardice. For, after all, it is not here, but in broad daylight, with the exhilaration of conflict, where he can assure himself at every blow he has the longest sword and the heaviest hand, that this man's physical bravery can keep him up; he is an unwieldy ship, and needs plenty of way on before he will steer.

In the banquet scene, while the first murderer gives account of what he has done, there comes a flash of truculent joy at the 'twenty trenchèd gashes' on Banquo's head. Thus Macbeth makes welcome to his imagination those very details of physical horror which are so soon to turn sour in him. As he runs out to embrace these cruel circumstances, as he seeks to realise to his mind's eye the reassuring spectacle of his dead enemy, he is dressing out the phantom to terrify himself; and his imagination, playing the part of justice, is to 'commend to his own lips the ingredients of his poisoned chalice.' With the recollection of Hamlet and his father's spirit still fresh upon him, and the holy awe with which that good man encountered things not dreamt of in his philosophy, it was not possible to avoid looking for resemblances between the two apparitions and the two men haunted. But there are none to be found. Macbeth has a purely physical dislike for Banquo's spirit and the 'twenty trenchèd gashes.' He is afraid of he knows not what. He is abject, and again blustering. In the end he so far forgets himself, his terror, and the nature of what is before him, that he rushes upon it as he would upon a man. When his wife tells him he needs repose, there is something really childish in the way he looks about the room, and, seeing nothing, with an expression of almost sensual relief, plucks up heart enough to go to bed. And what is the upshot of the visitation? It is written in Shakespeare, but should be read with the commentary of Salvini's voice and expression:—'O! siam nell' opra ancor fanciulli'—'We are yet but young in deed.' Circle below circle. He is looking with horrible satisfaction into the mouth of hell. There may still be a prick to-day; but to-morrow conscience will be dead, and he may move untroubled in this element of blood.

In the fifth act we see this lowest circle reached; and it is Salvini's finest moment throughout the play. From the first he was admirably made up, and looked Macbeth to the full as perfectly as ever he looked Othello. From the first moment he steps upon the stage you can see this character is a creation to the fullest meaning of the phrase; for the man before you is a type you know well already. He arrives with Banquo on the heath, fair and red-bearded, sparing of gesture, full of pride and the sense of animal wellbeing, and satisfied after the battle like a beast who has eaten his fill. But in the fifth act there is a change. This is still the big, burly, fleshly, handsome-looking Thane; here is still the same face which in the earlier acts could be superficially good-humoured and sometimes royally courteous. But now the atmosphere of blood, which pervades the whole tragedy, has entered into the man and subdued him to its own nature; and an indescribable degradation, a slackness and puffiness, has overtaken his features. He has breathed the air of carnage, and supped full of horrors. Lady Macbeth complains of the smell of blood on her hand: Macbeth makes no complaint—he has ceased to notice it now; but the same smell is in his nostrils. A contained fury and disgust possesses him. He taunts the messenger and the doctor as people would taunt their mortal enemies. And, indeed, as he knows right well, every one is his enemy now, except his wife. About her he questions the doctor with something like a last human anxiety; and, in tones of grisly mystery, asks him if he can 'minister to a mind diseased.' When the news of her death is brought him, he is staggered and falls into a seat; but somehow it is not anything we can call grief that he displays. There had been two of them against God and man; and now, when there is only one, it makes perhaps less difference than he had expected. And so her death is not only an affliction, but one more disillusion; and he redoubles in bitterness. The speech that follows, given with tragic cynicism in every word, is a dirge, not so much for her as for himself. From that time forth there is nothing human left in him, only 'the fiend of Scotland,' Macduff's 'hell-hound,' whom, with a stern glee, we see baited like a bear and hunted down like a wolf. He is inspired and set above fate by a demoniacal energy, a lust of wounds and slaughter. Even after he meets Macduff his courage does not fail; but when he hears the Thane was not born of woman, all virtue goes out of him; and though he speaks sounding words of defiance, the last combat is little better than a suicide.

The whole performance is, as I said, so full of gusto and a headlong unity; the personality of Macbeth is so sharp and powerful; and within these somewhat narrow limits there is so much play and saliency that, so far as concerns Salvini himself, a third great success seems indubitable. Unfortunately, however, a great actor cannot fill more than a very small fraction of the boards; and though Banquo's ghost will probably be more seasonable in his future apparitions, there are some more inherent difficulties in the piece. The company at large did not distinguish themselves. Macduff, to the huge delight of the gallery, out-Macduff'd the average ranter. The lady who filled the principal female part has done better on other occasions, but I fear she has not metal for what she tried last week. Not to succeed in the sleep-walking scene is to make a memorable failure. As it was given, it succeeded in being wrong in art without being true to nature.

And there is yet another difficulty, happily easy to reform, which somewhat interfered with the success of the performance. At the end of the incantation scene the Italian translator has made Macbeth fall insensible upon the stage. This is a change of questionable propriety from a psychological point of view; while in point of view of effect it leaves the stage for some moments empty of all business. To remedy this, a bevy of green ballet-girls came forth and pointed their toes about the prostrate king. A dance of High

Church curates, or a hornpipe by Mr. T. P. Cooke, would not be more out of the key; though the gravity of a Scots audience was not to be overcome, and they merely expressed their disapprobation by a round of moderate hisses, a similar irruption of Christmas fairies would most likely convulse a London theatre from pit to gallery with inextinguishable laughter. It is, I am told, the Italian tradition; but it is one more honoured in the breach than the observance. With the total disappearance of these damsels, with a stronger Lady Macbeth, and, if possible, with some compression of those scenes in which Salvini does not appear, and the spectator is left at the mercy of Macduffs and Duncans, the play would go twice as well, and we should be better able to follow and enjoy an admirable work of dramatic art.

CHAPTER III—BAGSTER'S 'PILGRIM'S PROGRESS'

I have here before me an edition of the Pilgrim's Progress, bound in green, without a date, and described as 'illustrated by nearly three hundred engravings, and memoir of Bunyan.' On the outside it is lettered 'Bagster's Illustrated Edition,' and after the author's apology, facing the first page of the tale, a folding pictorial 'Plan of the Road' is marked as 'drawn by the late Mr. T. Conder,' and engraved by J. Basire. No further information is anywhere vouchsafed; perhaps the publishers had judged the work too unimportant; and we are still left ignorant whether or not we owe the woodcuts in the body of the volume to the same hand that drew the plan. It seems, however, more than probable. The literal particularity of mind which, in the map, laid down the flower-plots in the devil's garden, and carefully introduced the court-house in the town of Vanity, is closely paralleled in many of the cuts; and in both, the architecture of the buildings and the disposition of the gardens have a kindred and entirely English air. Whoever he was, the author of these wonderful little pictures may lay claim to be the best illustrator of Bunyan. [183] They are not only good illustrations, like so many others; but they are like so few, good illustrations of Bunyan. Their spirit, in defect and quality, is still the same as his own. The designer also has lain down and dreamed a dream, as literal, as quaint, and almost as apposite as Bunyan's; and text and pictures make but the two sides of the same homespun yet impassioned story. To do justice to the designs, it will be necessary to say, for the hundredth time, a word or two about the masterpiece which they adorn.

All allegories have a tendency to escape from the purpose of their creators; and as the characters and incidents become more and more interesting in themselves, the moral, which these were to show forth, falls more and more into neglect. An architect may command a wreath of vine-leaves round the cornice of a monument; but if, as each leaf came from the chisel, it took proper life and fluttered freely on the wall, and if the vine grew, and the building were hidden over with foliage and fruit, the architect would stand in much the same situation as the writer of allegories. The Faëry Queen was an allegory, I am willing to believe; but it survives as an imaginative tale in incomparable verse. The case of Bunyan is widely different; and yet in this also Allegory, poor nymph, although never quite forgotten, is sometimes rudely thrust against the wall. Bunyan was fervently in earnest; with 'his fingers in his ears, he ran on,' straight for his mark. He tells us himself, in the conclusion to the first part, that he did not fear to raise a laugh; indeed, he feared nothing, and said anything; and he was greatly served in this by a certain rustic privilege of his style, which, like the talk of strong uneducated men, when it does not impress by its force, still charms by its simplicity. The mere story and the allegorical design enjoyed perhaps his equal favour. He believed in both with an energy of faith that was capable of moving mountains. And we have to remark in him, not the parts where inspiration fails and is supplied by cold and merely decorative invention, but the parts where faith has grown to be credulity, and his characters become so real to him that he forgets the end of their creation. We can follow him step by step into the trap which he lays for himself by his own entire good faith and triumphant literality of vision, till the trap closes and shuts him in an inconsistency. The allegories of the Interpreter and of the Shepherds of the Delectable Mountains are all actually performed, like stage-plays, before the pilgrims. The son of Mr. Great-grace visibly 'tumbles hills about with his words.' Adam the First has his condemnation written visibly on his forehead, so that Faithful reads it. At the very instant the net closes round the pilgrims, 'the white robe falls from the black man's body.' Despair 'getteth him a grievous crab-tree cudgel'; it was in 'sunshiny weather' that he had his fits; and the birds in the grove about the House Beautiful, 'our country birds,' only sing their little pious verses 'at the spring, when the flowers appear and the sun shines warm.' 'I often,' says Piety, 'go out to hear them; we also ofttimes keep them tame on our house.' The post between Beulah and the Celestial City sounds his horn, as you may yet hear in country places. Madam Bubble, that 'tall, comely dame, something of a swarthy complexion, in very pleasant attire, but old,' 'gives you a smile at the end of each sentence'—a real woman she; we all know her. Christiana dying 'gave Mr. Stand-fast a ring,' for no possible reason in the allegory, merely because the touch was human and affecting. Look at Great-heart, with his soldierly ways, garrison ways, as I had almost called them; with his taste in weapons; his delight in any that 'he found to be a man of his hands'; his chivalrous point of honour, letting Giant Maul get up again when he was down, a thing fairly flying in the teeth of the moral; above all, with his language in the inimitable tale of Mr. Fearing: 'I thought I should have lost my man'—'chicken-hearted'—'at last he came in, and I will say that for my lord, he carried it wonderful lovingly to him.' This is no Independent minister; this is a stout, honest, big-busted ancient, adjusting his shoulder-belts, twirling his long moustaches as he speaks. Last and most remarkable, 'My sword,' says the dying Valiant-for-Truth, he in whom Great-heart delighted, 'my sword I give to him that shall succeed me in my pilgrimage, and my courage and skill to him that can get it.' And after this boast, more arrogantly unorthodox than was ever dreamed of by the rejected Ignorance, we are told that 'all the trumpets sounded for him on the other side.'

In every page the book is stamped with the same energy of vision and the same energy of belief. The quality is equally and indifferently displayed in the spirit of the fighting, the tenderness of the pathos, the startling vigour and strangeness of the incidents, the natural strain of the conversations, and the humanity and charm of the characters. Trivial talk over a meal, the dying words of heroes, the delights of Beulah or the Celestial City, Apollyon and my Lord Hate-good, Great-heart, and Mr. Worldly-Wiseman, all have been imagined with the same clearness, all written of with equal gusto and precision, all created in the same mixed element, of simplicity that is almost comical, and art that, for its purpose, is faultless.

It was in much the same spirit that our artist sat down to his drawings. He is by nature a Bunyan of the pencil. He, too, will draw anything, from a butcher at work on a dead sheep, up to the courts of Heaven. 'A Lamb for Supper' is the name of one of his designs, 'Their Glorious Entry' of another. He has the same disregard for the ridiculous, and enjoys somewhat of the same privilege of style, so that we are pleased even when we laugh the most. He is literal to the verge of folly. If dust is to be raised from the unswept parlour, you may be sure it will 'fly abundantly' in the picture. If Faithful is to lie 'as dead' before Moses, dead he shall lie with a warrant—dead and stiff like granite; nay (and here the artist must enhance upon the symbolism of the author), it is with the identical stone tables of the law that Moses fells the sinner. Good and bad people, whom we at once distinguish in the text by their names, Hopeful, Honest, and Valiant-for-Truth, on the one hand, as against By-ends, Sir Having Greedy, and the Lord Old-man on the other, are in these drawings as simply distinguished by their costume. Good people, when not armed cap-à-pie, wear a speckled tunic girt about the waist, and low hats, apparently of straw. Bad people swagger in tail-coats and chimney-pots, a few with knee-breeches, but the large majority in trousers, and for all the world like guests at a garden-party. Worldly-Wiseman alone, by some inexplicable quirk, stands before Christian in laced hat, embroidered waistcoat, and trunk-hose. But above all examples of this artist's intrepidity, commend me to the print entitled 'Christian Finds it Deep.' 'A great darkness and horror,' says the text, have fallen on the pilgrim; it is the comfortless deathbed with which Bunyan so strikingly concludes the sorrows and conflicts of his hero. How to represent this worthily the artist knew not; and yet he was determined to represent it somehow. This was how he did: Hopeful is still shown to his neck above the water of death; but Christian has bodily disappeared, and a blot of solid blackness indicates his place.

As you continue to look at these pictures, about an inch square for the most part, sometimes printed three or more to the page, and each having a printed legend of its own, however trivial the event recorded, you will soon become aware of two things: first, that the man can draw, and, second, that he possesses the gift of an imagination. 'Obstinate reviles,' says the legend; and you should see Obstinate reviling. 'He warily retraces his steps'; and there is Christian, posting through the plain, terror and speed in every muscle. 'Mercy yearns to go' shows you a plain interior with packing going forward, and, right in the middle, Mercy yearning to go—every line of the girl's figure yearning. In 'The Chamber called Peace' we see a simple English room, bed with white curtains, window valance and door, as may be found in many thousand unpretentious houses; but far off, through the open window, we behold the sun uprising out of a great plain, and Christian hails it with his hand:

'Where am I now! is this the love and care

Of Jesus, for the men that pilgrims are!

Thus to provide! That I should be forgiven!

And dwell already the next door to heaven!'

A page or two further, from the top of the House Beautiful, the damsels point his gaze toward the Delectable Mountains: 'The Prospect,' so the cut is ticketed—and I shall be surprised, if on less than a square inch of paper you can show me one so wide and fair. Down a cross road on an English plain, a cathedral city outlined on the horizon, a hazel shaw upon the left, comes Madam Wanton dancing with her fair enchanted cup, and Faithful, book in hand, half pauses. The cut is perfect as a symbol; the giddy movement of the sorceress, the uncertain poise of the man struck to the heart by a temptation, the contrast of that even plain of life whereon he journeys with the bold, ideal bearing of the wanton—the artist who invented and portrayed this had not merely read Bunyan, he had also thoughtfully lived. The Delectable Mountains—I continue skimming the first part—are not on the whole happily rendered. Once, and once only, the note is struck, when Christian and Hopeful are seen coming, shoulder-high, through a thicket of green shrubs—box, perhaps, or perfumed nutmeg; while behind them, domed or pointed, the hills stand ranged against the sky. A little further, and we come to that masterpiece of Bunyan's insight into life, the Enchanted Ground; where, in a few traits, he has set down the latter end of such a number of the would-be good; where his allegory goes so deep that, to people looking seriously on life, it cuts like satire. The true significance of this invention lies, of course, far out of the way of drawing; only one feature, the great tedium of the land, the growing weariness in well-doing, may be somewhat represented in a symbol.

The pilgrims are near the end: 'Two Miles Yet,' says the legend. The road goes ploughing up and down over a rolling heath; the wayfarers, with outstretched arms, are already sunk to the knees over the brow of the nearest hill; they have just passed a milestone with the cipher two; from overhead a great, piled, summer cumulus, as of a slumberous summer afternoon, beshadows them: two miles! it might be hundreds. In dealing with the Land of Beulah the artist lags, in both parts, miserably behind the text, but in the distant prospect of the Celestial City more than regains his own. You will remember when Christian and Hopeful 'with desire fell sick.' 'Effect of the Sunbeams' is the artist's title. Against the sky, upon a cliffy mountain, the radiant temple beams upon them over deep, subjacent woods; they, behind a mound, as if seeking shelter from the splendour—one prostrate on his face, one kneeling, and with hands ecstatically lifted—yearn with passion after that immortal city. Turn the page, and we behold them walking by the very shores of death; Heaven, from this nigher view, has risen half-way to the zenith, and sheds a wider glory; and the two pilgrims, dark against that brightness, walk and sing out of the fulness of their hearts. No cut more thoroughly illustrates at once the merit and the weakness of the artist. Each pilgrim sings with a book in his grasp—a family Bible at the least for bigness; tomes so recklessly enormous that our second, impulse is to laughter. And yet that is not the first thought, nor perhaps the last. Something in the attitude of the manikins—faces they have none, they are too small for that—something in the way they swing these monstrous volumes to their singing, something perhaps borrowed from the text, some subtle differentiation from the cut that went before and the cut that follows after—something, at least, speaks clearly of a fearful joy, of Heaven seen from the deathbed, of the horror of the last passage no less than of the glorious coming home. There is that in the action of one of them which always reminds me, with a difference, of that haunting last glimpse of Thomas Idle, travelling to Tyburn in the cart. Next come the Shining Ones, wooden and trivial enough; the pilgrims pass into the river; the blot already mentioned settles over and obliterates Christian. In two more cuts we behold them drawing nearer to the other shore; and then, between two radiant angels, one of whom points upward, we see them mounting in new weeds, their former lendings left behind them on the inky river. More angels meet them; Heaven is displayed, and if no better, certainly no worse, than it has been shown by others—a place, at least, infinitely populous and glorious with light—a place that haunts solemnly the hearts of children. And then this symbolic draughtsman once more strikes into his proper vein. Three cuts conclude the first part. In the first the gates close, black against the glory struggling from within. The second shows us Ignorance—alas! poor Arminian!—hailing, in a sad twilight, the ferryman Vain-Hope; and in the third we behold him, bound hand and foot, and black already with the hue of his eternal fate, carried high over the mountain-tops of the world by two angels of the anger of the Lord. 'Carried to Another Place,' the artist enigmatically names his plate—a terrible design.

Wherever he touches on the black side of the supernatural his pencil grows more daring and incisive. He has many true inventions in the perilous and diabolic; he has many startling nightmares realised. It is not easy to select the best; some may like one and some another; the nude, depilated devil bounding and casting darts against the Wicket Gate; the scroll of flying horrors that hang over Christian by the Mouth of Hell; the horned shade that comes behind him whispering blasphemies; the daylight breaking through that rent cave-mouth of the mountains and falling chill adown the haunted tunnel; Christian's further progress along the causeway, between the two black pools, where, at every yard or two, a gin, a pitfall, or a snare awaits the passer-by—loathsome white devilkins harbouring close under the bank to work the springes, Christian himself pausing and pricking with his sword's point at the nearest noose, and pale discomfortable mountains rising on the farther side; or yet again, the two ill-favoured ones that beset the first of Christian's journey, with the frog-like structure of the skull, the frog-like limberness of limbs—crafty, slippery, lustful-looking devils, drawn always in outline as though possessed of a dim, infernal luminosity. Horrid fellows are they, one and all; horrid fellows and horrific scenes. In another spirit that Good-Conscience 'to whom Mr. Honest had spoken in his lifetime,' a cowled, grey, awful figure, one hand pointing to the heavenly shore, realises, I will not say all, but some at least of the strange impressiveness of Bunyan's words. It is no easy nor pleasant thing to speak in one's lifetime with Good-Conscience; he is an austere, unearthly friend, whom maybe Torquemada knew; and the folds of his raiment are not merely claustral, but have something of the horror of the pall. Be not afraid, however; with the hand of that appearance Mr. Honest will get safe across.

Yet perhaps it is in sequences that this artist best displays himself. He loves to look at either side of a thing: as, for instance, when he shows us both sides of the wall—'Grace Inextinguishable' on the one side, with the devil vainly pouring buckets on the flame, and 'The Oil of Grace' on the other, where the Holy Spirit, vessel in hand, still secretly supplies the fire. He loves, also, to show us the same event twice over, and to repeat his instantaneous photographs at the interval of but a moment. So we have, first, the whole troop of pilgrims coming up to Valiant, and Great-heart to the front, spear in hand and parleying; and next, the same cross-roads, from a more distant view, the convoy now scattered and looking safely and curiously on, and Valiant handing over for inspection his 'right Jerusalem blade.' It is true that this designer has no great care after consistency: Apollyon's spear is laid by, his quiver of darts will disappear, whenever they might hinder the designer's freedom; and the fiend's tail is blobbed or forked at his good pleasure. But this is not unsuitable to the illustration of the fervent Bunyan, breathing hurry and momentary inspiration. He, with his hot purpose, hunting sinners with a lasso, shall himself forget the things that he has written yesterday. He shall first slay Heedless in the Valley of the Shadow, and then take leave of him talking in his sleep, as if nothing had happened, in an arbour on the Enchanted Ground. And again, in his rhymed prologue, he shall assign some of the glory of the siege of Doubting Castle to his favourite Valiant-for-the-Truth, who did not meet with the besiegers till long after, at that dangerous corner by Deadman's Lane. And, with all inconsistencies and freedoms, there is a power shown in these sequences of cuts: a power of joining on one action or one humour to another; a power of following out the moods, even of the dismal subterhuman fiends engendered by the artist's fancy; a power of sustained continuous realisation, step by step, in nature's order, that can tell a story, in all its ins and outs, its pauses and surprises, fully and figuratively, like the art of words.

One such sequence is the fight of Christian and Apollyon—six cuts, weird and fiery, like the text. The pilgrim is throughout a pale and stockish figure; but the devil covers a multitude of defects. There is no better devil of the conventional order than our artist's Apollyon, with his mane, his wings, his bestial legs, his changing and terrifying expression, his infernal energy to slay. In cut the first you see him afar off, still obscure in form, but already formidable in suggestion. Cut the second, 'The Fiend in Discourse,' represents him, not reasoning, railing rather, shaking his spear at the pilgrim, his shoulder advanced, his tail writhing in the air, his foot ready for a spring, while Christian stands back a little, timidly defensive. The third illustrates these magnificent words: 'Then Apollyon straddled quite over the whole breadth of the way, and said, I am void of fear in this matter: prepare thyself to die; for I swear by my infernal den that thou shalt go no farther: here will I spill thy soul! And with that he threw a flaming dart at his breast.' In the cut he throws a dart with either hand, belching pointed flames out of his mouth, spreading his broad vans, and straddling the while across the path, as only a fiend can straddle who has just sworn by his infernal den. The defence will not be long against such vice, such flames, such red-hot nether energy. And in the fourth cut, to be sure, he has leaped bodily upon his victim, sped by foot and pinion, and roaring as he leaps. The fifth shows the climacteric of the battle; Christian has reached nimbly out and got his sword, and dealt that deadly home-thrust, the fiend still stretched upon him, but 'giving back, as one that had received his mortal wound.' The raised head, the bellowing mouth, the paw clapped upon the sword, the one wing relaxed in agony, all realise vividly these words of the text. In the sixth and last, the trivial armed figure of the pilgrim is seen kneeling with clasped hands on the betrodden scene of contest and among the shivers of the darts; while just at the margin the hinder quarters and the tail of Apollyon are whisking off, indignant and discounted.

In one point only do these pictures seem to be unworthy of the text, and that point is one rather of the difference of arts than the difference of artists. Throughout his best and worst, in his highest and most divine imaginations as in the narrowest sallies of his sectarianism, the human-hearted piety of Bunyan touches and ennobles, convinces, accuses the reader. Through no art beside the art of words can the kindness of a man's affections be expressed. In the cuts you shall find faithfully parodied the quaintness and the power, the triviality and the surprising freshness of the author's fancy; there you shall find him out-stripped in ready symbolism and the art of bringing things essentially invisible before the eyes: but to feel the contact of essential goodness, to be made in love with piety, the book must be read and not the prints examined.

Farewell should not be taken with a grudge; nor can I dismiss in any other words than those of gratitude a series of pictures which have, to one at least, been the visible embodiment of Bunyan from childhood up, and shown him, through all his years, Great-heart lungeing at Giant Maul, and Apollyon breathing fire at Christian, and every turn and town along the road to the Celestial City, and that bright place itself, seen as to a stave of music, shining afar off upon the hill-top, the candle of the world.

SKETCHES

I. THE SATIRIST

My companion enjoyed a cheap reputation for wit and insight. He was by habit and repute a satirist. If he did occasionally condemn anything or anybody who richly deserved it, and whose demerits had hitherto escaped, it was simply because he condemned everything and everybody. While I was with him he disposed of St. Paul with an epigram, shook my reverence for Shakespeare in a neat antithesis, and fell foul of the Almighty Himself, on the score of one or two out of the ten commandments. Nothing escaped his blighting censure. At every sentence he overthrew an idol, or lowered my estimation of a friend. I saw everything with new eyes, and could only marvel at my former blindness. How was it possible that I had not before observed A's false hair, B's selfishness, or C's boorish manners? I and my companion, methought, walked the streets like a couple of gods among a swarm of vermin; for every one we saw seemed to bear openly upon his brow the mark of the apocalyptic beast. I half expected that these miserable beings, like the people of Lystra, would recognise their betters and force us to the altar; in which case, warned by the late of Paul and Barnabas, I do not know that my modesty would have prevailed upon me to decline. But there was no need for such churlish virtue. More blinded than the Lycaonians, the people saw no divinity in our gait; and as our temporary godhead lay more in the way of observing than healing their infirmities, we were content to pass them by in scorn.

I could not leave my companion, not from regard or even from interest, but from a very natural feeling, inseparable from the case. To understand it, let us take a simile. Suppose yourself walking down the street with a man who continues to sprinkle the crowd out of a flask of vitriol. You would be much diverted with the grimaces and contortions of his victims; and at the same time you would fear to leave his arm until his bottle was empty, knowing that, when once among the crowd, you would run a good chance yourself of baptism with his biting liquor. Now my companion's vitriol was inexhaustible.

It was perhaps the consciousness of this, the knowledge that I was being anointed already out of the vials of his wrath, that made me fall to criticising the critic, whenever we had parted.

After all, I thought, our satirist has just gone far enough into his neighbours to find that the outside is false, without caring to go farther and discover what is really true. He is content to find that things are not what they seem, and broadly generalises from it that they do not exist at all. He sees our virtues are not what they pretend they are; and, on the strength of that, he denies us the possession of virtue altogether. He has learnt the first lesson, that no man is wholly good; but he has not even suspected that there is another equally true, to wit, that no man is wholly bad. Like the inmate of a coloured star, he has eyes for one colour alone. He has a keen scent after evil, but his nostrils are plugged against all good, as people plugged their nostrils before going about the streets of the plague-struck city.

Why does he do this? It is most unreasonable to flee the knowledge of good like the infection of a horrible disease, and batten and grow fat in the real atmosphere of a lazar-house. This was my first thought; but my second was not like unto it, and I saw that our satirist was wise, wise in his generation, like the unjust steward. He does not want light, because the darkness is more pleasant. He does not wish to see the good, because he is happier without it. I recollect that when I walked with him, I was in a state of divine exaltation, such as Adam and Eve must have enjoyed when the savour of the fruit was still unfaded between their lips; and I recognise that this must be the man's habitual state. He has the forbidden fruit in his waist-coat pocket, and can make himself a god as often and as long as he likes. He has raised himself upon a glorious pedestal above his fellows; he has touched the summit of ambition; and he envies neither King nor Kaiser, Prophet nor Priest, content in an elevation as high as theirs, and much more easily attained. Yes, certes, much more easily attained. He has not risen by climbing himself, but by pushing others down. He has grown great in his own estimation, not by blowing himself out, and risking the fate of Æsop's frog, but simply by the habitual use of a diminishing glass on everybody else. And I think altogether that his is a better, a safer, and a surer recipe than most others.

After all, however, looking back on what I have written, I detect a spirit suspiciously like his own. All through, I have been comparing myself with our satirist, and all through, I have had the best of the comparison. Well, well, contagion is as often mental as physical; and I do not think my readers, who have all been under his lash, will blame me very much for giving the headsman a mouthful of his own sawdust.

II. NUITS BLANCHES

If any one should know the pleasure and pain of a sleepless night, it should be I. I remember, so long ago, the sickly child that woke from his few hours' slumber with the sweat of a nightmare on his brow, to lie awake and listen and long for the first signs of life among the silent streets. These nights of pain and weariness are graven on my mind; and so when the same thing happened to me again, everything that I heard or saw was rather a recollection than a discovery.

Weighed upon by the opaque and almost sensible darkness, I listened eagerly for anything to break the sepulchral quiet. But nothing came, save, perhaps, an emphatic crack from the old cabinet that was made by Deacon Brodie, or the dry rustle of the coals on the extinguished fire. It was a calm; or I know that I should have heard in the roar and clatter of the storm, as I have not heard it for so many years, the wild career of a horseman, always scouring up from the distance and passing swiftly below the window; yet always returning again from the place whence first he came, as though, baffled by some higher power, he had retraced his steps to gain impetus for another and another attempt.

As I lay there, there arose out of the utter stillness the rumbling of a carriage a very great way off, that drew near, and passed within a few streets of the house, and died away as gradually as it had arisen. This, too, was as a reminiscence.

I rose and lifted a corner of the blind. Over the black belt of the garden I saw the long line of Queen Street, with here and there a lighted window. How often before had my nurse lifted me out of bed and pointed them out to me, while we wondered together if, there also, there were children that could not sleep, and if these lighted oblongs were signs of those that waited like us for the morning.

I went out into the lobby, and looked down into the great deep well of the staircase. For what cause I know not, just as it used to be in the old days that the feverish child might be the better served, a peep of gas illuminated a narrow circle far below me. But where I was, all was darkness and silence, save the dry monotonous ticking of the clock that came ceaselessly up to my ear.

The final crown of it all, however, the last touch of reproduction on the pictures of my memory, was the arrival of that time for which, all night through, I waited and longed of old. It was my custom, as the hours dragged on, to repeat the question, 'When will the carts come in?' and repeat it again and again until at last those sounds arose in the street that I have heard once more this morning. The road before our house is a great thoroughfare for early carts. I know not, and I never have known, what they carry, whence they come, or whither they go. But I know that, long ere dawn, and for hours together, they stream continuously past, with the same rolling and jerking of wheels and the same clink of horses' feet. It was not for nothing that they made the burthen of my wishes all night through. They are really the first throbbings of life, the harbingers of day; and it pleases you as much to hear them as it must please a shipwrecked seaman once again to grasp a hand of flesh and blood after years of miserable solitude. They have the freshness of the daylight life about them. You can hear the carters cracking their whips and crying hoarsely to their horses or to one another; and sometimes even a peal of healthy, harsh horse-laughter comes up to you through the darkness. There is now an end of mystery and fear. Like the knocking at the door in Macbeth, [205] or the cry of the watchman in the Tour de Nesle, they show that the horrible cæsura is over and the nightmares have fled away, because the day is breaking and the ordinary life of men is beginning to bestir itself among the streets.

In the middle of it all I fell asleep, to be wakened by the officious knocking at my door, and I find myself twelve years older than I had dreamed myself all night.

III. THE WREATH OF IMMORTELLES

It is all very well to talk of death as 'a pleasant potion of immortality', but the most of us, I suspect, are of 'queasy stomachs,' and find it none of the sweetest. [206a] The graveyard may be cloak-room to Heaven; but we must admit that it is a very ugly and offensive vestibule in itself, however fair may be the life to which it leads. And though Enoch and Elias went into the temple through a gate which certainly may be called Beautiful, the rest of us have to find our way to it through Ezekiel's low-bowed door and the vault full of creeping things and all manner of abominable beasts. Nevertheless, there is a certain frame of mind to which a cemetery is, if not an antidote, at least an alleviation. If you are in a fit of the blues, go nowhere else. It was in obedience to this wise regulation that the other morning found me lighting my pipe at the entrance to Old Greyfriars', thoroughly sick of the town, the country, and myself.

Two of the men were talking at the gate, one of them carrying a spade in hands still crusted with the soil of graves. Their very aspect was delightful to me; and I crept nearer to them, thinking to pick up some snatch of sexton gossip, some 'talk fit for a charnel,' [206b] something, in fine, worthy of that fastidious logician, that adept in coroner's law, who has come down to us as the patron of Yaughan's liquor, and the very prince of gravediggers. Scots people in general are so much wrapped up in their profession that I had a good chance of overhearing such conversation: the talk of fish-mongers running usually on stockfish and haddocks; while of the Scots sexton I could repeat stories and speeches that positively smell of the graveyard. But on this occasion I was doomed to disappointment. My two friends were far into the region of generalities. Their profession was forgotten in their electorship. Politics had engulfed the narrower economy of grave-digging. 'Na, na,' said the one, 'ye're a' wrang.' 'The English and Irish Churches,' answered the other, in a tone as if he had made the remark before, and it had been called in question—'The English and Irish Churches have impoverished the country.'

'Such are the results of education,' thought I as I passed beside them and came fairly among the tombs. Here, at least, there were no commonplace politics, no diluted this-morning's leader, to distract or offend me. The old shabby church showed, as usual, its quaint extent of roofage and the relievo skeleton on one gable, still blackened with the fire of thirty years ago. A chill dank mist lay over all. The Old Greyfriars' churchyard was in perfection that morning, and one could go round and reckon up the associations with no fear of vulgar interruption. On this stone the Covenant was signed. In that vault, as the story goes, John Knox took hiding in some Reformation broil. From that window Burke the murderer looked out many a time across the tombs, and perhaps o' nights let himself down over the sill to rob some new-made grave. Certainly he would have a selection here. The very walks have been carried over forgotten resting-places; and the whole ground is uneven, because (as I was once quaintly told) 'when the wood rots it stands to reason the soil should fall in,' which, from the law of gravitation, is certainly beyond denial. But it is round the boundary that there are the finest tombs. The whole irregular space is, as it were, fringed with quaint old monuments, rich in death's-heads and scythes and hour-glasses, and doubly rich in pious epitaphs and Latin mottoes—rich in them to such an extent that their proper space has run over, and they have crawled end-long up the shafts of columns and ensconced themselves in all sorts of odd corners among the sculpture. These tombs raise their backs against the rabble of squalid dwelling-houses, and every here and there a clothes-pole projects between two monuments its fluttering trophy of white and yellow and red. With a grim irony they recall the banners in the Invalides, banners as appropriate perhaps over the sepulchres of tailors and weavers as these others above the dust of armies. Why they put things out to dry on that particular morning it was hard to imagine. The grass was grey with drops of rain, the headstones black with moisture. Yet, in despite of weather and common sense, there they hung between the tombs; and beyond them I could see through open windows into miserable rooms where whole families were born and fed, and slept and died. At one a girl sat singing merrily with her back to the graveyard; and from another came the shrill tones of a scolding woman. Every here and there was a town garden full of sickly flowers, or a pile of crockery inside upon the window-seat. But you do not grasp the full connection between these houses of the dead and the living, the unnatural marriage of stately sepulchres and squalid houses, till, lower down, where the road has sunk far below the surface of the cemetery, and the very roofs are scarcely on a level with its wall, you observe that a proprietor has taken advantage of a tall monument and trained a chimney-stack against its back. It startles you to see the red, modern pots peering over the shoulder of the tomb.

A man was at work on a grave, his spade clinking away the drift of bones that permeates the thin brown soil; but my first disappointment had taught me to expect little from Greyfriars' sextons, and I passed him by in silence. A slater on the slope of a neighbouring roof eyed me curiously. A lean black cat, looking as if it had battened on strange meats, slipped past me. A little boy at a window put his finger to his nose in so offensive a manner that I was put upon my dignity, and turned grandly off to read old epitaphs and peer through the gratings into the shadow of vaults.

Just then I saw two women coming down a path, one of them old, and the other younger, with a child in her arms. Both had faces eaten with famine and hardened with sin, and both had reached that stage of degradation, much lower in a woman than a man, when all care for dress is lost. As they came down they neared a grave, where some pious friend or relative had laid a wreath of immortelles, and put a bell glass over it, as is the custom. The effect of that ring of dull yellow among so many blackened and dusty sculptures was more pleasant than it is in modern cemeteries, where every second mound can boast a similar coronal; and here, where it was the exception and not the rule, I could even fancy the drops of moisture that dimmed the covering were the tears of those who laid it where it was. As the two women came up to it, one of them kneeled down on the wet grass and looked long and silently through the clouded shade, while the second stood above her, gently oscillating to and fro to lull the muling baby. I was struck a great way off with something religious in the attitude of these two unkempt and haggard women; and I drew near faster, but still cautiously, to hear what they were saying. Surely on them the spirit of death and decay had descended; I had no education to dread here: should I not have a chance of seeing nature? Alas! a pawnbroker could not have been more practical and commonplace, for this was what the kneeling woman said to the woman upright—this and nothing more: 'Eh, what extravagance!'

O nineteenth century, wonderful art thou indeed—wonderful, but wearisome in thy stale and deadly uniformity. Thy men are more like numerals than men. They must bear their idiosyncrasies or their professions written on a placard about their neck, like the scenery in Shakespeare's theatre. Thy precepts of economy have pierced into the lowest ranks of life; and there is now a decorum in vice, a respectability among the disreputable, a pure spirit of Philistinism among the waifs and strays of thy Bohemia. For lo! thy very gravediggers talk politics; and thy castaways kneel upon new graves, to discuss the cost of the monument and grumble at the improvidence of love.

Such was the elegant apostrophe that I made as I went out of the gates again, happily satisfied in myself, and feeling that I alone of all whom I had seen was able to profit by the silent poem of these green mounds and blackened headstones.

IV. NURSES

I knew one once, and the room where, lonely and old, she waited for death. It was pleasant enough, high up above the lane, and looking forth upon a hill-side, covered all day with sheets and yellow blankets, and with long lines of underclothing fluttering between the battered posts. There were any number of cheap prints, and a drawing by one of 'her children,' and there were flowers in the window, and a sickly canary withered into consumption in an ornamental cage. The bed, with its checked coverlid, was in a closet. A great Bible lay on the table; and her drawers were full of 'scones,' which it was her pleasure to give to young visitors such as I was then.

You may not think this a melancholy picture; but the canary, and the cat, and the white mouse that she had for a while, and that died, were all indications of the want that ate into her heart. I think I know a little of what that old woman felt; and I am as sure as if I had seen her, that she sat many an hour in silent tears, with the big Bible open before her clouded eyes.

If you could look back upon her life, and feel the great chain that had linked her to one child after another, sometimes to be wrenched suddenly through, and sometimes, which is infinitely worse, to be torn gradually off through years of growing neglect, or perhaps growing dislike! She had, like the mother, overcome that natural repugnance—repugnance which no man can conquer—towards the infirm and helpless mass of putty of the earlier stage. She had spent her best and happiest years in tending, watching, and learning to love like a mother this child, with which she has no connection and to which she has no tie. Perhaps she refused some sweetheart (such things have been), or put him off and off, until he lost heart and turned to some one else, all for fear of leaving this creature that had wound itself about her heart. And the end of it all—her month's warning, and a present perhaps, and the rest of the life to vain regret. Or, worse still, to see the child gradually forgetting and forsaking her, fostered in disrespect and neglect on the plea of growing manliness, and at last beginning to treat her as a servant whom he had treated a few years before as a mother. She sees the Bible or the Psalm-book, which with gladness and love unutterable in her heart she had bought for him years ago out of her slender savings, neglected for some newer gift of his father, lying in dust in the lumber-room or given away to a poor child, and the act applauded for its unfeeling charity. Little wonder if she becomes hurt and angry, and attempts to tyrannise and to grasp her old power back again. We are not all patient Grizzels, by good fortune, but the most of us human beings with feelings and tempers of our own.

And so, in the end, behold her in the room that I described. Very likely and very naturally, in some fling of feverish misery or recoil of thwarted love, she has quarrelled with her old employers and the children are forbidden to see her or to speak to her; or at best she gets her rent paid and a little to herself, and now and then her late charges are sent up (with another nurse, perhaps) to pay her a short visit. How bright these visits seem as she looks forward to them on her lonely bed! How unsatisfactory their realisation, when the forgetful child, half wondering, checks with every word and action the outpouring of her maternal love! How bitter and restless the memories that they leave behind! And for the rest, what else has she?—to watch them with eager eyes as they go to school, to sit in church where she can see them every Sunday, to be passed some day unnoticed in the street, or deliberately cut because the great man or the great woman are with friends before whom they are ashamed to recognise the old woman that loved them.

When she goes home that night, how lonely will the room appear to her! Perhaps the neighbours may hear her sobbing to herself in the dark, with the fire burnt out for want of fuel, and the candle still unlit upon the table.

And it is for this that they live, these quasi-mothers—mothers in everything but the travail and the thanks. It is for this that they have remained virtuous in youth, living the dull life of a household servant. It is for this that they refused the old sweetheart, and have no fireside or offspring of their own.

I believe in a better state of things, that there will be no more nurses, and that every mother will nurse her own offspring; for what can be more hardening and demoralising than to call forth the tenderest feelings of a woman's heart and cherish them yourself as long as you need them, as long as your children require a nurse to love them, and then to blight and thwart and destroy them, whenever your own use for them is at an end. This may be Utopian; but it is always a little thing if one mother or two mothers can be brought to feel more tenderly to those who share their toil and have no part in their reward.

V. A CHARACTER

The man has a red, bloated face, and his figure is short and squat. So far there is nothing in him to notice, but when you see his eyes, you can read in these hard and shallow orbs a depravity beyond measure depraved, a thirst after wickedness, the pure, disinterested love of Hell for its own sake. The other night, in the street, I was watching an omnibus passing with lit-up windows, when I heard some one coughing at my side as though he would cough his soul out; and turning round, I saw him stopping under a lamp, with a brown greatcoat buttoned round him and his whole face convulsed. It seemed as if he could not live long; and so the sight set my mind upon a train of thought, as I finished my cigar up and down the lighted streets.

He is old, but all these years have not yet quenched his thirst for evil, and his eyes still delight themselves in wickedness. He is dumb; but he will not let that hinder his foul trade, or perhaps I should say, his yet fouler amusement, and he has pressed a slate into the service of corruption. Look at him, and he will sign to you with his bloated head, and when you go to him in answer to the sign, thinking perhaps that the poor dumb man has lost his way, you will see what he writes upon his slate. He haunts the doors of schools, and shows such inscriptions as these to the innocent children that come out. He hangs about picture-galleries, and makes the noblest pictures the text for some silent homily of vice. His industry is a lesson to ourselves. Is it not wonderful how he can triumph over his infirmities and do such an amount of harm without a tongue? Wonderful industry—strange, fruitless, pleasureless toil? Must not the very devil feel a soft emotion to see his disinterested and laborious service? Ah, but the devil knows better than this: he knows that this man is penetrated with the love of evil and that all his pleasure is shut up in wickedness: he recognises him, perhaps, as a fit type for mankind of his satanic self, and watches over his effigy as we might watch over a favourite likeness. As the business man comes to love the toil, which he only looked upon at first as a ladder towards other desires and less unnatural gratifications, so the dumb man has felt the charm of his trade and fallen captivated before the eyes of sin. It is a mistake when preachers tell us that vice is hideous and loathsome; for even vice has her Hörsel and her devotees, who love her for her own sake.

THE GREAT NORTH ROAD

CHAPTER I—NANCE AT THE 'GREEN DRAGON'

Nance Holdaway was on her knees before the fire blowing the green wood that voluminously smoked upon the dogs, and only now and then shot forth a smothered flame; her knees already ached and her eyes smarted, for she had been some while at this ungrateful task, but her mind was gone far away to meet the coming stranger. Now she met him in the wood, now at the castle gate, now in the kitchen by candle-light; each fresh presentment eclipsed the one before; a form so elegant, manners so sedate, a countenance so brave and comely, a voice so winning and resolute—sure such a man was never seen! The thick-coming fancies poured and brightened in her head like the smoke and flames upon the hearth.

Presently the heavy foot of her uncle Jonathan was heard upon the stair, and as he entered the room she bent the closer to her work. He glanced at the green fagots with a sneer, and looked askance at the bed and the white sheets, at the strip of carpet laid, like an island, on the great expanse of the stone floor, and at the broken glazing of the casement clumsily repaired with paper.

'Leave that fire a-be,' he cried. 'What, have I toiled all my life to turn innkeeper at the hind end? Leave it a-be, I say.'

'La, uncle, it doesn't burn a bit; it only smokes,' said Nance, looking up from her position.

'You are come of decent people on both sides,' returned the old man. 'Who are you to blow the coals for any Robin-run-agate? Get up, get on your hood, make yourself useful, and be off to the "Green Dragon."'

'I thought you was to go yourself,' Nance faltered.

'So did I,' quoth Jonathan; 'but it appears I was mistook.'

The very excess of her eagerness alarmed her, and she began to hang back. 'I think I would rather not, dear uncle,' she said. 'Night is at hand, and I think, dear, I would rather not.'

'Now you look here,' replied Jonathan, 'I have my lord's orders, have I not? Little he gives me, but it's all my livelihood. And do you fancy, if I disobey my lord, I'm likely to turn round for a lass like you? No, I've that hell-fire of pain in my old knee, I wouldn't walk a mile, not for King George upon his bended knees.' And he walked to the window and looked down the steep scarp to where the river foamed in the bottom of the dell.

Nance stayed for no more bidding. In her own room, by the glimmer of the twilight, she washed her hands and pulled on her Sunday mittens; adjusted her black hood, and tied a dozen times its cherry ribbons; and in less than ten minutes, with a fluttering heart and excellently bright eyes, she passed forth under the arch and over the bridge, into the thickening shadows of the groves. A well-marked wheel-track conducted her. The wood, which upon both sides of the river dell was a mere scrambling thicket of hazel, hawthorn, and holly, boasted on the level of more considerable timber. Beeches came to a good growth, with here and there an oak; and the track now passed under a high arcade of branches, and now ran under the open sky in glades. As the girl proceeded these glades became more frequent, the trees began again to decline in size, and the wood to degenerate into furzy coverts. Last of all there was a fringe of elders; and beyond that the track came forth upon an open, rolling moorland, dotted with wind-bowed and scanty bushes, and all golden brown with the winter, like a grouse. Right over against the girl the last red embers of the sunset burned under horizontal clouds; the night fell clear and still and frosty, and the track in low and marshy passages began to crackle under foot with ice.

Some half a mile beyond the borders of the wood the lights of the 'Green Dragon' hove in sight, and running close beside them, very faint in the dying dusk, the pale ribbon of the Great North Road. It was the back of the post-house that was presented to Nance Holdaway; and as she continued to draw near and the night to fall more completely, she became aware of an unusual brightness and bustle. A post-chaise stood in the yard, its lamps already lighted: light shone hospitably in the windows and from the open door; moving lights and shadows testified to the activity of servants bearing lanterns. The clank of pails, the stamping of hoofs on the firm causeway, the jingle of harness, and, last of all, the energetic hissing of a groom, began to fall upon her ear. By the stir you would have thought the mail was at the door, but it was still too early in the night. The down mail was not due at the 'Green Dragon' for hard upon an hour; the up mail from Scotland not before two in the black morning.

Nance entered the yard somewhat dazzled. Sam, the tall ostler, was polishing a curb-chain wit sand; the lantern at his feet letting up spouts of candle-light through the holes with which its conical roof was peppered.

'Hey, miss,' said he jocularly, 'you won't look at me any more, now you have gentry at the castle.'

Her cheeks burned with anger.

'That's my lord's chay,' the man continued, nodding at the chaise, 'Lord Windermoor's. Came all in a fluster—dinner, bowl of punch, and put the horses to. For all the world like a runaway match, my dear—bar the bride. He brought Mr. Archer in the chay with him.'

'Is that Holdaway?' cried the landlord from the lighted entry, where he stood shading his eyes.

'Only me, sir,' answered Nance.

'O, you, Miss Nance,' he said. 'Well, come in quick, my pretty. My lord is waiting for your uncle.'

And he ushered Nance into a room cased with yellow wainscot and lighted by tall candles, where two gentlemen sat at a table finishing a bowl of punch. One of these was stout, elderly, and irascible, with a face like a full moon, well dyed with liquor, thick tremulous lips, a short, purple hand, in which he brandished a long pipe, and an abrupt and gobbling utterance. This was my Lord Windermoor. In his companion Nance beheld a younger man, tall, quiet, grave, demurely dressed, and wearing his own hair. Her

153

glance but lighted on him, and she flushed, for in that second she made sure that she had twice betrayed herself—betrayed by the involuntary flash of her black eyes her secret impatience to behold this new companion, and, what was far worse, betrayed her disappointment in the realisation of her dreams. He, meanwhile, as if unconscious, continued to regard her with unmoved decorum.

'O, a man of wood,' thought Nance.

'What—what?' said his lordship. 'Who is this?'

'If you please, my lord, I am Holdaway's niece,' replied Nance, with a curtsey.

'Should have been here himself,' observed his lordship. 'Well, you tell Holdaway that I'm aground, not a stiver—not a stiver. I'm running from the beagles—going abroad, tell Holdaway. And he need look for no more wages: glad of 'em myself, if I could get 'em. He can live in the castle if he likes, or go to the devil. O, and here is Mr. Archer; and I recommend him to take him in—a friend of mine—and Mr. Archer will pay, as I wrote. And I regard that in the light of a precious good thing for Holdaway, let me tell you, and a set-off against the wages.'

'But O, my lord!' cried Nance, 'we live upon the wages, and what are we to do without?'

'What am I to do?—what am I to do?' replied Lord Windermoor with some exasperation. 'I have no wages. And there is Mr. Archer. And if Holdaway doesn't like it, he can go to the devil, and you with him!—and you with him!'

'And yet, my lord,' said Mr. Archer, 'these good people will have as keen a sense of loss as you or I; keener, perhaps, since they have done nothing to deserve it.'

'Deserve it?' cried the peer. 'What? What? If a rascally highwayman comes up to me with a confounded pistol, do you say that I've deserved it? How often am I to tell you, sir, that I was cheated—that I was cheated?'

'You are happy in the belief,' returned Mr. Archer gravely.

'Archer, you would be the death of me!' exclaimed his lordship. 'You know you're drunk; you know it, sir; and yet you can't get up a spark of animation.'

'I have drunk fair, my lord,' replied the younger man; 'but I own I am conscious of no exhilaration.'

'If you had as black a look-out as me, sir,' cried the peer, 'you would be very glad of a little innocent exhilaration, let me tell you. I am glad of it—glad of it, and I only wish I was drunker. For let me tell you it's a cruel hard thing upon a man of my time of life and my position, to be brought down to beggary because the world is full of thieves and rascals—thieves and rascals. What? For all I know, you may be a thief and a rascal yourself; and I would fight you for a pinch of snuff—a pinch of snuff,' exclaimed his lordship.

Here Mr. Archer turned to Nance Holdaway with a pleasant smile, so full of sweetness, kindness, and composure that, at one bound, her dreams returned to her. 'My good Miss Holdaway,' said he, 'if you are willing to show me the road, I am even eager to be gone. As for his lordship and myself, compose yourself; there is no fear; this is his lordship's way.'

'What? what?' cried his lordship. 'My way? Ish no such a thing, my way.'

'Come, my lord,' cried Archer; 'you and I very thoroughly understand each other; and let me suggest, it is time that both of us were gone. The mail will soon be due. Here, then, my lord, I take my leave of you, with the most earnest assurance of my gratitude for the past, and a sincere offer of any services I may be able to render in the future.'

'Archer,' exclaimed Lord Windermoor, 'I love you like a son. Le' 's have another bowl.'

'My lord, for both our sakes, you will excuse me,' replied Mr. Archer. 'We both require caution; we must both, for some while at least, avoid the chance of a pursuit.'

'Archer,' quoth his lordship, 'this is a rank ingratishood. What? I'm to go firing away in the dark in the cold po'chaise, and not so much as a game of écarté possible, unless I stop and play with the postillion, the postillion; and the whole country swarming with thieves and rascals and highwaymen.'

'I beg your lordship's pardon,' put in the landlord, who now appeared in the doorway to announce the chaise, 'but this part of the North Road is known for safety. There has not been a robbery, to call a robbery, this five years' time. Further south, of course, it's nearer London, and another story,' he added.

'Well, then, if that's so,' concluded my lord, 'le' 's have t'other bowl and a pack of cards.'

'My lord, you forget,' said Archer, 'I might still gain; but it is hardly possible for me to lose.'

'Think I'm a sharper?' inquired the peer. 'Gen'leman's parole's all I ask.'

But Mr. Archer was proof against these blandishments, and said farewell gravely enough to Lord Windermoor, shaking his hand and at the same time bowing very low. 'You will never know,' says he, 'the service you have done me.' And with that, and before my lord had finally taken up his meaning, he had slipped about the table, touched Nance lightly but imperiously on the arm, and left the room. In face of the outbreak of his lordship's lamentations she made haste to follow the truant.

CHAPTER II—IN WHICH MR. ARCHER IS INSTALLED

The chaise had been driven round to the front door; the courtyard lay all deserted, and only lit by a lantern set upon a window-sill. Through this Nance rapidly led the way, and began to ascend the swellings of the moor with a heart that somewhat fluttered in her bosom. She was not afraid, but in the course of these last passages with Lord Windermoor Mr. Archer had ascended to that pedestal on which her fancy waited to instal him. The reality, she felt, excelled her dreams, and this cold night walk was the first romantic incident in her experience.

It was the rule in these days to see gentlemen unsteady after dinner, yet Nance was both surprised and amused when her companion, who had spoken so soberly, began to stumble and waver by her side with the most airy divagations. Sometimes he would get so close to her that she must edge away; and at others lurch clear out of the track and plough among deep heather. His courtesy and gravity meanwhile remained unaltered. He asked her how far they had to go; whether the way lay all upon the moorland, and when he learned they had to pass a wood expressed his pleasure. 'For,' said he, 'I am passionately fond of trees. Trees and fair lawns, if you consider of it rightly, are the ornaments of nature, as palaces and fine approaches—' And here he stumbled into a patch of slough and nearly fell. The girl had hard work not to laugh, but at heart she was lost in admiration for one who talked so elegantly.

They had got to about a quarter of a mile from the 'Green Dragon,' and were near the summit of the rise, when a sudden rush of wheels arrested them. Turning and looking back, they saw the post-house, now much declined in brightness; and speeding away northward the two tremulous bright dots of my Lord Windermoor's chaise-lamps. Mr. Archer followed these yellow and unsteady stars until they dwindled into points and disappeared.

'There goes my only friend,' he said. 'Death has cut off those that loved me, and change of fortune estranged my flatterers; and but for you, poor bankrupt, my life is as lonely as this moor.'

The tone of his voice affected both of them. They stood there on the side of the moor, and became thrillingly conscious of the void waste of the night, without a feature for the eye, and except for the fainting whisper of the carriage-wheels without a murmur for the ear. And instantly, like a mockery, there broke out, very far away, but clear and jolly, the note of the mail-guard's horn. 'Over the hills' was his air. It rose to the two watchers on the moor with the most cheerful sentiment of human company and travel, and at the same time in and around the 'Green Dragon' it woke up a great bustle of lights running to and fro and clattering hoofs. Presently after, out of the darkness to southward, the mail grew near with a growing rumble. Its lamps were very large and bright, and threw their radiance forward in overlapping cones; the four cantering horses swarmed and steamed; the body of the coach followed like a great shadow; and this lit picture slid with a sort of ineffectual swiftness over the black field of night, and was eclipsed by the buildings of the 'Green Dragon.'

Mr. Archer turned abruptly and resumed his former walk; only that he was now more steady, kept better alongside his young conductor, and had fallen into a silence broken by sighs. Nance waxed very pitiful over his fate, contrasting an imaginary past of courts and great society, and perhaps the King himself, with the tumbledown ruin in a wood to which she was now conducting him.

'You must try, sir, to keep your spirits up,' said she. 'To be sure this is a great change for one like you; but who knows the future?'

Mr. Archer turned towards her in the darkness, and she could clearly perceive that he smiled upon her very kindly. 'There spoke a sweet nature,' said he, 'and I must thank you for these words. But I would not have you fancy that I regret the past for any happiness found in it, or that I fear the simplicity and hardship of the country. I am a man that has been much tossed about in life; now up, now down; and do you think that I shall not be able to support what you support—you who are kind, and therefore know how to feel pain; who are beautiful, and therefore hope; who are young, and therefore (or am I the more mistaken?) discontented?'

'Nay, sir, not that, at least,' said Nance; 'not discontented. If I were to be discontented, how should I look those that have real sorrows in the face? I have faults enough, but not that fault; and I have my merits too, for I have a good opinion of myself. But for beauty, I am not so simple but that I can tell a banter from a compliment.'

'Nay, nay,' said Mr. Archer, 'I had half forgotten; grief is selfish, and I was thinking of myself and not of you, or I had never blurted out so bold a piece of praise. 'Tis the best proof of my sincerity. But come, now, I would lay a wager you are no coward?'

'Indeed, sir, I am not more afraid than another,' said Nance. 'None of my blood are given to fear.'

'And you are honest?' he returned.

'I will answer for that,' said she.

'Well, then, to be brave, to be honest, to be kind, and to be contented, since you say you are so—is not that to fill up a great part of virtue?'

'I fear you are but a flatterer,' said Nance, but she did not say it clearly, for what with bewilderment and satisfaction, her heart was quite oppressed.

There could be no harm, certainly, in these grave compliments; but yet they charmed and frightened her, and to find favour, for reasons however obscure, in the eyes of this elegant, serious, and most unfortunate young gentleman, was a giddy elevation, was almost an apotheosis, for a country maid.

But she was to be no more exercised; for Mr. Archer, disclaiming any thought of flattery, turned off to other subjects, and held her all through the wood in conversation, addressing her with an air of perfect sincerity, and listening to her answers with every mark of interest. Had open flattery continued, Nance would have soon found refuge in good sense; but the more subtle lure she could not suspect, much less avoid. It was the first time she had ever taken part in a conversation illuminated by any ideas. All was then true that she had heard and dreamed of gentlemen; they were a race apart, like deities knowing good and evil. And then there burst upon her soul a divine thought, hope's glorious sunrise: since she could understand, since it seemed that she too, even she, could interest this sorrowful Apollo, might she not learn? or was she not learning? Would not her soul awake and put forth wings? Was she not, in fact, an enchanted princess, waiting but a touch to become royal? She saw herself transformed, radiantly attired, but in the most exquisite taste: her face grown longer and more refined; her tint etherealised; and she heard herself with delighted wonder talking like a book.

Meanwhile they had arrived at where the track comes out above the river dell, and saw in front of them the castle, faintly shadowed on the night, covering with its broken battlements a bold projection of the bank, and showing at the extreme end, where were the habitable tower and wing, some crevices of candle-light. Hence she called loudly upon her uncle, and he was seen to issue, lantern in hand, from the tower door, and, where the ruins did not intervene, to pick his way over the swarded courtyard, avoiding treacherous cellars and winding among blocks of fallen masonry. The arch of the great gate was still entire, flanked by two tottering bastions, and it was here that Jonathan met them, standing at the edge of the bridge, bent somewhat forward, and blinking at them through the glow of his own lantern. Mr. Archer greeted him with civility; but the old man was in no humour of compliance. He guided the newcomer across the court-yard, looking sharply and quickly in his face, and grumbling all the time about the cold, and the discomfort and dilapidation of the castle. He was sure he hoped that Mr. Archer would like it; but in truth he could not think what brought him there. Doubtless he had a good reason—this with a look of cunning scrutiny—but, indeed, the place was quite unfit for any person of repute; he himself was eaten up with the rheumatics. It was the most rheumaticky place in England, and some fine day the whole habitable part (to call it habitable) would fetch away bodily and go down the slope into the river. He had seen the cracks widening; there was a plaguy issue in the bank below; he thought a spring was mining it; it might be to-morrow, it might be next day; but they were all sure of a come-down sooner or later. 'And that is a poor death,' said he, 'for any one, let alone a gentleman, to have a whole old ruin dumped upon his belly. Have a care to your left there; these cellar vaults have all broke down, and the grass and hemlock hide 'em. Well, sir, here is welcome to you, such as it is, and wishing you well away.'

And with that Jonathan ushered his guest through the tower door, and down three steps on the left hand into the kitchen or common room of the castle. It was a huge, low room, as large as a meadow, occupying the whole width of the habitable wing, with six barred windows looking on the court, and two into the river valley. A dresser, a table, and a few chairs stood dotted here and there upon the uneven flags. Under the great chimney a good fire burned in an iron fire-basket; a high old settee, rudely carved with figures and Gothic lettering, flanked it on either side; there was a hinge table and a stone bench in the chimney corner, and above the arch hung guns, axes, lanterns, and great sheaves of rusty keys.

Jonathan looked about him, holding up the lantern, and shrugged his shoulders, with a pitying grimace. 'Here it is,' he said. 'See the damp on the floor, look at the moss; where there's moss you may be sure that it's rheumaticky. Try and get near that fire for to warm yourself; it'll blow the coat off your back. And with a young gentleman with a face like yours, as pale as a tallow-candle, I'd be afeard of a churchyard cough and a galloping decline,' says Jonathan, naming the maladies with gloomy gusto, 'or the cold might strike and turn your blood,' he added.

Mr. Archer fairly laughed. 'My good Mr. Holdaway,' said he, 'I was born with that same tallow-candle face, and the only fear that you inspire me with is the fear that I intrude unwelcomely upon your private hours. But I think I can promise you that I am very little troublesome, and I am inclined to hope that the terms which I can offer may still pay you the derangement.'

'Yes, the terms,' said Jonathan, 'I was thinking of that. As you say, they are very small,' and he shook his head.

'Unhappily, I can afford no more,' said Mr. Archer. 'But this we have arranged already,' he added with a certain stiffness; 'and as I am aware that Miss Holdaway has matter to communicate, I will, if you permit, retire at once. To-night I must bivouac; to-morrow my trunk is to follow from the "Dragon." So if you will show me to my room I shall wish you a good slumber and a better awakening.'

Jonathan silently gave the lantern to Nance, and she, turning and curtseying in the doorway, proceeded to conduct their guest up the broad winding staircase of the tower. He followed with a very brooding face.

'Alas!' cried Nance, as she entered the room, 'your fire black out,' and, setting down the lantern, she clapped upon her knees before the chimney and began to rearrange the charred and still smouldering remains. Mr. Archer looked about the gaunt apartment with a sort of shudder. The great height, the bare stone, the shattered windows, the aspect of the uncurtained bed, with one of its four fluted columns broken short, all struck a chill upon his fancy. From this dismal survey his eyes returned to Nance crouching before the fire, the candle in one hand and artfully puffing at the embers; the flames as they broke forth played upon the soft outline of her cheek—she was alive and young, coloured with the bright hues of life, and a woman. He looked upon her, softening; and then sat down and continued to admire the picture.

'There, sir,' said she, getting upon her feet, 'your fire is doing bravely now. Good-night.'

He rose and held out his hand. 'Come,' said he, 'you are my only friend in these parts, and you must shake hands.'

She brushed her hand upon her skirt and offered it, blushing.

'God bless you, my dear,' said he.

And then, when he was alone, he opened one of the windows, and stared down into the dark valley. A gentle wimpling of the river among stones ascended to his ear; the trees upon the other bank stood very black against the sky; farther away an owl was hooting. It was dreary and cold, and as he turned back to the hearth and the fine glow of fire, 'Heavens!' said he to himself, 'what an unfortunate destiny is mine!'

He went to bed, but sleep only visited his pillow in uneasy snatches. Outbreaks of loud speech came up the staircase; he heard the old stones of the castle crack in the frosty night with sharp reverberations, and the bed complained under his tossings. Lastly, far on into the morning, he awakened from a doze to hear, very far off, in the extreme and breathless quiet, a wailing flourish on the horn. The down mail was drawing near to the 'Green Dragon.' He sat up in bed; the sound was tragical by distance, and the modulation appealed to his ear like human speech. It seemed to call upon him with a dreary insistence—to call him far away, to address him personally, and to have a meaning that he failed to seize. It was thus, at least, in this nodding castle, in a cold, miry woodland, and so far from men and society, that the traffic on the Great North Road spoke to him in the intervals of slumber.

CHAPTER III—JONATHAN HOLDAWAY

Nance descended the tower stair, pausing at every step. She was in no hurry to confront her uncle with bad news, and she must dwell a little longer on the rich note of Mr. Archer's voice, the charm of his kind words, and the beauty of his manner and person. But, once at the stair-foot, she threw aside the spell and recovered her sensible and workaday self.

Jonathan was seated in the middle of the settle, a mug of ale beside him, in the attitude of one prepared for trouble; but he did not speak, and suffered her to fetch her supper and eat of it, with a very excellent appetite, in silence. When she had done, she, too, drew a tankard of home-brewed, and came and planted herself in front of him upon the settle.

'Well?' said Jonathan.

'My lord has run away,' said Nance.

'What?' cried the old man.

'Abroad,' she continued; 'run away from creditors. He said he had not a stiver, but he was drunk enough. He said you might live on in the castle, and Mr. Archer would pay you; but you was to look for no more wages, since he would be glad of them himself.'

Jonathan's face contracted; the flush of a black, bilious anger mounted to the roots of his hair; he gave an inarticulate cry, leapt upon his feet, and began rapidly pacing the stone floor. At first he kept his hands behind his back in a tight knot; then he began to gesticulate as he turned.

'This man—this lord,' he shouted, 'who is he? He was born with a gold spoon in his mouth, and I with a dirty straw. He rolled in his coach when he was a baby. I have dug and toiled and laboured since I was that high—that high.' And he shouted again. 'I'm bent and broke, and full of pains. D' ye think I don't know the taste of sweat? Many's the gallon I've drunk of it—ay, in the midwinter, toiling like a slave. All through, what has my life been? Bend, bend, bend my old creaking back till it would ache like breaking; wade about in the foul mire, never a dry stitch; empty belly, sore hands, hat off to my Lord Redface; kicks and ha'pence; and now, here, at the hind end, when I'm worn to my poor bones, a kick and done with it.' He walked a little while in silence, and then, extending his hand, 'Now you, Nance Holdaway,' says he, 'you come of my blood, and you're a good girl. When that man was a boy, I used to carry his gun for him. I carried the gun all day on my two feet, and many a stitch I had, and chewed a bullet for. He rode upon a horse, with feathers in his hat; but it was him that had the shots and took the game home. Did I complain? Not I. I knew my station. What did I ask, but just the chance to live and die honest? Nance Holdaway, don't let them deny it to me—don't let them do it. I've been as poor as Job, and as honest as the day, but now, my girl, you mark these words of mine, I'm getting tired of it.'

'I wouldn't say such words, at least,' said Nance.

'You wouldn't?' said the old man grimly. 'Well, and did I when I was your age? Wait till your back's broke and your hands tremble, and your eyes fail, and you're weary of the battle and ask no more but to lie down in your bed and give the ghost up like an honest man; and then let there up and come some insolent, ungodly fellow—ah! if I had him in these hands! "Where's my money that you gambled?" I should say. "Where's my money that you drank and diced?" "Thief!" is what I would say; "Thief!" he roared, "'Thief'"

'Mr. Archer will hear you if you don't take care,' said Nance, 'and I would be ashamed, for one, that he should hear a brave, old, honest, hard-working man like Jonathan Holdaway talk nonsense like a boy.'

'D' ye think I mind for Mr. Archer?' he cried shrilly, with a clack of laughter; and then he came close up to her, stooped down with his two palms upon his knees, and looked her in the eyes, with a strange hard expression, something like a smile. 'Do I mind for God, my girl?' he said; 'that's what it's come to be now, do I mind for God?'

'Uncle Jonathan,' she said, getting up and taking him by the arm; 'you sit down again, where you were sitting. There, sit still; I'll have no more of this; you'll do yourself a mischief. Come, take a drink of this good ale, and I'll warm a tankard for you. La, we'll pull through, you'll see. I'm young, as you say, and it's my turn to carry the bundle; and don't you worry your bile, or we'll have sickness, too, as well as sorrow.'

'D' ye think that I'd forgotten you?' said Jonathan, with something like a groan; and thereupon his teeth clicked to, and he sat silent with the tankard in his hand and staring straight before him.

'Why,' says Nance, setting on the ale to mull, 'men are always children, they say, however old; and if ever I heard a thing like this, to set to and make yourself sick, just when the money's failing. Keep a good heart up; you haven't kept a good heart these seventy years, nigh hand, to break down about a pound or two. Here's this Mr. Archer come to lodge, that you disliked so much. Well, now you see it was a clear Providence. Come, let's think upon our mercies. And here is the ale mulling lovely; smell of it; I'll take a drop myself, it smells so sweet. And, Uncle Jonathan, you let me say one word. You've lost more than money before now; you lost my aunt, and bore it like a man. Bear this.'

His face once more contracted; his fist doubled, and shot forth into the air, and trembled. 'Let them look out!' he shouted. 'Here, I warn all men; I've done with this foul kennel of knaves. Let them look out!'

'Hush, hush! for pity's sake,' cried Nance.

And then all of a sudden he dropped his face into his hands, and broke out with a great hiccoughing dry sob that was horrible to hear. 'O,' he cried, 'my God, if my son hadn't left me, if my Dick was here!' and the sobs shook him; Nance sitting still and watching him, with distress. 'O, if he were here to help his father!' he went on again. 'If I had a son like other fathers, he would save me now, when all is breaking down; O, he would save me! Ay, but where is he? Raking taverns, a thief perhaps. My curse be on him!' he added, rising again into wrath.

'Hush!' cried Nance, springing to her feet: 'your boy, your dead wife's boy—Aunt Susan's baby that she loved—would you curse him? O, God forbid!'

The energy of her address surprised him from his mood. He looked upon her, tearless and confused. 'Let me go to my bed,' he said at last, and he rose, and, shaking as with ague, but quite silent, lighted his candle, and left the kitchen.

Poor Nance! the pleasant current of her dreams was all diverted. She beheld a golden city, where she aspired to dwell; she had spoken with a deity, and had told herself that she might rise to be his equal; and now the earthly ligaments that bound her down had been tightened. She was like a tree looking skyward, her roots were in the ground. It seemed to her a thing so coarse, so rustic, to be thus concerned about a loss in money; when Mr. Archer, fallen from the sky-level of counts and nobles, faced his changed destiny with so immovable a courage. To weary of honesty; that, at least, no one could do, but even to name it was already a disgrace; and she beheld in fancy her uncle, and the young lad, all laced and feathered, hand upon hip, bestriding his small horse. The opposition seemed to perpetuate itself from generation to generation; one side still doomed to the clumsy and the servile, the other born to beauty.

She thought of the golden zones in which gentlemen were bred, and figured with so excellent a grace; zones in which wisdom and smooth words, white linen and slim hands, were the mark of the desired inhabitants; where low temptations were unknown, and honesty no virtue, but a thing as natural as breathing.

CHAPTER IV—MINGLING THREADS

It was nearly seven before Mr. Archer left his apartment. On the landing he found another door beside his own opening on a roofless corridor, and presently he was walking on the top of the ruins. On one hand he could look down a good depth into the green court-yard; on the other his eye roved along the downward course of the river, the wet woods all smoking, the shadows long and blue, the mists golden and rosy in the sun, here and there the water flashing across an obstacle. His heart expanded and softened to a grateful melancholy, and with his eye fixed upon the distance, and no thought of present danger, he continued to stroll along the elevated and treacherous promenade.

A terror-stricken cry rose to him from the courtyard. He looked down, and saw in a glimpse Nance standing below with hands clasped in horror and his own foot trembling on the margin of a gulf. He recoiled and leant against a pillar, quaking from head to foot, and covering his face with his hands; and Nance had time to run round by the stair and rejoin him where he stood before he had changed a line of his position.

'Ah!' he cried, and clutched her wrist; 'don't leave me. The place rocks;

I have no head for altitudes.'

'Sit down against that pillar,' said Nance. 'Don't you be afraid; I won't leave you, and don't look up or down: look straight at me. How white you are!'

'The gulf,' he said, and closed his eyes again and shuddered.

'Why,' said Nance, 'what a poor climber you must be! That was where my cousin Dick used to get out of the castle after Uncle Jonathan had shut the gate. I've been down there myself with him helping me. I wouldn't try with you,' she said, and laughed merrily.

The sound of her laughter was sincere and musical, and perhaps its beauty barbed the offence to Mr. Archer. The blood came into his face with a quick jet, and then left it paler than before. 'It is a physical weakness,' he said harshly, 'and very droll, no doubt, but one that I can conquer on necessity. See, I am still shaking. Well, I advance to the battlements and look down. Show me your cousin's path.'

'He would go sure-foot along that little ledge,' said Nance, pointing as she spoke; 'then out through the breach and down by yonder buttress. It is easier coming back, of course, because you see where you are going. From the buttress foot a sheep-walk goes along the scarp—see, you can follow it from here in the dry grass. And now, sir,' she added, with a touch of womanly pity, 'I would come away from here if I were you, for indeed you are not fit.'

Sure enough Mr. Archer's pallor and agitation had continued to increase; his cheeks were deathly, his clenched fingers trembled pitifully. 'The weakness is physical,' he sighed, and had nearly fallen. Nance led him from the spot, and he was no sooner back in the tower-stair, than he fell heavily against the wall and put his arm across his eyes. A cup of brandy had to be brought him before he could descend to breakfast; and the perfection of Nance's dream was for the first time troubled.

Jonathan was waiting for them at table, with yellow, blood-shot eyes and a peculiar dusky complexion. He hardly waited till they found their seats, before, raising one hand, and stooping with his mouth above his plate, he put up a prayer for a blessing on the food and a spirit of gratitude in the eaters, and thereupon, and without more civility, fell to. But it was notable that he was no less speedily satisfied than he had been greedy to begin. He pushed his plate away and drummed upon the table.

'These are silly prayers,' said he, 'that they teach us. Eat and be thankful, that's no such wonder. Speak to me of starving—there's the touch. You're a man, they tell me, Mr. Archer, that has met with some reverses?'

'I have met with many,' replied Mr. Archer.

'Ha!' said Jonathan. 'None reckons but the last. Now, see; I tried to make this girl here understand me.'

'Uncle,' said Nance, 'what should Mr. Archer care for your concerns? He hath troubles of his own, and came to be at peace, I think.'

'I tried to make her understand me,' repeated Jonathan doggedly; 'and now I'll try you. Do you think this world is fair?'

'Fair and false!' quoth Mr. Archer.

The old man laughed immoderately. 'Good,' said he, 'very good, but what I mean is this: do you know what it is to get up early and go to bed late, and never take so much as a holiday but four: and one of these your own marriage day, and the other three the funerals of folk you loved, and all that, to have a quiet old age in shelter, and bread for your old belly, and a bed to lay your crazy bones upon, with a clear conscience?'

'Sir,' said Mr. Archer, with an inclination of his head, 'you portray a very brave existence.'

'Well,' continued Jonathan, 'and in the end thieves deceive you, thieves rob and rook you, thieves turn you out in your old age and send you begging. What have you got for all your honesty? A fine return! You that might have stole scores of pounds, there you are out in the rain with your rheumatics!'

Mr. Archer had forgotten to eat; with his hand upon his chin he was studying the old man's countenance. 'And you conclude?' he asked.

'Conclude!' cried Jonathan. 'I conclude I'll be upsides with them.'

'Ay,' said the other, 'we are all tempted to revenge.'

'You have lost money?' asked Jonathan.

'A great estate,' said Archer quietly.

'See now!' says Jonathan, 'and where is it?'

'Nay, I sometimes think that every one has had his share of it but me,' was the reply. 'All England hath paid his taxes with my patrimony: I was a sheep that left my wool on every briar.'

'And you sit down under that?' cried the old man. 'Come now, Mr. Archer, you and me belong to different stations; and I know mine—no man better—but since we have both been rooked, and are both sore with it, why, here's my hand with a very good heart, and I ask for yours, and no offence, I hope.'

'There is surely no offence, my friend,' returned Mr. Archer, as they shook hands across the table; 'for, believe me, my sympathies are quite acquired to you. This life is an arena where we fight with beasts; and, indeed,' he added, sighing, 'I sometimes marvel why we go down to it unarmed.'

In the meanwhile a creaking of ungreased axles had been heard descending through the wood; and presently after, the door opened, and the tall ostler entered the kitchen carrying one end of Mr. Archer's trunk. The other was carried by an aged beggar man of that district, known and welcome for some twenty miles about under the name of 'Old Cumberland.' Each was soon perched upon a settle, with a cup of ale; and the ostler, who valued himself upon his affability, began to entertain the company, still with half an eye on Nance, to whom in gallant terms he expressly dedicated every sip of ale. First he told of the trouble they had to get his Lordship started in the chaise; and how he had dropped a rouleau of gold on the threshold, and the passage and doorstep had been strewn with guinea-pieces. At this old Jonathan looked at Mr. Archer. Next the visitor turned to news of a more thrilling character: how the down mail had been stopped again near Grantham by three men on horseback—a white and two bays; how they had handkerchiefs on their faces; how Tom the guard's blunderbuss missed fire, but he swore he had winged one of them with a pistol; and how they had got clean away with seventy pounds in money, some valuable papers, and a watch or two.

'Brave! brave!' cried Jonathan in ecstasy. 'Seventy pounds! O, it's brave!'

'Well, I don't see the great bravery,' observed the ostler, misapprehending him. 'Three men, and you may call that three to one. I'll call it brave when some one stops the mail single-handed; that's a risk.'

'And why should they hesitate?' inquired Mr. Archer. 'The poor souls who are fallen to such a way of life, pray what have they to lose? If they get the money, well; but if a ball should put them from their troubles, why, so better.'

'Well, sir,' said the ostler, 'I believe you'll find they won't agree with you. They count on a good fling, you see; or who would risk it?—And here's my best respects to you, Miss Nance.'

'And I forgot the part of cowardice,' resumed Mr. Archer. 'All men fear.'

'O, surely not!' cried Nance.

'All men,' reiterated Mr. Archer.

'Ay, that's a true word,' observed Old Cumberland, 'and a thief, anyway, for it's a coward's trade.'

'But these fellows, now,' said Jonathan, with a curious, appealing manner—'these fellows with their seventy pounds! Perhaps, Mr. Archer, they were no true thieves after all, but just people who had been robbed and tried to get their own again. What was that you said, about all England and the taxes? One takes, another gives; why, that's almost fair. If I've been rooked and robbed, and the coat taken off my back, I call it almost fair to take another's.'

'Ask Old Cumberland,' observed the ostler; 'you ask Old Cumberland, Miss Nance!' and he bestowed a wink upon his favoured fair one.

'Why that?' asked Jonathan.

'He had his coat taken—ay, and his shirt too,' returned the ostler.

'Is that so?' cried Jonathan eagerly. 'Was you robbed too?'

'That was I,' replied Cumberland, 'with a warrant! I was a well-to-do man when I was young.'

'Ay! See that!' says Jonathan. 'And you don't long for a revenge?'

'Eh! Not me!' answered the beggar. 'It's too long ago. But if you'll give me another mug of your good ale, my pretty lady, I won't say no to that.'

'And shalt have! And shalt have!' cried Jonathan. 'Or brandy even, if you like it better.'

And as Cumberland did like it better, and the ostler chimed in, the party pledged each other in a dram of brandy before separating.

As for Nance, she slipped forth into the ruins, partly to avoid the ostler's gallantries, partly to lament over the defects of Mr. Archer. Plainly, he was no hero. She pitied him; she began to feel a protecting interest mingle with and almost supersede her admiration, and was at the same time disappointed and yet drawn to him. She was, indeed, conscious of such unshaken fortitude in her own heart, that she was almost tempted by an occasion to be bold for two. She saw herself, in a brave attitude, shielding her imperfect hero from the world; and she saw, like a piece of heaven, his gratitude for her protection.

CHAPTER V—LIFE IN THE CASTLE

From that day forth the life of these three persons in the ruin ran very smoothly. Mr. Archer now sat by the fire with a book, and now passed whole days abroad, returning late, dead weary. His manner was a mask; but it was half transparent; through the even tenor of his gravity and courtesy profound revolutions of feeling were betrayed, seasons of numb despair, of restlessness, of aching temper. For days he would say nothing beyond his usual courtesies and solemn compliments; and then, all of a sudden, some fine evening beside the kitchen fire, he would fall into a vein of elegant gossip, tell of strange and interesting events, the secrets of families, brave deeds of war, the miraculous discovery of crime, the visitations of the dead. Nance and her uncle would sit till the small hours with eyes wide open: Jonathan applauding the unexpected incidents with many a slap of his big hand; Nance, perhaps, more pleased with the narrator's eloquence and wise reflections; and then, again, days would follow of abstraction, of listless humming, of frequent apologies and long hours of silence. Once only, and then after a week of unrelieved melancholy, he went over to the 'Green Dragon,' spent the afternoon with the landlord and a bowl of punch, and returned as on the first night, devious in step but courteous and unperturbed of speech.

If he seemed more natural and more at his ease it was when he found Nance alone; and, laying by some of his reserve, talked before her rather than to her of his destiny, character and hopes. To Nance these interviews were but a doubtful privilege. At times he would seem to take a pleasure in her presence, to consult her gravely, to hear and to discuss her counsels; at times even, but these were rare and brief, he would talk of herself, praise the qualities that she possessed, touch indulgently on her defects, and lend her books to read and even examine her upon her reading; but far more often he would fall into a half unconsciousness, put her a question and then answer it himself, drop into the veiled tone of voice of one soliloquising, and leave her at last as though he had forgotten her existence. It was odd, too, that in all this random converse, not a fact of his past life, and scarce a name, should ever cross his lips. A profound reserve kept watch upon his most unguarded moments. He spoke continually of himself, indeed, but still in enigmas; a veiled prophet of egoism.

The base of Nance's feelings for Mr. Archer was admiration as for a superior being; and with this, his treatment, consciously or not, accorded happily. When he forgot her, she took the blame upon herself. His formal politeness was so exquisite that this essential brutality stood excused. His compliments, besides, were always grave and rational; he would offer reason for his praise, convict her of merit, and thus disarm suspicion. Nay, and the very hours when he forgot and remembered her alternately could by the ardent fallacies of youth be read in the light of an attention. She might be far from his confidence; but still she was nearer it than any one. He might ignore her presence, but yet he sought it.

Moreover, she, upon her side, was conscious of one point of superiority. Beside this rather dismal, rather effeminate man, who recoiled from a worm, who grew giddy on the castle wall, who bore so helplessly the weight of his misfortunes, she felt herself a head and shoulders taller in cheerful and sterling courage. She could walk head in air along the most precarious rafter; her hand feared neither the grossness nor the harshness of life's web, but was thrust cheerfully, if need were, into the briar bush, and could take hold of any crawling horror. Ruin was mining the walls of her cottage, as already it had mined and subverted Mr. Archer's palace. Well, she faced it with a bright countenance and a busy hand. She had got some washing, some rough seamstress work from the 'Green Dragon,' and from another neighbour ten miles away across the moor. At this she cheerfully laboured, and from that height she could afford to pity the useless talents and poor attitude of Mr. Archer. It did not change her admiration, but it made it bearable. He was above her in all ways; but she was above him in one. She kept it to herself, and hugged it. When, like all young creatures, she made long stories to justify, to nourish, and to forecast the course of her affection, it was this private superiority that made all rosy, that cut the knot, and that, at last, in some great situation, fetched to her knees the dazzling but imperfect hero. With this pretty exercise she beguiled the hours of labour, and consoled herself for Mr. Archer's bearing.

Pity was her weapon and her weakness. To accept the loved one's faults, although it has an air of freedom, is to kiss the chain, and this pity it was which, lying nearer to her heart, lent the one element of true emotion to a fanciful and merely brain-sick love.

Thus it fell out one day that she had gone to the 'Green Dragon' and brought back thence a letter to Mr. Archer. He, upon seeing it, winced like a man under the knife: pain, shame, sorrow, and the most trenchant edge of mortification cut into his heart and wrung the steady composure of his face.

'Dear heart! have you bad news?' she cried.

But he only replied by a gesture and fled to his room, and when, later on, she ventured to refer to it, he stopped her on the threshold, as if with words prepared beforehand. 'There are some pains,' said he, 'too acute for consolation, or I would bring them to my kind consoler. Let the memory of that letter, if you please, be buried.' And then as she continued to gaze at him, being, in spite of herself, pained by his elaborate phrase, doubtfully sincere in word and manner: 'Let it be enough,' he added haughtily, 'that if this matter wring my heart, it doth not touch my conscience. I am a man, I would have you to know, who suffers undeservedly.'

He had never spoken so directly: never with so convincing an emotion; and her heart thrilled for him. She could have taken his pains and died of them with joy.

Meanwhile she was left without support. Jonathan now swore by his lodger, and lived for him. He was a fine talker. He knew the finest sight of stories; he was a man and a gentleman, take him for all in all, and a perfect credit to Old England. Such were the old man's declared sentiments, and sure enough he clung to Mr. Archer's side, hung upon his utterance when he spoke, and watched him with unwearing interest when he was silent. And yet his feeling was not clear; in the partial wreck of his mind, which was leaning to decay, some after-thought was strongly present. As he gazed in Mr. Archer's face a sudden brightness would kindle in his rheumy eyes, his eyebrows would lift as with a sudden thought, his mouth would open as though to speak, and close again on silence. Once or twice he even called Mr. Archer mysteriously forth into the dark courtyard, took him by the button, and laid a demonstrative finger on his chest; but there his ideas or his courage failed him; he would shufflingly excuse himself and return to his position by the fire without a word of explanation. 'The good man was growing old,' said Mr. Archer with a suspicion of a shrug. But the good man had his idea, and even when he was alone the name of Mr. Archer fell from his lips continually in the course of mumbled and gesticulative conversation.

CHAPTER VI—THE BAD HALF-CROWN

However early Nance arose, and she was no sluggard, the old man, who had begun to outlive the earthly habit of slumber, would usually have been up long before, the fire would be burning brightly, and she would see him wandering among the ruins, lantern in hand, and talking assiduously to himself. One day, however, after he had returned late from the market town, she found that she had stolen a march upon that indefatigable early riser. The kitchen was all blackness. She crossed the castle-yard to the wood-cellar, her steps printing the thick hoarfrost. A scathing breeze blew out of the north-east and slowly carried a regiment of black and tattered clouds over the face of heaven, which was already kindled with the wild light of morning, but where she walked, in shelter of the ruins, the flame of her candle burned steady. The extreme cold smote upon her conscience. She could not bear to think this bitter business fell usually to the lot of one so old as Jonathan, and made desperate resolutions to be earlier in the future.

The fire was a good blaze before he entered, limping dismally into the kitchen. 'Nance,' said he, 'I be all knotted up with the rheumatics; will you rub me a bit?' She came and rubbed him where and how he bade her. 'This is a cruel thing that old age should be rheumaticky,' said he. 'When I was young I stood my turn of the teethache like a man! for why? because it couldn't last for ever; but these rheumatics come to live and die with you. Your aunt was took before the time came; never had an ache to mention. Now I lie all night in my single bed and the blood never warms in me; this knee of mine it seems like lighted up with rheumatics; it seems as though you could see to sew by it; and all the strings of my old body ache, as if devils was pulling 'em. Thank you kindly; that's someways easier now, but an old man, my dear, has little to look for; it's pain, pain, pain to the end of the business, and I'll never be rightly warm again till I get under the sod,' he said, and looked down at her with a face so aged and weary that she had nearly wept.

'I lay awake all night,' he continued; 'I do so mostly, and a long walk kills me. Eh, deary me, to think that life should run to such a puddle! And I remember long syne when I was strong, and the blood all hot and good about me, and I loved to run, too—deary me, to run! Well, that's all by. You'd better pray to be took early, Nance, and not live on till you get to be like me, and are robbed in your grey old age, your cold, shivering, dark old age, that's like a winter's morning'; and he bitterly shuddered, spreading his hands before the fire.

'Come now,' said Nance, 'the more you say the less you'll like it, Uncle Jonathan; but if I were you I would be proud for to have lived all your days honest and beloved, and come near the end with your good name: isn't that a fine thing to be proud of? Mr. Archer was telling me in some strange land they used to run races each with a lighted candle, and the art was to keep the candle burning. Well, now, I thought that was like life: a man's good conscience is the flame he gets to carry, and if he comes to the winning-post with that still burning, why, take it how you will, the man's a hero—even if he was low-born like you and me.'

'Did Mr. Archer tell you that?' asked Jonathan.

'No, dear,' said she, 'that's my own thought about it. He told me of the race. But see, now,' she continued, putting on the porridge, 'you say old age is a hard season, but so is youth. You're half out of the battle, I would say; you loved my aunt and got her, and buried her, and some of these days soon you'll go to meet her; and take her my love and tell her I tried to take good care of you; for so I do, Uncle Jonathan.'

Jonathan struck with his fist upon the settle. 'D' ye think I want to die, ye vixen?' he shouted. 'I want to live ten hundred years.'

This was a mystery beyond Nance's penetration, and she stared in wonder as she made the porridge.

'I want to live,' he continued, 'I want to live and to grow rich. I want to drive my carriage and to dice in hells and see the ring, I do. Is this a life that I lived? I want to be a rake, d' ye understand? I want to know what things are like. I don't want to die like a blind kitten, and me seventy-six.'

'O fie!' said Nance.

The old man thrust out his jaw at her, with the grimace of an irreverent schoolboy. Upon that aged face it seemed a blasphemy. Then he took out of his bosom a long leather purse, and emptying its contents on the settle, began to count and recount the pieces, ringing and examining each, and suddenly he leapt like a young man. 'What!' he screamed. 'Bad? O Lord! I'm robbed again!' And falling on his knees before the settle he began to pour forth the most dreadful curses on the head of his deceiver. His eyes were shut, for to him this vile solemnity was prayer. He held up the bad half-crown in his right hand, as though he were displaying it to Heaven, and what increased the horror of the scene, the curses he invoked were those whose efficacy he had tasted—old age and poverty, rheumatism and an ungrateful son. Nance listened appalled; then she sprang forward and dragged down his arm and laid her hand upon his mouth.

'Whist!' she cried. 'Whist ye, for God's sake! O my man, whist ye! If Heaven were to hear; if poor Aunt Susan were to hear! Think, she may be listening.' And with the histrionism of strong emotion she pointed to a corner of the kitchen.

His eyes followed her finger. He looked there for a little, thinking, blinking; then he got stiffly to his feet and resumed his place upon the settle, the bad piece still in his hand. So he sat for some time, looking upon the half-crown, and now wondering to himself on the injustice and partiality of the law, now computing again and again the nature of his loss. So he was still sitting when Mr. Archer entered the kitchen. At this a light came into his face, and after some seconds of rumination he dispatched Nance upon an errand.

'Mr. Archer,' said he, as soon as they were alone together, 'would you give me a guinea-piece for silver?'

'Why, sir, I believe I can,' said Mr. Archer.

And the exchange was just effected when Nance re-entered the apartment. The blood shot into her face.

'What's to do here?' she asked rudely.

'Nothing, my dearie,' said old Jonathan, with a touch of whine.

'What's to do?' she said again.

'Your uncle was but changing me a piece of gold,' returned Mr. Archer.

'Let me see what he hath given you, Mr. Archer,' replied the girl. 'I had a bad piece, and I fear it is mixed up among the good.'

'Well, well,' replied Mr. Archer, smiling, 'I must take the merchant's risk of it. The money is now mixed.'

'I know my piece,' quoth Nance. 'Come, let me see your silver, Mr. Archer. If I have to get it by a theft I'll see that money,' she cried.

'Nay, child, if you put as much passion to be honest as the world to steal, I must give way, though I betray myself,' said Mr. Archer. 'There it is as I received it.'

Nance quickly found the bad half-crown.

'Give him another,' she said, looking Jonathan in the face; and when that had been done, she walked over to the chimney and flung the guilty piece into the reddest of the fire. Its base constituents began immediately to run; even as she watched it the disc crumbled, and the lineaments of the King became confused. Jonathan, who had followed close behind, beheld these changes from over her shoulder, and his face darkened sorely.

'Now,' said she, 'come back to table, and to-day it is I that shall say grace, as I used to do in the old times, day about with Dick'; and covering her eyes with one hand, 'O Lord,' said she with deep emotion, 'make us thankful; and, O Lord, deliver us from evil! For the love of the poor souls that watch for us in heaven, O deliver us from evil.'

CHAPTER VII—THE BLEACHING-GREEN

The year moved on to March; and March, though it blew bitter keen from the North Sea, yet blinked kindly between whiles on the river dell. The mire dried up in the closest covert; life ran in the bare branches, and the air of the afternoon would be suddenly sweet with the fragrance of new grass.

Above and below the castle the river crooked like the letter 'S.' The lower loop was to the left, and embraced the high and steep projection which was crowned by the ruins; the upper loop enclosed a lawny promontory, fringed by thorn and willow. It was easy to reach it from the castle side, for the river ran in this part very quietly among innumerable boulders and over dam-like walls of rock. The place was all enclosed, the wind a stranger, the turf smooth and solid; so it was chosen by Nance to be her bleaching-green.

One day she brought a bucketful of linen, and had but begun to wring and lay them out when Mr. Archer stepped from the thicket on the far side, drew very deliberately near, and sat down in silence on the grass. Nance looked up to greet him with a smile, but finding her smile was not returned, she fell into embarrassment and stuck the more busily to her employment. Man or woman, the whole world looks well at any work to which they are accustomed; but the girl was ashamed of what she did. She was ashamed, besides, of the sun-bonnet that so well became her, and ashamed of her bare arms, which were her greatest beauty.

'Nausicaa,' said Mr. Archer at last, 'I find you like Nausicaa.'

'And who was she?' asked Nance, and laughed in spite of herself, an empty and embarrassed laugh, that sounded in Mr. Archer's ears, indeed, like music, but to her own like the last grossness of rusticity.

'She was a princess of the Grecian islands,' he replied. 'A king, being shipwrecked, found her washing by the shore. Certainly I, too, was shipwrecked,' he continued, plucking at the grass. 'There was never a more desperate castaway—to fall from polite life, fortune, a shrine of honour, a grateful conscience, duties willingly taken up and faithfully discharged; and to fall to this—idleness, poverty, inutility, remorse.' He seemed to have forgotten her presence, but here he remembered her again. 'Nance,' said he, 'would you have a man sit down and suffer or rise up and strive?'

'Nay,' she said. 'I would always rather see him doing.'

'Ha!' said Mr. Archer, 'but yet you speak from an imperfect knowledge. Conceive a man damned to a choice of only evil—misconduct upon either side, not a fault behind him, and yet naught before him but this choice of sins. How would you say then?'

'I would say that he was much deceived, Mr. Archer,' returned Nance. 'I would say there was a third choice, and that the right one.'

'I tell you,' said Mr. Archer, 'the man I have in view hath two ways open, and no more. One to wait, like a poor mewling baby, till Fate save or ruin him; the other to take his troubles in his hand, and to perish or be saved at once. It is no point of morals; both are wrong. Either way this step-child of Providence must fall; which shall he choose, by doing or not doing?'

'Fall, then, is what I would say,' replied Nance. 'Fall where you will, but do it! For O, Mr. Archer,' she continued, stooping to her work, 'you that are good and kind, and so wise, it doth sometimes go against my heart to see you live on here like a sheep in a turnip-field! If you were braver—' and here she paused, conscience-smitten.

'Do I, indeed, lack courage?' inquired Mr. Archer of himself. 'Courage, the footstool of the virtues, upon which they stand? Courage, that a poor private carrying a musket has to spare of; that does not fail a weasel or a rat; that is a brutish faculty? I to fail there, I wonder? But what is courage, then? The constancy to endure oneself or to see others suffer? The itch of ill-advised activity: mere shuttle-wittedness, or to be still and patient? To inquire of the significance of words is to rob ourselves of what we seem to know, and yet, of all things, certainly to stand still is the least heroic. Nance,' he said, 'did you ever hear of Hamlet?'

'Never,' said Nance.

''Tis an old play,' returned Mr. Archer, 'and frequently enacted. This while I have been talking Hamlet. You must know this Hamlet was a Prince among the Danes,' and he told her the play in a very good style, here and there quoting a verse or two with solemn emphasis.

'It is strange,' said Nance; 'he was then a very poor creature?'

'That was what he could not tell,' said Mr. Archer. 'Look at me, am I as poor a creature?'

She looked, and what she saw was the familiar thought of all her hours; the tall figure very plainly habited in black, the spotless ruffles, the slim hands; the long, well-shapen, serious, shaven face, the wide and somewhat thin-lipped mouth, the dark eyes that were so full of depth and change and colour. He was gazing at her with his brows a little knit, his chin upon one hand and that elbow resting on his knee.

'Ye look a man!' she cried, 'ay, and should be a great one! The more shame to you to lie here idle like a dog before the fire.'

'My fair Holdaway,' quoth Mr. Archer, 'you are much set on action. I cannot dig, to beg I am ashamed.' He continued, looking at her with a half-absent fixity, "Tis a strange thing, certainly, that in my years of fortune I should never taste happiness, and now when I am broke, enjoy so much of it, for was I ever happier than to-day? Was the grass softer, the stream pleasanter in sound, the air milder, the heart more at peace? Why should I not sink? To dig—why, after all, it should be easy. To take a mate, too? Love is of all grades since Jupiter; love fails to none; and children'—but here he passed his hand suddenly over his eyes. 'O fool and coward, fool and coward!' he said bitterly; 'can you forget your fetters? You did not know that I was fettered, Nance?' he asked, again addressing her.

But Nance was somewhat sore. 'I know you keep talking,' she said, and, turning half away from him, began to wring out a sheet across her shoulder. 'I wonder you are not wearied of your voice. When the hands lie abed the tongue takes a walk.'

Mr. Archer laughed unpleasantly, rose and moved to the water's edge. In this part the body of the river poured across a little narrow fell, ran some ten feet very smoothly over a bed of pebbles, then getting wind, as it were, of another shelf of rock which barred the channel, began, by imperceptible degrees, to separate towards either shore in dancing currents, and to leave the middle clear and stagnant. The set towards either side was nearly equal; about one half of the whole water plunged on the side of the castle, through a narrow gullet; about one half ran ripping past the margin of the green and slipped across a babbling rapid.

'Here,' said Mr. Archer, after he had looked for some time at the fine and shifting demarcation of these currents, 'come here and see me try my fortune.'

'I am not like a man,' said Nance; 'I have no time to waste.'

'Come here,' he said again. 'I ask you seriously, Nance. We are not always childish when we seem so.'

She drew a little nearer.

'Now,' said he, 'you see these two channels—choose one.'

'I'll choose the nearest, to save time,' said Nance.

'Well, that shall be for action,' returned Mr. Archer. 'And since I wish to have the odds against me, not only the other channel but yon stagnant water in the midst shall be for lying still. You see this?' he continued, pulling up a withered rush. 'I break it in three. I shall put each separately at the top of the upper fall, and according as they go by your way or by the other I shall guide my life.'

'This is very silly,' said Nance, with a movement of her shoulders.

'I do not think it so,' said Mr. Archer.

'And then,' she resumed, 'if you are to try your fortune, why not evenly?'

'Nay,' returned Mr. Archer with a smile, 'no man can put complete reliance in blind fate; he must still cog the dice.'

By this time he had got upon the rock beside the upper fall, and, bidding her look out, dropped a piece of rush into the middle of the intake. The rusty fragment was sucked at once over the fall, came up again far on the right hand, leaned ever more and more in the same direction, and disappeared under the hanging grasses on the castle side.

'One,' said Mr. Archer, 'one for standing still.'

But the next launch had a different fate, and after hanging for a while about the edge of the stagnant water, steadily approached the bleaching-green and danced down the rapid under Nance's eyes.

'One for me,' she cried with some exultation; and then she observed that Mr. Archer had grown pale, and was kneeling on the rock, with his hand raised like a person petrified. 'Why,' said she, 'you do not mind it, do you?'

'Does a man not mind a throw of dice by which a fortune hangs?' said Mr. Archer, rather hoarsely. 'And this is more than fortune. Nance, if you have any kindness for my fate, put up a prayer before I launch the next one.'

'A prayer,' she cried, 'about a game like this? I would not be so heathen.'

'Well,' said he, 'then without,' and he closed his eyes and dropped the piece of rush. This time there was no doubt. It went for the rapid as straight as any arrow.

'Action then!' said Mr. Archer, getting to his feet; 'and then God forgive us,' he added, almost to himself.

'God forgive us, indeed,' cried Nance, 'for wasting the good daylight! But come, Mr. Archer, if I see you look so serious I shall begin to think you was in earnest.'

'Nay,' he said, turning upon her suddenly, with a full smile; 'but is not this good advice? I have consulted God and demigod; the nymph of the river, and what I far more admire and trust, my blue-eyed Minerva. Both have said the same. My own heart was telling it already. Action, then, be mine; and into the deep sea with all this paralysing casuistry. I am happy to-day for the first time.'

CHAPTER VIII—THE MAIL GUARD

Somewhere about two in the morning a squall had burst upon the castle, a clap of screaming wind that made the towers rock, and a copious drift of rain that streamed from the windows. The wind soon blew itself out, but the day broke cloudy and dripping, and when the little party assembled at breakfast their humours appeared to have changed with the change of weather. Nance had been brooding on the scene at the river-side, applying it in various ways to her particular aspirations, and the result, which was hardly to her mind, had taken the colour out of her cheeks. Mr. Archer, too, was somewhat absent, his thoughts were of a mingled strain; and even upon his usually impassive countenance there were betrayed successive depths of depression and starts of exultation, which the girl translated in terms of her own hopes and fears. But Jonathan was the most altered: he was strangely silent, hardly passing a word, and watched Mr. Archer with an eager and furtive eye. It seemed as if the idea that had so long hovered before him had now taken a more solid shape, and, while it still attracted, somewhat alarmed his imagination.

At this rate, conversation languished into a silence which was only broken by the gentle and ghostly noises of the rain on the stone roof and about all that field of ruins; and they were all relieved when the note of a man whistling and the sound of approaching footsteps in the grassy court announced a visitor. It was the ostler from the 'Green Dragon' bringing a letter for Mr. Archer. Nance saw her hero's face contract and then relax again at sight of it; and she thought that she knew why, for the sprawling, gross black characters of the address were easily distinguishable from the fine writing on the former letter that had so much disturbed him. He opened it and began to read; while the ostler sat down to table with a pot of ale, and proceeded to make himself agreeable after his fashion.

'Fine doings down our way, Miss Nance,' said he. 'I haven't been abed this blessed night.'

Nance expressed a polite interest, but her eye was on Mr. Archer, who was reading his letter with a face of such extreme indifference that she was tempted to suspect him of assumption.

'Yes,' continued the ostler, 'not been the like of it this fifteen years: the North Mail stopped at the three stones.'

Jonathan's cup was at his lip, but at this moment he choked with a great splutter; and Mr. Archer, as if startled by the noise, made so sudden a movement that one corner of the sheet tore off and stayed between his finger and thumb. It was some little time before the old man was sufficiently recovered to beg the ostler to go on, and he still kept coughing and crying and rubbing his eyes. Mr. Archer, on his side, laid the letter down, and, putting his hands in his pocket, listened gravely to the tale.

'Yes,' resumed Sam, 'the North Mail was stopped by a single horseman; dash my wig, but I admire him! There were four insides and two out, and poor Tom Oglethorpe, the guard. Tom showed himself a man; let fly his blunderbuss at him; had him covered, too, and could swear to that; but the Captain never let on, up with a pistol and fetched poor Tom a bullet through the body. Tom, he squelched upon the seat, all over blood. Up comes the Captain to the window. "Oblige me," says he, "with what you have." Would you believe it? Not a man says cheep!—not them. "Thy hands over thy head." Four watches, rings, snuff-boxes, seven-and-forty pounds overhead in gold. One Dicksee, a grazier, tries it on: gives him a guinea. "Beg your pardon," says the Captain, "I think too highly of you to take it at your hand. I will not take less than ten from such a gentleman." This Dicksee had his money in his stocking, but there was the pistol at his eye. Down he goes, offs with his stocking, and there was thirty golden guineas. "Now," says the Captain, "you've tried it on with me, but I scorns the advantage. Ten I said," he says, "and ten I take." So, dash my buttons, I call that man a man!' cried Sam in cordial admiration.

'Well, and then?' says Mr. Archer.

'Then,' resumed Sam, 'that old fat fagot Engleton, him as held the ribbons and drew up like a lamb when he was told to, picks up his cattle, and drives off again. Down they came to the "Dragon," all singing like as if they was scalded, and poor Tom saying nothing. You would 'a' thought they had all lost the King's crown to hear them. Down gets this Dicksee. "Postmaster," he says, taking him by the arm, "this is a most abominable thing," he says. Down gets a Major Clayton, and gets the old man by the other arm. "We've been robbed," he cries, "robbed!" Down gets the others, and all around the old man telling their story, and what they had lost, and how they was all as good as ruined; till at last Old Engleton says, says he, "How about Oglethorpe?" says he. "Ay," says the others, "how about the guard?" Well, with that we bousted him down, as white as a rag and all blooded like a sop. I thought he was dead. Well, he ain't dead; but he's dying, I fancy.'

'Did you say four watches?' said Jonathan.

'Four, I think. I wish it had been forty,' cried Sam. 'Such a party of soused herrings I never did see—not a man among them bar poor Tom. But us that are the servants on the road have all the risk and none of the profit.'

'And this brave fellow,' asked Mr. Archer, very quietly, 'this Oglethorpe—how is he now?'

'Well, sir, with my respects, I take it he has a hole bang through him,' said Sam. 'The doctor hasn't been yet. He'd 'a' been bright and early if it had been a passenger. But, doctor or no, I'll make a good guess that Tom won't see to-morrow. He'll die on a Sunday, will poor Tom; and they do say that's fortunate.'

'Did Tom see him that did it?' asked Jonathan.

'Well, he saw him,' replied Sam, 'but not to swear by. Said he was a very tall man, and very big, and had a 'ankerchief about his face, and a very quick shot, and sat his horse like a thorough gentleman, as he is.'

'A gentleman!' cried Nance. 'The dirty knave!'

'Well, I calls a man like that a gentleman,' returned the ostler; 'that's what I mean by a gentleman.'

'You don't know much of them, then,' said Nance.

'A gentleman would scorn to stoop to such a thing. I call my uncle a better gentleman than any thief.'

'And you would be right,' said Mr. Archer.

'How many snuff-boxes did he get?' asked Jonathan.

'O, dang me if I know,' said Sam; 'I didn't take an inventory.'

'I will go back with you, if you please,' said Mr. Archer. 'I should like to see poor Oglethorpe. He has behaved well.'

'At your service, sir,' said Sam, jumping to his feet. 'I dare to say a gentleman like you would not forget a poor fellow like Tom—no, nor a plain man like me, sir, that went without his sleep to nurse him. And excuse me, sir,' added Sam, 'you won't forget about the letter neither?'

'Surely not,' said Mr. Archer.

Oglethorpe lay in a low bed, one of several in a long garret of the inn. The rain soaked in places through the roof and fell in minute drops; there was but one small window; the beds were occupied by servants, the air of the garret was both close and chilly. Mr. Archer's heart sank at the threshold to see a man lying perhaps mortally hurt in so poor a sick-room, and as he drew near the low bed he took his hat off. The guard was a big, blowsy, innocent-looking soul with a thick lip and a broad nose, comically turned up; his cheeks were crimson, and when Mr. Archer laid a finger on his brow he found him burning with fever.

'I fear you suffer much,' he said, with a catch in his voice, as he sat down on the bedside.

'I suppose I do, sir,' returned Oglethorpe; 'it is main sore.'

'I am used to wounds and wounded men,' returned the visitor. 'I have been in the wars and nursed brave fellows before now; and, if you will suffer me, I propose to stay beside you till the doctor comes.'

'It is very good of you, sir, I am sure,' said Oglethorpe. 'The trouble is they won't none of them let me drink.'

'If you will not tell the doctor,' said Mr. Archer, 'I will give you some water. They say it is bad for a green wound, but in the Low Countries we all drank water when we found the chance, and I could never perceive we were the worse for it.'

'Been wounded yourself, sir, perhaps?' called Oglethorpe.

'Twice,' said Mr. Archer, 'and was as proud of these hurts as any lady of her bracelets. 'Tis a fine thing to smart for one's duty; even in the pangs of it there is contentment.'

'Ah, well!' replied the guard, 'if you've been shot yourself, that explains. But as for contentment, why, sir, you see, it smarts, as you say. And then, I have a good wife, you see, and a bit of a brat—a little thing, so high.'

'Don't move,' said Mr. Archer.

'No, sir, I will not, and thank you kindly,' said Oglethorpe. 'At York

187

they are. A very good lass is my wife—far too good for me. And the little rascal—well, I don't know how to say it, but he sort of comes round you. If I were to go, sir, it would be hard on my poor girl—main hard on her!'

'Ay, you must feel bitter hardly to the rogue that laid you here,' said Archer.

'Why, no, sir, more against Engleton and the passengers,' replied the guard. 'He played his hand, if you come to look at it; and I wish he had shot worse, or me better. And yet I'll go to my grave but what I covered him,' he cried. 'It looks like witchcraft. I'll go to my grave but what he was drove full of slugs like a pepper-box.'

'Quietly,' said Mr. Archer, 'you must not excite yourself. These deceptions are very usual in war; the eye, in the moment of alert, is hardly to be trusted, and when the smoke blows away you see the man you fired at, taking aim, it may be, at yourself. You should observe, too, that you were in the dark night, and somewhat dazzled by the lamps, and that the sudden stopping of the mail had jolted you. In such circumstances a man may miss, ay, even with a blunder-buss, and no blame attach to his marksmanship.' . . .

THE YOUNG CHEVALIER

PROLOGUE—THE WINE-SELLER'S WIFE

There was a wine-seller's shop, as you went down to the river in the city of the Anti-popes. There a man was served with good wine of the country and plain country fare; and the place being clean and quiet, with a prospect on the river, certain gentlemen who dwelt in that city in attendance on a great personage made it a practice (when they had any silver in their purses) to come and eat there and be private.

They called the wine-seller Paradou. He was built more like a bullock than a man, huge in bone and brawn, high in colour, and with a hand like a baby for size. Marie-Madeleine was the name of his wife; she was of Marseilles, a city of entrancing women, nor was any fairer than herself. She was tall, being almost of a height with Paradou; full-girdled, point-device in every form, with an exquisite delicacy in the face; her nose and nostrils a delight to look at from the fineness of the sculpture, her eyes inclined a hair's-breadth inward, her colour between dark and fair, and laid on even like a flower's. A faint rose dwelt in it, as though she had been found unawares bathing, and had blushed from head to foot. She was of a grave countenance, rarely smiling; yet it seemed to be written upon every part of her that she rejoiced in life. Her husband loved the heels of her feet and the knuckles of her fingers; he loved her like a glutton and a brute; his love hung about her like an atmosphere; one that came by chance into the wine-shop was aware of that passion; and it might be said that by the strength of it the woman had been drugged or spell-bound. She knew not if she loved or loathed him; he was always in her eyes like something monstrous—monstrous in his love, monstrous in his person, horrific but imposing in his violence; and her sentiment swung back and forward from desire to sickness. But the mean, where it dwelt chiefly, was an apathetic fascination, partly of horror; as of

Europa in mid ocean with her bull.

On the 10th November 1749 there sat two of the foreign gentlemen in the wine-seller's shop. They were both handsome men of a good presence, richly dressed. The first was swarthy and long and lean, with an alert, black look, and a mole upon his cheek. The other was more fair. He seemed very easy and sedate, and a little melancholy for so young a man, but his smile was charming. In his grey eyes there was much abstraction, as of one recalling fondly that which was past and lost. Yet there was strength and swiftness in his limbs; and his mouth set straight across his face, the under lip a thought upon side, like that of a man accustomed to resolve. These two talked together in a rude outlandish speech that no frequenter of that wine-shop understood. The swarthy man answered to the name of Ballantrae; he of the dreamy eyes was sometimes called Balmile, and sometimes my Lord, or my Lord Gladsmuir; but when the title was given him, he seemed to put it by as if in jesting, not without bitterness.

The mistral blew in the city. The first day of that wind, they say in the countries where its voice is heard, it blows away all the dust, the second all the stones, and the third it blows back others from the mountains. It was now come to the third day; outside the pebbles flew like hail, and the face of the river was puckered, and the very building-stones in the walls of houses seemed to be curdled with the savage cold and fury of that continuous blast. It could be heard to hoot in all the chimneys of the city; it swept about the wine-shop, filling the room with eddies; the chill and gritty touch of it passed between the nearest clothes and the bare flesh; and the two gentlemen at the far table kept their mantles loose about their shoulders. The roughness of these outer hulls, for they were plain travellers' cloaks that had seen service, set the greater mark of richness on what showed below of their laced clothes; for the one was in scarlet and the other in violet and white, like men come from a scene of ceremony; as indeed they were.

It chanced that these fine clothes were not without their influence on the scene which followed, and which makes the prologue of our tale. For a long time Balmile was in the habit to come to the wine-shop and eat a meal or drink a measure of wine; sometimes with a comrade; more often alone, when he would sit and dream and drum upon the table, and the thoughts would show in the man's face in little glooms and lightenings, like the sun and the clouds upon a water. For a long time Marie-Madeleine had observed him apart. His sadness, the beauty of his smile when by any chance he remembered her existence and addressed her, the changes of his mind signalled forth by an abstruse play of feature, the mere fact that he was foreign and a thing detached from the local and the accustomed, insensibly attracted and affected her. Kindness was ready in her mind; it but lacked the touch of an occasion to effervesce and crystallise. Now Balmile had come hitherto in a very poor plain habit; and this day of the mistral, when his mantle was just open, and she saw beneath it the glancing of the violet and the velvet and the silver, and the clustering fineness of the lace, it seemed to set the man in a new light, with which he shone resplendent to her fancy.

The high inhuman note of the wind, the violence and continuity of its outpouring, and the fierce touch of it upon man's whole periphery, accelerated the functions of the mind. It set thoughts whirling, as it whirled the trees of the forest; it stirred them up in flights, as it stirred up the dust in chambers. As brief as sparks, the fancies glittered and succeeded each other in the mind of Marie-Madeleine; and the grave man with the smile, and the bright clothes under the plain mantle, haunted her with incongruous explanations. She considered him, the unknown, the speaker of an unknown tongue, the hero (as she placed him) of an unknown romance, the dweller upon unknown memories. She recalled him sitting there alone, so immersed, so stupefied; yet she was sure he was not stupid. She recalled one day when he had remained a long time motionless, with parted lips, like one in the act of starting up, his eyes fixed on vacancy. Any one else must have looked foolish; but not he. She tried to conceive what manner of memory had thus entranced him; she forged for him a past; she showed him to herself in every light of heroism and greatness and misfortune; she brooded with petulant intensity on all she knew and guessed of him. Yet, though she was already gone so deep, she was still unashamed, still unalarmed; her thoughts were still disinterested; she had still to reach the stage at which—beside the image of that other whom we love to contemplate and to adorn—we place the image of ourself and behold them together with delight.

She stood within the counter, her hands clasped behind her back, her shoulders pressed against the wall, her feet braced out. Her face was bright with the wind and her own thoughts; as a fire in a similar day of tempest glows and brightens on a hearth, so she seemed to glow, standing there, and to breathe out energy. It was the first time Ballantrae had visited that wine-seller's, the first time he had seen the wife; and his eyes were true to her.

'I perceive your reason for carrying me to this very draughty tavern,' he said at last.

'I believe it is propinquity,' returned Balmile.

'You play dark,' said Ballantrae, 'but have a care! Be more frank with me, or I will cut you out. I go through no form of qualifying my threat, which would be commonplace and not conscientious. There is only one point in these campaigns: that is the degree of admiration offered by the man; and to our hostess I am in a posture to make victorious love.'

'If you think you have the time, or the game worth the candle,' replied the other with a shrug.

'One would suppose you were never at the pains to observe her,' said Ballantrae.

'I am not very observant,' said Balmile. 'She seems comely.'

'You very dear and dull dog!' cried Ballantrae; 'chastity is the most besotting of the virtues. Why, she has a look in her face beyond singing! I believe, if you was to push me hard, I might trace it home to a trifle of a squint. What matters? The height of beauty is in the touch that's wrong, that's the modulation in a tune. 'Tis the devil we all love; I owe many a conquest to my mole'—he touched it as he spoke with a smile, and his eyes glittered;—'we are all hunchbacks, and beauty is only that kind of deformity that I happen to admire. But come! Because you are chaste, for which I am sure I pay you my respects, that is no reason why you should be blind. Look at her, look at the delicious nose of her, look at her cheek, look at her ear, look at her hand and wrist—look at the whole baggage from heels to crown, and tell me if she wouldn't melt on a man's tongue.'

As Ballantrae spoke, half jesting, half enthusiastic, Balmile was constrained to do as he was bidden. He looked at the woman, admired her excellences, and was at the same time ashamed for himself and his companion. So it befell that when Marie-Madeleine raised her eyes, she met those of the subject of her contemplations fixed directly on herself with a look that is unmistakable, the look of a person measuring and valuing another—and, to clench the false impression, that his glance was instantly and guiltily withdrawn. The blood beat back upon her heart and leaped again; her obscure thoughts flashed clear before her; she flew in fancy straight to his arms like a wanton, and fled again on the instant like a nymph. And at that moment there chanced an interruption, which not only spared her embarrassment, but set the last consecration on her now articulate love.

Into the wine-shop there came a French gentleman, arrayed in the last refinement of the fashion, though a little tumbled by his passage in the wind. It was to be judged he had come from the same formal gathering at which the others had preceded him; and perhaps that he had gone there in the hope to meet with them, for he came up to Ballantrae with unceremonious eagerness.

'At last, here you are!' he cried in French. 'I thought I was to miss you altogether.'

The Scotsmen rose, and Ballantrae, after the first greetings, laid his hand on his companion's shoulder.

'My lord,' said he, 'allow me to present to you one of my best friends and one of our best soldiers, the Lord Viscount Gladsmuir.'

The two bowed with the elaborate elegance of the period.

'Monseigneur,' said Balmile, 'je n'ai pas la prétention de m'affubler d'un titre que la mauvaise fortune de mon roi ne me permet pas de porter comma il sied. Je m'appelle, pour vous servir, Blair de Balmile tout court.' [My lord, I have not the effrontery to cumber myself with a title which the ill fortunes of my king will not suffer me to bear the way it should be. I call myself, at your service, plain Blair of Balmile.]

'Monsieur le Vicomte ou monsieur Blèr' de Balmaïl,' replied the newcomer, 'le nom n'y fait rien, et l'on connaît vos beaux faits.' [The name matters nothing, your gallant actions are known.]

A few more ceremonies, and these three, sitting down together to the table, called for wine. It was the happiness of Marie-Madeleine to wait unobserved upon the prince of her desires. She poured the wine, he drank of it; and that link between them seemed to her, for the moment, close as a caress. Though they lowered their tones, she surprised great names passing in their conversation, names of kings, the names of de Gesvre and Belle-Isle; and the man who dealt in these high matters, and she who was now coupled with him in her own thoughts, seemed to swim in mid air in a transfiguration. Love is a crude core, but it has singular and far-reaching fringes; in that passionate attraction for the stranger that now swayed and mastered her, his harsh incomprehensible language, and these names of grandees in his talk, were each an element.

The Frenchman stayed not long, but it was plain he left behind him matter of much interest to his companions; they spoke together earnestly, their heads down, the woman of the wine-shop totally forgotten; and they were still so occupied when Paradou returned.

This man's love was unsleeping. The even bluster of the mistral, with which he had been combating some hours, had not suspended, though it had embittered, that predominant passion. His first look was for his wife, a look of hope and suspicion, menace and humility and love, that made the over-blooming brute appear for the moment almost beautiful. She returned his glance, at first as though she knew him not, then with a swiftly waxing coldness of intent; and at last, without changing their direction, she had closed her eyes.

There passed across her mind during that period much that Paradou could not have understood had it been told to him in words: chiefly the sense of an enlightening contrast betwixt the man who talked of kings and the man who kept a wine-shop, betwixt the love she yearned for and that to which she had been long exposed like a victim bound upon the altar. There swelled upon her, swifter than the Rhone, a tide of abhorrence and disgust.

She had succumbed to the monster, humbling herself below animals; and now she loved a hero, aspiring to the semi-divine. It was in the pang of that humiliating thought that she had closed her eyes.

Paradou—quick as beasts are quick, to translate silence—felt the insult through his blood; his inarticulate soul bellowed within him for revenge. He glanced about the shop. He saw the two indifferent gentlemen deep in talk, and passed them over: his fancy flying not so high. There was but one other present, a country lout who stood swallowing his wine, equally unobserved by all and unobserving—to him he dealt a glance of murderous suspicion, and turned direct upon his wife. The wine-shop had lain hitherto, a space of shelter, the scene of a few ceremonial passages and some whispered conversation, in the howling river of the wind; the clock had not yet ticked a score of times since Paradou's appearance; and now, as he suddenly gave tongue, it seemed as though the mistral had entered at his heels.

'What ails you, woman?' he cried, smiting on the counter.

'Nothing ails me,' she replied. It was strange; but she spoke and stood at that moment like a lady of degree, drawn upward by her aspirations.

'You speak to me, by God, as though you scorned me!' cried the husband.

The man's passion was always formidable; she had often looked on upon its violence with a thrill, it had been one ingredient in her fascination; and she was now surprised to behold him, as from afar off, gesticulating but impotent. His fury might be dangerous like a torrent or a gust of wind, but it was inhuman; it might be feared or braved, it should never be respected. And with that there came in her a sudden glow of courage and that readiness to die which attends so closely upon all strong passions.

'I do scorn you,' she said.

'What is that?' he cried.

'I scorn you,' she repeated, smiling.

'You love another man!' said he.

'With all my soul,' was her reply.

The wine-seller roared aloud so that the house rang and shook with it.

'Is this the—?' he cried, using a foul word, common in the South; and he seized the young countryman and dashed him to the ground. There he lay for the least interval of time insensible; thence fled from the house, the most terrified person in the county. The heavy measure had escaped from his hands, splashing the wine high upon the wall. Paradou caught it. 'And you?' he roared to his wife, giving her the same name in the feminine, and he aimed at her the deadly missile. She expected it, motionless, with radiant eyes.

But before it sped, Paradou was met by another adversary, and the unconscious rivals stood confronted. It was hard to say at that moment which appeared the more formidable. In Paradou, the whole muddy and truculent depths of the half-man were stirred to frenzy; the lust of destruction raged in him; there was not a feature in his face but it talked murder. Balmile had dropped his cloak: he shone out at once in his finery, and stood to his full stature; girt in mind and body all his resources, all his temper, perfectly in command in his face the light of battle. Neither spoke; there was no blow nor threat of one; it was war reduced to its last element, the spiritual; and the huge wine-seller slowly lowered his weapon. Balmile was a noble, he a commoner; Balmile exulted in an honourable cause. Paradou already perhaps began to be ashamed of his violence. Of a sudden, at least, the tortured brute turned and fled from the shop in the footsteps of his former victim, to whose continued flight his reappearance added wings.

So soon as Balmile appeared between her husband and herself, Marie-Madeleine transferred to him her eyes. It might be her last moment, and she fed upon that face; reading there inimitable courage and illimitable valour to protect. And when the momentary peril was gone by, and the champion turned a little awkwardly towards her whom he had rescued, it was to meet, and quail before, a gaze of admiration more distinct than words. He bowed, he stammered, his words failed him; he who had crossed the floor a moment ago, like a young god, to smite, returned like one discomfited; got somehow to his place by the table, muffled himself again in his discarded cloak, and for a last touch of the ridiculous, seeking for anything to restore his countenance, drank of the wine before him, deep as a porter after a heavy lift. It was little wonder if Ballantrae, reading the scene with malevolent eyes, laughed out loud and brief, and drank with raised glass, 'To the champion of the Fair.'

Marie-Madeleine stood in her old place within the counter; she disdained the mocking laughter; it fell on her ears, but it did not reach her spirit. For her, the world of living persons was all resumed again into one pair, as in the days of Eden; there was but the one end in life, the one hope before her, the one thing needful, the one thing possible—to be his.

CHAPTER I—THE PRINCE

That same night there was in the city of Avignon a young man in distress of mind. Now he sat, now walked in a high apartment, full of draughts and shadows. A single candle made the darkness visible; and the light scarce sufficed to show upon the wall, where they had been recently and rudely nailed, a few miniatures and a copper medal of the young man's head. The same was being sold that year in London, to admiring thousands. The original was fair; he had beautiful brown eyes, a beautiful bright open face; a little feminine, a little hard, a little weak; still full of the light of youth, but already beginning to be vulgarised; a sordid bloom come upon it, the lines coarsened with a touch of puffiness. He was dressed, as for a gala, in peach-colour and silver; his breast sparkled with stars and was bright with ribbons; for he had held a levee in the afternoon and received a distinguished personage incognito. Now he sat with a bowed head, now walked precipitately to and fro, now went and gazed from the uncurtained window, where the wind was still blowing, and the lights winked in the darkness.

The bells of Avignon rose into song as he was gazing; and the high notes and the deep tossed and drowned, boomed suddenly near or were suddenly swallowed up, in the current of the mistral. Tears sprang in the pale blue eyes; the expression of his face was changed to that of a more active misery, it seemed as if the voices of the bells reached, and touched and pained him, in a waste of vacancy where even pain was welcome. Outside in the night they continued to sound on, swelling and fainting; and the listener heard in his memory, as it were their harmonies, joy-bells clashing in a northern city, and the acclamations of a multitude, the cries of battle, the gross voices of cannon, the stridor of an animated life. And then all died away, and he stood face to face with himself in the waste of vacancy, and a horror came upon his mind, and a faintness on his brain, such as seizes men upon the brink of cliffs.

On the table, by the side of the candle, stood a tray of glasses, a bottle, and a silver bell. He went thither swiftly, then his hand lowered first above the bell, then settled on the bottle. Slowly he filled a glass, slowly drank it out; and, as a tide of animal warmth recomforted the recesses of his nature, stood there smiling at himself. He remembered he was young; the funeral curtains rose, and he saw his life shine and broaden and flow out majestically, like a river sunward. The smile still on his lips, he lit a second candle and a third; a fire stood ready built in a chimney, he lit that also; and the fir-cones and the gnarled olive billets were swift to break in flame and to crackle on the hearth, and the room brightened and enlarged about him like his hopes. To and fro, to and fro, he went, his hands lightly clasped, his breath deeply and pleasurably taken. Victory walked with him; he marched to crowns and empires among shouting followers; glory was his dress. And presently again the shadows closed upon the solitary. Under the gilt of flame and candle-light, the stone walls of the apartment showed down bare and cold; behind the depicted triumph loomed up the actual failure: defeat, the long distress of the flight, exile, despair, broken followers, mourning faces, empty pockets, friends estranged. The memory of his father rose in his mind: he, too, estranged and defied; despair sharpened into wrath. There was one who had led armies in the field, who had staked his life upon the family enterprise, a man of action and experience, of the open air, the camp, the court, the council-room; and he was to accept direction from an old, pompous gentleman in a home in Italy, and buzzed about by priests? A pretty king, if he had not a martial son to lean upon! A king at all?

'There was a weaver (of all people) joined me at St. Ninians; he was more of a man than my papa!' he thought. 'I saw him lie doubled in his blood and a grenadier below him—and he died for my papa! All died for him, or risked the dying, and I lay for him all those months in the rain and skulked in heather like a fox; and now he writes me his advice! calls me Carluccio—me, the man of the house, the only king in that king's race.' He ground his teeth. 'The only king in Europe!' Who else? Who has done and suffered except me? who has lain and run and hidden with his faithful subjects, like a second Bruce? Not my accursed cousin, Louis of France, at least, the lewd effeminate traitor!' And filling the glass to the brim, he drank a king's damnation. Ah, if he had the power of Louis, what a king were here!

The minutes followed each other into the past, and still he persevered in this debilitating cycle of emotions, still fed the fire of his excitement with driblets of Rhine wine: a boy at odds with life, a boy with a spark of the heroic, which he was now burning out and drowning down in futile reverie and solitary excess.

From two rooms beyond, the sudden sound of a raised voice attracted him.

'By . . .

HEATHERCAT

CHAPTER I—TRAQUAIRS OF MONTROYMONT

The period of this tale is in the heat of the killing-time; the scene laid for the most part in solitary hills and morasses, haunted only by the so-called Mountain Wanderers, the dragoons that came in chase of them, the women that wept on their dead bodies, and the wild birds of the moorland that have cried there since the beginning. It is a land of many rain-clouds; a land of much mute history, written there in prehistoric symbols. Strange green raths are to be seen commonly in the country, above all by the kirkyards; barrows of the dead, standing stones; beside these, the faint, durable footprints and handmarks of the Roman; and an antiquity older perhaps than any, and still living and active—a complete Celtic nomenclature and a scarce-mingled Celtic population. These rugged and grey hills were once included in the boundaries of the Caledonian Forest. Merlin sat here below his apple-tree and lamented Gwendolen; here spoke with Kentigern; here fell into his enchanted trance. And the legend of his slumber seems to body forth the story of that Celtic race, deprived for so many centuries of their authentic speech, surviving with their ancestral inheritance of melancholy perversity and patient, unfortunate courage.

The Traquairs of Montroymont (Mons Romanus, as the erudite expound it) had long held their seat about the head-waters of the Dule and in the back parts of the moorland parish of Balweary. For two hundred years they had enjoyed in these upland quarters a certain decency (almost to be named distinction) of repute; and the annals of their house, or what is remembered of them, were obscure and bloody. Ninian Traquair was 'cruallie slochtered' by the Crozers at the kirk-door of Balweary, anno 1482. Francis killed Simon Ruthven of Drumshoreland, anno 1540; bought letters of slayers at the widow and heir, and, by a barbarous form of compounding, married (without tocher) Simon's daughter Grizzel, which is the way the Traquairs and Ruthvens came first to an intermarriage. About the last Traquair and Ruthven marriage, it is the business of this book, among many other things, to tell.

The Traquairs were always strong for the Covenant; for the King also, but the Covenant first; and it began to be ill days for Montroymont when the Bishops came in and the dragoons at the heels of them. Ninian (then laird) was an anxious husband of himself and the property, as the times required, and it may be said of him, that he lost both. He was heavily suspected of the Pentland Hills rebellion. When it came the length of Bothwell Brig, he stood his trial before the Secret Council, and was convicted of talking with some insurgents by the wayside, the subject of the conversation not very clearly appearing, and of the reset and maintenance of one Gale, a gardener man, who was seen before Bothwell with a musket, and afterwards, for a continuance of months, delved the garden at Montroymont. Matters went very ill with Ninian at the Council; some of the lords were clear for treason; and even the boot was talked of. But he was spared that torture; and at last, having pretty good friendship among great men, he came off with a fine of seven thousand marks, that caused the estate to groan. In this case, as in so many others, it was the wife that made the trouble. She was a great keeper of conventicles; would ride ten miles to one, and when she was fined, rejoiced greatly to suffer for the Kirk; but it was rather her husband that suffered. She had their only son, Francis, baptized privately by the hands of Mr. Kidd; there was that much the more to pay for! She could neither be driven nor wiled into the parish kirk; as for taking the sacrament at the hands of any Episcopalian curate, and tenfold more at those of Curate Haddo, there was nothing further from her purposes; and Montroymont had to put his hand in his pocket month by month and year by year. Once, indeed, the little lady was cast in prison, and the laird, worthy, heavy, uninterested man, had to ride up and take her place; from which he was not discharged under nine months and a sharp fine. It scarce seemed she had any gratitude to him; she came out of gaol herself, and plunged immediately deeper in conventicles, resetting recusants, and all her old, expensive folly, only with greater vigour and openness, because Montroymont was safe in the Tolbooth and she had no witness to consider. When he was liberated and came back, with his fingers singed, in December 1680, and late in the black night, my lady was from home. He came into the house at his alighting, with a riding-rod yet in his hand; and, on the servant-maid telling him, caught her by the scruff of the neck, beat her violently, flung her down in the passageway, and went upstairs to his bed fasting and without a light. It was three in the morning when my lady returned from that conventicle, and, hearing of the assault (because the maid had sat up for her, weeping), went to their common chamber with a lantern in hand and stamping with her shoes so as to wake the dead; it was supposed, by those that heard her, from a design to have it out with the good man at once. The house-servants gathered on the stair, because it was a main interest with them to know which of these two was the better horse; and for the space of two hours they were heard to go at the matter, hammer and tongs. Montroymont alleged he was at the end of possibilities; it was no longer within his power to pay the annual rents; she had served him basely by keeping conventicles while he lay in prison for her sake; his friends were weary, and there was nothing else before him but the entire loss of the family lands, and to begin life again by the wayside as a common beggar. She took him up very sharp and high: called upon him, if he were a Christian? and which he most considered, the loss of a few dirty, miry glebes, or of his soul? Presently he was heard to weep, and my lady's voice to go on continually like a running burn, only the words indistinguishable; whereupon it was supposed a victory for her ladyship, and the domestics took themselves to bed. The next day Traquair appeared like a man who had gone under the harrows; and his lady wife thenceforward continued in her old course without the least deflection.

Thenceforward Ninian went on his way without complaint, and suffered his wife to go on hers without remonstrance. He still minded his estate, of which it might be said he took daily a fresh farewell, and counted it already lost; looking ruefully on the acres and the graves of his fathers, on the moorlands where the wild-fowl consorted, the low, gurgling pool of the trout, and the high, windy place of the calling curlews—things that were yet his for the day and would be another's to-morrow; coming back again, and sitting ciphering till the dusk at his approaching ruin, which no device of arithmetic could postpone beyond a year or two. He was essentially the simple ancient man, the farmer and landholder; he would have been content to watch the seasons come and go, and his cattle increase, until the limit of age; he would have been content at any time to die, if he could have left the estates undiminished to an heir-male of his ancestors, that duty standing first in his instinctive calendar. And now he saw everywhere the image of the new proprietor come to meet him, and go sowing and reaping, or fowling for his pleasure on the red moors, or eating the very gooseberries in the Place garden; and saw always, on the other hand, the figure of Francis go forth, a beggar, into the broad world.

It was in vain the poor gentleman sought to moderate; took every test and took advantage of every indulgence; went and drank with the dragoons in Balweary; attended the communion and came regularly to the church to Curate Haddo, with his son beside him. The mad, raging, Presbyterian zealot of a wife at home made all of no avail; and indeed the house must have fallen years before if it had not been for the secret indulgence of the curate, who had a great sympathy with the laird, and winked hard at the doings in Montroymont. This curate was a man very ill reputed in the countryside, and indeed in all Scotland. 'Infamous Haddo' is Shield's expression. But Patrick Walker is more copious. 'Curate Hall Haddo,' says he, sub voce Peden, 'or Hell Haddo, as he was more justly to be called, a pokeful of old condemned errors and the filthy vile lusts of the flesh, a published whore-monger, a common gross drunkard, continually and godlessly scraping and skirling on a fiddle, continually breathing flames against the remnant of Israel. But the Lord put an end to his piping, and all these offences were composed into one bloody grave.' No doubt this was written to excuse his slaughter; and I have never heard it claimed for Walker that he was either a just witness or an indulgent judge. At least, in a merely human character, Haddo comes off not wholly amiss in the matter of these Traquairs: not that he showed any graces of the Christian, but had a sort of Pagan decency, which might almost tempt one to be concerned about his sudden, violent, and unprepared fate.

CHAPTER II—FRANCIE

Francie was eleven years old, shy, secret, and rather childish of his age, though not backward in schooling, which had been pushed on far by a private governor, one M'Brair, a forfeited minister harboured in that capacity at

Montroymont. The boy, already much employed in secret by his mother, was the most apt hand conceivable to run upon a message, to carry food to lurking fugitives, or to stand sentry on the skyline above a conventicle. It seemed no place on the moorlands was so naked but what he would find cover there; and as he knew every hag, boulder, and heather-bush in a circuit of seven miles about Montroymont, there was scarce any spot but what he could leave or approach it unseen. This dexterity had won him a reputation in that part of the country; and among the many children employed in these dangerous affairs, he passed under the by-name of Heathercat.

How much his father knew of this employment might be doubted. He took much forethought for the boy's future, seeing he was like to be left so poorly, and would sometimes assist at his lessons, sighing heavily, yawning deep, and now and again patting Francie on the shoulder if he seemed to be doing ill, by way of a private, kind encouragement. But a great part of the day was passed in aimless wanderings with his eyes sealed, or in his cabinet sitting bemused over the particulars of the coming bankruptcy; and the boy would be absent a dozen times for once that his father would observe it.

On 2nd of July 1682 the boy had an errand from his mother, which must be kept private from all, the father included in the first of them. Crossing the braes, he hears the clatter of a horse's shoes, and claps down incontinent in a hag by the wayside. And presently he spied his father come riding from one direction, and Curate Haddo walking from another; and Montroymont leaning down from the saddle, and Haddo getting on his toes (for he was a little, ruddy, bald-pated man, more like a dwarf), they greeted kindly, and came to a halt within two fathoms of the child.

'Montroymont,' the curate said, 'the deil's in 't but I'll have to denunciate your leddy again.'

'Deil's in 't indeed!' says the laird.

'Man! can ye no induce her to come to the kirk?' pursues Haddo; 'or to a communion at the least of it? For the conventicles, let be! and the same for yon solemn fule, M'Brair: I can blink at them. But she's got to come to the kirk, Montroymont.'

'Dinna speak of it,' says the laird. 'I can do nothing with her.'

'Couldn't ye try the stick to her? it works wonders whiles,' suggested Haddo. 'No? I'm wae to hear it. And I suppose ye ken where you're going?'

'Fine!' said Montroymont. 'Fine do I ken where: bankrup'cy and the Bass Rock!'

'Praise to my bones that I never married!' cried the curate. 'Well, it's a grievous thing to me to see an auld house dung down that was here before Flodden Field. But naebody can say it was with my wish.'

'No more they can, Haddo!' says the laird. 'A good friend ye've been to me, first and last. I can give you that character with a clear conscience.'

Whereupon they separated, and Montroymont rode briskly down into the Dule Valley. But of the curate Francis was not to be quit so easily. He went on with his little, brisk steps to the corner of a dyke, and stopped and whistled and waved upon a lassie that was herding cattle there. This Janet M'Clour was a big lass, being taller than the curate; and what made her look the more so, she was kilted very high. It seemed for a while she would not come, and Francie heard her calling Haddo a 'daft auld fule,' and saw her running and dodging him among the whins and hags till he was fairly blown. But at the last he gets a bottle from his plaid-neuk and holds it up to her; whereupon she came at once into a composition, and the pair sat, drinking of the bottle, and daffing and laughing together, on a mound of heather. The boy had scarce heard of these vanities, or he might have been minded of a nymph and satyr, if anybody could have taken long-leggit Janet for a nymph. But they seemed to be huge friends, he thought; and was the more surprised, when the curate had taken his leave, to see the lassie fling stones after him with screeches of laughter, and Haddo turn about and caper, and shake his staff at her, and laugh louder than herself. A wonderful merry pair, they seemed; and when Francie had crawled out of the hag, he had a great deal to consider in his mind. It was possible they were all fallen in error about Mr. Haddo, he reflected—having seen him so tender with Montroymont, and so kind and playful with the lass Janet; and he had a temptation to go out of his road and question her herself upon the matter. But he had a strong spirit of duty on him; and plodded on instead over the braes till he came near the House of Cairngorm. There, in a hollow place by the burnside that was shaded by some birks, he was aware of a barefoot boy, perhaps a matter of three years older than himself. The two approached with the precautions of a pair of strange dogs, looking at each other queerly.

'It's ill weather on the hills,' said the stranger, giving the watchword.

'For a season,' said Francie, 'but the Lord will appear.'

'Richt,' said the barefoot boy; 'wha're ye frae?'

'The Leddy Montroymont,' says Francie.

'Ha'e, then!' says the stranger, and handed him a folded paper, and they stood and looked at each other again. 'It's unco het,' said the boy.

'Dooms het,' says Francie.

'What do they ca' ye?' says the other.

'Francie,' says he. 'I'm young Montroymont. They ca' me Heathercat.'

'I'm Jock Crozer,' said the boy. And there was another pause, while each rolled a stone under his foot.

'Cast your jaiket and I'll fecht ye for a bawbee,' cried the elder boy with sudden violence, and dramatically throwing back his jacket.

'Na, I've nae time the now,' said Francie, with a sharp thrill of alarm, because Crozer was much the heavier boy.

'Ye're feared. Heathercat indeed!' said Crozer, for among this infantile army of spies and messengers, the fame of Crozer had gone forth and was resented by his rivals. And with that they separated.

On his way home Francie was a good deal occupied with the recollection of this untoward incident. The challenge had been fairly offered and basely refused: the tale would be carried all over the country, and the lustre of the name of Heathercat be dimmed. But the scene between Curate Haddo and Janet M'Clour had also given him much to think of: and he was still puzzling over the case of the curate, and why such ill words were said of him, and why, if he were so merry-spirited, he should yet preach so dry, when coming over a knowe, whom should he see but Janet, sitting with her back to him, minding her cattle! He was always a great child for secret, stealthy ways, having been employed by his mother on errands when the same was necessary; and he came behind the lass without her hearing.

'Jennet,' says he.

'Keep me,' cries Janet, springing up. 'O, it's you, Maister Francie! Save us, what a fricht ye gied me.'

'Ay, it's me,' said Francie. 'I've been thinking, Jennet; I saw you and the curate a while back—'

'Brat!' cried Janet, and coloured up crimson; and the one moment made as if she would have stricken him with a ragged stick she had to chase her bestial with, and the next was begging and praying that he would mention it to none. It was 'naebody's business, whatever,' she said; 'it would just start a clash in the country'; and there would be nothing left for her but to drown herself in Dule Water.

'Why?' says Francie.

The girl looked at him and grew scarlet again.

'And it isna that, anyway,' continued Francie. 'It was just that he seemed so good to ye—like our Father in heaven, I thought; and I thought that mebbe, perhaps, we had all been wrong about him from the first. But I'll have to tell Mr. M'Brair; I'm under a kind of a bargain to him to tell him all.'

'Tell it to the divil if ye like for me!' cried the lass. 'I've naething to be ashamed of. Tell M'Brair to mind his ain affairs,' she cried again: 'they'll be hot eneugh for him, if Haddie likes!' And so strode off, shoving her beasts before her, and ever and again looking back and crying angry words to the boy, where he stood mystified.

By the time he had got home his mind was made up that he would say nothing to his mother. My Lady Montroymont was in the keeping-room, reading a godly book; she was a wonderful frail little wife to make so much noise in the world and be able to steer about that patient sheep her husband; her eyes were like sloes, the fingers of her hands were like tobacco-pipe shanks, her mouth shut tight like a trap; and even when she was the most serious, and still more when she was angry, there hung about her face the terrifying semblance of a smile.

'Have ye gotten the billet, Francie said she; and when he had handed it over, and she had read and burned it, 'Did you see anybody?' she asked.

'I saw the laird,' said Francie.

'He didna see you, though?' asked his mother.

'Deil a fear,' from Francie.

'Francie!' she cried. 'What's that I hear? an aith? The Lord forgive me, have I broughten forth a brand for the burning, a fagot for hell-fire?'

'I'm very sorry, ma'am,' said Francie. 'I humbly beg the Lord's pardon, and yours, for my wickedness.'

'H'm,' grunted the lady. 'Did ye see nobody else?'

'No, ma'am,' said Francie, with the face of an angel, 'except Jock Crozer, that gied me the billet.'

'Jock Crozer!' cried the lady. 'I'll Crozer them! Crozers indeed! What next? Are we to repose the lives of a suffering remnant in Crozers? The whole clan of them wants hanging, and if I had my way of it, they wouldna want it long. Are you aware, sir, that these Crozers killed your forebear at the kirk-door?'

'You see, he was bigger 'n me,' said Francie.

'Jock Crozer!' continued the lady. 'That'll be Clement's son, the biggest thief and reiver in the country-side. To trust a note to him! But I'll give the benefit of my opinions to Lady Whitecross when we two forgather. Let her look to herself! I have no patience with half-hearted carlines, that complies on the Lord's day morning with the kirk, and comes taigling the same night to the conventicle. The one or the other! is what I say: hell or heaven—Haddie's abominations or the pure word of God dreeping from the lips of Mr. Arnot,

"'Like honey from the honeycomb

That dreepeth, sweeter far.'"

My lady was now fairly launched, and that upon two congenial subjects: the deficiencies of the Lady Whitecross and the turpitudes of the whole Crozer race—which, indeed, had never been conspicuous for respectability. She pursued the pair of them for twenty minutes on the clock with wonderful animation and detail, something of the pulpit manner, and the spirit of one possessed. 'O hellish compliance!' she exclaimed. 'I would not suffer a complier to break bread with Christian folk. Of all the sins of this day there is not one so God-defying, so Christ-humiliating, as damnable compliance': the boy standing before her meanwhile, and brokenly pursuing other thoughts, mainly of Haddo and Janet, and Jock Crozer stripping off his jacket. And yet, with all his distraction, it might be argued that he heard too much: his father and himself being 'compliers'—that is to say, attending the church of the parish as the law required.

Presently, the lady's passion beginning to decline, or her flux of ill words to be exhausted, she dismissed her audience. Francie bowed low, left the room, closed the door behind him: and then turned him about in the passage-way, and with a low voice, but a prodigious deal of sentiment, repeated the name of the evil one twenty times over, to the end of which, for the greater efficacy, he tacked on 'damnable' and 'hellish.' Fas est ab hoste doceri—disrespect is made more pungent by quotation; and there is no doubt but he felt relieved, and went upstairs into his tutor's chamber with a quiet mind. M'Brair sat by the cheek of the peat-fire and shivered, for he had a quartan ague and this was his day. The great night-cap and plaid, the dark unshaven cheeks of the man, and the white, thin hands that held the plaid about his chittering body, made a sorrowful picture. But Francie knew and loved him; came straight in, nestled close to the refugee, and told his story. M'Brair had been at the College with Haddo; the Presbytery had licensed both on the same day; and at this tale, told with so much innocency by the boy, the heart of the tutor was commoved.

'Woe upon him! Woe upon that man!' he cried. 'O the unfaithful shepherd! O the hireling and apostate minister! Make my matters hot for me? quo' she! the shameless limmer! And true it is, that he could repose me in that nasty, stinking hole, the Canongate Tolbooth, from which your mother drew me out—the Lord reward her for it!—or to that cold, unbieldy, marine place of the Bass Rock, which, with my delicate kist, would be fair ruin to me. But I will be valiant in my Master's service. I have a duty here: a duty to my God, to myself, and to Haddo: in His strength, I will perform it.'

Then he straitly discharged Francie to repeat the tale, and bade him in the future to avert his very eyes from the doings of the curate. 'You must go to his place of idolatry; look upon him there!' says he, 'but nowhere else. Avert your eyes, close your ears, pass him by like a three days' corp. He is like that damnable monster Basiliscus, which defiles—yea, poisons!—by the sight.'—All which was hardly claratory to the boy's mind.

Presently Montroymont came home, and called up the stairs to Francie. Traquair was a good shot and swordsman: and it was his pleasure to walk with his son over the braes of the moorfowl, or to teach him arms in the back court, when they made a mighty comely pair, the child being so lean, and light, and active, and the laird himself a man of a manly, pretty stature, his hair (the periwig being laid aside) showing already white with many anxieties, and his face of an even, flaccid red. But this day Francie's heart was not in the fencing.

'Sir,' says he, suddenly lowering his point, 'will ye tell me a thing if I was to ask it?'

'Ask away,' says the father.

'Well, it's this,' said Francie: 'Why do you and me comply if it's so wicked?'

'Ay, ye have the cant of it too!' cries Montroymont. 'But I'll tell ye for all that. It's to try and see if we can keep the rigging on this house, Francie. If she had her way, we would be beggar-folk, and hold our hands out by the wayside. When ye hear her—when ye hear folk,' he corrected himself briskly, 'call me a coward, and one that betrayed the Lord, and I kenna what else, just mind it was to keep a bed to ye to sleep in and a bite for ye to eat.—On guard!' he cried, and the lesson proceeded again till they were called to supper.

'There's another thing yet,' said Francie, stopping his father. 'There's another thing that I am not sure that I am very caring for. She—she sends me errands.'

'Obey her, then, as is your bounden duty,' said Traquair.

'Ay, but wait till I tell ye,' says the boy. 'If I was to see you I was to hide.'

Montroymont sighed. 'Well, and that's good of her too,' said he. 'The less that I ken of thir doings the better for me; and the best thing you can do is just to obey her, and see and be a good son to her, the same as ye are to me, Francie.'

At the tenderness of this expression the heart of Francie swelled within his bosom, and his remorse was poured out. 'Faither!' he cried, 'I said "deil" to-day; many's the time I said it, and damnable too, and hellitsh. I ken they're all right; they're beeblical. But I didna say them beeblically; I said them for sweir words—that's the truth of it.'

'Hout, ye silly bairn!' said the father, 'dinna do it nae mair, and come in by to your supper.' And he took the boy, and drew him close to him a moment, as they went through the door, with something very fond and secret, like a caress between a pair of lovers.

The next day M'Brair was abroad in the afternoon, and had a long advising with Janet on the braes where she herded cattle. What passed was never wholly known; but the lass wept bitterly, and fell on her knees to him among the whins. The same night, as soon as it was dark, he took the road again for Balweary. In the Kirkton, where the dragoons quartered, he saw many lights, and heard the noise of a ranting song and people laughing grossly, which was highly offensive to his mind. He gave it the wider berth, keeping among fields; and came down at last by the water-side, where the manse stands solitary between the river and the road. He tapped at the back door, and the old woman called upon him to come in, and guided him through the house to the study, as they still called it, though there was little enough study there in Haddo's days, and more song-books than theology.

'Here's yin to speak wi' ye, Mr. Haddie!' cries the old wife.

And M'Brair, opening the door and entering, found the little, round, red man seated in one chair and his feet upon another. A clear fire and a tallow dip lighted him barely. He was taking tobacco in a pipe, and smiling to himself; and a brandy-bottle and glass, and his fiddle and bow, were beside him on the table.

'Hech, Patey M'Briar, is this you?' said he, a trifle tipsily. 'Step in by, man, and have a drop brandy: for the stomach's sake! Even the deil can quote Scripture—eh, Patey?'

'I will neither eat nor drink with you,' replied M'Brair. 'I am come upon my Master's errand: woe be upon me if I should anyways mince the same. Hall Haddo, I summon you to quit this kirk which you encumber.'

'Muckle obleeged!' says Haddo, winking.

'You and me have been to kirk and market together,' pursued M'Brair; 'we have had blessed seasons in the kirk, we have sat in the same teaching-rooms and read in the same book; and I know you still retain for me some carnal kindness. It would be my shame if I denied it; I live here at your mercy and by your favour, and glory to acknowledge it. You have pity on my wretched body, which is but grass, and must soon be trodden under: but O, Haddo! how much greater is the yearning with which I yearn after and pity your immortal soul! Come now, let us reason together! I drop all points of controversy, weighty though these be; I take your defaced and damnified kirk on your own terms; and I ask you, Are you a worthy minister? The communion season approaches; how can you pronounce thir solemn words, "The elders will now bring forrit the elements," and not quail? A parishioner may be summoned to-night; you may have to rise from your miserable orgies; and I ask you, Haddo, what does your conscience tell you? Are you fit? Are you fit to smooth the pillow of a parting Christian? And if the summons

212

should be for yourself, how then?'

Haddo was startled out of all composure and the better part of his temper. 'What's this of it?' he cried. 'I'm no waur than my neebours. I never set up to be speeritual; I never did. I'm a plain, canty creature; godliness is cheerfulness, says I; give me my fiddle and a dram, and I wouldna hairm a flee.'

'And I repeat my question,' said M'Brair: 'Are you fit—fit for this great charge? fit to carry and save souls?'

'Fit? Blethers! As fit's yoursel',' cried Haddo.

'Are you so great a self-deceiver?' said M'Brair. 'Wretched man, trampler upon God's covenants, crucifier of your Lord afresh. I will ding you to the earth with one word: How about the young woman, Janet M'Clour?'

'Weel, what about her? what do I ken?' cries Haddo. 'M'Brair, ye daft auld wife, I tell ye as true's truth, I never meddled her. It was just daffing, I tell ye: daffing, and nae mair: a piece of fun, like! I'm no denying but what I'm fond of fun, sma' blame to me! But for onything sarious—hout, man, it might come to a deposeetion! I'll sweir it to ye. Where's a Bible, till you hear me sweir?'

'There is nae Bible in your study,' said M'Brair severely.

And Haddo, after a few distracted turns, was constrained to accept the fact.

'Weel, and suppose there isna?' he cried, stamping. 'What mair can ye say of us, but just that I'm fond of my joke, and so's she? I declare to God, by what I ken, she might be the Virgin Mary—if she would just keep clear of the dragoons. But me! na, deil haet o' me!'

'She is penitent at least,' says M'Brair.

'Do you mean to actually up and tell me to my face that she accused me?' cried the curate.

'I canna just say that,' replied M'Brair. 'But I rebuked her in the name of God, and she repented before me on her bended knees.'

'Weel, I daursay she's been ower far wi' the dragoons,' said Haddo. 'I never denied that. I ken naething by it.'

'Man, you but show your nakedness the more plainly,' said M'Brair. 'Poor, blind, besotted creature—and I see you stoytering on the brink of dissolution: your light out, and your hours numbered. Awake, man!' he shouted with a formidable voice, 'awake, or it be ower late.'

'Be damned if I stand this!' exclaimed Haddo, casting his tobacco-pipe violently on the table, where it was smashed in pieces. 'Out of my house with ye, or I'll call for the dragoons.'

'The speerit of the Lord is upon me,' said M'Brair with solemn ecstasy. 'I sist you to compear before the Great White Throne, and I warn you the summons shall be bloody and sudden.'

And at this, with more agility than could have been expected, he got clear of the room and slammed the door behind him in the face of the pursuing curate. The next Lord's day the curate was ill, and the kirk closed, but for all his ill words, Mr. M'Brair abode unmolested in the house of Montroymont.

CHAPTER III—THE HILL-END OF DRUMLOWE

This was a bit of a steep broken hill that overlooked upon the west a moorish valley, full of ink-black pools. These presently drained into a burn that made off, with little noise and no celerity of pace, about the corner of the hill. On the far side the ground swelled into a bare heath, black with junipers, and spotted with the presence of the standing stones for which the place was famous. They were many in that part, shapeless, white with lichen—you would have said with age: and had made their abode there for untold centuries, since first the heathens shouted for their installation. The ancients had hallowed them to some ill religion, and their neighbourhood had long been avoided by the prudent before the fall of day; but of late, on the upspringing of new requirements, these lonely stones on the moor had again become a place of assembly. A watchful picket on the Hill-end commanded all the northern and eastern approaches; and such was the disposition of the ground, that by certain cunningly posted sentries the west also could be made secure against surprise: there was no place in the country where a conventicle could meet with more quiet of mind or a more certain retreat open, in the case of interference from the dragoons. The minister spoke from a knowe close to the edge of the ring, and poured out the words God gave him on the very threshold of the devils of yore. When they pitched a tent (which was often in wet weather, upon a communion occasion) it was rigged over the huge isolated pillar that had the name of Anes-Errand, none knew why. And the congregation sat partly clustered on the slope below, and partly among the idolatrous monoliths and on the turfy soil of the Ring itself. In truth the situation was well qualified to give a zest to Christian doctrines, had there been any wanted. But these congregations assembled under conditions at once so formidable and romantic as made a zealot of the most cold. They were the last of the faithful; God, who had averted His face from all other countries of the world, still leaned from heaven to observe, with swelling sympathy, the doings of His moorland remnant; Christ was by them with His eternal wounds, with dropping tears; the Holy Ghost (never perfectly realised nor firmly adopted by Protestant imaginations) was dimly supposed to be in the heart of each and on the lips of the minister. And over against them was the army of the hierarchies, from the men Charles and James Stuart, on to King Lewie and the Emperor; and the scarlet Pope, and the muckle black devil himself, peering out the red mouth of hell in an ecstasy of hate and hope. 'One pull more!' he seemed to cry; 'one pull more, and it's done. There's only Clydesdale and the Stewartry, and the three Bailiaries of Ayr, left for God.' And with such an august assistance of powers and principalities looking on at the last conflict of good and evil, it was scarce possible to spare a thought to those old, infirm, debile, ab agendo devils whose holy place they were now violating.

There might have been three hundred to four hundred present. At least there were three hundred horses tethered for the most part in the ring; though some of the hearers on the outskirts of the crowd stood with their bridles in their hand, ready to mount at the first signal. The circle of faces was strangely characteristic; long, serious, strongly marked, the tackle standing out in the lean brown cheeks, the mouth set and the eyes shining with a fierce enthusiasm; the shepherd, the labouring man, and the rarer laird, stood there in their broad blue bonnets or laced hats, and presenting an essential identity of type. From time to time a long-drawn groan of adhesion rose in this audience, and was propagated like a wave to the outskirts, and died away among the keepers of the horses. It had a name; it was called 'a holy groan.'

A squall came up; a great volley of flying mist went out before it and whelmed the scene; the wind stormed with a sudden fierceness that carried away the minister's voice and twitched his tails and made him stagger, and turned the congregation for a moment into a mere pother of blowing plaid-ends and prancing horses; and the rain followed and was dashed straight into their faces. Men and women panted aloud in the shock of that violent shower-bath; the teeth were bared along all the line in an involuntary grimace; plaids, mantles, and riding-coats were proved vain, and the worshippers felt the water stream on their naked flesh. The minister, reinforcing his great and shrill voice, continued to contend against and triumph over the rising of the squall and the dashing of the rain.

'In that day ye may go thirty mile and not hear a crawing cock,' he said; 'and fifty mile and not get a light to your pipe; and an hundred mile and not see a smoking house. For there'll be naething in all Scotland but deid men's banes and blackness, and the living anger of the Lord. O, where to find a bield—O sirs, where to find a bield from the wind of the Lord's anger? Do ye call this a wind? Bethankit! Sirs, this is but a temporary dispensation; this is but a puff of wind, this is but a spit of rain and by with it. Already there's a blue bow in the west, and the sun will take the crown of the causeway again, and your things'll be dried upon ye, and your flesh will be warm upon your bones. But O, sirs, sirs! for the day of the Lord's anger!'

His rhetoric was set forth with an ear-piercing elocution, and a voice that sometimes crashed like cannon. Such as it was, it was the gift of all hill-preachers, to a singular degree of likeness or identity. Their images scarce ranged beyond the red horizon of the moor and the rainy hill-top, the shepherd and his sheep, a fowling-piece, a spade, a pipe, a dunghill, a crowing cock, the shining and the withdrawal of the sun. An occasional pathos of simple humanity, and frequent patches of big Biblical words, relieved the homely tissue. It was a poetry apart; bleak, austere, but genuine, and redolent of the soil.

A little before the coming of the squall there was a different scene enacting at the outposts. For the most part, the sentinels were faithful to their important duty; the Hill-end of Drumlowe was known to be a safe meeting-place; and the out-pickets on this particular day had been somewhat lax from the beginning, and grew laxer during the inordinate length of the discourse. Francie lay there in his appointed hiding-hole, looking abroad between two whin-bushes. His view was across the course of the burn, then over a piece of plain moorland, to a gap between two hills; nothing moved but grouse, and some cattle who slowly traversed his field of view, heading northward: he heard the psalms, and sang words of his own to the savage and melancholy music; for he had his own design in hand, and terror and cowardice prevailed in his bosom alternately, like the hot and the cold fit of an ague. Courage was uppermost during the singing, which he accompanied through all its length with this impromptu strain:

'And I will ding Jock Crozer down

No later than the day.'

Presently the voice of the preacher came to him in wafts, at the wind's will, as by the opening and shutting of a door; wild spasms of screaming, as of some undiscerned gigantic hill-bird stirred with inordinate passion, succeeded to intervals of silence; and Francie heard them with a critical ear. 'Ay,' he thought at last, 'he'll do; he has the bit in his mou' fairly.'

He had observed that his friend, or rather his enemy, Jock Crozer, had been established at a very critical part of the line of outposts; namely, where the burn issues by an abrupt gorge from the semicircle of high moors. If anything was calculated to nerve him to battle it was this. The post was important; next to the Hill-end itself, it might be called the key to the position; and it was where the cover was bad, and in which it was most natural to place a child. It should have been Heathercat's; why had it been given to Crozer? An exquisite fear of what should be the answer passed through his marrow every time he faced the question. Was it possible that Crozer could have boasted? that there were rumours abroad to his—Heathercat's—discredit? that his honour was publicly sullied? All the world went dark about him at the thought; he sank without a struggle into the midnight pool of despair; and every time he so sank, he brought back with him—not drowned heroism indeed, but half-drowned courage by the locks. His heart beat very slowly as he deserted his station, and began to crawl towards that of Crozer. Something pulled him back, and it was not the sense of duty, but a remembrance of Crozer's build and hateful readiness of fist. Duty, as he conceived it, pointed him forward on the rueful path that he was travelling. Duty bade him redeem his name if he were able, at the risk of broken bones; and his bones and every tooth in his head ached by anticipation. An awful subsidiary fear whispered him that if he were hurt, he should disgrace himself by weeping. He consoled himself, boy-like, with the consideration that he was not yet committed; he could easily steal over unseen to Crozer's post, and he had a continuous private idea that he would very probably steal back again. His course took him so near the minister that he could hear some of his words: 'What news, minister, of Claver'se? He's going round like a roaring rampaging lion. . . .

Footnotes:

[0] With special reference to Father Damien, pp. 63–81.

[65] From the Sydney Presbyterian, October 26, 1889.

[85] Theater of Mortality, p. 10; Edin. 1713.

[86] History of My Own Times, beginning 1660, by Bishop Gilbert Burnet, p. 158.

[87a] Wodrow's Church History, Book II. chap. i. sect. I.

[87b] Crookshank's Church History, 1751, second ed. p. 202.

[88] Burnet, p. 348.

[89] Fuller's Historie of the Holy Warre, fourth ed. 1651.

[90] Wodrow, vol. ii. p. 17.

[92] Sir J. Turner's Memoirs, pp. 148–50.

[93] A Cloud of Witnesses, p. 376.

[94a] Wodrow, pp. 19, 20.

[94b] A Hind Let Loose, p. 123.

[95] Turner, p. 163.

[96a] Turner, p. 198.

[96b] Ibid. p. 167.

[97] Wodrow, p. 29.

[98] Turner, Wodrow, and Church History by James Kirkton, an outed minister of the period.

[99] Kirkton, p. 244.

[101a] Kirkton.

[101b] Turner.

[102] Kirkton.

[103] Kirkton.

[104] Cloud of Witnesses, p. 389; Edin. 1765.

[105a] Kirkton, p. 247.

[105b] Ibid. p. 254.

[105c] Ibid. p. 247.

[105d] Ibid. pp. 247, 248.

[106] Kirkton, p. 248.

[107a] Kirkton, p. 249.

[107b] Naphtali, p. 205; Glasgow, 1721.

[107c] Wodrow, p. 59.

[108a] Kirkton, p. 246.

[108b] Defoe's History of the Church of Scotland.

[151] 'This paper was written in collaboration with James Waiter Ferrier, and if reprinted this is to be stated, though his principal collaboration was to lie back in an easy-chair and laugh.'—[R.L.S., Oct. 25, 1894.]

[183] The illustrator was, in fact, a lady, Miss Eunice Bagster, eldest daughter of the publisher, Samuel Bagster; except in the case of the cuts depicting the fight with Apollyon, which were designed by her brother, Mr. Jonathan Bagster. The edition was published in 1845. I am indebted for this information to the kindness of Mr. Robert Bagster, the present managing director of the firm.—[Sir Sidney Colvin's Note.]

[205] See a short essay of De Quincey's.

[206a] Religio Medici, Part ii.

[206b] Duchess of Malfi.

THE WEIR OF HERMISTON

TO MY WIFE

I saw rain falling and the rainbow drawn

On Lammermuir. Hearkening I heard again

In my precipitous city beaten bells

Winnow the keen sea wind. And here afar,

Intent on my own race and place, I wrote.

Take thou the writing: thine it is. For who

Burnished the sword, blew on the drowsy coal,

Held still the target higher, chary of praise

And prodigal of counsel—who but thou?

So now, in the end, if this the least be good,

If any deed be done, if any fire

Burn in the imperfect page, the praise be thine.

INTRODUCTORY

In the wild end of a moorland parish, far out of the sight of any house, there stands a cairn among the heather, and a little by east of it, in the going down of the brae-side, a monument with some verses half defaced. It was here that Claverhouse shot with his own hand the Praying Weaver of Balweary, and the chisel of Old Mortality has clinked on that lonely gravestone. Public and domestic history have thus marked with a bloody finger this hollow among the hills; and since the Cameronian gave his life there, two hundred years ago, in a glorious folly, and without comprehension or regret, the silence of the moss has been broken once again by the report of firearms and the cry of the dying.

The Deil's Hags was the old name. But the place is now called Francie's Cairn. For a while it was told that Francie walked. Aggie Hogg met him in the gloaming by the cairnside, and he spoke to her, with chattering teeth, so that his words were lost. He pursued Rob Todd (if any one could have believed Robbie) for the space of half a mile with pitiful entreaties. But the age is one of incredulity; these superstitious decorations speedily fell off; and the facts of the story itself, like the bones of a giant buried there and half dug up, survived, naked and imperfect, in the memory of the scattered neighbours. To this day, of winter nights, when the sleet is on the window and the cattle are quiet in the byre, there will be told again, amid the silence of the young and the additions and corrections of the old, the tale of the Justice-Clerk and of his son, young Hermiston, that vanished from men's knowledge; of the two Kirsties and the Four Black Brothers of the Cauldstaneslap; and of Frank Innes, "the young fool advocate," that came into these moorland parts to find his destiny.

CHAPTER I—LIFE AND DEATH OF MRS. WEIR

The Lord Justice-Clerk was a stranger in that part of the country; but his lady wife was known there from a child, as her race had been before her. The old "riding Rutherfords of Hermiston," of whom she was the last descendant, had been famous men of yore, ill neighbours, ill subjects, and ill husbands to their wives though not their properties. Tales of them were rife for twenty miles about; and their name was even printed in the page of our Scots histories, not always to their credit. One bit the dust at Flodden; one was hanged at his peel door by James the Fifth; another fell dead in a carouse with Tom Dalyell; while a fourth (and that was Jean's own father) died presiding at a Hell-Fire Club, of which he was the founder. There were many heads shaken in Crossmichael at that judgment; the more so as the man had a villainous reputation among high and low, and both with the godly and the worldly. At that very hour of his demise, he had ten going pleas before the Session, eight of them oppressive. And the same doom extended even to his agents; his grieve, that had been his right hand in many a left-hand business, being cast from his horse one night and drowned in a peat-hag on the Kye-skairs; and his very doer (although lawyers have long spoons) surviving him not long, and dying on a sudden in a bloody flux.

In all these generations, while a male Rutherford was in the saddle with his lads, or brawling in a change-house, there would be always a white-faced wife immured at home in the old peel or the later mansion-house. It seemed this succession of martyrs bided long, but took their vengeance in the end, and that was in the person of the last descendant, Jean. She bore the name of the Rutherfords, but she was the daughter of their trembling wives. At the first she was not wholly without charm. Neighbours recalled in her, as a child, a strain of elfin wilfulness, gentle little mutinies, sad little gaieties, even a morning gleam of beauty that was not to be fulfilled. She withered in the growing, and (whether it was the sins of her sires or the sorrows of her mothers) came to her maturity depressed, and, as it were, defaced; no blood of life in her, no grasp or gaiety; pious, anxious, tender, tearful, and incompetent.

It was a wonder to many that she had married—seeming so wholly of the stuff that makes old maids. But chance cast her in the path of Adam Weir, then the new Lord-Advocate, a recognised, risen man, the conqueror of many obstacles, and thus late in the day beginning to think upon a wife. He was one who looked rather to obedience than beauty, yet it would seem he was struck with her at the first look. "Wha's she?" he said, turning to his host; and, when he had been told, "Ay," says he, "she looks menseful. She minds me—"; and then, after a pause (which some have been daring enough to set down to sentimental recollections), "Is she releegious?" he asked, and was shortly after, at his own request, presented. The acquaintance, which it seems profane to call a courtship, was pursued with Mr. Weir's accustomed industry, and was long a legend, or rather a source of legends, in the Parliament House. He was described coming, rosy with much port, into the drawing-room, walking direct up to the lady, and assailing her with pleasantries, to which the embarrassed fair one responded, in what seemed a kind of agony, "Eh, Mr. Weir!" or "O, Mr. Weir!" or "Keep me, Mr. Weir!" On the very eve of their engagement, it was related that one had drawn near to the tender couple, and had overheard the lady cry out, with the tones of one who talked for the sake of talking, "Keep me, Mr. Weir, and what became of him?" and the profound accents of the suitor reply, "Haangit, mem, haangit." The motives upon either side were much debated. Mr. Weir must have supposed his bride to be somehow suitable; perhaps he belonged to that class of men who think a weak head the ornament of women—an opinion invariably punished in this life. Her descent and her estate were beyond question. Her wayfaring ancestors and her litigious father had done well by Jean. There was ready money and there were broad acres, ready to fall wholly to the husband, to lend dignity to his descendants, and to himself a title, when he should be called upon the Bench. On the side of Jean, there was perhaps some fascination of curiosity as to this unknown male animal that approached her with the roughness of a ploughman and the aplomb of an advocate. Being so trenchantly opposed to all she knew, loved, or understood, he may well have seemed to her the extreme, if scarcely the ideal, of his sex. And besides, he was an ill man to refuse. A little over forty at the period of his marriage, he looked already older, and to the force of manhood added the senatorial dignity of years; it was, perhaps, with an unreverend awe, but he was awful. The Bench, the Bar, and the most experienced and reluctant witness, bowed to his authority—and why not Jeannie Rutherford?

The heresy about foolish women is always punished, I have said, and Lord Hermiston began to pay the penalty at once. His house in George Square was wretchedly ill-guided; nothing answerable to the expense of maintenance but the cellar, which was his own private care. When things went wrong at dinner, as they continually did, my lord would look up the table at his wife: "I think these broth would be better to sweem in than to sup." Or else to the butler: "Here, M'Killop, awa' wi' this Raadical gigot—tak' it to the French, man, and bring me some puddocks! It seems rather a sore kind of a business that I should be all day in Court haanging Raadicals, and get nawthing to my denner." Of course this was but a manner of speaking, and he had never hanged a man for being a Radical in his life; the law, of which he was the faithful minister, directing otherwise. And of course these growls were in the nature of pleasantry, but it was of a recondite sort; and uttered as they were in his resounding voice, and commented on by that expression which they called in the Parliament House "Hermiston's hanging face"—they struck mere dismay into the wife. She sat before him speechless and fluttering; at each dish, as at a fresh ordeal, her eye hovered toward my lord's countenance and fell again; if he but ate in silence, unspeakable relief was her portion; if there were complaint, the world was darkened. She would seek out the cook, who was always her sister in the Lord. "O, my dear, this is the most dreidful thing that my lord can never be contented in his own house!" she would begin; and weep and pray with the cook; and then the cook would pray with Mrs. Weir; and the next day's meal would never be a penny the better—and the next cook (when she came) would be worse, if anything, but just as pious. It was often wondered that Lord Hermiston bore it as he did; indeed, he was a stoical old voluptuary, contented with sound wine and plenty of it. But there were moments when he overflowed. Perhaps half a dozen times in the history of his married life—"Here! tak' it awa', and bring me a piece bread and kebbuck!" he had exclaimed, with an appalling explosion of his voice and rare gestures. None thought to dispute or to make excuses; the service was arrested; Mrs. Weir sat at the head of the table whimpering without disguise; and his lordship opposite munched his bread and cheese in ostentatious disregard. Once only, Mrs. Weir had ventured to appeal. He was passing her chair on his way into the study.

"O, Edom!" she wailed, in a voice tragic with tears, and reaching out to him both hands, in one of which she held a sopping pocket-handkerchief.

He paused and looked upon her with a face of wrath, into which there stole, as he looked, a twinkle of humour.

"Noansense!" he said. "You and your noansense! What do I want with a Christian faim'ly? I want Christian broth! Get me a lass that can plain-boil a potato, if she was a whüre off the streets." And with these words, which echoed in her tender ears like blasphemy, he had passed on to his study and shut the door behind him.

Such was the housewifery in George Square. It was better at Hermiston, where Kirstie Elliott, the sister of a neighbouring bonnet-laird, and an eighteenth cousin of the lady's, bore the charge of all, and kept a trim house and a good country table. Kirstie was a woman in a thousand, clean, capable, notable; once a moorland Helen, and still comely as a blood horse and healthy as the hill wind. High in flesh and voice and colour, she ran the house with her whole intemperate soul, in a bustle, not without buffets. Scarce more pious than decency in those days required, she was the cause of many an anxious thought and many a tearful prayer to Mrs. Weir. Housekeeper and mistress renewed the parts of Martha and Mary; and though with a pricking conscience, Mary reposed on Martha's strength as on a rock. Even Lord Hermiston held Kirstie in a particular regard. There were few with whom he unbent so gladly, few whom he favoured with so many pleasantries. "Kirstie and me maun have our joke," he would declare in high good-humour, as he buttered Kirstie's scones, and she waited at table. A man who had no need either of love or of popularity, a keen reader of men and of events, there was perhaps only one truth for which he was quite unprepared: he would have been quite unprepared to learn that Kirstie hated him. He thought maid and master were well matched; hard, bandy, healthy, broad Scots folk, without a hair of nonsense to the pair of them. And the fact was that she made a goddess and an only child of the effete and tearful lady; and even as she waited at table her hands would sometimes itch for my lord's ears.

Thus, at least, when the family were at Hermiston, not only my lord, but Mrs. Weir too, enjoyed a holiday. Free from the dreadful looking-for of the miscarried dinner, she would mind her seam, read her piety books, and take her walk (which was my lord's orders), sometimes by herself, sometimes with Archie, the only child of that scarce natural union. The child was her next bond to life. Her frosted sentiment bloomed again, she breathed deep of life, she let loose her heart, in that society. The miracle of her motherhood was ever new to her. The sight of the little man at her skirt intoxicated her with the sense of power, and froze her with the consciousness of her responsibility. She looked forward, and, seeing him in fancy grow up and play his diverse part on the world's theatre, caught in her breath and lifted up her courage with a lively effort. It was only with the child that she forgot herself and was at moments natural; yet it was only with the child that she had conceived and managed to pursue a scheme of conduct. Archie was to be a great man and a good; a minister if possible, a saint for certain. She tried to engage his mind upon her favourite books, Rutherford's Letters, Scougalls Grace Abounding, and the like. It was a common practice of hers (and strange to remember now) that she would carry the child to the Deil's Hags, sit with him on the Praying Weaver's stone, and talk of the Covenanters till their tears ran down. Her view of history was wholly artless, a design in snow and ink; upon the one side, tender innocents with psalms upon their lips; upon the other, the persecutors, booted, bloody-minded, flushed with wine: a suffering Christ, a raging Beelzebub. Persecutor was a word that knocked upon the woman's heart; it was her highest thought of wickedness, and the mark of it was on her house. Her great-great-grandfather had drawn the sword against the Lord's anointed on the field of Rullion Green, and breathed his last (tradition said) in the arms of the detestable Dalyell. Nor could she blind herself to this, that had they lived in those old days, Hermiston himself would have been numbered alongside of Bloody MacKenzie and the politic Lauderdale and Rothes, in the band of God's immediate enemies. The sense of this moved her to the more fervour; she had a voice for that name of persecutor

231

that thrilled in the child's marrow; and when one day the mob hooted and hissed them all in my lord's travelling carriage, and cried, "Down with the persecutor! down with Hanging Hermiston!" and mamma covered her eyes and wept, and papa let down the glass and looked out upon the rabble with his droll formidable face, bitter and smiling, as they said he sometimes looked when he gave sentence, Archie was for the moment too much amazed to be alarmed, but he had scarce got his mother by herself before his shrill voice was raised demanding an explanation: why had they called papa a persecutor?

"Keep me, my precious!" she exclaimed. "Keep me, my dear! this is poleetical. Ye must never ask me anything poleetical, Erchie. Your faither is a great man, my dear, and it's no for me or you to be judging him. It would be telling us all, if we behaved ourselves in our several stations the way your faither does in his high office; and let me hear no more of any such disrespectful and undutiful questions! No that you meant to be undutiful, my lamb; your mother kens that—she kens it well, dearie!" And so slid off to safer topics, and left on the mind of the child an obscure but ineradicable sense of something wrong.

Mrs. Weir's philosophy of life was summed in one expression—tenderness. In her view of the universe, which was all lighted up with a glow out of the doors of hell, good people must walk there in a kind of ecstasy of tenderness. The beasts and plants had no souls; they were here but for a day, and let their day pass gently! And as for the immortal men, on what black, downward path were many of them wending, and to what a horror of an immortality! "Are not two sparrows," "Whosoever shall smite thee," "God sendeth His rain," "Judge not, that ye be not judged"—these texts made her body of divinity; she put them on in the morning with her clothes and lay down to sleep with them at night; they haunted her like a favourite air, they clung about her like a favourite perfume. Their minister was a marrowy expounder of the law, and my lord sat under him with relish; but Mrs. Weir respected him from far off; heard him (like the cannon of a beleaguered city) usefully booming outside on the dogmatic ramparts; and meanwhile, within and out of shot, dwelt in her private garden which she watered with grateful tears. It seems strange to say of this colourless and ineffectual woman, but she was a true enthusiast, and might have made the sunshine and the glory of a cloister. Perhaps none but Archie knew she could be eloquent; perhaps none but he had seen her—her colour raised, her hands clasped or quivering—glow with gentle ardour. There is a corner of the policy of Hermiston, where you come suddenly in view of the summit of Black Fell, sometimes like the mere grass top of a hill, sometimes (and this is her own expression) like a precious jewel in the heavens. On such days, upon the sudden view of it, her hand would tighten on the child's fingers, her voice rise like a song. "I to the hills!" she would repeat. "And O, Erchie, are nae these like the hills of Naphtali?" and her tears would flow.

Upon an impressionable child the effect of this continual and pretty accompaniment to life was deep. The woman's quietism and piety passed on to his different nature undiminished; but whereas in her it was a native sentiment, in him it was only an implanted dogma. Nature and the child's pugnacity at times revolted. A cad from the Potterrow once struck him in the mouth; he struck back, the pair fought it out in the back stable lane towards the Meadows, and Archie returned with a considerable decline in the number of his front teeth, and unregenerately boasting of the losses of the foe. It was a sore day for Mrs. Weir; she wept and prayed over the infant backslider until my lord was due from Court, and she must resume that air of tremulous composure with which she always greeted him. The judge was that day in an observant mood, and remarked upon the absent teeth.

"I am afraid Erchie will have been fechting with some of they blagyard lads," said Mrs. Weir.

My lord's voice rang out as it did seldom in the privacy of his own house. "I'll have norm of that, sir!" he cried. "Do you hear me?—nonn of that! No son of mine shall be speldering in the glaur with any dirty raibble."

The anxious mother was grateful for so much support; she had even feared the contrary. And that night when she put the child to bed—"Now, my dear, ye see!" she said, "I told you what your faither would think of it, if he heard ye had fallen into this dreidful sin; and let you and me pray to God that ye may be keepit from the like temptation or strengthened to resist it!"

The womanly falsity of this was thrown away. Ice and iron cannot be welded; and the points of view of the Justice-Clerk and Mrs. Weir were not less unassimilable. The character and position of his father had long been a stumbling-block to Archie, and with every year of his age the difficulty grew more instant. The man was mostly silent; when he spoke at all, it was to speak of the things of the world, always in a worldly spirit, often in language that the child had been schooled to think coarse, and sometimes with words that he knew to be sins in themselves. Tenderness was the first duty, and my lord was invariably harsh. God was love; the name of my lord (to all who knew him) was fear. In the world, as schematised for Archie by his mother, the place was marked for such a creature. There were some whom it was good to pity and well (though very likely useless) to pray for; they were named reprobates, goats, God's enemies, brands for the burning; and Archie tallied every mark of identification, and drew the inevitable private inference that the Lord Justice-Clerk was the chief of sinners.

The mother's honesty was scarce complete. There was one influence she feared for the child and still secretly combated; that was my lord's; and half unconsciously, half in a wilful blindness, she continued to undermine her husband with his son. As long as Archie remained silent, she did so ruthlessly, with a single eye to heaven and the child's salvation; but the day came when Archie spoke. It was 1801, and Archie was seven, and beyond his years for curiosity and logic, when he brought the case up openly. If judging were sinful and forbidden, how came papa to be a judge? to have that sin for a trade? to bear the name of it for a distinction?

"I can't see it," said the little Rabbi, and wagged his head.

Mrs. Weir abounded in commonplace replies.

"No, I cannae see it," reiterated Archie. "And I'll tell you what, mamma, I don't think you and me's justifeed in staying with him."

The woman awoke to remorse, she saw herself disloyal to her man, her sovereign and bread-winner, in whom (with what she had of worldliness) she took a certain subdued pride. She expatiated in reply on my lord's honour and greatness; his useful services in this world of sorrow and wrong, and the place in which he stood, far above where babes and innocents could hope to see or criticise. But she had builded too well—Archie had his answers pat: Were not babes and innocents the type of the kingdom of heaven? Were not honour and greatness the badges of the world? And at any rate, how about the mob that had once seethed about the carriage?

"It's all very fine," he concluded, "but in my opinion papa has no right to be it. And it seems that's not the worst yet of it. It seems he's called "The Hanging judge"—it seems he's crooool. I'll tell you what it is, mamma, there's a tex' borne in upon me: It were better for that man if a milestone were bound upon his back and him flung into the deepestmost pairts of the sea."

"O, my lamb, ye must never say the like of that!" she cried. "Ye're to honour faither and mother, dear, that your days may be long in the land. It's Atheists that cry out against him—French Atheists, Erchie! Ye would never surely even yourself down to be saying the same thing as French Atheists? It would break my heart to think that of you. And O, Erchie, here are'na you setting up to judge? And have ye no forgot God's plain command—the First with Promise, dear? Mind you upon the beam and the mote!"

Having thus carried the war into the enemy's camp, the terrified lady breathed again. And no doubt it is easy thus to circumvent a child with catchwords, but it may be questioned how far it is effectual. An instinct in his breast detects the quibble, and a voice condemns it. He will instantly submit, privately hold the same opinion. For even in this simple and antique relation of the mother and the child, hypocrisies are multiplied.

When the Court rose that year and the family returned to Hermiston, it was a common remark in all the country that the lady was sore failed. She seemed to loose and seize again her touch with life, now sitting inert in a sort of durable bewilderment, anon waking to feverish and weak activity. She dawdled about the lasses at their work, looking stupidly on; she fell to rummaging in old cabinets and presses, and desisted when half through; she would begin remarks with an air of animation and drop them without a struggle. Her common appearance was of one who has forgotten something and is trying to remember; and when she overhauled, one after another, the worthless and touching mementoes of her youth, she might have been seeking the clue to that lost thought. During this period, she gave many gifts to the neighbours and house lasses, giving them with a manner of regret that embarrassed the recipients.

The last night of all she was busy on some female work, and toiled upon it with so manifest and painful a devotion that my lord (who was not often curious) inquired as to its nature.

She blushed to the eyes. "O, Edom, it's for you!" she said. "It's slippers. I—I hae never made ye any."

"Ye daft auld wife!" returned his lordship. "A bonny figure I would be, palmering about in bauchles!"

The next day, at the hour of her walk, Kirstie interfered. Kirstie took this decay of her mistress very hard; bore her a grudge, quarrelled with and railed upon her, the anxiety of a genuine love wearing the disguise of temper. This day of all days she insisted disrespectfully, with rustic fury, that Mrs. Weir should stay at home. But, "No, no," she said, "it's my lord's orders," and set forth as usual. Archie was visible in the acre bog, engaged upon some childish enterprise, the instrument of which was mire; and she stood and looked at him a while like one about to call; then thought otherwise, sighed, and shook her head, and proceeded on her rounds alone. The house lasses were at the burnside washing, and saw her pass with her loose, weary, dowdy gait.

"She's a terrible feckless wife, the mistress!" said the one.

"Tut," said the other, "the wumman's seeck."

"Weel, I canna see nae differ in her," returned the first. "A fushionless quean, a feckless carline."

The poor creature thus discussed rambled a while in the grounds without a purpose. Tides in her mind ebbed and flowed, and carried her to and fro like seaweed. She tried a path, paused, returned, and tried another; questing, forgetting her quest; the spirit of choice extinct in her bosom, or devoid of sequency. On a sudden, it appeared as though she had remembered, or had formed a resolution, wheeled about, returned with hurried steps, and appeared in the dining-room, where Kirstie was at the cleaning, like one charged with an important errand.

"Kirstie!" she began, and paused; and then with conviction, "Mr. Weir isna speeritually minded, but he has been a good man to me."

It was perhaps the first time since her husband's elevation that she had forgotten the handle to his name, of which the tender, inconsistent woman was not a little proud. And when Kirstie looked up at the speaker's face, she was aware of a change.

"Godsake, what's the maitter wi' ye, mem?" cried the housekeeper, starting from the rug.

"I do not ken," answered her mistress, shaking her head. "But he is not speeritually minded, my dear."

"Here, sit down with ye! Godsake, what ails the wife?" cried Kirstie, and helped and forced her into my lord's own chair by the cheek of the hearth.

"Keep me, what's this?" she gasped. "Kirstie, what's this? I'm frich'ened."

They were her last words.

It was the lowering nightfall when my lord returned. He had the sunset in his back, all clouds and glory; and before him, by the wayside, spied Kirstie Elliott waiting. She was dissolved in tears, and addressed him in the high, false note of barbarous mourning, such as still lingers modified among Scots heather.

"The Lord peety ye, Hermiston! the Lord prepare ye!" she keened out. "Weary upon me, that I should have to tell it!"

He reined in his horse and looked upon her with the hanging face.

"Has the French landit?" cried he.

"Man, man," she said, "is that a' ye can think of? The Lord prepare ye:

the Lord comfort and support ye!"

"Is onybody deid?" said his lordship. "It's no Erchie?"

"Bethankit, no!" exclaimed the woman, startled into a more natural tone. "Na, na, it's no sae bad as that. It's the mistress, my lord; she just fair flittit before my e'en. She just gi'ed a sab and was by wi' it. Eh, my bonny Miss Jeannie, that I mind sae weel!" And forth again upon that pouring tide of lamentation in which women of her class excel and over-abound.

Lord Hermiston sat in the saddle beholding her. Then he seemed to recover command upon himself.

"Well, it's something of the suddenest," said he. "But she was a dwaibly body from the first."

And he rode home at a precipitate amble with Kirstie at his horse's heels.

Dressed as she was for her last walk, they had laid the dead lady on her bed. She was never interesting in life; in death she was not impressive; and as her husband stood before her, with his hands crossed behind his powerful back, that which he looked upon was the very image of the insignificant.

"Her and me were never cut out for one another," he remarked at last. "It was a daft-like marriage." And then, with a most unusual gentleness of tone, "Puir bitch," said he, "puir bitch!" Then suddenly: "Where's Erchie?"

Kirstie had decoyed him to her room and given him "a jeely-piece."

"Ye have some kind of gumption, too," observed the judge, and considered his housekeeper grimly. "When all's said," he added, "I micht have done waur—I micht have been marriet upon a skirting Jezebel like you!"

"There's naebody thinking of you, Hermiston!" cried the offended woman. "We think of her that's out of her sorrows. And could she have done waur? Tell me that, Hermiston—tell me that before her clay-cauld corp!"

"Weel, there's some of them gey an' ill to please," observed his lordship.

CHAPTER II—FATHER AND SON

My Lord Justice-Clerk was known to many; the man Adam Weir perhaps to none. He had nothing to explain or to conceal; he sufficed wholly and silently to himself; and that part of our nature which goes out (too often with false coin) to acquire glory or love, seemed in him to be omitted. He did not try to be loved, he did not care to be; it is probable the very thought of it was a stranger to his mind. He was an admired lawyer, a highly unpopular judge; and he looked down upon those who were his inferiors in either distinction, who were lawyers of less grasp or judges not so much detested. In all the rest of his days and doings, not one trace of vanity appeared; and he went on through life with a mechanical movement, as of the unconscious; that was almost august.

He saw little of his son. In the childish maladies with which the boy was troubled, he would make daily inquiries and daily pay him a visit, entering the sick-room with a facetious and appalling countenance, letting off a few perfunctory jests, and going again swiftly, to the patient's relief. Once, a court holiday falling opportunely, my lord had his carriage, and drove the child himself to Hermiston, the customary place of convalescence. It is conceivable he had been more than usually anxious, for that journey always remained in Archie's memory as a thing apart, his father having related to him from beginning to end, and with much detail, three authentic murder cases. Archie went the usual round of other Edinburgh boys, the high school and the college; and Hermiston looked on, or rather looked away, with scarce an affectation of interest in his progress. Daily, indeed, upon a signal after dinner, he was brought in, given nuts and a glass of port, regarded sardonically, sarcastically questioned. "Well, sir, and what have you donn with your book to-day?" my lord might begin, and set him posers in law Latin. To a child just stumbling into Corderius, Papinian and Paul proved quite invincible. But papa had memory of no other. He was not harsh to the little scholar, having a vast fund of patience learned upon the bench, and was at no pains whether to conceal or to express his disappointment. "Well, ye have a long jaunt before ye yet!"

he might observe, yawning, and fall back on his own thoughts (as like as not) until the time came for separation, and my lord would take the decanter and the glass, and be off to the back chamber looking on the Meadows, where he toiled on his cases till the hours were small. There was no "fuller man" on the bench; his memory was marvellous, though wholly legal; if he had to "advise" extempore, none did it better; yet there was none who more earnestly prepared. As he thus watched in the night, or sat at table and forgot the presence of his son, no doubt but he tasted deeply of recondite pleasures. To be wholly devoted to some intellectual exercise is to have succeeded in life; and perhaps only in law and the higher mathematics may this devotion be maintained, suffice to itself without reaction, and find continual rewards without excitement. This atmosphere of his father's sterling industry was the best of Archie's education. Assuredly it did not attract him; assuredly it rather rebutted and depressed. Yet it was still present, unobserved like the ticking of a clock, an arid ideal, a tasteless stimulant in the boy's life.

But Hermiston was not all of one piece. He was, besides, a mighty toper; he could sit at wine until the day dawned, and pass directly from the table to the bench with a steady hand and a clear head. Beyond the third bottle, he showed the plebeian in a larger print; the low, gross accent, the low, foul mirth, grew broader and commoner; he became less formidable, and infinitely more disgusting. Now, the boy had inherited from Jean Rutherford a shivering delicacy, unequally mated with potential violence. In the playing-fields, and amongst his own companions, he repaid a coarse expression with a blow; at his father's table (when the time came for him to join these revels) he turned pale and sickened in silence. Of all the guests whom he there encountered, he had toleration for only one: David Keith Carnegie, Lord Glenalmond. Lord Glenalmond was tall and emaciated, with long features and long delicate hands. He was often compared with the statue of Forbes of Culloden in the Parliament House; and his blue eye, at more than sixty, preserved some of the fire of youth. His exquisite disparity with any of his fellow-guests, his appearance as of an artist and an aristocrat stranded in rude company, riveted the boy's attention; and as curiosity and interest are the things in the world that are the most immediately and certainly rewarded, Lord Glenalmond was attracted by the boy.

240

"And so this is your son, Hermiston?" he asked, laying his hand on Archie's shoulder. "He's getting a big lad."

"Hout!" said the gracious father, "just his mother over again—daurna say boo to a goose!"

But the stranger retained the boy, talked to him, drew him out, found in him a taste for letters, and a fine, ardent, modest, youthful soul; and encouraged him to be a visitor on Sunday evenings in his bare, cold, lonely dining-room, where he sat and read in the isolation of a bachelor grown old in refinement. The beautiful gentleness and grace of the old judge, and the delicacy of his person, thoughts, and language, spoke to Archie's heart in its own tongue. He conceived the ambition to be such another; and, when the day came for him to choose a profession, it was in emulation of Lord Glenalmond, not of Lord Hermiston, that he chose the Bar. Hermiston looked on at this friendship with some secret pride, but openly with the intolerance of scorn. He scarce lost an opportunity to put them down with a rough jape; and, to say truth, it was not difficult, for they were neither of them quick. He had a word of contempt for the whole crowd of poets, painters, fiddlers, and their admirers, the bastard race of amateurs, which was continually on his lips. "Signor Feedle-eerie!" he would say. "O, for Goad's sake, no more of the Signor!"

"You and my father are great friends, are you not?" asked Archie once.

"There is no man that I more respect, Archie," replied Lord Glenalmond. "He is two things of price. He is a great lawyer, and he is upright as the day."

"You and he are so different," said the boy, his eyes dwelling on those of his old friend, like a lover's on his mistress's.

"Indeed so," replied the judge; "very different. And so I fear are you and he. Yet I would like it very ill if my young friend were to misjudge his father. He has all the Roman virtues: Cato and Brutus were such; I think a son's heart might well be proud of such an ancestry of one."

"And I would sooner he were a plaided herd," cried Archie, with sudden bitterness.

"And that is neither very wise, nor I believe entirely true," returned Glenalmond. "Before you are done you will find some of these expressions rise on you like a remorse. They are merely literary and decorative; they do not aptly express your thought, nor is your thought clearly apprehended, and no doubt your father (if he were here) would say, 'Signor Feedle-eerie!'"

With the infinitely delicate sense of youth, Archie avoided the subject from that hour. It was perhaps a pity. Had he but talked—talked freely—let himself gush out in words (the way youth loves to do and should), there might have been no tale to write upon the Weirs of Hermiston. But the shadow of a threat of ridicule sufficed; in the slight tartness of these words he read a prohibition; and it is likely that Glenalmond meant it so.

Besides the veteran, the boy was without confidant or friend. Serious and eager, he came through school and college, and moved among a crowd of the indifferent, in the seclusion of his shyness. He grew up handsome, with an open, speaking countenance, with graceful, youthful ways; he was clever, he took prizes, he shone in the Speculative Society. It should seem he must become the centre of a crowd of friends; but something that was in part the delicacy of his mother, in part the austerity of his father, held him aloof from all. It is a fact, and a strange one, that among his contemporaries Hermiston's son was thought to be a chip of the old block. "You're a friend of Archie Weir's?" said one to Frank Innes; and Innes replied, with his usual flippancy and more than his usual insight: "I know Weir, but I never met Archie." No one had met Archie, a malady most incident to only sons. He flew his private signal, and none heeded it; it seemed he was abroad in a world from which the very hope of intimacy was banished; and he looked round about him on the concourse of his fellow-students, and forward to the trivial days and acquaintances that were to come, without hope or interest.

As time went on, the tough and rough old sinner felt himself drawn to the son of his loins and sole continuator of his new family, with softnesses of sentiment that he could hardly credit and was wholly impotent to express. With a face, voice, and manner trained through forty years to terrify and repel, Rhadamanthus may be great, but he will scarce be engaging. It is a fact that he tried to propitiate Archie, but a fact that cannot be too lightly taken;

242

the attempt was so unconspicuously made, the failure so stoically supported. Sympathy is not due to these steadfast iron natures. If he failed to gain his son's friendship, or even his son's toleration, on he went up the great, bare staircase of his duty, uncheered and undepressed. There might have been more pleasure in his relations with Archie, so much he may have recognised at moments; but pleasure was a by-product of the singular chemistry of life, which only fools expected.

An idea of Archie's attitude, since we are all grown up and have forgotten the days of our youth, it is more difficult to convey. He made no attempt whatsoever to understand the man with whom he dined and breakfasted. Parsimony of pain, glut of pleasure, these are the two alternating ends of youth; and Archie was of the parsimonious. The wind blew cold out of a certain quarter—he turned his back upon it; stayed as little as was possible in his father's presence; and when there, averted his eyes as much as was decent from his father's face. The lamp shone for many hundred days upon these two at table—my lord, ruddy, gloomy, and unreverent; Archie with a potential brightness that was always dimmed and veiled in that society; and there were not, perhaps, in Christendom two men more radically strangers. The father, with a grand simplicity, either spoke of what interested himself, or maintained an unaffected silence. The son turned in his head for some topic that should be quite safe, that would spare him fresh evidences either of my lord's inherent grossness or of the innocence of his inhumanity; treading gingerly the ways of intercourse, like a lady gathering up her skirts in a by-path. If he made a mistake, and my lord began to abound in matter of offence, Archie drew himself up, his brow grew dark, his share of the talk expired; but my lord would faithfully and cheerfully continue to pour out the worst of himself before his silent and offended son.

"Well, it's a poor hert that never rejoices!" he would say, at the conclusion of such a nightmare interview. "But I must get to my plew-stilts." And he would seclude himself as usual in his back room, and Archie go forth into the night and the city quivering with animosity and scorn.

CHAPTER III—IN THE MATTER OF THE HANGING OF DUNCAN JOPP

It chanced in the year 1813 that Archie strayed one day into the Justiciary Court. The macer made room for the son of the presiding judge. In the dock, the centre of men's eyes, there stood a whey-coloured, misbegotten caitiff, Duncan Jopp, on trial for his life. His story, as it was raked out before him in that public scene, was one of disgrace and vice and cowardice, the very nakedness of crime; and the creature heard and it seemed at times as though he understood—as if at times he forgot the horror of the place he stood in, and remembered the shame of what had brought him there. He kept his head bowed and his hands clutched upon the rail; his hair dropped in his eyes and at times he flung it back; and now he glanced about the audience in a sudden fellness of terror, and now looked in the face of his judge and gulped. There was pinned about his throat a piece of dingy flannel; and this it was perhaps that turned the scale in Archie's mind between disgust and pity. The creature stood in a vanishing point; yet a little while, and he was still a man, and had eyes and apprehension; yet a little longer, and with a last sordid piece of pageantry, he would cease to be. And here, in the meantime, with a trait of human nature that caught at the beholder's breath, he was tending a sore throat.

Over against him, my Lord Hermiston occupied the bench in the red robes of criminal jurisdiction, his face framed in the white wig. Honest all through, he did not affect the virtue of impartiality; this was no case for refinement; there was a man to be hanged, he would have said, and he was hanging him. Nor was it possible to see his lordship, and acquit him of gusto in the task. It was plain he gloried in the exercise of his trained faculties, in the clear sight which pierced at once into the joint of fact, in the rude, unvarnished gibes with which he demolished every figment of defence. He took his ease and jested, unbending in that solemn place with some of the freedom of the tavern; and the rag of man with the flannel round his neck was hunted gallowsward with jeers.

Duncan had a mistress, scarce less forlorn and greatly older than himself, who came up, whimpering and curtseying, to add the weight of her betrayal. My lord gave her the oath in his most roaring voice, and added an intolerant warning.

"Mind what ye say now, Janet," said he. "I have an e'e upon ye, I'm ill to jest with."

Presently, after she was tremblingly embarked on her story, "And what made ye do this, ye auld runt?" the Court interposed. "Do ye mean to tell me ye was the panel's mistress?"

"If you please, ma loard," whined the female.

"Godsake! ye made a bonny couple," observed his lordship; and there was something so formidable and ferocious in his scorn that not even the galleries thought to laugh.

The summing up contained some jewels.

"These two peetiable creatures seem to have made up thegither, it's not for us to explain why."—"The panel, who (whatever else he may be) appears to be equally ill set-out in mind and boady."—"Neither the panel nor yet the old wife appears to have had so much common sense as even to tell a lie when it was necessary." And in the course of sentencing, my lord had this obiter dictum: "I have been the means, under God, of haanging a great number, but never just such a disjaskit rascal as yourself." The words were strong in themselves; the light and heat and detonation of their delivery, and the savage pleasure of the speaker in his task, made them tingle in the ears.

When all was over, Archie came forth again into a changed world. Had there been the least redeeming greatness in the crime, any obscurity, any dubiety, perhaps he might have understood. But the culprit stood, with his sore throat, in the sweat of his mortal agony, without defence or excuse: a thing to cover up with blushes: a being so much sunk beneath the zones of sympathy that pity might seem harmless. And the judge had pursued him with a monstrous, relishing gaiety, horrible to be conceived, a trait for nightmares. It is one thing to spear a tiger, another to crush a toad; there are æsthetics even of the slaughter-house; and the loathsomeness of Duncan Jopp enveloped and infected the image of his judge.

Archie passed by his friends in the High Street with incoherent words and gestures. He saw Holyrood in a dream, remembrance of its romance awoke in him and faded; he had a vision of the old radiant stories, of Queen Mary and Prince Charlie, of the hooded stag, of the splendour and crime, the velvet and bright iron of the past; and dismissed them with a cry of pain. He lay and moaned in the Hunter's Bog, and the heavens were dark above him and the grass of the field an offence. "This is my father," he said. "I draw my life from him; the flesh upon my bones is his, the bread I am fed with is the wages of these horrors." He recalled his mother, and ground his forehead in the earth. He thought of flight, and where was he to flee to? of other lives, but was there any life worth living in this den of savage and jeering animals?

The interval before the execution was like a violent dream. He met his father; he would not look at him, he could not speak to him. It seemed there was no living creature but must have been swift to recognise that imminent animosity; but the hide of the Justice-Clerk remained impenetrable. Had my lord been talkative, the truce could never have subsisted; but he was by fortune in one of his humours of sour silence; and under the very guns of his broadside, Archie nursed the enthusiasm of rebellion. It seemed to him, from the top of his nineteen years' experience, as if he were marked at birth to be the perpetrator of some signal action, to set back fallen Mercy, to overthrow the usurping devil that sat, horned and hoofed, on her throne. Seductive Jacobin figments, which he had often refuted at the Speculative, swam up in his mind and startled him as with voices: and he seemed to himself to walk accompanied by an almost tangible presence of new beliefs and duties.

On the named morning he was at the place of execution. He saw the fleering rabble, the flinching wretch produced. He looked on for a while at a certain parody of devotion, which seemed to strip the wretch of his last claim to manhood. Then followed the brutal instant of extinction, and the paltry dangling of the remains like a broken jumping-jack. He had been prepared for something terrible, not for this tragic meanness. He stood a moment silent, and then—"I denounce this God-defying murder," he shouted; and his father, if he must have disclaimed the sentiment, might have owned the stentorian voice with which it was uttered.

Frank Innes dragged him from the spot. The two handsome lads followed the same course of study and recreation, and felt a certain mutual attraction, founded mainly on good looks. It had never gone deep; Frank was by nature a thin, jeering creature, not truly susceptible whether of feeling or inspiring friendship; and the relation between the pair was altogether on the outside, a thing of common knowledge and the pleasantries that spring from a common acquaintance. The more credit to Frank that he was appalled by Archie's outburst, and at least conceived the design of keeping him in sight, and, if possible, in hand, for the day. But Archie, who had just defied—was it God or Satan?—would not listen to the word of a college companion.

"I will not go with you," he said. "I do not desire your company, sir; I would be alone."

"Here, Weir, man, don't be absurd," said Innes, keeping a tight hold upon his sleeve. "I will not let you go until I know what you mean to do with yourself; it's no use brandishing that staff." For indeed at that moment Archie had made a sudden—perhaps a warlike—movement. "This has been the most insane affair; you know it has. You know very well that I'm playing the good Samaritan. All I wish is to keep you quiet."

"If quietness is what you wish, Mr. Innes," said Archie, "and you will promise to leave me entirely to myself, I will tell you so much, that I am going to walk in the country and admire the beauties of nature."

"Honour bright?" asked Frank.

"I am not in the habit of lying, Mr. Innes," retorted Archie. "I have the honour of wishing you good-day."

"You won't forget the Spec.?" asked Innes.

"The Spec.?" said Archie. "O no, I won't forget the Spec."

And the one young man carried his tortured spirit forth of the city and all the day long, by one road and another, in an endless pilgrimage of misery; while the other hastened smilingly to spread the news of Weir's access of

247

insanity, and to drum up for that night a full attendance at the Speculative, where further eccentric developments might certainly be looked for. I doubt if Innes had the least belief in his prediction; I think it flowed rather from a wish to make the story as good and the scandal as great as possible; not from any ill-will to Archie—from the mere pleasure of beholding interested faces. But for all that his words were prophetic. Archie did not forget the Spec.; he put in an appearance there at the due time, and, before the evening was over, had dealt a memorable shock to his companions. It chanced he was the president of the night. He sat in the same room where the Society still meets—only the portraits were not there: the men who afterwards sat for them were then but beginning their career. The same lustre of many tapers shed its light over the meeting; the same chair, perhaps, supported him that so many of us have sat in since. At times he seemed to forget the business of the evening, but even in these periods he sat with a great air of energy and determination. At times he meddled bitterly, and launched with defiance those fines which are the precious and rarely used artillery of the president. He little thought, as he did so, how he resembled his father, but his friends remarked upon it, chuckling. So far, in his high place above his fellow-students, he seemed set beyond the possibility of any scandal; but his mind was made up—he was determined to fulfil the sphere of his offence. He signed to Innes (whom he had just fined, and who just impeached his ruling) to succeed him in the chair, stepped down from the platform, and took his place by the chimney-piece, the shine of many wax tapers from above illuminating his pale face, the glow of the great red fire relieving from behind his slim figure. He had to propose, as an amendment to the next subject in the case-book, "Whether capital punishment be consistent with God's will or man's policy?"

A breath of embarrassment, of something like alarm, passed round the room, so daring did these words appear upon the lips of Hermiston's only son. But the amendment was not seconded; the previous question was promptly moved and unanimously voted, and the momentary scandal smuggled by. Innes triumphed in the fulfilment of his prophecy. He and Archie were now become the heroes of the night; but whereas every one crowded about Innes, when the meeting broke up, but one of all his companions came to speak to

Archie.

"Weir, man! That was an extraordinary raid of yours!" observed this courageous member, taking him confidentially by the arm as they went out.

"I don't think it a raid," said Archie grimly. "More like a war. I saw that poor brute hanged this morning, and my gorge rises at it yet."

"Hut-tut," returned his companion, and, dropping his arm like something hot, he sought the less tense society of others.

Archie found himself alone. The last of the faithful—or was it only the boldest of the curious?—had fled. He watched the black huddle of his fellow-students draw off down and up the street, in whispering or boisterous gangs. And the isolation of the moment weighed upon him like an omen and an emblem of his destiny in life. Bred up in unbroken fear himself, among trembling servants, and in a house which (at the least ruffle in the master's voice) shuddered into silence, he saw himself on the brink of the red valley of war, and measured the danger and length of it with awe. He made a detour in the glimmer and shadow of the streets, came into the back stable lane, and watched for a long while the light burn steady in the Judge's room. The longer he gazed upon that illuminated window-blind, the more blank became the picture of the man who sat behind it, endlessly turning over sheets of process, pausing to sip a glass of port, or rising and passing heavily about his book-lined walls to verify some reference. He could not combine the brutal judge and the industrious, dispassionate student; the connecting link escaped him; from such a dual nature, it was impossible he should predict behaviour; and he asked himself if he had done well to plunge into a business of which the end could not be foreseen? and presently after, with a sickening decline of confidence, if he had done loyally to strike his father? For he had struck him—defied him twice over and before a cloud of witnesses—struck him a public buffet before crowds. Who had called him to judge his father in these precarious and high questions? The office was usurped. It might have become a stranger; in a son—there was no blinking it—in a son, it was disloyal. And now, between these two natures so antipathetic, so hateful to each other, there was depending an unpardonable affront: and the providence of God alone might foresee the manner in which it would be resented by Lord Hermiston.

These misgivings tortured him all night and arose with him in the winter's morning; they followed him from class to class, they made him shrinkingly sensitive to every shade of manner in his companions, they sounded in his ears through the current voice of the professor; and he brought them home with him at night unabated and indeed increased. The cause of this increase lay in a chance encounter with the celebrated Dr. Gregory. Archie stood looking vaguely in the lighted window of a book shop, trying to nerve himself for the approaching ordeal. My lord and he had met and parted in the morning as they had now done for long, with scarcely the ordinary civilities of life; and it was plain to the son that nothing had yet reached the father's ears. Indeed, when he recalled the awful countenance of my lord, a timid hope sprang up in him that perhaps there would be found no one bold enough to carry tales. If this were so, he asked himself, would he begin again? and he found no answer. It was at this moment that a hand was laid upon his arm, and a voice said in his ear, "My dear Mr. Archie, you had better come and see me."

He started, turned round, and found himself face to face with Dr. Gregory. "And why should I come to see you?" he asked, with the defiance of the miserable.

"Because you are looking exceedingly ill," said the doctor, "and you very evidently want looking after, my young friend. Good folk are scarce, you know; and it is not every one that would be quite so much missed as yourself. It is not every one that Hermiston would miss."

And with a nod and a smile, the doctor passed on.

A moment after, Archie was in pursuit, and had in turn, but more roughly, seized him by the arm.

"What do you mean? what did you mean by saying that? What makes you think that Hermis—my father would have missed me?"

The doctor turned about and looked him all over with a clinical eye. A far more stupid man than Dr. Gregory might have guessed the truth;

but ninety-nine out of a hundred, even if they had been equally inclined to kindness, would have blundered by some touch of charitable exaggeration. The doctor was better inspired. He knew the father well; in that white face of intelligence and suffering, he divined something of the son; and he told, without apology or adornment, the plain truth.

"When you had the measles, Mr. Archibald, you had them gey and ill; and I thought you were going to slip between my fingers," he said. "Well, your father was anxious. How did I know it? says you. Simply because I am a trained observer. The sign that I saw him make, ten thousand would have missed; and perhaps—perhaps, I say, because he's a hard man to judge of—but perhaps he never made another. A strange thing to consider! It was this. One day I came to him: 'Hermiston,' said I, 'there's a change.' He never said a word, just glowered at me (if ye'll pardon the phrase) like a wild beast. 'A change for the better,' said I. And I distinctly heard him take his breath."

The doctor left no opportunity for anti-climax; nodding his cocked hat (a piece of antiquity to which he clung) and repeating "Distinctly" with raised eye-brows, he took his departure, and left Archie speechless in the street.

The anecdote might be called infinitely little, and yet its meaning for Archie was immense. "I did not know the old man had so much blood in him." He had never dreamed this sire of his, this aboriginal antique, this adamantine Adam, had even so much of a heart as to be moved in the least degree for another—and that other himself, who had insulted him! With the generosity of youth, Archie was instantly under arms upon the other side: had instantly created a new image of Lord Hermiston, that of a man who was all iron without and all sensibility within. The mind of the vile jester, the tongue that had pursued Duncan Jopp with unmanly insults, the unbeloved countenance that he had known and feared for so long, were all forgotten; and he hastened home, impatient to confess his misdeeds, impatient to throw himself on the mercy of this imaginary character.

He was not to be long without a rude awakening. It was in the gloaming when he drew near the door-step of the lighted house, and was aware of the figure of his father approaching from the opposite side. Little daylight lingered; but on the door being opened, the strong yellow shine of the lamp gushed out upon the landing and shone full on Archie, as he stood, in the old-fashioned observance of respect, to yield precedence. The judge came without haste, stepping stately and firm; his chin raised, his face (as he entered the lamplight) strongly illumined, his mouth set hard. There was never a wink of change in his expression; without looking to the right or left, he mounted the stair, passed close to Archie, and entered the house. Instinctively, the boy, upon his first coming, had made a movement to meet him; instinctively he recoiled against the railing, as the old man swept by him in a pomp of indignation. Words were needless; he knew all—perhaps more than all—and the hour of judgment was at hand.

It is possible that, in this sudden revulsion of hope, and before these symptoms of impending danger, Archie might have fled. But not even that was left to him. My lord, after hanging up his cloak and hat, turned round in the lighted entry, and made him an imperative and silent gesture with his thumb, and with the strange instinct of obedience, Archie followed him into the house.

All dinner-time there reigned over the Judge's table a palpable silence, and as soon as the solids were despatched he rose to his feet.

"M'Killup, tak' the wine into my room," said he; and then to his son: "Archie, you and me has to have a talk."

It was at this sickening moment that Archie's courage, for the first and last time, entirely deserted him. "I have an appointment," said he.

"It'll have to be broken, then," said Hermiston, and led the way into his study.

The lamp was shaded, the fire trimmed to a nicety, the table covered deep with orderly documents, the backs of law books made a frame upon all sides that was only broken by the window and the doors.

For a moment Hermiston warmed his hands at the fire, presenting his back to Archie; then suddenly disclosed on him the terrors of the Hanging Face.

252

"What's this I hear of ye?" he asked.

There was no answer possible to Archie.

"I'll have to tell ye, then," pursued Hermiston. "It seems ye've been skirting against the father that begot ye, and one of his Maijesty's Judges in this land; and that in the public street, and while an order of the Court was being executit. Forbye which, it would appear that ye've been airing your opeenions in a Coallege Debatin' Society"; he paused a moment: and then, with extraordinary bitterness, added: "Ye damned eediot."

"I had meant to tell you," stammered Archie. "I see you are well informed."

"Muckle obleeged to ye," said his lordship, and took his usual seat. "And so you disapprove of Caapital Punishment?" he added.

"I am sorry, sir, I do," said Archie.

"I am sorry, too," said his lordship. "And now, if you please, we shall approach this business with a little more parteecularity. I hear that at the hanging of Duncan Jopp—and, man! ye had a fine client there—in the middle of all the riff-raff of the ceety, ye thought fit to cry out, 'This is a damned murder, and my gorge rises at the man that haangit him.'"

"No, sir, these were not my words," cried Archie.

"What were yer words, then?" asked the Judge.

"I believe I said, 'I denounce it as a murder!'" said the son. "I beg your pardon—a God-defying murder. I have no wish to conceal the truth," he added, and looked his father for a moment in the face.

"God, it would only need that of it next!" cried Hermiston. "There was nothing about your gorge rising, then?"

"That was afterwards, my lord, as I was leaving the Speculative. I said I had been to see the miserable creature hanged, and my gorge rose at it."

"Did ye, though?" said Hermiston. "And I suppose ye knew who

253

haangit him?"

"I was present at the trial, I ought to tell you that, I ought to explain. I ask your pardon beforehand for any expression that may seem undutiful. The position in which I stand is wretched," said the unhappy hero, now fairly face to face with the business he had chosen. "I have been reading some of your cases. I was present while Jopp was tried. It was a hideous business. Father, it was a hideous thing! Grant he was vile, why should you hunt him with a vileness equal to his own? It was done with glee—that is the word—you did it with glee; and I looked on, God help me! with horror."

"You're a young gentleman that doesna approve of Caapital Punishment," said Hermiston. "Weel, I'm an auld man that does. I was glad to get Jopp haangit, and what for would I pretend I wasna? You're all for honesty, it seems; you couldn't even steik your mouth on the public street. What for should I steik mines upon the bench, the King's officer, bearing the sword, a dreid to evil-doers, as I was from the beginning, and as I will be to the end! Mair than enough of it! Heedious! I never gave twa thoughts to heediousness, I have no call to be bonny. I'm a man that gets through with my day's business, and let that suffice."

The ring of sarcasm had died out of his voice as he went on; the plain words became invested with some of the dignity of the Justice-seat.

"It would be telling you if you could say as much," the speaker resumed. "But ye cannot. Ye've been reading some of my cases, ye say. But it was not for the law in them, it was to spy out your faither's nakedness, a fine employment in a son. You're splairging; you're running at lairge in life like a wild nowt. It's impossible you should think any longer of coming to the Bar. You're not fit for it; no splairger is. And another thing: son of mines or no son of mines, you have flung fylement in public on one of the Senators of the Coallege of Justice, and I would make it my business to see that ye were never admitted there yourself. There is a kind of a decency to be observit. Then comes the next of it—what am I to do with ye next? Ye'll have to find some kind of a trade, for I'll never support ye in idleset. What do ye fancy ye'll be fit for? The pulpit? Na, they could never get diveenity into that bloackhead.

Him that the law of man whammles is no likely to do muckle better by the law of God. What would ye make of hell? Wouldna your gorge rise at that? Na, there's no room for splairgers under the fower quarters of John Calvin. What else is there? Speak up. Have ye got nothing of your own?"

"Father, let me go to the Peninsula," said Archie. "That's all I'm fit for—to fight."

"All? quo' he!" returned the Judge. "And it would be enough too, if I thought it. But I'll never trust ye so near the French, you that's so Frenchi-feed."

"You do me injustice there, sir," said Archie. "I am loyal; I will not boast; but any interest I may have ever felt in the French—"

"Have ye been so loyal to me?" interrupted his father.

There came no reply.

"I think not," continued Hermiston. "And I would send no man to be a servant to the King, God bless him! that has proved such a shauchling son to his own faither. You can splairge here on Edinburgh street, and where's the hairm? It doesna play buff on me! And if there were twenty thousand eediots like yourself, sorrow a Duncan Jopp would hang the fewer. But there's no splairging possible in a camp; and if ye were to go to it, you would find out for yourself whether Lord Well'n'ton approves of caapital punishment or not. You a sodger!" he cried, with a sudden burst of scorn. "Ye auld wife, the sodgers would bray at ye like cuddies!"

As at the drawing of a curtain, Archie was aware of some illogicality in his position, and stood abashed. He had a strong impression, besides, of the essential valour of the old gentleman before him, how conveyed it would be hard to say.

"Well, have ye no other proposeetion?" said my lord again.

"You have taken this so calmly, sir, that I cannot but stand ashamed," began Archie.

"I'm nearer voamiting, though, than you would fancy," said my lord.

The blood rose to Archie's brow.

"I beg your pardon, I should have said that you had accepted my affront. . . . I admit it was an affront; I did not think to apologise, but I do, I ask your pardon; it will not be so again, I pass you my word of honour. . . . I should have said that I admired your magnanimity with—this—offender," Archie concluded with a gulp.

"I have no other son, ye see," said Hermiston. "A bonny one I have gotten! But I must just do the best I can wi' him, and what am I to do? If ye had been younger, I would have wheepit ye for this rideeculous exhibeetion. The way it is, I have just to grin and bear. But one thing is to be clearly understood. As a faither, I must grin and bear it; but if I had been the Lord Advocate instead of the Lord Justice-Clerk, son or no son, Mr. Erchibald Weir would have been in a jyle the night."

Archie was now dominated. Lord Hermiston was coarse and cruel; and yet the son was aware of a bloomless nobility, an ungracious abnegation of the man's self in the man's office. At every word, this sense of the greatness of Lord Hermiston's spirit struck more home; and along with it that of his own impotence, who had struck—and perhaps basely struck—at his own father, and not reached so far as to have even nettled him.

"I place myself in your hands without reserve," he said.

"That's the first sensible word I've had of ye the night," said Hermiston. "I can tell ye, that would have been the end of it, the one way or the other; but it's better ye should come there yourself, than what I would have had to hirstle ye. Weel, by my way of it—and my way is the best—there's just the one thing it's possible that ye might be with decency, and that's a laird. Ye'll be out of hairm's way at the least of it. If ye have to rowt, ye can rowt amang the kye; and the maist feck of the caapital punishment ye're like to come across'll be guddling trouts. Now, I'm for no idle lairdies; every man has to work, if it's only at peddling ballants; to work, or to be wheeped, or to be haangit. If I set ye down at Hermiston I'll have to see you work that place the way it has never been workit yet; ye must ken about the sheep like a herd; ye must be my grieve there, and I'll see that I gain by ye. Is that understood?"

"I will do my best," said Archie.

"Well, then, I'll send Kirstie word the morn, and ye can go yourself the day after," said Hermiston. "And just try to be less of an eediot!" he concluded with a freezing smile, and turned immediately to the papers on his desk.

CHAPTER IV—OPINIONS OF THE BENCH

Late the same night, after a disordered walk, Archie was admitted into Lord Glenalmond's dining-room, where he sat with a book upon his knee, beside three frugal coals of fire. In his robes upon the bench, Glenalmond had a certain air of burliness: plucked of these, it was a may-pole of a man that rose unsteadily from his chair to give his visitor welcome. Archie had suffered much in the last days, he had suffered again that evening; his face was white and drawn, his eyes wild and dark. But Lord Glenalmond greeted him without the least mark of surprise or curiosity.

"Come in, come in," said he. "Come in and take a seat. Carstairs" (to his servant), "make up the fire, and then you can bring a bit of supper," and again to Archie, with a very trivial accent: "I was half expecting you," he added.

"No supper," said Archie. "It is impossible that I should eat."

"Not impossible," said the tall old man, laying his hand upon his shoulder, "and, if you will believe me, necessary."

"You know what brings me?" said Archie, as soon as the servant had left the room.

"I have a guess, I have a guess," replied Glenalmond. "We will talk of it presently—when Carstairs has come and gone, and you have had a piece of my good Cheddar cheese and a pull at the porter tankard: not before."

"It is impossible I should eat" repeated Archie.

"Tut, tut!" said Lord Glenalmond. "You have eaten nothing to-day, and I venture to add, nothing yesterday. There is no case that may not be made worse; this may be a very disagreeable business, but if you were to fall sick and die, it would be still more so, and for all concerned—for all concerned."

"I see you must know all," said Archie. "Where did you hear it?"

"In the mart of scandal, in the Parliament House," said Glenalmond. "It runs riot below among the bar and the public, but it sifts up to us upon the bench, and rumour has some of her voices even in the divisions."

Carstairs returned at this moment, and rapidly laid out a little supper; during which Lord Glenalmond spoke at large and a little vaguely on indifferent subjects, so that it might be rather said of him that he made a cheerful noise, than that he contributed to human conversation; and Archie sat upon the other side, not heeding him, brooding over his wrongs and errors.

But so soon as the servant was gone, he broke forth again at once. "Who told my father? Who dared to tell him? Could it have been you?"

"No, it was not me," said the Judge; "although—to be quite frank with you, and after I had seen and warned you—it might have been me—I believe it was Glenkindie."

"That shrimp!" cried Archie.

"As you say, that shrimp," returned my lord; "although really it is scarce a fitting mode of expression for one of the senators of the College of Justice. We were hearing the parties in a long, crucial case, before the fifteen; Creech was moving at some length for an infeftment; when I saw Glenkindie lean forward to Hermiston with his hand over his mouth and make him a secret communication. No one could have guessed its nature from your father: from Glenkindie, yes, his malice sparked out of him a little grossly. But your father, no. A man of granite. The next moment he pounced upon Creech. 'Mr. Creech,' says he, 'I'll take a look of that sasine,' and for thirty minutes after," said Glenalmond, with a smile, "Messrs. Creech and Co. were fighting a pretty up-hill battle, which resulted, I need hardly add, in their total rout. The case was dismissed. No, I doubt if ever I heard Hermiston better inspired. He was literally rejoicing in apicibus juris."

Archie was able to endure no longer. He thrust his plate away and interrupted the deliberate and insignificant stream of talk. "Here," he said, "I have made a fool of myself, if I have not made something worse. Do you judge between us—judge between a father and a son. I can speak to you; it is not like . . . I will tell you what I feel and what I mean to do; and you shall be the judge," he repeated.

"I decline jurisdiction," said Glenalmond, with extreme seriousness. "But, my dear boy, if it will do you any good to talk, and if it will interest you at all to hear what I may choose to say when I have heard you, I am quite at your command. Let an old man say it, for once, and not need to blush: I love you like a son."

There came a sudden sharp sound in Archie's throat. "Ay," he cried, "and there it is! Love! Like a son! And how do you think I love my father?"

"Quietly, quietly," says my lord.

"I will be very quiet," replied Archie. "And I will be baldly frank. I do not love my father; I wonder sometimes if I do not hate him. There's my shame; perhaps my sin; at least, and in the sight of God, not my fault. How was I to love him? He has never spoken to me, never smiled upon me; I do not think he ever touched me. You know the way he talks? You do not talk so, yet you can sit and hear him without shuddering, and I cannot. My soul is sick when he begins with it; I could smite him in the mouth. And all that's nothing. I was at the trial of this Jopp. You were not there, but you must have heard him often; the man's notorious for it, for being—look at my position! he's my father and this is how I have to speak of him—notorious for being a brute and cruel and a coward. Lord Glenalmond, I give you my word, when I came out of that Court, I longed to die—the shame of it was beyond my strength: but I—I—" he rose from his seat and began to pace the room in a disorder. "Well, who am I? A boy, who have never been tried, have never done anything except this twopenny impotent folly with my father. But I tell you, my lord, and I know myself, I am at least that kind of a man—or that kind of a boy, if you prefer it—that I could die in torments rather than that any one should suffer as that scoundrel suffered. Well, and what have I done? I see it now. I have made a fool of myself, as I said in the beginning; and I have gone back, and asked my father's pardon, and placed myself wholly in his hands—and he has sent me to Hermiston," with a wretched smile, "for life, I suppose—and what can I say? he strikes me as having done quite right, and let me off better than I had deserved."

"My poor, dear boy!" observed Glenalmond. "My poor dear and, if you will allow me to say so, very foolish boy! You are only discovering where you are; to one of your temperament, or of mine, a painful discovery. The world was not made for us; it was made for ten hundred millions of men, all different from each other and from us; there's no royal road there, we just have to sclamber and tumble. Don't think that I am at all disposed to be surprised; don't suppose that I ever think of blaming you; indeed I rather admire! But there fall to be offered one or two observations on the case which occur to me and which (if you will listen to them dispassionately) may be the means of inducing you to view the matter more calmly. First of all, I cannot acquit you of a good deal of what is called intolerance. You seem to have been very much offended because your father talks a little sculduddery after dinner, which it is perfectly licit for him to do, and which (although I am not very fond of it myself) appears to be entirely an affair of taste. Your father, I scarcely like to remind you, since it is so trite a commonplace, is older than yourself. At least, he is major and sui juris, and may please himself in the matter of his conversation. And, do you know, I wonder if he might not have as good an answer against you and me? We say we sometimes find him coarse, but I suspect he might retort that he finds us always dull. Perhaps a relevant exception."

He beamed on Archie, but no smile could be elicited.

"And now," proceeded the Judge, "for 'Archibald on Capital Punishment.' This is a very plausible academic opinion; of course I do not and I cannot hold it; but that's not to say that many able and excellent persons have not done so in the past. Possibly, in the past also, I may have a little dipped myself in the same heresy. My third client, or possibly my fourth, was the means of a return in my opinions. I never saw the man I more believed in; I would have put my hand in the fire, I would have gone to the cross for him; and when it came to trial he was gradually pictured before me, by undeniable probation, in the light of so gross, so cold-blooded, and so black-hearted a villain, that I had a mind to have cast my brief upon the table. I was then boiling against

261

the man with even a more tropical temperature than I had been boiling for him. But I said to myself: 'No, you have taken up his case; and because you have changed your mind it must not be suffered to let drop. All that rich tide of eloquence that you prepared last night with so much enthusiasm is out of place, and yet you must not desert him, you must say something.' So I said something, and I got him off. It made my reputation. But an experience of that kind is formative. A man must not bring his passions to the bar—or to the bench," he added.

The story had slightly rekindled Archie's interest. "I could never deny," he began—"I mean I can conceive that some men would be better dead. But who are we to know all the springs of God's unfortunate creatures? Who are we to trust ourselves where it seems that God Himself must think twice before He treads, and to do it with delight? Yes, with delight. *Tigris ut aspera.*"

"Perhaps not a pleasant spectacle," said Glenalmond. "And yet, do you know, I think somehow a great one."

"I've had a long talk with him to-night," said Archie.

"I was supposing so," said Glenalmond.

"And he struck me—I cannot deny that he struck me as something very big," pursued the son. "Yes, he is big. He never spoke about himself; only about me. I suppose I admired him. The dreadful part—"

"Suppose we did not talk about that," interrupted Glenalmond. "You know it very well, it cannot in any way help that you should brood upon it, and I sometimes wonder whether you and I—who are a pair of sentimentalists— are quite good judges of plain men."

"How do you mean?" asked Archie.

"Fair judges, mean," replied Glenalmond. "Can we be just to them? Do we not ask too much? There was a word of yours just now that impressed me a little when you asked me who we were to know all the springs of God's unfortunate creatures. You applied that, as I understood, to capital cases only. But does it—I ask myself—does it not apply all through? Is it any less difficult to judge of a good man or of a half-good man, than of the worst criminal at the bar? And may not each have relevant excuses?"

"Ah, but we do not talk of punishing the good," cried Archie.

"No, we do not talk of it," said Glenalmond. "But I think we do it. Your father, for instance."

"You think I have punished him?" cried Archie.

Lord Glenalmond bowed his head.

"I think I have," said Archie. "And the worst is, I think he feels it! How much, who can tell, with such a being? But I think he does."

"And I am sure of it," said Glenalmond.

"Has he spoken to you, then?" cried Archie.

"O no," replied the judge.

"I tell you honestly," said Archie, "I want to make it up to him. I will go, I have already pledged myself to go to Hermiston. That was to him. And now I pledge myself to you, in the sight of God, that I will close my mouth on capital punishment and all other subjects where our views may clash, for—how long shall I say? when shall I have sense enough?—ten years. Is that well?"

"It is well," said my lord.

"As far as it goes," said Archie. "It is enough as regards myself, it is to lay down enough of my conceit. But as regards him, whom I have publicly insulted? What am I to do to him? How do you pay attentions to a—an Alp like that?"

"Only in one way," replied Glenalmond. "Only by obedience, punctual, prompt, and scrupulous."

"And I promise that he shall have it," answered Archie. "I offer you my hand in pledge of it."

"And I take your hand as a solemnity," replied the judge. "God bless you, my dear, and enable you to keep your promise. God guide you in the true way, and spare your days, and preserve to you your honest heart." At that, he kissed the young man upon the forehead in a gracious, distant, antiquated way; and instantly launched, with a marked change of voice, into another subject. "And now, let us replenish the tankard; and I believe if you will try my Cheddar again, you would find you had a better appetite. The Court has spoken, and the case is dismissed."

"No, there is one thing I must say," cried Archie. "I must say it in justice to himself. I know—I believe faithfully, slavishly, after our talk—he will never ask me anything unjust. I am proud to feel it, that we have that much in common, I am proud to say it to you."

The Judge, with shining eyes, raised his tankard. "And I think perhaps that we might permit ourselves a toast," said he. "I should like to propose the health of a man very different from me and very much my superior—a man from whom I have often differed, who has often (in the trivial expression) rubbed me the wrong way, but whom I have never ceased to respect and, I may add, to be not a little afraid of. Shall I give you his name?"

"The Lord Justice-Clerk, Lord Hermiston," said Archie, almost with gaiety; and the pair drank the toast deeply.

It was not precisely easy to re-establish, after these emotional passages, the natural flow of conversation. But the Judge eked out what was wanting with kind looks, produced his snuff-box (which was very rarely seen) to fill in a pause, and at last, despairing of any further social success, was upon the point of getting down a book to read a favourite passage, when there came a rather startling summons at the front door, and Carstairs ushered in my Lord Glenkindie, hot from a midnight supper. I am not aware that Glenkindie was ever a beautiful object, being short, and gross-bodied, and with an expression of sensuality comparable to a bear's. At that moment, coming in hissing from many potations, with a flushed countenance and blurred eyes, he was strikingly contrasted with the tall, pale, kingly figure of Glenalmond. A rush of confused thought came over Archie—of shame that this was one of his father's elect friends; of pride, that at the least of it Hermiston could carry his liquor; and last of all, of rage, that he should have here under his eyes the man that had betrayed him. And then that too passed away; and he sat quiet, biding his opportunity.

The tipsy senator plunged at once into an explanation with Glenalmond. There was a point reserved yesterday, he had been able to make neither head nor tail of it, and seeing lights in the house, he had just dropped in for a glass of porter—and at this point he became aware of the third person. Archie saw the cod's mouth and the blunt lips of Glenkindie gape at him for a moment, and the recognition twinkle in his eyes.

"Who's this?" said he. "What? is this possibly you, Don Quickshot? And how are ye? And how's your father? And what's all this we hear of you? It seems you're a most extraordinary leveller, by all tales. No king, no parliaments, and your gorge rises at the macers, worthy men! Hoot, toot! Dear, dear me! Your father's son too! Most rideeculous!"

Archie was on his feet, flushing a little at the reappearance of his unhappy figure of speech, but perfectly self-possessed. "My lord—and you, Lord Glenalmond, my dear friend," he began, "this is a happy chance for me, that I can make my confession and offer my apologies to two of you at once."

"Ah, but I don't know about that. Confession? It'll be judeecial, my young friend," cried the jocular Glenkindie. "And I'm afraid to listen to ye. Think if ye were to make me a coanvert!"

"If you would allow me, my lord," returned Archie, "what I have to say is very serious to me; and be pleased to be humorous after I am gone!"

"Remember, I'll hear nothing against the macers!" put in the incorrigible Glenkindie.

But Archie continued as though he had not spoken. "I have played, both yesterday and to-day, a part for which I can only offer the excuse of youth. I was so unwise as to go to an execution; it seems I made a scene at the gallows; not content with which, I spoke the same night in a college society against capital punishment. This is the extent of what I have done, and in case you hear more alleged against me, I protest my innocence. I have expressed my regret already to my father, who is so good as to pass my conduct over—in a degree, and upon the condition that I am to leave my law studies." . . .

CHAPTER V—WINTER ON THE MOORS

I. At Hermiston

The road to Hermiston runs for a great part of the way up the valley of a stream, a favourite with anglers and with midges, full of falls and pools, and shaded by willows and natural woods of birch. Here and there, but at great distances, a byway branches off, and a gaunt farmhouse may be descried above in a fold of the hill; but the more part of the time, the road would be quite empty of passage and the hills of habitation. Hermiston parish is one of the least populous in Scotland; and, by the time you came that length, you would scarce be surprised at the inimitable smallness of the kirk, a dwarfish, ancient place seated for fifty, and standing in a green by the burn-side among two-score gravestones. The manse close by, although no more than a cottage, is surrounded by the brightness of a flower-garden and the straw roofs of bees; and the whole colony, kirk and manse, garden and graveyard, finds harbourage in a grove of rowans, and is all the year round in a great silence broken only by the drone of the bees, the tinkle of the burn, and the bell on Sundays. A mile beyond the kirk the road leaves the valley by a precipitous ascent, and brings you a little after to the place of Hermiston, where it comes to an end in the back-yard before the coach-house. All beyond and about is the great field, of the hills; the plover, the curlew, and the lark cry there; the wind blows as it blows in a ship's rigging, hard and cold and pure; and the hill-tops huddle one behind another like a herd of cattle into the sunset.

The house was sixty years old, unsightly, comfortable; a farmyard and a kitchen-garden on the left, with a fruit wall where little hard green pears came to their maturity about the end of October.

The policy (as who should say the park) was of some extent, but very ill reclaimed; heather and moorfowl had crossed the boundary wall and spread and roosted within; and it would have tasked a landscape gardener to say where policy ended and unpolicied nature began. My lord had been led by the influence of Mr. Sheriff Scott into a considerable design of planting; many acres were accordingly set out with fir, and the little feathery besoms gave a false scale and lent a strange air of a toy-shop to the moors. A great, rooty sweetness of bogs was in the air, and at all seasons an infinite melancholy piping of hill birds. Standing so high and with so little shelter, it was a cold, exposed house, splashed by showers, drenched by continuous rains that made the gutters to spout, beaten upon and buffeted by all the winds of heaven; and the prospect would be often black with tempest, and often white with the snows of winter. But the house was wind and weather proof, the hearths were kept bright, and the rooms pleasant with live fires of peat; and Archie might sit of an evening and hear the squalls bugle on the moorland, and watch the fire prosper in the earthy fuel, and the smoke winding up the chimney, and drink deep of the pleasures of shelter.

Solitary as the place was, Archie did not want neighbours. Every night, if he chose, he might go down to the manse and share a "brewst" of toddy with the minister—a hare-brained ancient gentleman, long and light and still active, though his knees were loosened with age, and his voice broke continually in childish trebles—and his lady wife, a heavy, comely dame, without a word to say for herself beyond good-even and good-day. Harum-scarum, clodpole young lairds of the neighbourhood paid him the compliment of a visit. Young Hay of Romanes rode down to call, on his crop-eared pony; young Pringle of Drumanno came up on his bony grey. Hay remained on the hospitable field, and must be carried to bed; Pringle got somehow to his saddle about 3 A.M., and (as Archie stood with the lamp on the upper doorstep) lurched, uttered a senseless view-holloa, and vanished out of the small circle of illumination like a wraith. Yet a minute or two longer the clatter of his break-neck flight was audible, then it was cut off by the intervening steepness of the hill; and again, a great while after, the renewed beating of phantom horse-hoofs, far in the valley of the Hermiston, showed that the horse at least, if not his rider, was still on the homeward way.

There was a Tuesday club at the "Cross-keys" in Crossmichael, where the young bloods of the country-side congregated and drank deep on a percentage of the expense, so that he was left gainer who should have drunk the most. Archie had no great mind to this diversion, but he took it like a duty laid upon him, went with a decent regularity, did his manfullest with the liquor, held up his head in the local jests, and got home again and was able to put up his horse, to the admiration of Kirstie and the lass that helped her. He dined at Driffel, supped at Windielaws. He went to the new year's ball at Huntsfield and was made welcome, and thereafter rode to hounds with my Lord Muirfell, upon whose name, as that of a legitimate Lord of Parliament, in a work so full of Lords of Session, my pen should pause reverently. Yet the same fate attended him here as in Edinburgh. The habit of solitude tends to perpetuate itself, and an austerity of which he was quite unconscious, and a pride which seemed arrogance, and perhaps was chiefly shyness, discouraged and offended his new companions. Hay did not return more than twice, Pringle never at all, and there came a time when Archie even desisted from the Tuesday Club, and became in all things—what he had had the name of almost from the first—the Recluse of Hermiston. High-nosed Miss Pringle of Drumanno and high-stepping Miss Marshall of the Mains were understood to have had a difference of opinion about him the day after the ball—he was none the wiser, he could not suppose himself to be remarked by these entrancing ladies. At the ball itself my Lord Muirfell's daughter, the Lady Flora, spoke to him twice, and the second time with a touch of appeal, so that her colour rose and her voice trembled a little in his ear, like a passing grace in music. He stepped back with a heart on fire, coldly and not ungracefully excused himself, and a little after watched her dancing with young Drumanno of the empty laugh, and was harrowed at the sight, and raged to himself that this was a world in which it was given to Drumanno to please, and to himself only to stand aside and envy. He seemed excluded, as of right, from the favour of such society—seemed to extinguish mirth wherever he came, and was quick to feel the wound, and desist, and retire into solitude. If he had but understood the figure he presented, and the impression he made on these bright eyes and tender hearts; if he had but guessed that the Recluse of Hermiston, young, graceful, well spoken, but always cold, stirred the maidens of the county with the charm of Byronism when Byronism was new, it may be questioned whether his destiny might not even yet have been modified. It may be questioned, and I think it should be doubted. It was in his horoscope to be parsimonious of pain to himself, or of the chance of pain, even to the avoidance of any opportunity of pleasure; to have a Roman sense of duty, an instinctive aristocracy of manners and taste; to be the son of Adam Weir and Jean Rutherford.

2. Kirstie

Kirstie was now over fifty, and might have sat to a sculptor. Long of limb, and still light of foot, deep-breasted, robust-loined, her golden hair not yet mingled with any trace of silver, the years had but caressed and embellished her. By the lines of a rich and vigorous maternity, she seemed destined to be the bride of heroes and the mother of their children; and behold, by the iniquity of fate, she had passed through her youth alone, and drew near to the confines of age, a childless woman. The tender ambitions that she had received at birth had been, by time and disappointment, diverted into a certain barren zeal of industry and fury of interference. She carried her thwarted ardours into housework, she washed floors with her empty heart. If she could not win the love of one with love, she must dominate all by her temper. Hasty, wordy, and wrathful, she had a drawn quarrel with most of her neighbours, and with the others not much more than armed neutrality. The grieve's wife had been "sneisty"; the sister of the gardener who kept house for him had shown herself "upsitten"; and she wrote to Lord Hermiston about once a year demanding the discharge of the offenders, and justifying the demand by much wealth of detail. For it must not be supposed that the quarrel rested with the wife and did not take in the husband also—or with the gardener's sister, and did not speedily include the gardener himself. As the upshot of all this petty quarrelling and intemperate speech, she was practically excluded (like a lightkeeper on his tower) from the comforts of human association; except with her own indoor drudge, who, being but a lassie and entirely at her mercy, must submit to the shifty weather of "the mistress's" moods without complaint, and be willing to take buffets or caresses according to the temper of the hour. To Kirstie, thus situate and in the Indian summer of her heart, which was slow to submit to age, the gods sent this equivocal good thing of Archie's presence. She had known him in the cradle and paddled him when he misbehaved; and yet, as she had not so much as set eyes on him since he was eleven and had his last serious illness, the tall, slender, refined, and rather melancholy young gentleman of twenty came upon her with the shock of a new acquaintance. He was "Young Hermiston," "the laird himsel'": he had an air of distinctive superiority, a cold straight glance of his black eyes, that abashed the woman's tantrums in the beginning, and therefore the possibility of any quarrel was excluded. He was new, and therefore immediately aroused her curiosity; he was reticent, and kept it awake. And lastly he was dark and she fair, and he was male and she female, the everlasting fountains of interest.

Her feeling partook of the loyalty of a clanswoman, the hero-worship of a maiden aunt, and the idolatry due to a god. No matter what he had asked of her, ridiculous or tragic, she would have done it and joyed to do it. Her passion, for it was nothing less, entirely filled her. It was a rich physical pleasure to make his bed or light his lamp for him when he was absent, to pull off his wet boots or wait on him at dinner when he returned. A young man who should have so doted on the idea, moral and physical, of any woman, might be properly described as being in love, head and heels, and would have behaved himself accordingly. But Kirstie—though her heart leaped at his coming footsteps—though, when he patted her shoulder, her face brightened for the day—had not a hope or thought beyond the present moment and its perpetuation to the end of time. Till the end of time she would have had nothing altered, but still continue delightedly to serve her idol, and be repaid (say twice in the month) with a clap on the shoulder.

I have said her heart leaped—it is the accepted phrase. But rather, when she was alone in any chamber of the house, and heard his foot passing on the corridors, something in her bosom rose slowly until her breath was suspended, and as slowly fell again with a deep sigh, when the steps had passed and she was disappointed of her eyes' desire. This perpetual hunger and thirst of his presence kept her all day on the alert. When he went forth at morning, she would stand and follow him with admiring looks. As it grew late and drew to the time of his return, she would steal forth to a corner of the policy wall and be seen standing there sometimes by the hour together, gazing with shaded eyes, waiting the exquisite and barren pleasure of his view a mile off on the mountains. When at night she had trimmed and gathered the fire, turned down his bed, and laid out his night-gear—when there was no more to be done for the king's pleasure, but to remember him fervently in her usually very tepid prayers, and go to bed brooding upon his perfections, his future career, and what she should give him the next day for dinner—there still remained before her one more opportunity; she was still to take in the tray and say good-night. Sometimes Archie would glance up from his book with a preoccupied nod and a perfunctory salutation which was in truth a dismissal; sometimes—and by degrees more often—the volume would be laid aside, he would meet her coming with a look of relief; and the conversation would be engaged, last out the supper, and be prolonged till the small hours by the waning fire. It was no wonder that Archie was fond of company after his solitary days; and Kirstie, upon her side, exerted all the arts of her vigorous nature to ensnare his attention. She would keep back some piece of news during dinner to be fired off with the entrance of the supper tray, and form as it were the lever de rideau of the evening's entertainment. Once he had heard her tongue wag, she made sure of the result. From one subject to another she moved by insidious transitions, fearing the least silence, fearing almost to give him time for an answer lest it should slip into a hint of separation. Like so many people of her class, she was a brave narrator; her place was on the hearth-rug and she made it a rostrum, mimeing her stories as she told them, fitting them with vital detail, spinning them out with endless "quo' he's" and "quo' she's," her voice sinking into a whisper over the supernatural or the horrific; until she would suddenly spring up in affected surprise, and pointing to the clock, "Mercy, Mr. Archie!" she would say, "whatten a time o' night is this of it! God forgive me for a daft wife!" So it befell, by good management, that she was not only the first to begin these nocturnal conversations, but invariably the first to break them off; so she managed to retire and not to be dismissed.

3. A Border Family

Such an unequal intimacy has never been uncommon in Scotland, where the clan spirit survives; where the servant tends to spend her life in the same service, a helpmeet at first, then a tyrant, and at last a pensioner; where, besides, she is not necessarily destitute of the pride of birth, but is, perhaps, like Kirstie, a connection of her master's, and at least knows the legend of her own family, and may count kinship with some illustrious dead. For that is the mark of the Scot of all classes: that he stands in an attitude towards the past unthinkable to Englishmen, and remembers and cherishes the memory of his forebears, good or bad; and there burns alive in him a sense of identity with the dead even to the twentieth generation. No more characteristic instance could be found than in the family of Kirstie Elliott. They were all, and Kirstie the first of all, ready and eager to pour forth the particulars of their genealogy, embellished with every detail that memory had handed down or fancy fabricated; and, behold! from every ramification of that tree there dangled a halter. The Elliotts themselves have had a chequered history; but these Elliotts deduced, besides, from three of the most unfortunate of the border clans—the Nicksons, the Ellwalds, and the Crozers. One ancestor after another might be seen appearing a moment out of the rain and the hill mist upon his furtive business, speeding home, perhaps, with a paltry booty of lame horses and lean kine, or squealing and dealing death in some moorland feud of the ferrets and the wild cats. One after another closed his obscure adventures in mid-air, triced up to the arm of the royal gibbet or the Baron's dule-tree. For the rusty blunderbuss of Scots criminal justice, which usually hurt nobody but jurymen, became a weapon of precision for the Nicksons, the Ellwalds, and the Crozers. The exhilaration of their exploits seemed to haunt the memories of their descendants alone, and the shame to be forgotten. Pride glowed in their bosoms to publish their relationship to "Andrew Ellwald of the Laverockstanes, called 'Unchancy Dand,' who was justifeed wi' seeven mair of the same name at Jeddart in the days of King James the Sax." In all this tissue of crime and misfortune, the Elliotts of Cauldstaneslap had one boast which must appear legitimate: the males were gallows-birds, born outlaws, petty thieves, and deadly brawlers; but, according to the same tradition, the females were all chaste and faithful. The power of ancestry on the character is not limited to the inheritance of cells. If I buy ancestors by the gross from the benevolence of Lyon King of Arms, my grandson (if he is Scottish) will feel a quickening emulation of their deeds. The men of the Elliotts were proud, lawless, violent as of right, cherishing and prolonging a tradition. In like manner with the women. And the woman, essentially passionate and reckless, who crouched on the rug, in the shine of the peat fire, telling these tales, had cherished through life a wild integrity of virtue.

272

Her father Gilbert had been deeply pious, a savage disciplinarian in the antique style, and withal a notorious smuggler. "I mind when I was a bairn getting mony a skelp and being shoo'd to bed like pou'try," she would say. "That would be when the lads and their bit kegs were on the road. We've had the riffraff of two-three counties in our kitchen, mony's the time, betwix' the twelve and the three; and their lanterns would be standing in the forecourt, ay, a score o' them at once. But there was nae ungodly talk permitted at Cauldstaneslap. My faither was a consistent man in walk and conversation; just let slip an aith, and there was the door to ye! He had that zeal for the Lord, it was a fair wonder to hear him pray, but the family has aye had a gift that way." This father was twice married, once to a dark woman of the old Ellwald stock, by whom he had Gilbert, presently of Cauldstaneslap; and, secondly, to the mother of Kirstie. "He was an auld man when he married her, a fell auld man wi' a muckle voice—you could hear him rowting from the top o' the Kye-skairs," she said; "but for her, it appears she was a perfit wonder. It was gentle blood she had, Mr. Archie, for it was your ain. The country-side gaed gyte about her and her gowden hair. Mines is no to be mentioned wi' it, and there's few weemen has mair hair than what I have, or yet a bonnier colour. Often would I tell my dear Miss Jeannie—that was your mother, dear, she was cruel ta'en up about her hair, it was unco' tender, ye see—'Houts, Miss Jeannie,' I would say, 'just fling your washes and your French dentifrishes in the back o' the fire, for that's the place for them; and awa' down to a burn side, and wash yersel' in cauld hill water, and dry your bonny hair in the caller wind o' the muirs, the way that my mother aye washed hers, and that I have aye made it a practice to have wishen mines— just you do what I tell ye, my dear, and ye'll give me news of it! Ye'll have hair, and routh of hair, a pigtail as thick's my arm,' I said, 'and the bonniest colour like the clear gowden guineas, so as the lads in kirk'll no can keep their eyes off it!' Weel, it lasted out her time, puir thing! I cuttit a lock of it upon her corp that was lying there sae cauld. I'll show it ye some of thir days if ye're good. But, as I was sayin', my mither—"

On the death of the father there remained golden-haired Kirstie, who took service with her distant kinsfolk, the Rutherfords, and black-a-vised Gilbert, twenty years older, who farmed the Cauldstaneslap, married, and

273

begot four sons between 1773 and 1784, and a daughter, like a postscript, in '97, the year of Camperdown and Cape St. Vincent. It seemed it was a tradition in the family to wind up with a belated girl. In 1804, at the age of sixty, Gilbert met an end that might be called heroic. He was due home from market any time from eight at night till five in the morning, and in any condition from the quarrelsome to the speechless, for he maintained to that age the goodly customs of the Scots farmer. It was known on this occasion that he had a good bit of money to bring home; the word had gone round loosely. The laird had shown his guineas, and if anybody had but noticed it, there was an ill-looking, vagabond crew, the scum of Edinburgh, that drew out of the market long ere it was dusk and took the hill-road by Hermiston, where it was not to be believed that they had lawful business. One of the country-side, one Dickieson, they took with them to be their guide, and dear he paid for it! Of a sudden in the ford of the Broken Dykes, this vermin clan fell on the laird, six to one, and him three parts asleep, having drunk hard. But it is ill to catch an Elliott. For a while, in the night and the black water that was deep as to his saddle-girths, he wrought with his staff like a smith at his stithy, and great was the sound of oaths and blows. With that the ambuscade was burst, and he rode for home with a pistol-ball in him, three knife wounds, the loss of his front teeth, a broken rib and bridle, and a dying horse. That was a race with death that the laird rode! In the mirk night, with his broken bridle and his head swimming, he dug his spurs to the rowels in the horse's side, and the horse, that was even worse off than himself, the poor creature! screamed out loud like a person as he went, so that the hills echoed with it, and the folks at Cauldstaneslap got to their feet about the table and looked at each other with white faces. The horse fell dead at the yard gate, the laird won the length of the house and fell there on the threshold. To the son that raised him he gave the bag of money. "Hae," said he. All the way up the thieves had seemed to him to be at his heels, but now the hallucination left him—he saw them again in the place of the ambuscade—and the thirst of vengeance seized on his dying mind. Raising himself and pointing with an imperious finger into the black night from which he had come, he uttered the single command, "Brocken Dykes," and fainted. He had never been loved, but he had been feared in honour. At that sight, at that word, gasped out at them from a toothless and bleeding mouth, the old Elliott spirit awoke with a shout in the four sons. "Wanting the hat," continues my author, Kirstie, whom I but haltingly follow, for she told this tale like one inspired, "wanting guns, for there wasna twa grains o' pouder in the house, wi' nae mair weepons than their sticks into their hands, the fower o' them took the road. Only Hob, and that was the eldest, hunkered at the doorsill where the blood had rin, fyled his hand wi' it—and haddit it up to Heeven in the way o' the auld Border aith. 'Hell shall have her ain again this nicht!' he raired, and rode forth upon his earrand." It was three miles to Broken Dykes, down hill, and a sore road. Kirstie has seen men from Edinburgh dismounting there in plain day to lead their horses. But the four brothers rode it as if Auld Hornie were behind and Heaven in front. Come to the ford, and there was Dickieson. By all tales, he was not dead, but breathed and reared upon his elbow, and cried out to them for help. It was at a graceless face that he asked mercy. As soon as Hob saw, by the glint of the lantern, the eyes shining and the whiteness of the teeth in the man's face, "Damn you!" says he; "ye hae your teeth, hae ye?" and rode his horse to and fro upon that human remnant. Beyond that, Dandie must dismount with the lantern to be their guide; he was the youngest son, scarce twenty at the time. "A' nicht long they gaed in the wet heath and jennipers, and whaur they gaed they neither knew nor cared, but just followed the bluid stains and the footprints o' their faither's murderers. And a' nicht Dandie had his nose to the grund like a tyke, and the ithers followed and spak' naething, neither black nor white. There was nae noise to be heard, but just the sough of the swalled burns, and Hob, the dour yin, risping his teeth as he gaed." With the first glint of the morning they saw they were on the drove road, and at that the four stopped and had a dram to their breakfasts, for they knew that Dand must have guided them right, and the rogues could be but little ahead, hot foot for Edinburgh by the way of the Pentland Hills. By eight o'clock they had word of them—a shepherd had seen four men "uncoly mishandled" go by in the last hour. "That's yin a piece," says Clem, and swung his cudgel. "Five o' them!" says Hob. "God's death, but the faither was a man! And him drunk!" And then there befell them what my author termed "a sair misbegowk," for they were overtaken by a posse of mounted neighbours come to aid in the pursuit. Four sour faces looked on the reinforcement. "The Deil's broughten you!" said Clem, and they rode thenceforward in the rear of the party with hanging heads. Before ten they had found and secured the rogues, and by three of the afternoon, as they rode up the Vennel with their prisoners, they were aware of a concourse of people bearing in their midst something that dripped. "For the boady of the saxt," pursued Kirstie, "wi' his head smashed like a hazelnit, had been a' that nicht in the chairge o' Hermiston Water, and it dunting it on the stanes, and grunding it on the shallows, and flinging the deid thing heels-ower-hurdie at the Fa's o' Spango; and in the first o' the day, Tweed had got a hold o' him and carried him off like a wind, for it was uncoly swalled, and raced wi' him, bobbing under brae-sides, and was long playing with the creature in the drumlie lynns under the castle, and at the hinder end of all cuist him up on the starling of Crossmichael brig. Sae there they were a'thegither at last (for Dickieson had been brought in on a cart long syne), and folk could see what mainner o'man my brither had been that had held his head again sax and saved the siller, and him drunk!" Thus died of honourable injuries and in the savour of fame Gilbert Elliott of the Cauldstaneslap; but his sons had scarce less glory out of the business. Their savage haste, the skill with which Dand had found and followed the trail, the barbarity to the wounded Dickieson (which was like an open secret in the county), and the doom which it was currently supposed they had intended for the others, struck and stirred popular imagination. Some century earlier the last of the minstrels might have fashioned the last of the ballads out of that Homeric fight and chase; but the spirit was dead, or had been reincarnated already in Mr. Sheriff Scott, and the degenerate moorsmen must be content to tell the tale in prose, and to make of the "Four Black Brothers" a unit after the fashion of the "Twelve Apostles" or the "Three Musketeers."

Robert, Gilbert, Clement, and Andrew—in the proper Border diminutives, Hob, Gib, Clem, and Dand Elliott—these ballad heroes, had much in common; in particular, their high sense of the family and the family honour; but they went diverse ways, and prospered and failed in different businesses. According to Kirstie, "they had a' bees in their bonnets but Hob." Hob the laird was, indeed, essentially a decent man. An elder of the Kirk, nobody had heard an oath upon his lips, save perhaps thrice or so at the sheep-washing, since the chase of his father's murderers. The figure he had shown on that eventful night disappeared as if swallowed by a trap. He who had ecstatically dipped his hand in the red blood, he who had ridden down Dickieson, became, from that moment on, a stiff and rather graceless model of the rustic proprieties; cannily profiting by the high war prices, and yearly stowing away a little nest-egg in the bank against calamity; approved of and sometimes consulted by the greater lairds for the massive and placid sense of what he said, when he could be induced to say anything; and particularly valued by the minister, Mr. Torrance, as a right-hand man in the parish, and a model to parents. The transfiguration had been for the moment only; some Barbarossa, some old Adam of our ancestors, sleeps in all of us till the fit circumstance shall call it into action; and, for as sober as he now seemed, Hob had given once for all the measure of the devil that haunted him. He was married, and, by reason of the effulgence of that legendary night, was adored by his wife. He had a mob of little lusty, barefoot children who marched in a caravan the long miles to school, the stages of whose pilgrimage were marked by acts of spoliation and mischief, and who were qualified in the country-side as "fair pests." But in the house, if "faither was in," they were quiet as mice. In short, Hob moved through life in a great peace—the reward of any one who shall have killed his man, with any formidable and figurative circumstance, in the midst of a country gagged and swaddled with civilisation.

It was a current remark that the Elliotts were "guid and bad, like sanguishes"; and certainly there was a curious distinction, the men of business coming alternately with the dreamers. The second brother, Gib, was a weaver by trade, had gone out early into the world to Edinburgh, and come home again with his wings singed. There was an exaltation in his nature which had led him to embrace with enthusiasm the principles of the French Revolution, and had ended by bringing him under the hawse of my Lord Hermiston in that furious onslaught of his upon the Liberals, which sent Muir and Palmer into exile and dashed the party into chaff. It was whispered that my lord, in his great scorn for the movement, and prevailed upon a little by a sense of neighbourliness, had given Gib a hint. Meeting him one day in the Potterrow, my lord had stopped in front of him: "Gib, ye eediot," he had said, "what's this I hear of you? Poalitics, poalitics, poalitics, weaver's poalitics, is the way of it, I hear. If ye arena a'thegither dozened with cediocy, ye'll gang your ways back to Cauldstaneslap, and ca' your loom, and ca' your loom, man!" And Gilbert had taken him at the word and returned, with an expedition almost to be called flight, to the house of his father. The clearest of his inheritance was that family gift of prayer of which Kirstie had boasted; and the baffled politician now turned his attention to religious matters—or, as others said, to heresy and schism. Every Sunday morning he was in Crossmichael, where he had gathered together, one by one, a sect of about a dozen persons, who called themselves "God's Remnant of the True Faithful," or, for short, "God's Remnant." To the profane, they were known as "Gib's Deils." Bailie Sweedie, a noted humorist in the town, vowed that the proceedings always opened to the tune of "The Deil Fly Away with the Exciseman," and that the sacrament was dispensed in the form of hot whisky-toddy; both wicked hits at the evangelist, who had been suspected of smuggling in his youth, and had been overtaken (as the phrase went) on the streets of Crossmichael one Fair day. It was known that every Sunday they prayed for a blessing on the arms of Bonaparte. For this "God's Remnant," as they were "skailing" from the cottage that did duty for a temple, had been repeatedly stoned by the bairns, and Gib himself hooted by a squadron of Border volunteers in which his own brother, Dand, rode in a uniform and with a drawn sword. The "Remnant" were believed, besides, to be "antinomian in principle," which might otherwise have been a serious charge, but the way public opinion then blew it was quite swallowed up and forgotten in the scandal about Bonaparte. For the rest, Gilbert had set up his loom in an outhouse at Cauldstaneslap, where he laboured assiduously six days of the week. His brothers, appalled by his political opinions, and willing to avoid dissension in the household, spoke but little to him; he less to them, remaining absorbed in the study of the Bible and almost constant prayer. The gaunt weaver was dry-nurse at Cauldstaneslap, and the bairns loved him dearly. Except when he was carrying an infant in his arms, he was rarely seen to smile—as, indeed, there were few smilers in that family. When his sister-in-law rallied him, and proposed that he should get a wife and bairns of his own, since he was so fond of them, "I have no clearness of mind upon that point," he would reply. If nobody called him in to dinner, he stayed out. Mrs. Hob, a hard, unsympathetic woman, once tried the experiment.

He went without food all day, but at dusk, as the light began to fail him, he came into the house of his own accord, looking puzzled. "I've had a great gale of prayer upon my speerit," said he. "I canna mind sae muckle's what I had for denner." The creed of God's Remnant was justified in the life of its founder. "And yet I dinna ken," said Kirstie. "He's maybe no more stockfish than his neeghbours! He rode wi' the rest o' them, and had a good stamach to the work, by a' that I hear! God's Remnant! The deil's clavers! There wasna muckle Christianity in the way Hob guided Johnny Dickieson, at the least of it; but Guid kens! Is he a Christian even? He might be a Mahommedan or a Deevil or a Fire-worshipper, for what I ken."

The third brother had his name on a door-plate, no less, in the city of Glasgow, "Mr. Clement Elliott," as long as your arm. In his case, that spirit of innovation which had shown itself timidly in the case of Hob by the admission of new manures, and which had run to waste with Gilbert in subversive politics and heretical religions, bore useful fruit in many ingenious mechanical improvements. In boyhood, from his addiction to strange devices of sticks and string, he had been counted the most eccentric of the family. But that was all by now; and he was a partner of his firm, and looked to die a bailie. He too had married, and was rearing a plentiful family in the smoke and din of Glasgow; he was wealthy, and could have bought out his brother, the cock-laird, six times over, it was whispered; and when he slipped away to Cauldstaneslap for a well-earned holiday, which he did as often as he was able, he astonished the neighbours with his broadcloth, his beaver hat, and the ample plies of his neckcloth. Though an eminently solid man at bottom, after the pattern of Hob, he had contracted a certain Glasgow briskness and aplomb which set him off. All the other Elliotts were as lean as a rake, but Clement was laying on fat, and he panted sorely when he must get into his boots. Dand said, chuckling: "Ay, Clem has the elements of a corporation." "A provost and corporation," returned Clem. And his readiness was much admired.

The fourth brother, Dand, was a shepherd to his trade, and by starts, when he could bring his mind to it, excelled in the business. Nobody could train a dog like Dandie; nobody, through the peril of great storms in the

279

winter time, could do more gallantly. But if his dexterity were exquisite, his diligence was but fitful; and he served his brother for bed and board, and a trifle of pocket-money when he asked for it. He loved money well enough, knew very well how to spend it, and could make a shrewd bargain when he liked. But he preferred a vague knowledge that he was well to windward to any counted coins in the pocket; he felt himself richer so. Hob would expostulate: "I'm an amature herd." Dand would reply, "I'll keep your sheep to you when I'm so minded, but I'll keep my liberty too. Thir's no man can coandescend on what I'm worth." Clein would expound to him the miraculous results of compound interest, and recommend investments. "Ay, man?" Dand would say; "and do you think, if I took Hob's siller, that I wouldna drink it or wear it on the lassies? And, anyway, my kingdom is no of this world. Either I'm a poet or else I'm nothing." Clem would remind him of old age. "I'll die young, like, Robbie Burns," he would say stoutly. No question but he had a certain accomplishment in minor verse. His "Hermiston Burn," with its pretty refrain—

"I love to gang thinking whaur ye gang linking,

Hermiston burn, in the howe;"

his "Auld, auld Elliotts, clay-cauld Elliotts, dour, bauld Elliotts of auld," and his really fascinating piece about the Praying Weaver's Stone, had gained him in the neighbourhood the reputation, still possible in Scotland, of a local bard; and, though not printed himself, he was recognised by others who were and who had become famous. Walter Scott owed to Dandie the text of the "Raid of Wearie" in the Minstrelsy; and made him welcome at his house, and appreciated his talents, such as they were, with all his usual generosity. The Ettrick Shepherd was his sworn crony; they would meet, drink to excess, roar out their lyrics in each other's faces, and quarrel and make it up again till bedtime. And besides these recognitions, almost to be called official, Dandie was made welcome for the sake of his gift through the farmhouses of several contiguous dales, and was thus exposed to manifold temptations which he rather sought than fled. He had figured on the stool of repentance, for once fulfilling to the letter the tradition of his hero and model. His humorous verses to Mr. Torrance on that occasion—"Kenspeckle here my lane I stand"—unfortunately too indelicate for further citation, ran through the country like a fiery cross—they were recited, quoted, paraphrased, and laughed over as far away as Dumfries on the one hand and Dunbar on the other.

These four brothers were united by a close bond, the bond of that mutual admiration—or rather mutual hero-worship—which is so strong among the members of secluded families who have much ability and little culture. Even the extremes admired each other. Hob, who had as much poetry as the tongs, professed to find pleasure in Dand's verses; Clem, who had no more religion than Claverhouse, nourished a heartfelt, at least an open-mouthed, admiration of Gib's prayers; and Dandie followed with relish the rise of Clem's fortunes. Indulgence followed hard on the heels of admiration. The laird, Clem, and Dand, who were Tories and patriots of the hottest quality, excused to themselves, with a certain bashfulness, the radical and revolutionary heresies of Gib. By another division of the family, the laird, Clem, and Gib, who were men exactly virtuous, swallowed the dose of Dand's irregularities as a kind of clog or drawback in the mysterious providence of God affixed to bards, and distinctly probative of poetical genius. To appreciate the simplicity of their mutual admiration it was necessary to hear Clem, arrived upon one of his visits, and dealing in a spirit of continuous irony with the affairs and personalities of that great city of Glasgow where he lived and transacted business. The various personages, ministers of the church, municipal officers, mercantile big-wigs, whom he had occasion to introduce, were all alike denigrated, all served but as reflectors to cast back a flattering side-light on the house of Cauldstaneslap. The Provost, for whom Clem by exception entertained a measure of respect, he would liken to Hob. "He minds me o' the laird there," he would say. "He has some of Hob's grand, whunstane sense, and the same way with him of steiking his mouth when he's no very pleased." And Hob, all unconscious, would draw down his upper lip and produce, as if for comparison, the formidable grimace referred to. The unsatisfactory incumbent of St. Enoch's Kirk was thus briefly dismissed: "If he had but twa fingers o' Gib's, he would waken them up." And Gib, honest man! would look down and secretly smile. Clem was a spy whom they had sent out into the world of men. He had come back with the good

281

news that there was nobody to compare with the Four Black Brothers, no position that they would not adorn, no official that it would not be well they should replace, no interest of mankind, secular or spiritual, which would not immediately bloom under their supervision. The excuse of their folly is in two words: scarce the breadth of a hair divided them from the peasantry. The measure of their sense is this: that these symposia of rustic vanity were kept entirely within the family, like some secret ancestral practice. To the world their serious faces were never deformed by the suspicion of any simper of self-contentment. Yet it was known. "They hae a guid pride o' themsel's!" was the word in the country-side.

Lastly, in a Border story, there should be added their "two-names." Hob was The Laird. "Roy ne puis, prince ne daigne"; he was the laird of Cauldstaneslap—say fifty acres—ipsissimus. Clement was Mr. Elliott, as upon his door-plate, the earlier Dafty having been discarded as no longer applicable, and indeed only a reminder of misjudgment and the imbecility of the public; and the youngest, in honour of his perpetual wanderings, was known by the sobriquet of Randy Dand.

It will be understood that not all this information was communicated by the aunt, who had too much of the family failing herself to appreciate it thoroughly in others. But as time went on, Archie began to observe an omission in the family chronicle.

"Is there not a girl too?" he asked.

"Ay: Kirstie. She was named for me, or my grandmother at least—it's the same thing," returned the aunt, and went on again about Dand, whom she secretly preferred by reason of his gallantries.

"But what is your niece like?" said Archie at the next opportunity.

"Her? As black's your hat! But I dinna suppose she would maybe be what you would ca' ill-looked a'thegither. Na, she's a kind of a handsome jaud—a kind o' gipsy," said the aunt, who had two sets of scales for men and women—or perhaps it would be more fair to say that she had three, and the third and the most loaded was for girls.

"How comes it that I never see her in church?" said Archie.

"'Deed, and I believe she's in Glesgie with Clem and his wife. A heap good she's like to get of it! I dinna say for men folk, but where weemen folk are born, there let them bide. Glory to God, I was never far'er from here than Crossmichael."

In the meanwhile it began to strike Archie as strange, that while she thus sang the praises of her kinsfolk, and manifestly relished their virtues and (I may say) their vices like a thing creditable to herself, there should appear not the least sign of cordiality between the house of Hermiston and that of Cauldstaneslap. Going to church of a Sunday, as the lady housekeeper stepped with her skirts kilted, three tucks of her white petticoat showing below, and her best India shawl upon her back (if the day were fine) in a pattern of radiant dyes, she would sometimes overtake her relatives preceding her more leisurely in the same direction. Gib of course was absent: by skreigh of day he had been gone to Crossmichael and his fellow-heretics; but the rest of the family would be seen marching in open order: Hob and Dand, stiff-necked, straight-backed six-footers, with severe dark faces, and their plaids about their shoulders; the convoy of children scattering (in a state of high polish) on the wayside, and every now and again collected by the shrill summons of the mother; and the mother herself, by a suggestive circumstance which might have afforded matter of thought to a more experienced observer than Archie, wrapped in a shawl nearly identical with Kirstie's, but a thought more gaudy and conspicuously newer. At the sight, Kirstie grew more tall— Kirstie showed her classical profile, nose in air and nostril spread, the pure blood came in her cheek evenly in a delicate living pink.

"A braw day to ye, Mistress Elliott," said she, and hostility and gentility were nicely mingled in her tones. "A fine day, mem," the laird's wife would reply with a miraculous curtsey, spreading the while her plumage—setting off, in other words, and with arts unknown to the mere man, the pattern of her India shawl. Behind her, the whole Cauldstaneslap contingent marched in closer order, and with an indescribable air of being in the presence of the foe; and while Dandie saluted his aunt with a certain familiarity as of one who was well in court, Hob marched on in awful immobility. There appeared upon the face of this attitude in the family the consequences of some dreadful feud. Presumably the two women had been principals in the original encounter, and the laird had probably been drawn into the quarrel by the ears, too late to be included in the present skin-deep reconciliation.

"Kirstie," said Archie one day, "what is this you have against your family?"

"I dinna complean," said Kirstie, with a flush. "I say naething."

"I see you do not—not even good-day to your own nephew," said he.

"I hae naething to be ashamed of," said she. "I can say the Lord's prayer with a good grace. If Hob was ill, or in preeson or poverty, I would see to him blithely. But for curtchying and complimenting and colloguing, thank ye kindly!"

Archie had a bit of a smile: he leaned back in his chair. "I think you and Mrs. Robert are not very good friends," says he slyly, "when you have your India shawls on?"

She looked upon him in silence, with a sparkling eye but an indecipherable expression; and that was all that Archie was ever destined to learn of the battle of the India shawls.

"Do none of them ever come here to see you?" he inquired.

"Mr. Archie," said she, "I hope that I ken my place better. It would be a queer thing, I think, if I was to clamjamfry up your faither's house—that I should say it!—wi' a dirty, black-a-vised clan, no ane o' them it was worth while to mar soap upon but just mysel'! Na, they're all damnifeed wi' the black Ellwalds. I have nae patience wi' black folk." Then, with a sudden consciousness of the case of Archie, "No that it maitters for men sae muckle," she made haste to add, "but there's naebody can deny that it's unwomanly. Long hair is the ornament o' woman only way; we've good warrandise for that—it's in the Bible—and wha can doubt that the Apostle had some gowden-haired lassie in his mind—Apostle and all, for what was he but just a man like yersel'?"

284

CHAPTER VI—A LEAF FROM CHRISTINA'S PSALM-BOOK

Archie was sedulous at church. Sunday after Sunday he sat down and stood up with that small company, heard the voice of Mr. Torrance leaping like an ill-played clarionet from key to key, and had an opportunity to study his moth-eaten gown and the black thread mittens that he joined together in prayer, and lifted up with a reverent solemnity in the act of benediction. Hermiston pew was a little square box, dwarfish in proportion with the kirk itself, and enclosing a table not much bigger than a footstool. There sat Archie, an apparent prince, the only undeniable gentleman and the only great heritor in the parish, taking his ease in the only pew, for no other in the kirk had doors. Thence he might command an undisturbed view of that congregation of solid plaided men, strapping wives and daughters, oppressed children, and uneasy sheep-dogs. It was strange how Archie missed the look of race; except the dogs, with their refined foxy faces and inimitably curling tails, there was no one present with the least claim to gentility. The Cauldstaneslap party was scarcely an exception; Dandie perhaps, as he amused himself making verses through the interminable burden of the service, stood out a little by the glow in his eye and a certain superior animation of face and alertness of body; but even Dandie slouched like a rustic. The rest of the congregation, like so many sheep, oppressed him with a sense of hob-nailed routine, day following day—of physical labour in the open air, oatmeal porridge, peas bannock the somnolent fireside in the evening, and the night-long nasal slumbers in a box-bed. Yet he knew many of them to be shrewd and humorous, men of character, notable women, making a bustle in the world and radiating an influence from their low-browed doors. He knew besides they were like other men; below the crust of custom, rapture found a way; he had heard them beat the timbrel before Bacchus—had heard them shout and carouse over their whisky-toddy; and not the most Dutch-bottomed and severe faces among them all, not even the solemn elders themselves, but were capable of singular gambols at the voice of love. Men drawing near to an end of life's adventurous journey—maids thrilling with fear and curiosity on the threshold of entrance—women who had borne and perhaps buried children, who could remember the clinging of the small dead hands and the patter of the little feet now silent—he marvelled that among all those faces there should be no face of expectation, none that was mobile, none into which the rhythm and poetry of life had entered. "O for a live face," he thought; and at times he had a memory of Lady Flora; and at times he would study the living gallery before him with despair, and would see himself go on to waste his days in that joyless pastoral place, and death come to him, and his grave be dug under the rowans, and the Spirit of the Earth laugh out in a thunder-peal at the huge fiasco.

On this particular Sunday, there was no doubt but that the spring had come at last. It was warm, with a latent shiver in the air that made the warmth only the more welcome. The shallows of the stream glittered and tinkled among bunches of primrose. Vagrant scents of the earth arrested Archie by the way with moments of ethereal intoxication. The grey Quakerish dale was still only awakened in places and patches from the sobriety of its winter colouring; and he wondered at its beauty; an essential beauty of the old earth it seemed to him, not resident in particulars but breathing to him from the whole. He surprised himself by a sudden impulse to write poetry—he did so sometimes, loose, galloping octo-syllabics in the vein of Scott—and when he had taken his place on a boulder, near some fairy falls and shaded by a whip of a tree that was already radiant with new leaves, it still more surprised him that he should have nothing to write. His heart perhaps beat in time to some vast indwelling rhythm of the universe. By the time he came to a corner of the valley and could see the kirk, he had so lingered by the way that the first psalm was finishing. The nasal psalmody, full of turns and trills and graceless graces, seemed the essential voice of the kirk itself upraised in thanksgiving, "Everything's alive," he said; and again cries it aloud, "thank God, everything's alive!" He lingered yet a while in the kirk-yard. A tuft of primroses was blooming hard by the leg of an old black table tombstone, and he stopped to contemplate the random apologue. They stood forth on the cold earth with a trenchancy of contrast; and he was struck with a sense of incompleteness in the day, the season, and the beauty that surrounded him—the chill there was in the warmth, the gross black clods about the opening primroses, the damp earthy smell that was everywhere intermingled with the scents. The voice of the aged Torrance within rose in an ecstasy. And he wondered if Torrance also felt in his old bones the joyous influence of the spring morning; Torrance, or the shadow of what once was Torrance, that must come so soon to lie outside here in the sun and rain with all his rheumatisms, while a new minister stood in his room and thundered from his own familiar pulpit? The pity of it, and something of the chill of the grave, shook him for a moment as he made haste to enter.

He went up the aisle reverently, and took his place in the pew with lowered eyes, for he feared he had already offended the kind old gentleman in the pulpit, and was sedulous to offend no further. He could not follow the prayer, not even the heads of it. Brightnesses of azure, clouds of fragrance, a tinkle of falling water and singing birds, rose like exhalations from some deeper, aboriginal memory, that was not his, but belonged to the flesh on his bones. His body remembered; and it seemed to him that his body was in no way gross, but ethereal and perishable like a strain of music; and he felt for it an exquisite tenderness as for a child, an innocent, full of beautiful instincts and destined to an early death. And he felt for old Torrance—of the many supplications, of the few days—a pity that was near to tears. The prayer ended. Right over him was a tablet in the wall, the only ornament in the roughly masoned chapel—for it was no more; the tablet commemorated, I was about to say the virtues, but rather the existence of a former Rutherford of Hermiston; and Archie, under that trophy of his long descent and local greatness, leaned back in the pew and contemplated vacancy with the shadow of a smile between playful and sad, that became him strangely. Dandie's sister, sitting by the side of Clem in her new Glasgow finery, chose that moment to observe the young laird. Aware of the stir of his entrance, the little formalist had kept her eyes fastened and her face prettily composed during the prayer. It was not hypocrisy, there was no one further from a hypocrite. The girl had been taught to behave: to look up, to look down, to look unconscious, to look seriously impressed in church, and in every conjuncture to look her best. That was the game of female life, and she played it frankly. Archie was the one person in church who was of interest, who was somebody new, reputed eccentric, known to be young, and a laird, and still unseen by Christina.

Small wonder that, as she stood there in her attitude of pretty decency, her mind should run upon him! If he spared a glance in her direction, he should know she was a well-behaved young lady who had been to Glasgow. In reason he must admire her clothes, and it was possible that he should think her pretty. At that her heart beat the least thing in the world; and she proceeded, by way of a corrective, to call up and dismiss a series of fancied pictures of the young man who should now, by rights, be looking at her. She settled on the plainest of them,—a pink short young man with a dish face and no figure, at whose admiration she could afford to smile; but for all that, the consciousness of his gaze (which was really fixed on Torrance and his mittens) kept her in something of a flutter till the word Amen. Even then, she was far too well-bred to gratify her curiosity with any impatience. She resumed her seat languidly—this was a Glasgow touch—she composed her dress, rearranged her nosegay of primroses, looked first in front, then behind upon the other side, and at last allowed her eyes to move, without hurry, in the direction of the Hermiston pew. For a moment, they were riveted. Next she had plucked her gaze home again like a tame bird who should have meditated flight. Possibilities crowded on her; she hung over the future and grew dizzy; the image of this young man, slim, graceful, dark, with the inscrutable half-smile, attracted and repelled her like a chasm. "I wonder, will I have met my fate?" she thought, and her heart swelled.

Torrance was got some way into his first exposition, positing a deep layer of texts as he went along, laying the foundations of his discourse, which was to deal with a nice point in divinity, before Archie suffered his eyes to wander. They fell first of all on Clem, looking insupportably prosperous, and patronising Torrance with the favour of a modified attention, as of one who was used to better things in Glasgow. Though he had never before set eyes on him, Archie had no difficulty in identifying him, and no hesitation in pronouncing him vulgar, the worst of the family. Clem was leaning lazily forward when Archie first saw him. Presently he leaned nonchalantly back; and that deadly instrument, the maiden, was suddenly unmasked in profile. Though not quite in the front of the fashion (had anybody cared!), certain artful Glasgow mantua-makers, and her own inherent taste, had arrayed her to great advantage. Her accoutrement was, indeed, a cause of heart-burning, and almost of scandal, in that infinitesimal kirk company. Mrs. Hob had said her say at Cauldstaneslap. "Daft-like!" she had pronounced it. "A jaiket that'll no meet! Whaur's the sense of a jaiket that'll no button upon you, if it should come to be weet? What do ye ca' thir things? Demmy brokens, d'ye say? They'll be brokens wi' a vengeance or ye can win back! Weel, I have nae thing to do wi' it—it's no good taste." Clem, whose purse had thus metamorphosed his sister, and who was not insensible to the advertisement, had come to the rescue with a "Hoot, woman! What do you ken of good taste that has never been to the ceety?" And Hob, looking on the girl with pleased smiles, as she timidly displayed her finery in the midst of the dark kitchen, had thus ended the dispute: "The cutty looks weel," he had said, "and it's no very like rain. Wear them the day, hizzie; but it's no a thing to make a practice o'." In the breasts of her rivals, coming to the kirk very conscious of white under-linen, and their faces splendid with much soap, the sight of the toilet had raised a storm of varying emotion, from the mere unenvious admiration that was expressed in a long-drawn "Eh!" to the angrier feeling that found vent in an emphatic "Set her up!" Her frock was of straw-coloured jaconet muslin, cut low at the bosom and short at the ankle, so as to display her demi-broquins of Regency violet, crossing with many straps upon a yellow cobweb stocking. According to the pretty fashion in which our grandmothers did not hesitate to appear, and our great-aunts went forth armed for the pursuit and capture of our great-uncles, the dress was drawn up so as to mould the contour of both breasts, and in the nook between, a cairngorm brooch maintained it. Here, too, surely in a very enviable position, trembled the nosegay of primroses. She wore on her shoulders—or rather on her back and not her shoulders, which it scarcely passed—a French coat of sarsenet, tied in front with Margate braces, and of the same colour with her violet shoes. About her face clustered a disorder of dark ringlets, a little garland of yellow French roses surmounted her brow, and the whole was crowned by a village hat of chipped straw. Amongst all the rosy and all the weathered faces that surrounded her in church, she glowed like an open flower—girl and raiment, and the cairngorm that caught the daylight and returned it in a fiery flash, and the threads of bronze and gold that played in her hair.

Archie was attracted by the bright thing like a child. He looked at her again and yet again, and their looks crossed. The lip was lifted from her little teeth. He saw the red blood work vividly under her tawny skin. Her eye, which was great as a stag's, struck and held his gaze. He knew who she must be—Kirstie, she of the harsh diminutive, his housekeeper's niece, the sister of the rustic prophet, Gib—and he found in her the answer to his wishes.

Christina felt the shock of their encountering glances, and seemed to rise, clothed in smiles, into a region of the vague and bright. But the gratification was not more exquisite than it was brief. She looked away abruptly, and immediately began to blame herself for that abruptness. She knew what she should have done, too late—turned slowly with her nose in the air. And meantime his look was not removed, but continued to play upon her like a battery of cannon constantly aimed, and now seemed to isolate her alone with him, and now seemed to uplift her, as on a pillory, before the congregation. For Archie continued to drink her in with his eyes, even as a wayfarer comes to a well-head on a mountain, and stoops his face, and drinks with thirst unassuageable. In the cleft of her little breasts the fiery eye of the topaz and the pale florets of primrose fascinated him. He saw the breasts heave, and the flowers shake with the heaving, and marvelled what should so much discompose the girl. And Christina was conscious of his gaze—saw it, perhaps, with the dainty plaything of an ear that peeped among her ringlets; she was conscious of changing colour, conscious of her unsteady breath. Like a creature tracked, run down, surrounded, she sought in a dozen ways to give herself a countenance. She used her handkerchief—it was a really fine one—then she desisted in a panic: "He would only think I was too warm." She took to reading in the metrical psalms, and then remembered it was sermon-time. Last she put a "sugar-bool" in her mouth, and the next moment repented of the step. It was such a homely-like thing! Mr. Archie would never be eating sweeties in kirk; and, with a palpable effort, she swallowed it whole, and her colour flamed high. At this signal of distress Archie awoke to a sense of his ill-behaviour. What had he been doing? He had been exquisitely rude in church to the niece of his housekeeper; he had stared like a lackey and a libertine at a beautiful and modest girl. It was possible, it was even likely, he would be presented to her after service in the kirk-yard, and then how was he to look? And there was no excuse. He had marked the tokens of her shame, of her increasing indignation, and he was such a fool that he had not understood them. Shame bowed him down, and he looked resolutely at Mr. Torrance; who little supposed, good, worthy man, as he continued to expound justification by faith, what was his true business: to play the part of derivative to a pair of children at the old game of falling in love.

Christina was greatly relieved at first. It seemed to her that she was clothed again. She looked back on what had passed. All would have been right if she had not blushed, a silly fool! There was nothing to blush at, if she had taken a sugar-bool. Mrs. MacTaggart, the elder's wife in St. Enoch's, took them often. And if he had looked at her, what was more natural than that a young gentleman should look at the best-dressed girl in church? And at the same time, she knew far otherwise, she knew there was nothing casual or ordinary in the look, and valued herself on its memory like a decoration. Well, it was a blessing he had found something else to look at! And presently she began to have other thoughts. It was necessary, she fancied, that she should put herself right by a repetition of the incident, better managed. If the wish was father to the thought, she did not know or she would not recognise it. It was simply as a manœuvre of propriety, as something called for to lessen the significance of what had gone before, that she should a second time meet his eyes, and this time without blushing. And at the memory of the blush, she blushed again, and became one general blush burning from head to foot. Was ever anything so indelicate, so forward, done by a girl before? And here she was, making an exhibition of herself before the congregation about nothing! She stole a glance upon her neighbours, and behold! they were steadily indifferent, and Clem had gone to sleep. And still the one idea was becoming more and more potent with her, that in common prudence she must look again before the service ended. Something of the same sort was going forward in the mind of Archie, as he struggled with the load of penitence. So it chanced that, in the flutter of the moment when the last psalm was given out, and Torrance was reading the verse, and the leaves of every psalm-book in church were rustling under busy fingers, two stealthy glances were sent out like antennæ among the pews and on the indifferent and absorbed occupants, and drew timidly nearer to the straight line between Archie and Christina. They met, they lingered together for the least fraction of time, and that was enough. A charge as of electricity passed through Christina, and behold! the leaf of her psalm-book was torn across.

Archie was outside by the gate of the graveyard, conversing with Hob and the minister and shaking hands all round with the scattering congregation, when Clem and Christina were brought up to be presented. The laird took off his hat and bowed to her with grace and respect. Christina made her Glasgow curtsey to the laird, and went on again up the road for Hermiston and Cauldstaneslap, walking fast, breathing hurriedly with a heightened colour, and in this strange frame of mind, that when she was alone she seemed in high happiness, and when any one addressed her she resented it like a contradiction. A part of the way she had the company of some neighbour girls and a loutish young man; never had they seemed so insipid, never had she made herself so disagreeable. But these struck aside to their various destinations or were out-walked and left behind; and when she had driven off with sharp words the proffered convoy of some of her nephews and nieces, she was free to go on alone up Hermiston brae, walking on air, dwelling intoxicated among clouds of happiness. Near to the summit she heard steps behind her, a man's steps, light and very rapid. She knew the foot at once and walked the faster. "If it's me he's wanting, he can run for it," she thought, smiling.

Archie overtook her like a man whose mind was made up.

"Miss Kirstie," he began.

"Miss Christina, if you please, Mr. Weir," she interrupted. "I canna bear the contraction."

"You forget it has a friendly sound for me. Your aunt is an old friend of mine, and a very good one. I hope we shall see much of you at Hermiston?"

"My aunt and my sister-in-law doesna agree very well. Not that I have much ado with it. But still when I'm stopping in the house, if I was to be visiting my aunt, it would not look considerate-like."

"I am sorry," said Archie.

"I thank you kindly, Mr. Weir," she said. "I whiles think myself it's a great peety."

"Ah, I am sure your voice would always be for peace!" he cried.

"I wouldna be too sure of that," she said. "I have my days like other folk, I suppose."

"Do you know, in our old kirk, among our good old grey dames, you made an effect like sunshine."

"Ah, but that would be my Glasgow clothes!"

"I did not think I was so much under the influence of pretty frocks."

She smiled with a half look at him. "There's more than you!" she said. "But you see I'm only Cinderella. I'll have to put all these things by in my trunk; next Sunday I'll be as grey as the rest. They're Glasgow clothes, you see, and it would never do to make a practice of it. It would seem terrible conspicuous."

By that they were come to the place where their ways severed. The old grey moors were all about them; in the midst a few sheep wandered; and they could see on the one hand the straggling caravan scaling the braes in front of them for Cauldstaneslap, and on the other, the contingent from Hermiston bending off and beginning to disappear by detachments into the policy gate. It was in these circumstances that they turned to say farewell, and deliberately exchanged a glance as they shook hands. All passed as it should, genteelly; and in Christina's mind, as she mounted the first steep ascent for Cauldstaneslap, a gratifying sense of triumph prevailed over the recollection of minor lapses and mistakes. She had kilted her gown, as she did usually at that rugged pass; but when she spied Archie still standing and gazing after her, the skirts came down again as if by enchantment. Here was a piece of nicety for that upland parish, where the matrons marched with their coats kilted in the rain, and the lasses walked barefoot to kirk through the dust of summer, and went bravely down by the burn-side, and sat on stones to make a public toilet before entering! It was perhaps an air wafted from Glasgow; or perhaps it marked a stage of that dizziness of gratified vanity, in which the instinctive act passed unperceived. He was looking after! She unloaded her bosom of a prodigious sigh that was all pleasure, and betook herself to run. When she had overtaken the stragglers of her family, she caught up the niece whom she had so recently repulsed, and kissed and slapped her, and drove her away again, and ran after her with pretty cries and laughter. Perhaps she thought the laird might still be looking! But it chanced the little scene came under the view of eyes less favourable; for she overtook Mrs. Hob marching with Clem and Dand.

"You're shürely fey, lass!" quoth Dandie.

"Think shame to yersel', miss!" said the strident Mrs. Hob. "Is this the gait to guide yersel' on the way hame frae kirk? You're shiirely no sponsible the day! And anyway I would mind my guid claes."

"Hoot!" said Christina, and went on before them head in air, treading the rough track with the tread of a wild doe.

She was in love with herself, her destiny, the air of the hills, the benediction of the sun. All the way home, she continued under the intoxication of these sky-scraping spirits. At table she could talk freely of young Hermiston; gave her opinion of him off-hand and with a loud voice, that he was a handsome young gentleman, real well mannered and sensible-like, but it was a pity he looked doleful. Only—the moment after—a memory of his eyes in church embarrassed her. But for this inconsiderable check, all through meal-time she had a good appetite, and she kept them laughing at table, until Gib (who had returned before them from Crossmichael and his separative worship) reproved the whole of them for their levity.

Singing "in to herself" as she went, her mind still in the turmoil of a glad confusion, she rose and tripped upstairs to a little loft, lighted by four panes in the gable, where she slept with one of her nieces. The niece, who followed her, presuming on "Auntie's" high spirits, was flounced out of the apartment with small ceremony, and retired, smarting and half tearful, to bury her woes in the byre among the hay. Still humming, Christina divested herself of her finery, and put her treasures one by one in her great green trunk. The last of these was the psalm-book; it was a fine piece, the gift of Mistress Clem, in distinct old-faced type, on paper that had begun to grow foxy in the warehouse—not by service—and she was used to wrap it in a handkerchief every Sunday after its period of service was over, and bury it end-wise at the head of her trunk. As she now took it in hand the book fell open where the leaf was torn, and she stood and gazed upon that evidence of her bygone discomposure. There returned again the vision of the two brown eyes staring at her, intent and bright, out of that dark corner of the kirk. The whole appearance and attitude, the smile, the suggested gesture of young Hermiston came before her in a flash at the sight of the torn page. "I was surely fey!" she said, echoing the words of Dandie, and at the suggested doom her high spirits deserted her. She flung herself prone upon the bed, and lay there, holding the psalm-book in her hands for hours, for the more part in a mere stupor of unconsenting pleasure and unreasoning fear. The fear was superstitious; there came up again and again in her memory Dandie's ill-omened words, and a hundred grisly and black tales out of the immediate neighbourhood read her a commentary on their force. The pleasure was never realised. You might say the joints of her body thought and remembered, and were gladdened, but her essential self, in the immediate theatre of consciousness, talked feverishly of something else, like a nervous person at a fire. The image that she most complacently dwelt on was that of Miss Christina in her character of the Fair Lass of Cauldstaneslap, carrying all before her in the straw-coloured frock, the violet mantle, and the yellow cobweb stockings. Archie's image, on the other hand, when it presented itself was never welcomed—far less welcomed with any ardour, and it was exposed at times to merciless criticism. In the long vague dialogues she held in her mind, often with imaginary, often with unrealised interlocutors, Archie, if he were referred to at all came in for savage handling. He was described as "looking like a stork," "staring like a caulf," "a face like a ghaist's." "Do you call that manners?" she said; or, "I soon put him in his place." "'Miss Christina, if you please, Mr. Weir!' says I, and just flyped up my skirt tails." With gabble like this she would entertain herself long whiles together, and then her eye would perhaps fall on the torn leaf, and the eyes of Archie would appear again from the darkness of the wall, and the voluble words deserted her, and she would lie still and stupid, and think upon nothing with devotion, and be sometimes raised by a quiet sigh. Had a doctor of medicine come into that loft, he would have diagnosed a healthy, well-developed, eminently vivacious lass lying on her face in a fit of the sulks; not one who had just contracted, or was just contracting, a mortal sickness of the mind which should yet carry her towards death and despair. Had it been a doctor of psychology, he might have been pardoned for divining in the girl a passion of childish vanity, self-love in excelsis, and no more. It is to be understood that I have been painting chaos and describing the inarticulate. Every lineament that appears is too precise, almost every word used too strong. Take a finger-post in the mountains on a day of rolling mists; I have but copied the names that appear upon the pointers, the names of definite and famous cities far distant, and now perhaps basking in sunshine; but Christina remained all these hours, as it were, at the foot of the post itself, not moving, and enveloped in mutable and blinding wreaths of haze.

The day was growing late and the sunbeams long and level, when she sat suddenly up, and wrapped in its handkerchief and put by that psalm-book which had already played a part so decisive in the first chapter of her love-story. In the absence of the mesmerist's eye, we are told nowadays that the head of a bright nail may fill his place, if it be steadfastly regarded. So that torn page had riveted her attention on what might else have been but little, and perhaps soon forgotten; while the ominous words of Dandie—heard, not heeded, and still remembered—had lent to her thoughts, or rather to her mood, a cast of solemnity, and that idea of Fate—a pagan Fate, uncontrolled by any Christian deity, obscure, lawless, and august—moving indissuadably in the affairs of Christian men. Thus even that phenomenon of love at first sight, which is so rare and seems so simple and violent, like a disruption of life's tissue, may be decomposed into a sequence of accidents happily concurring.

She put on a grey frock and a pink kerchief, looked at herself a moment with approval in the small square of glass that served her for a toilet mirror, and went softly downstairs through the sleeping house that resounded with the sound of afternoon snoring. Just outside the door, Dandie was sitting with a book in his hand, not reading, only honouring the Sabbath by a sacred vacancy of mind. She came near him and stood still.

"I'm for off up the muirs, Dandie," she said.

There was something unusually soft in her tones that made him look up. She was pale, her eyes dark and bright; no trace remained of the levity of the morning.

"Ay, lass? Ye'll have yer ups and downs like me, I'm thinkin'," he observed.

"What for do ye say that?" she asked.

"O, for naething," says Dand. "Only I think ye're mair like me than the lave of them. Ye've mair of the poetic temper, tho' Guid kens little enough of the poetic taalent. It's an ill gift at the best. Look at yoursel'. At denner you were all sunshine and flowers and laughter, and now you're like the star of evening on a lake."

She drank in this hackneyed compliment like wine, and it glowed in her veins.

"But I'm saying, Dand"—she came nearer him—"I'm for the muirs. I must have a braith of air. If Clem was to be speiring for me, try and quaiet him, will ye no?"

"What way?" said Dandie. "I ken but the ae way, and that's leein'. I'll say ye had a sair heid, if ye like."

"But I havena," she objected.

"I daursay no," he returned. "I said I would say ye had; and if ye like to nay-say me when ye come back, it'll no mateerially maitter, for my chara'ter's clean gane a'ready past reca'."

"O, Dand, are ye a lecar?" she asked, lingering.

"Folks say sae," replied the bard.

"Wha says sae?" she pursued.

"Them that should ken the best," he responded. "The lassies, for ane."

"But, Dand, you would never lee to me?" she asked.

"I'll leave that for your pairt of it, ye girzie," said he. "Ye'll lee to me fast eneuch, when ye hae gotten a jo. I'm tellin' ye and it's true; when you have a jo, Miss Kirstie, it'll be for guid and ill. I ken: I was made that way mysel', but the deil was in my luck! Here, gang awa wi' ye to your muirs, and let me be; I'm in an hour of inspiraution, ye upsetting tawpie!"

But she clung to her brother's neighbourhood, she knew not why.

"Will ye no gie's a kiss, Dand?" she said. "I aye likit ye fine."

He kissed her and considered her a moment; he found something strange in her. But he was a libertine through and through, nourished equal contempt and suspicion of all womankind, and paid his way among them habitually with idle compliments.

"Gae wa' wi' ye!" said he. "Ye're a dentie baby, and be content wi' that!"

That was Dandie's way; a kiss and a comfit to Jenny—a bawbee and my blessing to Jill—and goodnight to the whole clan of ye, my dears! When anything approached the serious, it became a matter for men, he both thought and said. Women, when they did not absorb, were only children to be shoo'd away. Merely in his character of connoisseur, however, Dandie glanced carelessly after his sister as she crossed the meadow. "The brat's no that bad!" he thought with surprise, for though he had just been paying her compliments, he had not really looked at her. "Hey! what's yon?" For the grey dress was cut with short sleeves and skirts, and displayed her trim strong legs clad in pink stockings of the same shade as the kerchief she wore round her shoulders, and that shimmered as she went. This was not her way in undress; he knew her ways and the ways of the whole sex in the country-side, no one better; when they did not go barefoot, they wore stout "rig and furrow" woollen hose of an invisible blue mostly, when they were not black outright; and Dandie, at sight of this daintiness, put two and two together. It was a silk handkerchief, then they would be silken hose; they matched—then the whole outfit was a present of Clem's, a costly present, and not something to be worn through bog and briar, or on a late afternoon of Sunday. He whistled. "My denty May, either your heid's fair turned, or there's some ongoings!" he observed, and dismissed the subject.

She went slowly at first, but ever straighter and faster for the

Cauldstaneslap, a pass among the hills to which the farm owed its name. The Slap opened like a doorway between two rounded hillocks; and through this ran the short cut to Hermiston. Immediately on the other side it went down through the Deil's Hags, a considerable marshy hollow of the hill tops, full of springs, and crouching junipers, and pools where the black peat-water slumbered. There was no view from here. A man might have sat upon the Praying Weaver's stone a half century, and seen none but the Cauldstaneslap children twice in the twenty-four hours on their way to the school and back again, an occasional shepherd, the irruption of a clan of sheep, or the birds who haunted about the springs, drinking and shrilly piping. So, when she had once passed the Slap, Kirstie was received into seclusion. She looked back a last time at the farm. It still lay deserted except for the figure of Dandie, who was now seen to be scribbling in his lap, the hour of expected inspiration having come to him at last. Thence she passed rapidly through the morass, and came to the farther end of it, where a sluggish burn discharges, and the path for Hermiston accompanies it on the beginning of its downward path. From this corner a wide view was opened to her of the whole stretch of braes upon the other side, still sallow and in places rusty with the winter, with the path marked boldly, here and there by the burn-side a tuft of birches, and— two miles off as the crow flies—from its enclosures and young plantations, the windows of Hermiston glittering in the western sun.

Here she sat down and waited, and looked for a long time at these far-away bright panes of glass. It amused her to have so extended a view, she thought. It amused her to see the house of Hermiston—to see "folk"; and there was an indistinguishable human unit, perhaps the gardener, visibly sauntering on the gravel paths.

By the time the sun was down and all the easterly braes lay plunged in clear shadow, she was aware of another figure coming up the path at a most unequal rate of approach, now half running, now pausing and seeming to hesitate. She watched him at first with a total suspension of thought. She held her thought as a person holds his breathing. Then she consented to recognise him. "He'll no be coming here, he canna be; it's no possible." And there began to grow upon her a subdued choking suspense. He was coming; his hesitations had quite ceased, his step grew firm and swift; no doubt remained; and the question loomed up before her instant: what was she to do? It was all very well to say that her brother was a laird himself: it was all very well to speak of casual intermarriages and to count cousinship, like Auntie Kirstie. The difference in their social station was trenchant; propriety, prudence, all that she had ever learned, all that she knew, bade her flee. But on the other hand the cup of life now offered to her was too enchanting. For one moment, she saw the question clearly, and definitely made her choice. She stood up and showed herself an instant in the gap relieved upon the sky line; and the next, fled trembling and sat down glowing with excitement on the Weaver's stone. She shut her eyes, seeking, praying for composure. Her hand shook in her lap, and her mind was full of incongruous and futile speeches. What was there to make a work about? She could take care of herself, she supposed! There was no harm in seeing the laird. It was the best thing that could happen. She would mark a proper distance to him once and for all. Gradually the wheels of her nature ceased to go round so madly, and she sat in passive expectation, a quiet, solitary figure in the midst of the grey moss. I have said she was no hypocrite, but here I am at fault. She never admitted to herself that she had come up the hill to look for Archie. And perhaps after all she did not know, perhaps came as a stone falls. For the steps of love in the young, and especially in girls, are instinctive and unconscious.

In the meantime Archie was drawing rapidly near, and he at least was consciously seeking her neighbourhood. The afternoon had turned to ashes in his mouth; the memory of the girl had kept him from reading and drawn him as with cords; and at last, as the cool of the evening began to come on, he had taken his hat and set forth, with a smothered ejaculation, by the moor path to Cauldstaneslap. He had no hope to find her; he took the off chance without expectation of result and to relieve his uneasiness. The greater was his surprise, as he surmounted the slope and came into the hollow of the Deil's Hags, to see there, like an answer to his wishes, the little womanly figure in the grey dress and the pink kerchief sitting little, and low, and lost, and acutely solitary, in these desolate surroundings and on the weather-beaten stone of the dead weaver. Those things that still smacked of winter were all rusty about her, and those things that already relished of the spring had put forth the tender and lively colours of the season. Even in the unchanging face of the death-stone, changes were to be remarked; and in the channeled lettering, the moss began to renew itself in jewels of green. By an afterthought that was a stroke of art, she had turned up over her head the back of the kerchief; so that it now framed becomingly her vivacious and yet pensive face. Her feet were gathered under her on the one side, and she leaned on her bare arm, which showed out strong and round, tapered to a slim wrist, and shimmered in the fading light.

Young Hermiston was struck with a certain chill. He was reminded that he now dealt in serious matters of life and death. This was a grown woman he was approaching, endowed with her mysterious potencies and attractions, the treasury of the continued race, and he was neither better nor worse than the average of his sex and age. He had a certain delicacy which had preserved him hitherto unspotted, and which (had either of them guessed it) made him a more dangerous companion when his heart should be really stirred. His throat was dry as he came near; but the appealing sweetness of her smile stood between them like a guardian angel.

For she turned to him and smiled, though without rising. There was a shade in this cavalier greeting that neither of them perceived; neither he, who simply thought it gracious and charming as herself; nor yet she, who did not observe (quick as she was) the difference between rising to meet the laird, and remaining seated to receive the expected admirer.

"Are ye stepping west, Hermiston?" said she, giving him his territorial name after the fashion of the country-side.

"I was," said he, a little hoarsely, "but I think I will be about the end of my stroll now. Are you like me, Miss Christina? The house would not hold me. I came here seeking air."

He took his seat at the other end of the tombstone and studied her, wondering what was she. There was infinite import in the question alike for her and him.

"Ay," she said. "I couldna bear the roof either. It's a habit of mine to come up here about the gloaming when it's quaiet and caller."

"It was a habit of my mother's also," he said gravely. The recollection half startled him as he expressed it. He looked around. "I have scarce been here since. It's peaceful," he said, with a long breath.

"It's no like Glasgow," she replied. "A weary place, yon Glasgow! But what a day have I had for my homecoming, and what a bonny evening!"

"Indeed, it was a wonderful day," said Archie. "I think I will remember it years and years until I come to die. On days like this—I do not know if you feel as I do—but everything appears so brief, and fragile, and exquisite, that I am afraid to touch life. We are here for so short a time; and all the old people before us—Rutherfords of Hermiston, Elliotts of the Cauldstaneslap—that were here but a while since riding about and keeping up a great noise in this quiet corner—making love too, and marrying—why, where are they now? It's deadly commonplace, but, after all, the commonplaces are the great poetic truths."

He was sounding her, semi-consciously, to see if she could understand him; to learn if she were only an animal the colour of flowers, or had a soul in her to keep her sweet. She, on her part, her means well in hand, watched, womanlike, for any opportunity to shine, to abound in his humour, whatever that might be. The dramatic artist, that lies dormant or only half awake in most human beings, had in her sprung to his feet in a divine fury, and chance had served her well. She looked upon him with a subdued twilight look that became the hour of the day and the train of thought; earnestness shone through her like stars in the purple west; and from the great but controlled upheaval of her whole nature there passed into her voice, and rang in her lightest words, a thrill of emotion.

"Have you mind of Dand's song?" she answered. "I think he'll have been trying to say what you have been thinking."

"No, I never heard it," he said. "Repeat it to me, can you?"

"It's nothing wanting the tune," said Kirstie.

"Then sing it me," said he.

"On the Lord's Day? That would never do, Mr. Weir!"

"I am afraid I am not so strict a keeper of the Sabbath, and there is no one in this place to hear us, unless the poor old ancient under the stone."

"No that I'm thinking that really," she said. "By my way of thinking, it's just as serious as a psalm. Will I sooth it to ye, then?"

"If you please," said he, and, drawing near to her on the tombstone, prepared to listen.

She sat up as if to sing. "I'll only can sooth it to ye," she explained. "I wouldna like to sing out loud on the Sabbath. I think the birds would carry news of it to Gilbert," and she smiled. "It's about the Elliotts," she continued, "and I think there's few bonnier bits in the book-poets, though Dand has never got printed yet."

And she began, in the low, clear tones of her half voice, now sinking almost to a whisper, now rising to a particular note which was her best, and which Archie learned to wait for with growing emotion:—

"O they rade in the rain, in the days that are gane,

In the rain and the wind and the lave,

They shoutit in the ha' and they routit on the hill,

But they're a' quaitit noo in the grave.

Auld, auld Elliotts, clay-cauld Elliotts, dour, bauld Elliotte of auld!"

All the time she sang she looked steadfastly before her, her knees straight, her hands upon her knee, her head cast back and up. The expression was admirable throughout, for had she not learned it from the lips and under the criticism of the author? When it was done, she turned upon Archie a face softly bright, and eyes gently suffused and shining in the twilight, and his heart rose and went out to her with boundless pity and sympathy. His question was answered. She was a human being tuned to a sense of the tragedy of life; there were pathos and music and a great heart in the girl.

He arose instinctively, she also; for she saw she had gained a point, and scored the impression deeper, and she had wit enough left to flee upon a victory. They were but commonplaces that remained to be exchanged, but the low, moved voices in which they passed made them sacred in the memory. In the falling greyness of the evening he watched her figure winding through the morass, saw it turn a last time and wave a hand, and then pass through the Slap; and it seemed to him as if something went along with her out of the deepest of his heart. And something surely had come, and come to dwell there. He had retained from childhood a picture, now half obliterated by the passage of time and the multitude of fresh impressions, of his mother telling him, with the fluttered earnestness of her voice, and often with dropping tears, the tale of the "Praying Weaver," on the very scene of his brief tragedy and long repose. And now there was a companion piece; and he beheld, and he should behold for ever, Christina perched on the same tomb, in the grey colours of the evening, gracious, dainty, perfect as a flower, and she also singing—

"Of old, unhappy far off things,

And battles long ago,"

of their common ancestors now dead, of their rude wars composed, their weapons buried with them, and of these strange changelings, their descendants, who lingered a little in their places, and would soon be gone also, and perhaps sung of by others at the gloaming hour. By one of the unconscious arts of tenderness the two women were enshrined together in his memory. Tears, in that hour of sensibility, came into his eyes indifferently at the thought of either; and the girl, from being something merely bright and shapely, was caught up into the zone of things serious as life and death and his dead mother. So that in all ways and on either side, Fate played his game artfully with this poor pair of children. The generations were prepared, the pangs were made ready, before the curtain rose on the dark drama.

In the same moment of time that she disappeared from Archie, there opened before Kirstie's eyes the cup-like hollow in which the farm lay. She saw, some five hundred feet below her, the house making itself bright with candles, and this was a broad hint to her to hurry. For they were only kindled on a Sabbath night with a view to that family worship which rounded in the incomparable tedium of the day and brought on the relaxation of supper. Already she knew that Robert must be within-sides at the head of the table, "waling the portions"; for it was Robert in his quality of family priest and judge, not the gifted Gilbert, who officiated. She made good time accordingly down the steep ascent, and came up to the door panting as the three younger brothers, all roused at last from slumber, stood together in the cool and the dark of the evening with a fry of nephews and nieces about them, chatting and awaiting the expected signal. She stood back; she had no mind to direct attention to her late arrival or to her labouring breath.

"Kirstie, ye have shaved it this time, my lass?" said Clem. "Whaur were ye?"

"O, just taking a dander by mysel'," said Kirstie.

And the talk continued on the subject of the American War, without further reference to the truant who stood by them in the covert of the dusk, thrilling with happiness and the sense of guilt.

The signal was given, and the brothers began to go in one after another, amid the jostle and throng of Hob's children.

Only Dandie, waiting till the last, caught Kirstie by the arm. "When did ye begin to dander in pink hosen, Mistress Elliott?" he whispered slyly.

She looked down; she was one blush. "I maun have forgotten to change them," said she; and went into prayers in her turn with a troubled mind, between anxiety as to whether Dand should have observed her yellow stockings at church, and should thus detect her in a palpable falsehood, and shame that she had already made good his prophecy. She remembered the words of it, how it was to be when she had gotten a jo, and that that would be for good and evil. "Will I have gotten my jo now?" she thought with a secret rapture.

And all through prayers, where it was her principal business to conceal the pink stockings from the eyes of the indifferent Mrs. Hob—and all through supper, as she made a feint of eating and sat at the table radiant and constrained—and again when she had left them and come into her chamber, and was alone with her sleeping niece, and could at last lay aside the armour of society—the same words sounded within her, the same profound note of happiness, of a world all changed and renewed, of a day that had been passed in Paradise, and of a night that was to be heaven opened. All night she seemed to be conveyed smoothly upon a shallow stream of sleep and waking, and through the bowers of Beulah; all night she cherished to her heart that exquisite hope; and if, towards morning, she forgot it a while in a more profound unconsciousness, it was to catch again the rainbow thought with her first moment of awaking.

CHAPTER VII—ENTER MEPHISTOPHELES

Two days later a gig from Crossmichael deposited Frank Innes at the doors of Hermiston. Once in a way, during the past winter, Archie, in some acute phase of boredom, had written him a letter. It had contained something in the nature of an invitation or a reference to an invitation—precisely what, neither of them now remembered. When Innes had received it, there had been nothing further from his mind than to bury himself in the moors with Archie; but not even the most acute political heads are guided through the steps of life with unerring directness. That would require a gift of prophecy which has been denied to man. For instance, who could have imagined that, not a month after he had received the letter, and turned it into mockery, and put off answering it, and in the end lost it, misfortunes of a gloomy cast should begin to thicken over Frank's career? His case may be briefly stated. His father, a small Morayshire laird with a large family, became recalcitrant and cut off the supplies; he had fitted himself out with the beginnings of quite a good law library, which, upon some sudden losses on the turf, he had been obliged to sell before they were paid for; and his bookseller, hearing some rumour of the event, took out a warrant for his arrest. Innes had early word of it, and was able to take precautions. In this immediate welter of his affairs, with an unpleasant charge hanging over him, he had judged it the part of prudence to be off instantly, had written a fervid letter to his father at Inverauld, and put himself in the coach for Crossmichael. Any port in a storm! He was manfully turning his back on the Parliament House and its gay babble, on porter and oysters, the race-course and the ring; and manfully prepared, until these clouds should have blown by, to share a living grave with Archie Weir at Hermiston.

To do him justice, he was no less surprised to be going than Archie was to see him come; and he carried off his wonder with an infinitely better grace.

"Well, here I am!" said he, as he alighted. "Pylades has come to Orestes at last. By the way, did you get my answer? No? How very provoking! Well, here I am to answer for myself, and that's better still."

"I am very glad to see you, of course," said Archie. "I make you heartily welcome, of course. But you surely have not come to stay, with the Courts still sitting; is that not most unwise?"

"Damn the Courts!" says Frank. "What are the Courts to friendship and a little fishing?"

And so it was agreed that he was to stay, with no term to the visit but the term which he had privily set to it himself—the day, namely, when his father should have come down with the dust, and he should be able to pacify the bookseller. On such vague conditions there began for these two young men (who were not even friends) a life of great familiarity and, as the days drew on, less and less intimacy. They were together at meal times, together o' nights when the hour had come for whisky-toddy; but it might have been noticed (had there been any one to pay heed) that they were rarely so much together by day. Archie had Hermiston to attend to, multifarious activities in the hills, in which he did not require, and had even refused, Frank's escort. He would be off sometimes in the morning and leave only a note on the breakfast table to announce the fact; and sometimes, with no notice at all, he would not return for dinner until the hour was long past. Innes groaned under these desertions; it required all his philosophy to sit down to a solitary breakfast with composure, and all his unaffected good-nature to be able to greet Archie with friendliness on the more rare occasions when he came home late for dinner.

"I wonder what on earth he finds to do, Mrs. Elliott?" said he one morning, after he had just read the hasty billet and sat down to table.

"I suppose it will be business, sir," replied the housekeeper drily, measuring his distance off to him by an indicated curtsy.

"But I can't imagine what business!" he reiterated.

"I suppose it will be his business," retorted the austere Kirstie.

He turned to her with that happy brightness that made the charm of his disposition, and broke into a peal of healthy and natural laughter.

"Well played, Mrs. Elliott!" he cried; and the housekeeper's face relaxed into the shadow of an iron smile. "Well played indeed!" said he. "But you must not be making a stranger of me like that. Why, Archie and I were at the High School together, and we've been to college together, and we were going to the Bar together, when—you know! Dear, dear me! what a pity that was! A life spoiled, a fine young fellow as good as buried here in the wilderness with rustics; and all for what? A frolic, silly, if you like, but no more. God, how good your scones are, Mrs. Elliott!"

"They're no mines, it was the lassie made them," said Kirstie; "and, saving your presence, there's little sense in taking the Lord's name in vain about idle vivers that you fill your kyte wi'."

"I daresay you're perfectly right, ma'am," quoth the imperturbable Frank. "But as I was saying, this is a pitiable business, this about poor Archie; and you and I might do worse than put our heads together, like a couple of sensible people, and bring it to an end. Let me tell you, ma'am, that Archie is really quite a promising young man, and in my opinion he would do well at the Bar. As for his father, no one can deny his ability, and I don't fancy any one would care to deny that he has the deil's own temper—"

"If you'll excuse me, Mr. Innes, I think the lass is crying on me," said Kirstie, and flounced from the room.

"The damned, cross-grained, old broomstick!" ejaculated Innes.

In the meantime, Kirstie had escaped into the kitchen, and before her vassal gave vent to her feelings.

"Here, ettercap! Ye'll have to wait on yon Innes! I canna haud myself in. 'Puir Erchie!' I'd 'puir Erchie' him, if I had my way! And Hermiston with the deil's ain temper! God, let him take Hermiston's scones out of his mouth first. There's no a hair on ayther o' the Weirs that hasna mair spunk and dirdum to it than what he has in his hale dwaibly body! Settin' up his snash to me! Let him gang to the black toon where he's mebbe wantit—birling in a curricle—wi' pimatum on his heid—making a mess o' himsel' wi' nesty hizzies—a fair disgrace!" It was impossible to hear without admiration Kirstie's graduated disgust, as she brought forth, one after another, these somewhat baseless charges. Then she remembered her immediate purpose, and turned again on her fascinated auditor. "Do ye no hear me, tawpie? Do ye no hear what I'm tellin' ye? Will I have to shoo ye in to him? If I come to attend to ye, mistress!" And the maid fled the kitchen, which had become practically dangerous, to attend on Innes' wants in the front parlour.

Tantaene irae? Has the reader perceived the reason? Since Frank's coming there were no more hours of gossip over the supper tray! All his blandishments were in vain; he had started handicapped on the race for Mrs. Elliott's favour.

But it was a strange thing how misfortune dogged him in his efforts to be genial. I must guard the reader against accepting Kirstie's epithets as evidence; she was more concerned for their vigour than for their accuracy. Dwaibly, for instance; nothing could be more calumnious. Frank was the very picture of good looks, good humour, and manly youth. He had bright eyes with a sparkle and a dance to them, curly hair, a charming smile, brilliant teeth, an admirable carriage of the head, the look of a gentleman, the address of one accustomed to please at first sight and to improve the impression. And with all these advantages, he failed with every one about Hermiston; with the silent shepherd, with the obsequious grieve, with the groom who was also the ploughman, with the gardener and the gardener's sister—a pious, down-hearted woman with a shawl over her ears—he failed equally and flatly. They did not like him, and they showed it. The little maid, indeed, was an exception; she admired him devoutly, probably dreamed of him in her private hours; but she was accustomed to play the part of silent auditor to Kirstie's tirades and silent recipient of Kirstie's buffets, and she had learned not only to be a very capable girl of her years, but a very secret and prudent one besides. Frank was thus conscious that he had one ally and sympathiser in the midst of that general union of disfavour that surrounded, watched, and waited on him in the house of Hermiston; but he had little comfort or society from that alliance, and the demure little maid (twelve on her last birthday) preserved her own counsel, and tripped on his service, brisk, dumbly responsive, but inexorably unconversational. For the others, they were beyond hope and beyond endurance. Never had a young Apollo been cast among such rustic barbarians. But perhaps the cause of his ill-success lay in one trait which was habitual and unconscious with him, yet diagnostic of the man. It was his practice to approach any one person at the expense of some one else. He offered you an alliance against the some one else; he flattered you by slighting him; you were drawn into a small intrigue against him before you knew how. Wonderful are the virtues of this process generally; but Frank's mistake was in the choice of the some one else. He was not politic in that; he listened to the voice of irritation. Archie had offended him at first by what he had felt to be rather a dry reception, had offended him since by his frequent absences. He was besides the one figure continually present in Frank's eye; and it was to his immediate dependants that Frank could offer the snare of his sympathy. Now the truth is that the Weirs, father and son, were surrounded by a posse of strenuous loyalists. Of my lord they were vastly proud. It was a distinction in itself to be one of the vassals of the "Hanging Judge," and his gross, formidable joviality was far from unpopular in the neighbourhood of his home. For Archie they had, one and all, a sensitive affection and respect which recoiled from a word of belittlement.

Nor was Frank more successful when he went farther afield. To the Four Black Brothers, for instance, he was antipathetic in the highest degree. Hob thought him too light, Gib too profane. Clem, who saw him but for a day or two before he went to Glasgow, wanted to know what the fule's business was, and whether he meant to stay here all session time! "Yon's a drone," he pronounced. As for Dand, it will be enough to describe their first meeting, when Frank had been whipping a river and the rustic celebrity chanced to come along the path.

"I'm told you're quite a poet," Frank had said.

"Wha tell't ye that, mannie?" had been the unconciliating answer.

"O, everybody!" says Frank.

"God! Here's fame!" said the sardonic poet, and he had passed on his way.

Come to think of it, we have here perhaps a truer explanation of Frank's failures. Had he met Mr. Sheriff Scott he could have turned a neater compliment, because Mr. Scott would have been a friend worth making. Dand, on the other hand, he did not value sixpence, and he showed it even while he tried to flatter. Condescension is an excellent thing, but it is strange how one-sided the pleasure of it is! He who goes fishing among the Scots peasantry with condescension for a bait will have an empty basket by evening.

In proof of this theory Frank made a great success of it at the Crossmichael Club, to which Archie took him immediately on his arrival; his own last appearance on that scene of gaiety. Frank was made welcome there at once, continued to go regularly, and had attended a meeting (as the members ever after loved to tell) on the evening before his death. Young Hay and young Pringle appeared again. There was another supper at Windiclaws, another dinner at Driffel; and it resulted in Frank being taken to the bosom of the county people as unreservedly as he had been repudiated by the country folk. He occupied Hermiston after the manner of an invader in a conquered capital. He was perpetually issuing from it, as from a base, to toddy parties, fishing parties, and dinner parties, to which Archie was not invited, or to which Archie would not go. It was now that the name of The Recluse became general for the young man. Some say that Innes invented it; Innes, at least, spread it abroad.

"How's all with your Recluse to-day?" people would ask.

"O, reclusing away!" Innes would declare, with his bright air of saying something witty; and immediately interrupt the general laughter which he had provoked much more by his air than his words, "Mind you, it's all very well laughing, but I'm not very well pleased. Poor Archie is a good fellow, an excellent fellow, a fellow I always liked. I think it small of him to take his little disgrace so hard, and shut himself up. 'Grant that it is a ridiculous story, painfully ridiculous,' I keep telling him. 'Be a man! Live it down, man!' But not he. Of course, it's just solitude, and shame, and all that. But I confess I'm beginning to fear the result. It would be all the pities in the world if a really promising fellow like Weir was to end ill. I'm seriously tempted to write to Lord Hermiston, and put it plainly to him."

"I would if I were you," some of his auditors would say, shaking the head, sitting bewildered and confused at this new view of the matter, so deftly indicated by a single word. "A capital idea!" they would add, and wonder at the aplomb and position of this young man, who talked as a matter of course of writing to Hermiston and correcting him upon his private affairs.

And Frank would proceed, sweetly confidential: "I'll give you an idea, now. He's actually sore about the way that I'm received and he's left out in the county—actually jealous and sore. I've rallied him and I've reasoned with him, told him that every one was most kindly inclined towards him, told him even that I was received merely because I was his guest. But it's no use. He will neither accept the invitations he gets, nor stop brooding about the ones where he's left out. What I'm afraid of is that the wound's ulcerating. He had always one of those dark, secret, angry natures—a little underhand and plenty of bile—you know the sort. He must have inherited it from the Weirs, whom I suspect to have been a worthy family of weavers somewhere; what's the cant phrase?—sedentary occupation. It's precisely the kind of character to go wrong in a false position like what his father's made for him, or he's making for himself, whichever you like to call it. And for my part, I think it a disgrace," Frank would say generously.

Presently the sorrow and anxiety of this disinterested friend took shape. He began in private, in conversations of two, to talk vaguely of bad habits and low habits. "I must say I'm afraid he's going wrong altogether," he would say. "I'll tell you plainly, and between ourselves, I scarcely like to stay there any longer; only, man, I'm positively afraid to leave him alone. You'll see, I shall be blamed for it later on. I'm staying at a great sacrifice. I'm hindering my chances at the Bar, and I can't blind my eyes to it. And what I'm afraid of is that I'm going to get kicked for it all round before all's done. You see, nobody believes in friendship nowadays."

"Well, Innes," his interlocutor would reply, "it's very good of you, I must say that. If there's any blame going, you'll always be sure of my good word, for one thing."

"Well," Frank would continue, "candidly, I don't say it's pleasant. He has a very rough way with him; his father's son, you know. I don't say he's rude—of course, I couldn't be expected to stand that—but he steers very near the wind. No, it's not pleasant; but I tell ye, man, in conscience I don't think it would be fair to leave him. Mind you, I don't say there's anything actually wrong. What I say is that I don't like the looks of it, man!" and he would press the arm of his momentary confidant.

In the early stages I am persuaded there was no malice. He talked but for the pleasure of airing himself. He was essentially glib, as becomes the young advocate, and essentially careless of the truth, which is the mark of the young ass; and so he talked at random. There was no particular bias, but that one which is indigenous and universal, to flatter himself and to please and interest the present friend. And by thus milling air out of his mouth, he had presently built up a presentation of Archie which was known and talked of in all corners of the county. Wherever there was a residential house and a walled garden, wherever there was a dwarfish castle and a park, wherever a quadruple cottage by the ruins of a peel-tower showed an old family going down, and wherever a handsome villa with a carriage approach and a shrubbery marked the coming up of a new one—probably on the wheels of machinery—Archie began to be regarded in the light of a dark, perhaps a vicious mystery, and the future developments of his career to be looked for with uneasiness and confidential whispering. He had done something disgraceful, my dear. What, was not precisely known, and that good kind young man, Mr. Innes, did his best to make light of it. But there it was. And Mr. Innes was very anxious about him now; he was really uneasy, my dear; he was positively wrecking his own prospects because he dared not leave him alone. How wholly we all lie at the mercy of a single prater, not needfully with any malign purpose! And if a man but talks of himself in the right spirit, refers to his virtuous actions by the way, and never applies to them the name of virtue, how easily his evidence is accepted in the court of public opinion!

All this while, however, there was a more poisonous ferment at work between the two lads, which came late indeed to the surface, but had modified and magnified their dissensions from the first. To an idle, shallow, easy-going customer like Frank, the smell of a mystery was attractive. It gave his mind something to play with, like a new toy to a child; and it took him on the weak side, for like many young men coming to the Bar, and before they had been tried and found wanting, he flattered himself he was a fellow of unusual quickness and penetration. They knew nothing of Sherlock Holmes in those days, but there was a good deal said of Talleyrand. And if you could have caught Frank off his guard, he would have confessed with a smirk that, if he resembled any one, it was the Marquis de Talleyrand-Perigord. It was on the occasion of Archie's first absence that this interest took root. It was vastly deepened when Kirstie resented his curiosity at breakfast, and that same afternoon there occurred another scene which clinched the business. He was fishing Swingleburn, Archie accompanying him, when the latter looked at his watch.

"Well, good-bye," said he. "I have something to do. See you at dinner."

"Don't be in such a hurry," cries Frank. "Hold on till I get my rod up. I'll go with you; I'm sick of flogging this ditch."

And he began to reel up his line.

Archie stood speechless. He took a long while to recover his wits under this direct attack; but by the time he was ready with his answer, and the angle was almost packed up, he had become completely Weir, and the hanging face gloomed on his young shoulders. He spoke with a laboured composure, a laboured kindness even; but a child could see that his mind was made up.

"I beg your pardon, Innes; I don't want to be disagreeable, but let us understand one another from the beginning. When I want your company, I'll let you know."

"O!" cries Frank, "you don't want my company, don't you?"

"Apparently not just now," replied Archie. "I even indicated to you when I did, if you'll remember—and that was at dinner. If we two fellows are to live together pleasantly—and I see no reason why we should not—it can only be by respecting each other's privacy. If we begin intruding—"

"O, come! I'll take this at no man's hands. Is this the way you treat a guest and an old friend?" cried Innes.

"Just go home and think over what I said by yourself," continued Archie, "whether it's reasonable, or whether it's really offensive or not; and let's meet at dinner as though nothing had happened, I'll put it this way, if you like— that I know my own character, that I'm looking forward (with great pleasure, I assure you) to a long visit from you, and that I'm taking precautions at the first. I see the thing that we—that I, if you like—might fall out upon, and I step in and obsto principiis. I wager you five pounds you'll end by seeing that I mean friendliness, and I assure you, Francie, I do," he added, relenting.

Bursting with anger, but incapable of speech, Innes shouldered his rod, made a gesture of farewell, and strode off down the burn-side. Archie watched him go without moving. He was sorry, but quite unashamed. He hated to be inhospitable, but in one thing he was his father's son. He had a strong sense that his house was his own and no man else's; and to lie at a guest's mercy was what he refused. He hated to seem harsh. But that was Frank's lookout. If Frank had been commonly discreet, he would have been decently courteous. And there was another consideration. The secret he was protecting was not his own merely; it was hers: it belonged to that inexpressible she who was fast taking possession of his soul, and whom he would soon have defended at the cost of burning cities. By the time he had watched Frank as far as the Swingleburn-foot, appearing and disappearing in the tarnished heather, still stalking at a fierce gait but already dwindled in the distance into less than the smallness of Lilliput, he could afford to smile at the occurrence. Either Frank would go, and that would be a relief—or he would continue to stay, and his host must continue to endure him. And Archie was now free—by devious paths, behind hillocks and in the hollow of burns—to make for the trysting-place where Kirstie, cried about by the curlew and the plover, waited and burned for his coming by the Covenanter's stone.

Innes went off down-hill in a passion of resentment, easy to be understood, but which yielded progressively to the needs of his situation. He cursed Archie for a cold-hearted, unfriendly, rude, rude dog; and himself still more passionately for a fool in having come to Hermiston when he might have sought refuge in almost any other house in Scotland. But the step once taken, was practically irretrievable. He had no more ready money to go anywhere else; he would have to borrow from Archie the next club-night; and ill as he thought of his host's manners, he was sure of his practical generosity. Frank's resemblance to Talleyrand strikes me as imaginary; but at least not Talleyrand himself could have more obediently taken his lesson from the facts. He met Archie at dinner without resentment, almost with cordiality. You must take your friends as you find them, he would have said. Archie couldn't help being his father's son, or his grandfather's, the hypothetical weaver's, grandson. The son of a hunks, he was still a hunks at heart, incapable of true generosity and consideration; but he had other qualities with which Frank could divert himself in the meanwhile, and to enjoy which it was necessary that Frank should keep his temper.

So excellently was it controlled that he awoke next morning with his head full of a different, though a cognate subject. What was Archie's little game? Why did he shun Frank's company? What was he keeping secret? Was he keeping tryst with somebody, and was it a woman? It would be a good joke and a fair revenge to discover. To that task he set himself with a great deal of patience, which might have surprised his friends, for he had been always credited not with patience so much as brilliancy; and little by little, from one point to another, he at last succeeded in piecing out the situation. First he remarked that, although Archie set out in all the directions of the compass, he always came home again from some point between the south and west. From the study of a map, and in consideration of the great expanse of untenanted moorland running in that direction towards the sources of the Clyde, he laid his finger on Cauldstaneslap and two other neighbouring farms, Kingsmuirs and Polintarf. But it was difficult to advance farther. With his rod for a pretext, he vainly visited each of them in turn; nothing was to be seen suspicious about this trinity of moorland settlements. He would have tried to follow Archie, had it been the least possible, but the nature of the land precluded the idea. He did the next best, ensconced himself in a quiet corner, and pursued his movements with a telescope. It was equally in vain, and he soon wearied of his futile vigilance, left the telescope at home, and had almost given the matter up in despair, when, on the twenty-seventh day of his visit, he was suddenly confronted with the person whom he sought. The first Sunday

Kirstie had managed to stay away from kirk on some pretext of indisposition, which was more truly modesty; the pleasure of beholding Archie seeming too sacred, too vivid for that public place. On the two following, Frank had himself been absent on some of his excursions among the neighbouring families. It was not until the fourth, accordingly, that Frank had occasion to set eyes on the enchantress. With the first look, all hesitation was over. She came with the Cauldstaneslap party; then she lived at Cauldstaneslap. Here was Archie's secret, here was the woman, and more than that—though I have need here of every manageable attenuation of language—with the first look, he had already entered himself as rival. It was a good deal in pique, it was a little in revenge, it was much in genuine admiration: the devil may decide the proportions! I cannot, and it is very likely that Frank could not.

"Mighty attractive milkmaid," he observed, on the way home.

"Who?" said Archie.

"O, the girl you're looking at—aren't you? Forward there on the road. She came attended by the rustic bard; presumably, therefore, belongs to his exalted family. The single objection! for the four black brothers are awkward customers. If anything were to go wrong, Gib would gibber, and Clem would prove inclement; and Dand fly in danders, and Hob blow up in gobbets. It would be a Helliott of a business!"

"Very humorous, I am sure," said Archie.

"Well, I am trying to be so," said Frank. "It's none too easy in this place, and with your solemn society, my dear fellow. But confess that the milkmaid has found favour in your eyes, or resign all claim to be a man of taste."

"It is no matter," returned Archie.

But the other continued to look at him, steadily and quizzically, and his colour slowly rose and deepened under the glance, until not impudence itself could have denied that he was blushing. And at this Archie lost some of his control. He changed his stick from one hand to the other, and—"O, for God's sake, don't be an ass!" he cried.

"Ass? That's the retort delicate without doubt," says Frank. "Beware of the homespun brothers, dear. If they come into the dance, you'll see who's an ass. Think now, if they only applied (say) a quarter as much talent as I have applied to the question of what Mr. Archie does with his evening hours, and why he is so unaffectedly nasty when the subject's touched on—"

"You are touching on it now," interrupted Archie with a wince.

"Thank you. That was all I wanted, an articulate confession," said Frank.

"I beg to remind you—" began Archie.

But he was interrupted in turn. "My dear fellow, don't. It's quite needless. The subject's dead and buried."

And Frank began to talk hastily on other matters, an art in which he was an adept, for it was his gift to be fluent on anything or nothing. But although Archie had the grace or the timidity to suffer him to rattle on, he was by no means done with the subject. When he came home to dinner, he was greeted with a sly demand, how things were looking "Cauldstaneslap ways." Frank took his first glass of port out after dinner to the toast of Kirstie, and later in the evening he returned to the charge again.

"I say, Weir, you'll excuse me for returning again to this affair. I've been thinking it over, and I wish to beg you very seriously to be more careful. It's not a safe business. Not safe, my boy," said he.

"What?" said Archie.

"Well, it's your own fault if I must put a name on the thing; but really, as a friend, I cannot stand by and see you rushing head down into these dangers. My dear boy," said he, holding up a warning cigar, "consider! What is to be the end of it?"

"The end of what?"—Archie, helpless with irritation, persisted in this dangerous and ungracious guard.

"Well, the end of the milkmaid; or, to speak more by the card, the end of Miss Christina Elliott of the Cauldstaneslap."

"I assure you," Archie broke out, "this is all a figment of your imagination.

There is nothing to be said against that young lady; you have no right to introduce her name into the conversation."

"I'll make a note of it," said Frank. "She shall henceforth be nameless, nameless, nameless, Grigalach! I make a note besides of your valuable testimony to her character. I only want to look at this thing as a man of the world. Admitted she's an angel—but, my good fellow, is she a lady?"

This was torture to Archie. "I beg your pardon," he said, struggling to be composed, "but because you have wormed yourself into my confidence—"

"O, come!" cried Frank. "Your confidence? It was rosy but unconsenting. Your confidence, indeed? Now, look! This is what I must say, Weir, for it concerns your safety and good character, and therefore my honour as your friend. You say I wormed myself into your confidence. Wormed is good. But what have I done? I have put two and two together, just as the parish will be doing tomorrow, and the whole of Tweeddale in two weeks, and the black brothers—well, I won't put a date on that; it will be a dark and stormy morning! Your secret, in other words, is poor Poll's. And I want to ask of you as a friend whether you like the prospect? There are two horns to your dilemma, and I must say for myself I should look mighty ruefully on either. Do you see yourself explaining to the four Black Brothers? or do you see yourself presenting the milkmaid to papa as the future lady of Hermiston? Do you? I tell you plainly, I don't!"

Archie rose. "I will hear no more of this," he said, in a trembling voice.

But Frank again held up his cigar. "Tell me one thing first. Tell me if this is not a friend's part that I am playing?"

"I believe you think it so," replied Archle. "I can go as far as that. I can do so much justice to your motives. But I will hear no more of it. I am going to bed."

"That's right, Weir," said Frank heartily. "Go to bed and think over it; and I say, man, don't forget your prayers! I don't often do the moral—don't go in for that sort of thing—but when I do there's one thing sure, that I mean it."

So Archie marched off to bed, and Frank sat alone by the table for another hour or so, smiling to himself richly. There was nothing vindictive in his nature; but, if revenge came in his way, it might as well be good, and the thought of Archie's pillow reflections that night was indescribably sweet to him. He felt a pleasant sense of power. He looked down on Archie as on a very little boy whose strings he pulled—as on a horse whom he had backed and bridled by sheer power of intelligence, and whom he might ride to glory or the grave at pleasure. Which was it to be? He lingered long, relishing the details of schemes that he was too idle to pursue. Poor cork upon a torrent, he tasted that night the sweets of omnipotence, and brooded like a deity over the strands of that intrigue which was to shatter him before the summer waned.

CHAPTER VIII—A NOCTURNAL VISIT

Kirstie had many causes of distress. More and more as we grow old—and yet more and more as we grow old and are women, frozen by the fear of age—we come to rely on the voice as the single outlet of the soul. Only thus, in the curtailment of our means, can we relieve the straitened cry of the passion within us; only thus, in the bitter and sensitive shyness of advancing years, can we maintain relations with those vivacious figures of the young that still show before us and tend daily to become no more than the moving wall-paper of life. Talk is the last link, the last relation. But with the end of the conversation, when the voice stops and the bright face of the listener is turned away, solitude falls again on the bruised heart. Kirstie had lost her "cannie hour at e'en"; she could no more wander with Archie, a ghost if you will, but a happy ghost, in fields Elysian. And to her it was as if the whole world had fallen silent; to him, but an unremarkable change of amusements. And she raged to know it. The effervescency of her passionate and irritable nature rose within her at times to bursting point.

This is the price paid by age for unseasonable ardours of feeling. It must have been so for Kirstie at any time when the occasion chanced; but it so fell out that she was deprived of this delight in the hour when she had most need of it, when she had most to say, most to ask, and when she trembled to recognise her sovereignty not merely in abeyance but annulled. For, with the clairvoyance of a genuine love, she had pierced the mystery that had so long embarrassed Frank. She was conscious, even before it was carried out, even on that Sunday night when it began, of an invasion of her rights; and a voice told her the invader's name. Since then, by arts, by accident, by small things observed, and by the general drift of Archie's humour, she had passed beyond all possibility of doubt. With a sense of justice that Lord Hermiston might have envied, she had that day in church considered and admitted the attractions of the younger Kirstie; and with the profound humanity and sentimentality of her nature, she had recognised the coming of fate. Not thus would she have chosen. She had seen, in imagination, Archie wedded to some tall, powerful, and rosy heroine of the golden locks, made in her own image, for whom she would have strewed the bride-bed with delight; and now she could have wept to see the ambition falsified. But the gods had pronounced, and her doom was otherwise.

She lay tossing in bed that night, besieged with feverish thoughts. There were dangerous matters pending, a battle was toward, over the fate of which she hung in jealousy, sympathy, fear, and alternate loyalty and disloyalty to either side. Now she was reincarnated in her niece, and now in Archie. Now she saw, through the girl's eyes, the youth on his knees to her, heard his persuasive instances with a deadly weakness, and received his overmastering caresses. Anon, with a revulsion, her temper raged to see such utmost favours of fortune and love squandered on a brat of a girl, one of her own house, using her own name—a deadly ingredient—and that "didna ken her ain mind an' was as black's your hat." Now she trembled lest her deity should plead in vain, loving the idea of success for him like a triumph of nature; anon, with returning loyalty to her own family and sex, she trembled for Kirstie and the credit of the Elliotts. And again she had a vision of herself, the day over for her old-world tales and local gossip, bidding farewell to her last link with life and brightness and love; and behind and beyond, she saw but the blank butt-end where she must crawl to die. Had she then come to the lees? she, so great, so beautiful, with a heart as fresh as a girl's and strong as womanhood? It could not be, and yet it was so; and for a moment her bed was horrible to her as the sides of the grave. And she looked forward over a waste of hours, and saw herself go on to rage, and tremble, and be softened, and rage again, until the day came and the labours of the day must be renewed.

Suddenly she heard feet on the stairs—his feet, and soon after the sound of a window-sash flung open. She sat up with her heart beating. He had gone to his room alone, and he had not gone to bed. She might again have one of her night cracks; and at the entrancing prospect, a change came over her mind; with the approach of this hope of pleasure, all the baser metal became immediately obliterated from her thoughts. She rose, all woman, and all the best of woman, tender, pitiful, hating the wrong, loyal to her own sex— and all the weakest of that dear miscellany, nourishing, cherishing next her soft heart, voicelessly flattering, hopes that she would have died sooner than have acknowledged. She tore off her nightcap, and her hair fell about her shoulders in profusion. Undying coquetry awoke. By the faint light of her nocturnal rush, she stood before the looking-glass, carried her shapely arms above her head, and gathered up the treasures of her tresses. She was never backward to admire herself; that kind of modesty was a stranger to her nature; and she paused, struck with a pleased wonder at the sight. "Ye daft auld wife!" she said, answering a thought that was not; and she blushed with the innocent consciousness of a child. Hastily she did up the massive and shining coils, hastily donned a wrapper, and with the rushlight in her hand, stole into the hall. Below stairs she heard the clock ticking the deliberate seconds, and Frank jingling with the decanters in the dining-room. Aversion rose in her, bitter and momentary. "Nesty, tippling puggy!" she thought; and the next moment she had knocked guardedly at Archie's door and was bidden enter.

Archie had been looking out into the ancient blackness, pierced here and there with a rayless star; taking the sweet air of the moors and the night into his bosom deeply; seeking, perhaps finding, peace after the manner of the unhappy. He turned round as she came in, and showed her a pale face against the window-frame.

"Is that you, Kirstie?" he asked. "Come in!"

"It's unco late, my dear," said Kirstie, affecting unwillingness.

"No, no," he answered, "not at all. Come in, if you want a crack. I am not sleepy, God knows!"

She advanced, took a chair by the toilet table and the candle, and set the rushlight at her foot. Something—it might be in the comparative disorder of her dress, it might be the emotion that now welled in her bosom—had touched her with a wand of transformation, and she seemed young with the youth of goddesses.

"Mr. Erchie," she began, "what's this that's come to ye?"

"I am not aware of anything that has come," said Archie, and blushed, and repented bitterly that he had let her in.

"O, my dear, that'll no dae!" said Kirstie. "It's ill to blend the eyes of love. O, Mr. Erchie, tak a thocht ere it's ower late. Ye shouldna be impatient o' the braws o' life, they'll a' come in their saison, like the sun and the rain. Ye're young yet; ye've mony cantie years afore ye. See and dinna wreck yersel' at the outset like sae mony ithers! Hae patience—they telled me aye that was the owercome o' life—hae patience, there's a braw day coming yet. Gude kens it never cam to me; and here I am, wi' nayther man nor bairn to ca' my ain, wearying a' folks wi' my ill tongue, and you just the first, Mr. Erchie!"

"I have a difficulty in knowing what you mean," said Archie.

"Weel, and I'll tell ye," she said. "It's just this, that I'm feared. I'm feared for ye, my dear. Remember, your faither is a hard man, reaping where he hasna sowed and gaithering where he hasna strawed. It's easy speakin', but mind! Ye'll have to look in the gurly face o'm, where it's ill to look, and vain to look for mercy. Ye mind me o' a bonny ship pitten oot into the black and gowsty seas—ye're a' safe still, sittin' quait and crackin' wi' Kirstie in your lown chalmer; but whaur will ye be the morn, and in whatten horror o' the fearsome tempest, cryin' on the hills to cover ye?"

"Why, Kirstie, you're very enigmatical to-night—and very eloquent," Archie put in.

"And, my dear Mr. Erchie," she continued, with a change of voice, "ye mauna think that I canna sympathise wi' ye. Ye mauna think that I havena been young mysel'. Lang syne, when I was a bit lassie, no twenty yet—" She paused and sighed. "Clean and caller, wi' a fit like the hinney bee," she continned. "I was aye big and buirdly, ye maun understand; a bonny figure o' a woman, though I say it that suldna—built to rear bairns—braw bairns they suld hae been, and grand I would hae likit it! But I was young, dear, wi' the bonny glint o' youth in my e'en, and little I dreamed I'd ever be tellin' ye this, an auld, lanely, rudas wife! Weel, Mr. Erchie, there was a lad cam' courtin' me, as was but naetural. Mony had come before, and I would nane o' them. But this yin had a tongue to wile the birds frae the lift and the bees frae the foxglove bells. Deary me, but it's lang syne! Folk have dee'd sinsyne and been buried, and are forgotten, and bairns been born and got merrit and got bairns o' their ain. Sinsyne woods have been plantit, and have grawn up and are bonny trees, and the joes sit in their shadow, and sinsyne auld estates have changed hands, and there have been wars and rumours of wars on the face of the earth. And here I'm still—like an auld droopit craw—lookin' on and craikin'! But, Mr. Erchie, do ye no think that I have mind o' it a' still? I was dwalling then in my faither's house; and it's a curious thing that we were whiles trysted in the Deil's Hags. And do ye no think that I have mind of the bonny simmer days, the lang miles o' the bluid-red heather, the cryin' of the whaups, and the lad and the lassie that was trysted? Do ye no think that I mind how the hilly sweetness ran about my hairt? Ay, Mr. Erchie, I ken the way o' it—fine do I ken the way—how the grace o' God takes them, like Paul of Tarsus, when they think it least, and drives the pair o' them into a land which is like a dream, and the world and the folks in't are nae mair than clouds to the puir lassie, and heeven nae mair than windle-straes, if she can but pleesure him! Until Tam dee'd—that was my story," she broke off to say, "he dee'd, and I wasna at the buryin'. But while he was here, I could take care o' mysel'. And can yon puir lassie?"

Kirstie, her eyes shining with unshed tears, stretched out her hand towards him appealingly; the bright and the dull gold of her hair flashed and smouldered in the coils behind her comely head, like the rays of an eternal youth; the pure colour had risen in her face; and Archie was abashed alike by her beauty and her story. He came towards her slowly from the window, took up her hand in his and kissed it.

"Kirstie," he said hoarsely, "you have misjudged me sorely. I have always thought of her, I wouldna harm her for the universe, my woman!"

"Eh, lad, and that's easy sayin'," cried Kirstie, "but it's nane sae easy doin'! Man, do ye no comprehend that it's God's wull we should be blendit and glamoured, and have nae command over our ain members at a time like that? My bairn," she cried, still holding his hand, "think o' the puir lass! have pity upon her, Erchie! and O, be wise for twa! Think o' the risk she rins! I have seen ye, and what's to prevent ithers! I saw ye once in the Hags, in my ain howl, and I was wae to see ye there—in pairt for the omen, for I think there's a weird on the place—and in pairt for pure nakit envy and bitterness o' hairt. It's strange ye should forgather there tae! God! but yon puir, thrawn, auld Covenanter's seen a heap o' human natur since he lookit his last on the musket barrels, if he never saw nane afore," she added, with a kind of wonder in her eyes.

"I swear by my honour I have done her no wrong," said Archie. "I swear by my honour and the redemption of my soul that there shall none be done her. I have heard of this before. I have been foolish, Kirstie, not unkind, and, above all, not base."

"There's my bairn!" said Kirstie, rising. "I'll can trust ye noo, I'll can gang to my bed wi' an easy hairt." And then she saw in a flash how barren had been her triumph. Archie had promised to spare the girl, and he would keep it; but who had promised to spare Archie? What was to be the end of it? Over a maze of difficulties she glanced, and saw, at the end of every passage, the flinty countenance of Hermiston. And a kind of horror fell upon her at what she had done. She wore a tragic mask. "Erchie, the Lord peety you, dear, and peety me! I have buildit on this foundation"—laying her hand heavily on his shoulder—"and buildit hie, and pit my hairt in the buildin' of it. If the hale hypothec were to fa', I think, laddie, I would dee! Excuse a daft wife that loves ye, and that kenned your mither. And for His name's sake keep yersel' frae inordinate desires; haud your heart in baith your hands, carry it canny and laigh; dinna send it up like a hairn's kite into the collieshangie o' the wunds! Mind, Maister Erchie dear, that this life's a' disappointment, and a mouthfu' o' mools is the appointed end."

"Ay, but Kirstie, my woman, you're asking me ower much at last," said Archie, profoundly moved, and lapsing into the broad Scots. "Ye're asking what nae man can grant ye, what only the Lord of heaven can grant ye if He see fit. Ay! And can even He! I can promise ye what I shall do, and you can depend on that. But how I shall feel—my woman, that is long past thinking of!"

They were both standing by now opposite each other. The face of Archie wore the wretched semblance of a smile; hers was convulsed for a moment.

"Promise me ae thing," she cried in a sharp voice. "Promise me ye'll never do naething without telling me."

"No, Kirstie, I canna promise ye that," he replied. "I have promised enough, God kens!"

"May the blessing of God lift and rest upon ye dear!" she said.

"God bless ye, my old friend," said he.

CHAPTER IX—AT THE WEAVER'S STONE

It was late in the afternoon when Archie drew near by the hill path to the Praying Weaver's stone. The Hags were in shadow. But still, through the gate of the Slap, the sun shot a last arrow, which sped far and straight across the surface of the moss, here and there touching and shining on a tussock, and lighted at length on the gravestone and the small figure awaiting him there. The emptiness and solitude of the great moors seemed to be concentrated there, and Kirstie pointed out by that figure of sunshine for the only inhabitant. His first sight of her was thus excruciatingly sad, like a glimpse of a world from which all light, comfort, and society were on the point of vanishing. And the next moment, when she had turned her face to him and the quick smile had enlightened it, the whole face of nature smiled upon him in her smile of welcome. Archie's slow pace was quickened; his legs hasted to her though his heart was hanging back. The girl, upon her side, drew herself together slowly and stood up, expectant; she was all languor, her face was gone white; her arms ached for him, her soul was on tip-toes. But he deceived her, pausing a few steps away, not less white than herself, and holding up his hand with a gesture of denial.

"No, Christina, not to-day," he said. "To-day I have to talk to you seriously. Sit ye down, please, there where you were. Please!" he repeated.

The revulsion of feeling in Christina's heart was violent. To have longed and waited these weary hours for him, rehearsing her endearments—to have seen him at last come—to have been ready there, breathless, wholly passive, his to do what he would with—and suddenly to have found herself confronted with a grey-faced, harsh schoolmaster—it was too rude a shock. She could have wept, but pride withheld her. She sat down on the stone, from which she had arisen, part with the instinct of obedience, part as though she had been thrust there. What was this? Why was she rejected? Had she ceased to please? She stood here offering her wares, and he would none of them! And yet they were all his! His to take and keep, not his to refuse though! In her quick petulant nature, a moment ago on fire with hope, thwarted love and wounded vanity wrought. The schoolmaster that there is in all men, to the despair of all girls and most women, was now completely in possession of Archie. He had passed a night of sermons, a day of reflection; he had come wound up to do his duty; and the set mouth, which in him only betrayed the effort of his will, to her seemed the expression of an averted heart. It was the same with his constrained voice and embarrassed utterance; and if so—if it was all over—the pang of the thought took away from her the power of thinking.

He stood before her some way off. "Kirstie, there's been too much of this. We've seen too much of each other." She looked up quickly and her eyes contracted. "There's no good ever comes of these secret meetings. They're not frank, not honest truly, and I ought to have seen it. People have begun to talk; and it's not right of me. Do you see?"

"I see somebody will have been talking to ye," she said sullenly.

"They have, more than one of them," replied Archie.

"And whae were they?" she cried. "And what kind o' love do ye ca' that, that's ready to gang round like a whirligig at folk talking? Do ye think they havena talked to me?"

"Have they indeed?" said Archie, with a quick breath. "That is what I feared. Who were they? Who has dared—?"

Archie was on the point of losing his temper.

As a matter of fact, not any one had talked to Christina on the matter; and she strenuously repeated her own first question in a panic of self-defence.

"Ah, well! what does it matter?" he said. "They were good folk that wished well to us, and the great affair is that there are people talking. My dear girl, we have to be wise. We must not wreck our lives at the outset. They may be long and happy yet, and we must see to it, Kirstie, like God's rational creatures and not like fool children. There is one thing we must see to before all. You're worth waiting for, Kirstie! worth waiting for a generation; it would be enough reward."—And here he remembered the schoolmaster again, and very unwisely took to following wisdom. "The first thing that we must see to, is that there shall be no scandal about for my father's sake. That would ruin all; do ye no see that?"

Kirstie was a little pleased, there had been some show of warmth of sentiment in what Archie had said last. But the dull irritation still persisted in her bosom; with the aboriginal instinct, having suffered herself, she wished to make Archie suffer.

And besides, there had come out the word she had always feared to hear from his lips, the name of his father. It is not to be supposed that, during so many days with a love avowed between them, some reference had not been made to their conjoint future. It had in fact been often touched upon, and from the first had been the sore point. Kirstie had wilfully closed the eye of thought; she would not argue even with herself; gallant, desperate little heart, she had accepted the command of that supreme attraction like the call of fate and marched blindfold on her doom. But Archie, with his masculine sense of responsibility, must reason; he must dwell on some future good, when the present good was all in all to Kirstie; he must talk—and talk lamely, as necessity drove him—of what was to be. Again and again he had touched on marriage; again and again been driven back into indistinctness by a memory of Lord Hermiston. And Kirstie had been swift to understand and quick to choke down and smother the understanding; swift to leap up in flame at a mention of that hope, which spoke volumes to her vanity and her love, that she might one day be Mrs. Weir of Hermiston; swift, also, to recognise in his stumbling or throttled utterance the death-knell of these expectations, and constant, poor girl! in her large-minded madness, to go on and to reck nothing of the future. But these unfinished references, these blinks in which his heart spoke, and his memory and reason rose up to silence it before the words were well uttered, gave her unqualifiable agony. She was raised up and dashed down again bleeding. The recurrence of the subject forced her, for however short a time, to open her eyes on what she did not wish to see; and it had invariably ended in another disappointment. So now again, at the mere wind of its coming, at the mere mention of his father's name—who might seem indeed to have accompanied them in their whole moorland courtship, an awful figure in a wig with an ironical and bitter smile, present to guilty consciousness—she fled from it head down.

"Ye havena told me yet," she said, "who was it spoke?"

"Your aunt for one," said Archie.

"Auntie Kirstie?" she cried. "And what do I care for my Auntie Kirstie?"

"She cares a great deal for her niece," replied Archie, in kind reproof.

"Troth, and it's the first I've heard of it," retorted the girl.

"The question here is not who it is, but what they say, what they have noticed," pursued the lucid schoolmaster. "That is what we have to think of in self-defence."

"Auntie Kirstie, indeed! A bitter, thrawn auld maid that's fomented trouble in the country before I was born, and will be doing it still, I daur say, when I'm deid! It's in her nature; it's as natural for her as it's for a sheep to eat."

"Pardon me, Kirstie, she was not the only one," interposed Archie. "I had two warnings, two sermons, last night, both most kind and considerate. Had you been there, I promise you-you would have grat, my dear! And they opened my eyes. I saw we were going a wrong way."

"Who was the other one?" Kirstie demanded.

By this time Archie was in the condition of a hunted beast. He had come, braced and resolute; he was to trace out a line of conduct for the pair of them in a few cold, convincing sentences; he had now been there some time, and he was still staggering round the outworks and undergoing what he felt to be a savage cross-examination.

"Mr. Frank!" she cried. "What nex', I would like to ken?"

"He spoke most kindly and truly."

"What like did he say?"

"I am not going to tell you; you have nothing to do with that," cried Archie, startled to find he had admitted so much.

"O, I have naething to do with it!" she repeated, springing to her feet. "A'body at Hermiston's free to pass their opinions upon me, but I have naething to do wi' it! Was this at prayers like? Did ye ca' the grieve into the consultation? Little wonder if a'body's talking, when ye make a'body yer confidants! But as you say, Mr. Weir,—most kindly, most considerately, most truly, I'm sure,—I have naething to do with it. And I think I'll better be going. I'll be wishing you good evening, Mr. Weir." And she made him a stately curtsey, shaking as she did so from head to foot, with the barren ecstasy of temper.

Poor Archie stood dumbfounded. She had moved some steps away from him before he recovered the gift of articulate speech.

"Kirstie!" he cried. "O, Kirstie woman!"

There was in his voice a ring of appeal, a clang of mere astonishment that showed the schoolmaster was vanquished.

She turned round on him. "What do ye Kirstie me for?" she retorted. "What have ye to do wi' me! Gang to your ain freends and deave them!"

He could only repeat the appealing "Kirstie!"

"Kirstie, indeed!" cried the girl, her eyes blazing in her white face. "My name is Miss Christina Elliott, I would have ye to ken, and I daur ye to ca' me out of it. If I canna get love, I'll have respect, Mr. Weir. I'm come of decent people, and I'll have respect. What have I done that ye should lightly me? What have I done? What have I done? O, what have I done?" and her voice rose upon the third repetition. "I thocht—I thocht—I thocht I was sae happy!" and the first sob broke from her like the paroxysm of some mortal sickness.

Archie ran to her. He took the poor child in his arms, and she nestled to his breast as to a mother's, and clasped him in hands that were strong like vices. He felt her whole body shaken by the throes of distress, and had pity upon her beyond speech. Pity, and at the same time a bewildered fear of this explosive engine in his arms, whose works he did not understand, and yet had been tampering with. There arose from before him the curtains of boyhood, and he saw for the first time the ambiguous face of woman as she is. In vain he looked back over the interview; he saw not where he had offended. It seemed unprovoked, a wilful convulsion of brute nature. . . .

EDITORIAL NOTE

With the words last printed, "a wilful convulsion of brute nature," the romance of Weir of Hermiston breaks off. They were dictated, I believe, on the very morning of the writer's sudden seizure and death. Weir of Hermiston thus remains in the work of Stevenson what Edwin Droid is in the work of Dickens or Denis Duval in that of Thackeray: or rather it remains relatively more, for if each of those fragments holds an honourable place among its author's writings, among Stevenson's the fragment of Weir holds certainly the highest.

Readers may be divided in opinion on the question whether they would or they would not wish to hear more of the intended course of the story and destinies of the characters. To some, silence may seem best, and that the mind should be left to its own conjectures as to the sequel, with the help of such indications as the text affords. I confess that this is the view which has my sympathy. But since others, and those almost certainly a majority, are anxious to be told all they can, and since editors and publishers join in the request, I can scarce do otherwise than comply. The intended argument, then, so far as it was known at the time of the writer's death to his step-daughter and devoted amanuensis, Mrs. Strong, was nearly as follows:—

Archie persists in his good resolution of avoiding further conduct compromising to young Kirstie's good name. Taking advantage of the situation thus created, and of the girl's unhappiness and wounded vanity, Frank Innes pursues his purpose of seduction; and Kirstie, though still caring for Archie in her heart, allows herself to become Frank's victim. Old Kirstie is the first to perceive something amiss with her, and believing Archie to be the culprit, accuses him, thus making him aware for the first time that mischief has happened. He does not at once deny the charge, but seeks out and questions young Kirstie, who confesses the truth to him; and he, still loving her, promises to protect and defend her in her trouble. He then has an interview with Frank Innes on the moor, which ends in a quarrel, and in

Archie killing Frank beside the Weaver's Stone. Meanwhile the Four Black Brothers, having become aware of their sister's betrayal, are bent on vengeance against Archie as her supposed seducer. They are about to close in upon him with this purpose when he is arrested by the officers of the law for the murder of Frank. He is tried before his own father, the Lord Justice-Clerk, found guilty, and condemned to death. Meanwhile the elder Kirstie, having discovered from the girl how matters really stand, informs her nephews of the truth; and they, in a great revulsion of feeling in Archie's favour, determine on an action after the ancient manner of their house. They gather a following, and after a great fight break the prison where Archie lies confined, and rescue him. He and young Kirstie thereafter escape to America. But the ordeal of taking part in the trial of his own son has been too much for the Lord Justice-Clerk, who dies of the shock. "I do not know," adds the amanuensis, "what becomes of old Kirstie, but that character grew and strengthened so in the writing that I am sure he had some dramatic destiny for her."

The plan of every imaginative work is subject, of course, to change under the artist's hand as he carries it out; and not merely the character of the elder Kirstie, but other elements of the design no less, might well have deviated from the lines originally traced. It seems certain, however, that the next stage in the relations of Archie and the younger Kirstie would have been as above foreshadowed; and this conception of the lover's unconventional chivalry and unshaken devotion to his mistress after her fault is very characteristic of the writer's mind. The vengeance to be taken on the seducer beside the Weaver's Stone is prepared for in the first words of the Introduction; while the situation and fate of the judge, confronting like a Brutus, but unable to survive, the duty of sending his own son to the gallows, seem clearly to have been destined to furnish the climax and essential tragedy of the tale.

How this last circumstance was to have been brought about, within the limits of legal usage and possibility, seems hard to conjecture; but it was a point to which the author had evidently given careful consideration. Mrs. Strong says simply that the Lord Justice-Clerk, like an old Roman, condemns his son to death; but I am assured on the best legal authority of Scotland that no judge, however powerful either by character or office, could have insisted on presiding at the trial of a near kinsman of his own. The Lord Justice-Clerk was head of the criminal justiciary of the country; he might have insisted on his right of being present on the bench when his son was tried: but he would never have been allowed to preside or to pass sentence. Now in a letter of Stevenson's to Mr. Baxter, of October 1892, I find him asking for materials in terms which seem to indicate that he knew this quite well:—"I wish Pitcairn's 'Criminal Trials,' quam primum. Also an absolutely correct text of the Scots judiciary oath. Also, in case Pitcairn does not come down late enough, I wish as full a report as possible of a Scots murder trial between 1790–1820. Understand the fullest possible. Is there any book which would guide me to the following facts? The Justice-Clerk tries some people capitally on circuit. Certain evidence cropping up, the charge is transferred to the Justice-Clerk's own son. Of course in the next trial the Justice-Clerk is excluded, and the case is called before the Lord Justice-General. Where would this trial have to be? I fear in Edinburgh, which would not suit my view. Could it be again at the circuit town?" The point was referred to a quondam fellow-member with Stevenson of the Edinburgh Speculative Society, Mr. Graham Murray, the present Solicitor-General for Scotland; whose reply was to the effect that there would be no difficulty in making the new trial take place at the circuit town; that it would have to be held there in spring or autumn, before two Lords of Justiciary; and that the Lord Justice-General would have nothing to do with it, this title being at the date in question only a nominal one held by a layman (which is no longer the case). On this Stevenson writes, "Graham Murray's note re the venue was highly satisfactory, and did me all the good in the world." The terms of his inquiry seem to imply that he intended other persons, before Archie, to have fallen first under suspicion of the murder; and also—doubtless in order to make the rescue by the Black Brothers possible—that he wanted Archie to be imprisoned not in Edinburgh but in the circuit town. But they do not show how he meant to get over the main difficulty, which at the same time he fully recognises. Can it have been that Lord Hermiston's part was to have been limited to presiding at the first trial, where the evidence incriminating Archie was unexpectedly brought forward, and to directing that the law should take its course?

Whether the final escape and union of Archie and Christina would have proved equally essential to the plot may perhaps to some readers seem questionable. They may rather feel that a tragic destiny is foreshadowed from the beginning for all concerned, and is inherent in the very conditions of the tale. But on this point, and other matters of general criticism connected with it, I find an interesting discussion by the author himself in his correspondence. Writing to Mr. J. M. Barrie, under date November 1, 1892, and criticising that author's famous story of The Little Minister, Stevenson says:—

"Your descriptions of your dealings with Lord Rintoul are frightfully unconscientious. . . . The Little Minister ought to have ended badly; we all know it did, and we are infinitely grateful to you for the grace and good feeling with which you have lied about it. If you had told the truth, I for one could never have forgiven you. As you had conceived and written the earlier parts, the truth about the end, though indisputably true to fact, would have been a lie, or what is worse, a discord, in art. If you are going to make a book end badly, it must end badly from the beginning. Now, your book began to end well. You let yourself fall in love with, and fondle, and smile at your puppets. Once you had done that, your honour was committed—at the cost of truth to life you were bound to save them. It is the blot on Richard Feverel for instance, that it begins to end well; and then tricks you and ends ill. But in this case, there is worse behind, for the ill ending does not inherently issue from the plot—the story had, in fact, ended well after the great last interview between Richard and Lucy—and the blind, illogical bullet which smashes all has no more to do between the boards than a fly has to do with a room into whose open window it comes buzzing. It might have so happened; it needed not; and unless needs must, we have no right to pain our readers. I have had a heavy case of conscience of the same kind about my Braxfield story. Braxfield—only his name is Hermiston—has a son who is condemned to death; plainly there is a fine tempting fitness about this—and I meant he was to hang. But on considering my minor characters, I saw there were five people who would—in a sense, who must—break prison and attempt his rescue. They are capable hardy folks too, who might very well succeed. Why should they not then? Why should not young Hermiston escape clear out of the country? and be happy, if he could, with his—but soft! I will not betray my secret nor my heroine. . . ."

To pass, now, from the question how the story would have ended to the question how it originated and grew in the writer's mind. The character of the hero, Weir of Hermiston, is avowedly suggested by the historical personality of Robert Macqueen, Lord Braxfield. This famous judge has been for generations the subject of a hundred Edinburgh tales and anecdotes. Readers of Stevenson's essay on the Raeburn exhibition, in Virginibus Puerisque, will remember how he is fascinated by Raeburn's portrait of Braxfield, even as Lockhart had been fascinated by a different portrait of the same worthy sixty years before (see Peter's Letters to his Kinsfolk); nor did his interest in the character diminish in later life. Again, the case of a judge involved by the exigencies of his office in a strong conflict between public duty and private interest or affection, was one which had always attracted and exercised Stevenson's imagination. In the days when he and Mr. Henley were collaborating with a view to the stage, Mr. Henley once proposed a plot founded on the story of Mr. Justice Harbottle in Sheridan Le Fanu's In a Glass Darkly, in which the wicked judge goes headlong per fas et nefas to his object of getting the husband of his mistress hanged. Some time later Stevenson and his wife together wrote a play called The Hanging Judge. In this, the title character is tempted for the first time in his life to tamper with the course of justice, in order to shield his wife from persecution by a former husband who reappears after being supposed dead. Bulwer's novel of Paul Clifford, with its final situation of the worldly-minded judge, Sir William Brandon, learning that the highwayman whom he is in the act of sentencing is his own son, and dying of the knowledge, was also well known to Stevenson, and no doubt counted for something in the suggestion of the present story.

Once more, the difficulties often attending the relation of father and son in actual life had pressed heavily on Stevenson's mind and conscience from the days of his youth, when in obeying the law of his own nature he had been constrained to disappoint, distress, and for a time to be much misunderstood by, a father whom he justly loved and admired with all his heart. Difficulties of this kind he had already handled in a lighter vein once or twice in fiction— as for instance in the Story of a Lie and in The Wrecker—before he grappled with them in the acute and tragic phase in which they occur in the present story.

These three elements, then, the interest of the historical personality of Lord Braxfield, the problems and emotions arising from a violent conflict between duty and nature in a judge, and the difficulties due to incompatibility and misunderstanding between father and son, lie at the foundations of the present story. To touch on minor matters, it is perhaps worth notice, as Mr. Henley reminds me, that the name of Weir had from of old a special significance for Stevenson's imagination, from the traditional fame in Edinburgh of Major Weir, burned as a warlock, together with his sister, under circumstances of peculiar atrocity. Another name, that of the episodical personage of Mr. Torrance the minister, is borrowed direct from life, as indeed are the whole figure and its surroundings—kirkyard, kirk, and manse—down even to the black thread mittens: witness the following passage from a letter of the early seventies:—"I've been to church and am not depressed—a great step. It was at that beautiful church" [of Glencorse in the Pentlands, three miles from his father's country house at Swanston]. "It is a little cruciform place, with a steep slate roof. The small kirkyard is full of old grave-stones; one of a Frenchman from Dunkerque, I suppose he died prisoner in the military prison hard by. And one, the most pathetic memorial I ever saw: a poor school-slate, in a wooden frame, with the inscription cut into it evidently by the father's own hand. In church, old Mr. Torrance preached, over eighty and a relic of times forgotten, with his black thread gloves and mild old face." A side hint for a particular trait in the character of Mrs. Weir we can trace in some family traditions concerning the writer's own grandmother, who is reported to have valued piety much more than efficiency in her domestic servants. The other women characters seem, so far at least as I know, to have been pure creation, and especially that new and admirable incarnation of the eternal feminine in the elder Kirstie. The little that he says about her himself is in a letter written a few days before his death to Mr. Gosse. The allusions are to the various moods and attitudes of people in regard to middle age, and are suggested by Mr. Gosse's volume of poems, In Russet and Silver. "It seems rather funny," he writes, "that this matter should come up just now, as I am at present engaged in treating a severe case of middle age in one of my stories, The Justice-Clerk. The case is that of a woman, and I think I am doing her justice. You will be interested, I believe, to see the difference in our treatments.

Secreta Vitæ [the title of one of Mr. Gosse's poems] comes nearer to the case of my poor Kirstie." From the wonderful midnight scene between her and Archie, we may judge what we have lost in those later scenes where she was to have taxed him with the fault that was not his—to have presently learned his innocence from the lips of his supposed victim—to have then vindicated him to her kinsmen and fired them to the action of his rescue. The scene of the prison-breaking here planned by Stevenson would have gained interest (as will already have occurred to readers) from comparison with the two famous precedents in Scott, the Porteous mob and the breaking of Portanferry jail.

The best account of Stevenson's methods of imaginative work is in the following sentences from a letter of his own to Mr. W. Craibe Angus of Glasgow:—"I am still 'a slow study,' and sit for a long while silent on my eggs. Unconscious thought, there is the only method: macerate your subject, let it boil slow, then take the lid off and look in—and there your stuff is—good or bad." The several elements above noted having been left to work for many years in his mind, it was in the autumn of 1892 that he was moved to "take the lid off and look in,"—under the influence, it would seem, of a special and overmastering wave of that feeling for the romance of Scottish scenery and character which was at all times so strong in him, and which his exile did so much to intensify. I quote again from his letter to Mr. Barrie on November 1st in that year:—"It is a singular thing that I should live here in the South Seas under conditions so new and so striking, and yet my imagination so continually inhabit the cold old huddle of grey hills from which we come. I have finished David Balfour, I have another book on the stocks, The Young Chevalier, which is to be part in France and part in Scotland, and to deal with Prince Charlie about the year 1749; and now what have I done but begun a third, which is to be all moorland together, and is to have for a centre-piece a figure that I think you will appreciate—that of the immortal Braxfield. Braxfield himself is my grand premier—or since you are so much involved in the British drama, let me say my heavy lead." Writing to me at the same date he makes the same announcement more briefly, with a list of the characters and an indication of the scene and date of the story. To Mr. Baxter he writes a month later, "I have a novel on the stocks to be called The Justice-Clerk. It is pretty Scotch; the grand premier is taken from Braxfield

(O, by the by, send me Cockburn's Memorials), and some of the story is, well, queer. The heroine is seduced by one man, and finally disappears with the other man who shot him. . . . Mind you, I expect The Justice-Clerk to be my masterpiece. My Braxfield is already a thing of beauty and a joy for ever, and so far as he has gone, far my best character." From the last extract it appears that he had already at this date drafted some of the earlier chapters of the book. He also about the same time composed the dedication to his wife, who found it pinned to her bed-curtains one morning on awaking. It was always his habit to keep several books in progress at the same time, turning from one to another as the fancy took him, and finding relief in the change of labour; and for many months after the date of this letter, first illness,—then a voyage to Auckland,—then work on the Ebb-Tide, on a new tale called St. Ives, which was begun during an attack of influenza, and on his projected book of family history,—prevented his making any continuous progress with Weir. In August 1893 he says he has been recasting the beginning. A year later, still only the first four or five chapters had been drafted. Then, in the last weeks of his life, he attacked the task again, in a sudden heat of inspiration, and worked at it ardently and without interruption until the end came. No wonder if during these weeks he was sometimes aware of a tension of the spirit difficult to sustain. "How can I keep this pitch?" he is reported to have said after finishing one of the chapters; and all the world knows how that frail organism in fact betrayed him in mid effort. The greatness of the loss to his country's letters can for the first time be fully measured from the foregoing pages.

There remains one more point to be mentioned, as to the speech and manners of the Hanging Judge himself. That these are not a whit exaggerated, in comparison with what is recorded of his historic prototype, Lord Braxfield, is certain. The locus classicus in regard to this personage is in Lord Cockburn's Memorials of his Time. "Strong built and dark, with rough eyebrows, powerful eyes, threatening lips, and a low growling voice, he was like a formidable blacksmith. His accent and dialect were exaggerated Scotch; his language, like his thoughts, short, strong, and conclusive. Illiterate and without any taste for any refined enjoyment, strength of understanding, which gave him power without cultivation, only encouraged him to a more contemptuous disdain of all natures less coarse than his own. It may be doubted if he was ever so much in his element as when tauntingly repelling the last despairing claim of a wretched culprit, and sending him to Botany Bay or the gallows with an insulting jest. Yet this was not from cruelty, for which he was too strong and too jovial, but from cherished coarseness." Readers, nevertheless, who are at all acquainted with the social history of Scotland will hardly have failed to make the observation that Braxfield's is an extreme case of eighteenth-century manners, as he himself was an eighteenth-century personage (he died in 1799, in his seventy-eighth year); and that for the date in which the story is cast (1814) such manners are somewhat of an anachronism. During the generation contemporary with the French Revolution and the Napoleonic wars—or to put it another way, the generation that elapsed between the days when Scott roamed the country as a High School and University student and those when he settled in the fulness of fame and prosperity at Abbotsford,—or again (the allusions will appeal to readers of the admirable Galt) during the interval between the first and the last provostry of Bailie Pawkie in the borough of Gudetown, or between the earlier and the final ministrations of Mr. Balwhidder in the parish of Dalmailing,—during this period a great softening had taken place in Scottish manners generally, and in those of the Bar and Bench not least. "Since the death of Lord Justice-Clerk Macqueen of Braxfield," says Lockhart, writing about 1817, "the whole exterior of judicial deportment has been quite altered." A similar criticism may probably hold good on the picture of border life contained in the chapter concerning the Four Black Brothers of Cauldstaneslap, namely, that it rather suggests the ways of an earlier generation; nor have I any clue to the reasons which led Stevenson to choose this particular date, in the year preceding Waterloo, for a story which, in regard to some of its features at least, might seem more naturally placed some twenty-five or thirty years before.

If the reader seeks, further, to know whether the scenery of Hermiston can be identified with any one special place familiar to the writer's early experience, the answer, I think, must be in the negative. Rather it is distilled from a number of different haunts and associations among the moorlands of southern Scotland. In the dedication and in a letter to me he indicates the Lammermuirs as the scene of his tragedy. And Mrs. Stevenson (his

343

mother) tells me that she thinks he was inspired by recollections of a visit paid in boyhood to an uncle living at a remote farmhouse in that district called Overshiels, in the parish of Stow. But though he may have thought of the Lammermuirs in the first instance, we have already found him drawing his description of the kirk and manse from another haunt of his youth, namely, Glencorse in the Pentlands; while passages in chapters v. and viii. point explicitly to a third district, that is, Upper Tweeddale, with the country stretching thence towards the wells of Clyde. With this country also holiday rides and excursions from Peebles had made him familiar as a boy: and this seems certainly the most natural scene of the story, if only from its proximity to the proper home of the Elliotts, which of course is in the heart of the Border, especially Teviotdale and Ettrick. Some of the geographical names mentioned are clearly not meant to furnish literal indications. The Spango, for instance, is a water running, I believe, not into the Tweed but into the Nith, and Crossmichael as the name of a town is borrowed from Galloway.

But it is with the general and essential that the artist deals, and questions of strict historical perspective or local definition are beside the mark in considering his work. Nor will any reader expect, or be grateful for, comment in this place on matters which are more properly to the point—on the seizing and penetrating power of the author's ripened art as exhibited in the foregoing pages, the wide range of character and emotion over which he sweeps with so assured a hand, his vital poetry of vision and magic of presentment. Surely no son of Scotland has died leaving with his last breath a worthier tribute to the land he loved.

S. C.

GLOSSARY

Ae, one.

Antinomian, one of a sect which holds that under the gospel dispensation the moral law is not obligatory.

Auld Hornie, the Devil.

Ballant, ballad.

Bauchles, brogues, old shoes.

Bauld, bold.

Bees in their bonnet, eccentricities.

Birling, whirling.

Black-a-vised, dark-complexioned.

Bonnet-laird, small landed proprietor, yeoman.

Bool, ball.

Brae, rising ground.

Brig, bridge.

Buff, play buff on, to make a fool of, to deceive.

Burn, stream.

Butt end, end of a cottage.

Byre, cow-house.

Ca', drive.

Caller, fresh.

Canna, cannot.

Canny, careful, shrewd.

Cantie, cheerful.

Carline, old woman.

Cauld, cold.

Chalmer, chamber.

Claes, clothes.

Clamjamfry, crowd.

Clavers, idle talk.

Cock-laird. See Bonnet-laird.

Collieshangie, turmoil.

Crack, to converse.

Cuist, cast.

Cuddy, donkey.

Cutty, jade, also used playfully = brat.

Daft, mad, frolicsome.

Dander, to saunter.

Danders, cinders.

Daurna, dare not.

Deave, to deafen.

Denty, dainty.

Dirdum, vigour.

Disjaskit, worn out, disreputable-looking.

Doer, law agent.

Dour, hard.

Drumlie, dark.

Dunting, knocking.

Dwaibly, infirm, rickety.

Dule-tree, the tree of lamentation, the hanging-tree.

Earrand, errand.

Ettercap, vixen.

Fechting, fighting.

Feck, quantity, portion.

Feckless, feeble, powerless.

Fell, strong and fiery.

Fey, unlike yourself, strange, as if urged on by fate, or as persons are observed to be in the hour of approaching death or disaster.

Fit, foot.

Flit, to depart.

Flyped, turned up, turned in-side out.

Forbye, in addition to.

Forgather, to fall in with.

Fower, four.

Fushionless, pithless, weak.

Fyle, to soil, to defile.

Fylement, obloquy, defilement.

Gaed, Went.

Gang, to go.

Gey an', very.

Gigot, leg of mutton.

Girzie, lit. diminutive of Grizel, here a playful nickname.

Glaur, mud.

Glint, glance, sparkle.

Gloaming, twilight.

Glower, to scowl.

Gobbets, small lumps.

Gowden, golden.

Gowsty, gusty.

Grat, wept.

Grieve, land-steward.

Guddle, to catch fish with the hands by groping under the stones or banks.

Gumption, common sense, judgment.

Guid, good.

Gurley, stormy, surly.

Gyte, beside itself.

Hae, have, take.

Haddit, held.

Hale, whole.

Heels-ower-hurdie, heels over head.

Hinney, honey.

Hirstle, to bustle.

Hizzie, wench.

Howe, hollow.

Howl, hovel.

Hunkered, crouched.

Hypothec, lit. in Scots law the furnishings of a house, and formerly the produce and stock of a farm hypothecated by law to the landlord as security for rent; colloquially "the whole structure," "the whole concern."

Idleset, idleness.

Infeftment, a term in Scots law originally synonymous with investiture.

Jaud, jade.

Jeely-piece, a slice of bread and jelly.

Jennipers, juniper.

Jo, sweetheart.

Justifeed, executed, made the victim of justice.

Jyle, jail

Kebbuck, cheese.

Ken, to know.

Kenspeckle, conspicuous.

Kilted, tucked up.

Kyte, belly.

Laigh, low.

Laird, landed proprietor.

Lane, alone.

Lave, rest, remainder.

Linking, tripping.

Lown, lonely, still.

Lynn, cataract.

Lyon King of Arms, the chief of the Court of Heraldry in Scotland.

Macers, offiers of the supreme court. [Cf. Guy Mannering, last chapter.]

Maun, must.

Menseful, of good manners.

Mirk, dark.

Misbegowk, deception, disappointment.

Mools, mould, earth.

Muckle, much, great, big.

My lane, by myself.

Nowt, black cattle.

Palmering, walking infirmly.

Panel, in Scots law, the accused person in a criminal action, the prisoner.

Peel, fortified watch-tower.

Plew-stilts, plough-handles.

Policy, ornamental grounds of a country mansion.

Puddock, frog.

Quean, wench.

Rair, to roar.

Riff-raff, rabble.

Risping, grating.

Rout, rowt, to roar, to rant.

Rowth, abundance.

Rudas, haggard old woman.

Runt, an old cow past breeding; opprobriously, an old woman.

Sab, sob.

Sanguishes, sandwiches.

Sasine, in Scots law, the act of giving legal possession of feudal property, or, colloquially, the deed by which that possession is proved.

Sclamber, to scramble.

Sculduddery, impropriety, grossness.

Session, the Court of Session, the supreme court of Scotland.

Shauchling, shuffling, slipshod.

Shoo, to chase gently.

Siller, money.

Sinsyne, since then.

Skailing, dispersing.

Skelp, slap.

Skirling, screaming.

Skriegh-o'day, daybreak.

Snash, abuse.

Sneisty, supercilious.

Sooth, to hum.

Sough, sound, murmur.

Spec, The Speculative Society, a debating Society connected with

Edingburgh University.

Speir, to ask.

Speldering, sprawling.

Splairge, to splash.

Spunk, spirit, fire.

Steik, to shut.

Stockfish, hard, savourless.

Suger-bool, suger-plum.

Syne, since, then.

Tawpie, a slow foolish slut, also used playfully = monkey.

Telling you, a good thing for you.

Thir, these.

Thrawn, cross-grained.

Toon, town.

Two-names, local soubriquets in addition to patronymic.

Tyke, dog.

Unchancy, unlucky.

Unco, strange, extraordinary, very.

Upsitten, impertinent.

Vennel, alley, lane. The Vennel, a narrow lane in Edinburgh, running out of the Grassmarket.

Vivers, victuals.

Wae, sad, unhappy.

Waling, choosing.

Warrandise, warranty.

Waur, worse.

Weird, destiny.

Whammle, to upset.

Whaup, curlew.

Whiles, sometimes.

Windlestae, crested dog's-tail, grass.

Wund, wind.

Yin, one.

About Author

Childhood and youth

Stevenson was born at 8 Howard Place, Edinburgh, Scotland on 13 November 1850 to Thomas Stevenson (1818–87), a leading lighthouse engineer, and his wife Margaret Isabella (born Balfour, 1829–97). He was christened Robert Lewis Balfour Stevenson. At about age 18, he changed the spelling of "Lewis" to "Louis", and he dropped "Balfour" in 1873.

Lighthouse design was the family's profession; Thomas's father (Robert's grandfather) was civil engineer Robert Stevenson, and Thomas's brothers (Robert's uncles) Alan and David were in the same field. Thomas's maternal grandfather Thomas Smith had been in the same profession. However, Robert's mother's family were gentry, tracing their lineage back to Alexander Balfour who had held the lands of Inchyra in Fife in the fifteenth century. His mother's father Lewis Balfour (1777–1860) was a minister of the Church of Scotland at nearby Colinton, and her siblings included physician George William Balfour and marine engineer James Balfour. Stevenson spent the greater part of his boyhood holidays in his maternal grandfather's house. "Now I often wonder what I inherited from this old minister," Stevenson wrote. "I must suppose, indeed, that he was fond of preaching sermons, and so am I, though I never heard it maintained that either of us loved to hear them."

Lewis Balfour and his daughter both had weak chests, so they often needed to stay in warmer climates for their health. Stevenson inherited a tendency to coughs and fevers, exacerbated when the family moved to a damp, chilly house at 1 Inverleith Terrace in 1851. The family moved again to the sunnier 17 Heriot Row when Stevenson was six years old, but the tendency to extreme sickness in winter remained with him until he was 11. Illness was a recurrent feature of his adult life and left him extraordinarily thin. Contemporaneous views were that he had tuberculosis, but more recent views are that it was bronchiectasis or even sarcoidosis.

Stevenson's parents were both devout Presbyterians, but the household was not strict in its adherence to Calvinist principles. His nurse Alison Cunningham (known as Cummy) was more fervently religious. Her mix of Calvinism and folk beliefs were an early source of nightmares for the child, and he showed a precocious concern for religion. But she also cared for him tenderly in illness, reading to him from John Bunyan and the Bible as he lay sick in bed and telling tales of the Covenanters. Stevenson recalled this time of sickness in "The Land of Counterpane" in A Child's Garden of Verses (1885), dedicating the book to his nurse.

Stevenson was an only child, both strange-looking and eccentric, and he found it hard to fit in when he was sent to a nearby school at age 6, a problem repeated at age 11 when he went on to the Edinburgh Academy; but he mixed well in lively games with his cousins in summer holidays at Colinton. His frequent illnesses often kept him away from his first school, so he was taught for long stretches by private tutors. He was a late reader, learning at age 7 or 8, but even before this he dictated stories to his mother and nurse, and he compulsively wrote stories throughout his childhood. His father was proud of this interest; he had also written stories in his spare time until his own father found them and told him to "give up such nonsense and mind your business." He paid for the printing of Robert's first publication at 16, entitled The Pentland Rising: A Page of History, 1666. It was an account of the Covenanters' rebellion which was published in 1866, the 200th anniversary of the event.

Education

In September 1857, Stevenson went to Mr Henderson's School in India Street, Edinburgh, but because of poor health stayed only a few weeks and did not return until October 1859. During his many absences he was taught by private tutors. In October 1861, he went to Edinburgh Academy, an independent school for boys, and stayed there sporadically for about fifteen months. In the autumn of 1863, he spent one term at an English boarding school at Spring Grove in Isleworth in Middlesex (now an urban area of West London). In October 1864, following an improvement to his health, he was sent to Robert Thomson's private school in Frederick Street, Edinburgh, where he remained until he went to university. In November 1867, Stevenson entered the University of Edinburgh to study engineering. He showed from the start no enthusiasm for his studies and devoted much energy to avoiding lectures. This time was more important for the friendships he made with other students in the Speculative Society (an exclusive debating club), particularly with Charles Baxter, who would become Stevenson's financial agent, and with a professor, Fleeming Jenkin, whose house staged amateur drama in which Stevenson took part, and whose biography he would later write. Perhaps most important at this point in his life was a cousin, Robert Alan Mowbray Stevenson (known as "Bob"), a lively and light-hearted young man who, instead of the family profession, had chosen to study art. Each year during vacations, Stevenson travelled to inspect the family's engineering works—to Anstruther and Wick in 1868, with his father on his official tour of Orkney and Shetland islands lighthouses in 1869, and for three weeks to the island of Erraid in 1870. He enjoyed the travels more for the material they gave for his writing than for any engineering interest. The voyage with his father pleased him because a similar journey of Walter Scott with Robert Stevenson had provided the inspiration for Scott's 1822 novel The Pirate. In April 1871, Stevenson notified his father of his decision to pursue a life of letters. Though the elder Stevenson was naturally disappointed, the surprise cannot have been great, and Stevenson's mother reported that he was "wonderfully resigned" to his son's choice. To provide some security, it was agreed that Stevenson should read Law (again at Edinburgh University) and be called to the Scottish bar. In his 1887 poetry collection Underwoods, Stevenson muses on his having turned from the family profession:

> Say not of me that weakly I declined
>
> The labours of my sires, and fled the sea,
>
> The towers we founded and the lamps we lit,
>
> To play at home with paper like a child.
>
> But rather say: In the afternoon of time

A strenuous family dusted from its hands

The sand of granite, and beholding far

Along the sounding coast its pyramids

And tall memorials catch the dying sun,

Smiled well content, and to this childish task

Around the fire addressed its evening hours.

In other respects too, Stevenson was moving away from his upbringing. His dress became more Bohemian; he already wore his hair long, but he now took to wearing a velveteen jacket and rarely attended parties in conventional evening dress. Within the limits of a strict allowance, he visited cheap pubs and brothels. More importantly, he had come to reject Christianity and declared himself an atheist. In January 1873, his father came across the constitution of the LJR (Liberty, Justice, Reverence) Club, of which Stevenson and his cousin Bob were members, which began: "Disregard everything our parents have taught us". Questioning his son about his beliefs, he discovered the truth, leading to a long period of dissension with both parents:

What a damned curse I am to my parents! As my father said "You have rendered my whole life a failure". As my mother said "This is the heaviest affliction that has ever befallen me". O Lord, what a pleasant thing it is to have damned the happiness of (probably) the only two people who care a damn about you in the world.

Early writing and travels

Stevenson was visiting a cousin in England in late 1873 when he met two people who became very important to him: Sidney Colvin and Fanny (Frances Jane) Sitwell. Sitwell was a 34-year-old woman with a son, who was separated from her husband. She attracted the devotion of many who met her, including Colvin, who married her in 1901. Stevenson was also drawn to her, and they kept up a warm correspondence over several years in which he wavered between the role of a suitor and a son (he addressed her as "Madonna"). Colvin became Stevenson's literary adviser and was the first editor of his letters after his death. He placed Stevenson's first paid contribution in The Portfolio, an essay entitled "Roads".

Stevenson was soon active in London literary life, becoming acquainted with many of the writers of the time, including Andrew Lang, Edmund Gosse, and Leslie Stephen, the editor of the Cornhill Magazine who took an interest in Stevenson's work. Stephen took Stevenson to visit a patient at the Edinburgh Infirmary named William Ernest Henley, an energetic and talkative man with a wooden leg. Henley became a close friend and occasional literary collaborator, until a quarrel broke up the friendship in 1888, and he is often considered to be the model for Long John Silver in Treasure Island.

Stevenson was sent to Menton on the French Riviera in November 1873 to recuperate after his health failed. He returned in better health in April 1874 and settled down to his studies, but he returned to France several times after that. He made long and frequent trips to the neighborhood of the Forest of Fontainebleau, staying at Barbizon, Grez-sur-Loing, and Nemours and becoming a member of the artists' colonies there. He also traveled to Paris to visit galleries and the theatres. He qualified for the Scottish bar in July 1875, and his father added a brass plate to the Heriot Row house reading "R.L. Stevenson, Advocate". His law studies did influence his books, but he never practised law; all his energies were spent in travel and writing. One of his journeys was a canoe voyage in Belgium and France with Sir Walter Simpson, a friend from the Speculative Society, a frequent travel companion, and the author of The Art of Golf (1887). This trip was the basis of his first travel book An Inland Voyage (1878).

Marriage

The canoe voyage with Simpson brought Stevenson to Grez in September 1876 where he met Fanny Van de Grift Osbourne (1840–1914), born in Indianapolis. She had married at age 17 and moved to Nevada to rejoin husband Samuel after his participation in the American Civil War. Their children were Isobel (or "Belle"), Lloyd, and Hervey (who died in 1875). But anger over her husband's infidelities led to a number of separations. In 1875, she had taken her children to France where she and Isobel studied art.

Stevenson returned to Britain shortly after this first meeting, but Fanny apparently remained in his thoughts, and he wrote the essay "On falling in love" for the Cornhill Magazine. They met again early in 1877 and became lovers. Stevenson spent much of the following year with her and her children in France. In August 1878, she returned to San Francisco and Stevenson remained in Europe, making the walking trip that formed the basis for Travels with a Donkey in the Cévennes (1879). But he set off to join her in August 1879, against the advice of his friends and without notifying his parents. He took second-class passage on the steamship Devonia, in part to save money but also to learn how others traveled and to increase the adventure of the journey. He then traveled overland by train from New York City to California. He later wrote about the experience in The Amateur Emigrant. It was good experience for his writing, but it broke his health.

He was near death when he arrived in Monterey, California, where some local ranchers nursed him back to health. He stayed for a time at the French Hotel located at 530 Houston Street, now a museum dedicated to his memory called the "Stevenson House". While there, he often dined "on the cuff," as he said, at a nearby restaurant run by Frenchman Jules Simoneau which stood at what is now Simoneau Plaza; several years later, he sent Simoneau an inscribed copy of his novel Strange Case of Dr Jekyll and Mr Hyde (1886), writing that it would be a stranger case still if Robert Louis Stevenson ever forgot Jules Simoneau. While in Monterey, he wrote an evocative article about "the Old Pacific Capital" of Monterey.

By December 1879, Stevenson had recovered his health enough to continue to San Francisco where he struggled "all alone on forty-five cents a day, and sometimes less, with quantities of hard work and many heavy thoughts," in an effort to support himself through his writing. But by the end of the winter, his health was broken again and he found himself at death's door. Fanny was now divorced and recovered from her own illness, and she came to his bedside and nursed him to recovery. "After a while," he wrote, "my spirit got up again in a divine frenzy, and has since kicked and spurred my vile body forward with great emphasis and success." When his father heard of his condition, he cabled him money to help him through this period.

Fanny and Robert were married in May 1880, although he said that he was "a mere complication of cough and bones, much fitter for an emblem of mortality than a bridegroom." He travelled with his new wife and her son Lloyd north of San Francisco to Napa Valley and spent a summer honeymoon at an abandoned mining camp on Mount Saint Helena. He wrote about this experience in The Silverado Squatters. He met Charles Warren Stoddard, co-editor of the Overland Monthly and author of South Sea Idylls, who urged Stevenson to travel to the South Pacific, an idea which returned to him many years later. In August 1880, he sailed with Fanny and Lloyd from New York to Britain and found his parents and his friend Sidney Colvin on the wharf at Liverpool, happy to see him return home. Gradually, his wife was able to patch up differences between father and son and make herself a part of the family through her charm and wit.

Attempted settlement in Europe and the US

Stevenson searched in vain between 1880 and 1887 for a residence suitable to his health. He spent his summers at various places in Scotland and England, including Westbourne, Dorset, a residential area in Bournemouth. It was during his time in Bournemouth that he wrote the story Strange Case of Dr Jekyll and Mr Hyde, naming the character Mr. Poole after the town of Poole which is situated next to Bournemouth. In Westbourne, he named his house Skerryvore after the tallest lighthouse in Scotland, which his uncle Alan had built (1838–44). In the wintertime, Stevenson travelled to France and lived at Davos Platz and the Chalet de Solitude at Hyères, where he was very happy for a time. "I have so many things to make life sweet for me," he wrote, "it seems a pity I cannot have that other one thing—health. But though you will be angry to hear it, I believe, for myself at least, what is is best." In spite of his ill health, he produced the bulk of his best-known work during these years. Treasure Island was published under the pseudonym "Captain George North" and became his first widely popular book; he wrote it during this time, along with Kidnapped, Strange Case of Dr Jekyll and Mr Hyde (which established his wider reputation), The Black Arrow: A Tale of the Two Roses, A Child's Garden of Verses, and Underwoods. He gave a copy of Kidnapped to his friend and frequent Skerryvore visitor Henry James.

His father died in 1887 and Stevenson felt free to follow the advice of his physician to try a complete change of climate, so he headed for Colorado with his mother and family. But after landing in New York, they decided to spend the winter in the Adirondacks at a cure cottage now known as Stevenson Cottage at Saranac Lake, New York. During the intensely cold winter, Stevenson wrote some of his best essays, including Pulvis et Umbra. He also began The Master of Ballantrae and lightheartedly planned a cruise to the southern Pacific Ocean for the following summer.

Politics

Stevenson believed in Conservatism for most of his life. His cousin and biographer Sir Graham Balfour said that "he probably throughout life would, if compelled to vote, have always supported the Conservative candidate." In 1866, Stevenson voted for Benjamin Disraeli, future Conservative Prime Minister of the United Kingdom, over Thomas Carlyle for the Lord Rectorship of the University of Edinburgh. During his college years, he briefly identified himself as a "red-hot socialist". He wrote at age 26: "I look back to the time when I was a Socialist with something like regret.... Now I know that in thus turning Conservative with years, I am going through the normal cycle of change and travelling in the common orbit of men's opinions."

Journey to the Pacific

In June 1888, Stevenson chartered the yacht Casco and set sail with his family from San Francisco. The vessel "plowed her path of snow across the empty deep, far from all track of commerce, far from any hand of help." The sea air and thrill of adventure for a time restored his health, and for nearly three years he wandered the eastern and central Pacific, stopping for extended stays at the Hawaiian Islands where he became a good friend of King Kalākaua. He befriended the king's niece Princess Victoria Kaiulani, who also had Scottish heritage. He spent time at the Gilbert Islands, Tahiti, New Zealand, and the Samoan Islands. During this period, he completed The Master of Ballantrae, composed two ballads based on the legends of the islanders, and wrote The Bottle Imp. He preserved the experience of these years in his various letters and in his In the South Seas (which was published posthumously). He made a voyage in 1889 with Lloyd on the trading schooner Equator, visiting Butaritari, Mariki, Apaiang, and Abemama in the Gilbert Islands. They spent several months on Abemama with tyrant-chief Tem Binoka, whom Stevenson described in In the South Seas.

Stevenson left Sydney on the Janet Nicoll in April 1890 for his third and final voyage among the South Seas islands. He intended to produce another book of travel writing to follow his earlier book In the South Seas, but it was his wife who eventually published her journal of their third voyage. (Fanny misnames the ship in her account The Cruise of the Janet Nichol.) A fellow passenger was Jack Buckland, whose stories of life as an island trader became the inspiration for the character of Tommy Hadden in The Wrecker (1892), which Stevenson and Lloyd Osbourne wrote together. Buckland visited the Stevensons at Vailima in 1894.

Last years

In 1890, Stevenson purchased a tract of about 400 acres (1.6 km^2) in Upolu, an island in Samoa where he established himself on his estate in the village of Vailima after two aborted attempts to visit Scotland. He took the native name Tusitala (Samoan for "Teller of Tales"). His influence spread among the Samoans, who consulted him for advice, and he soon became involved in local politics. He was convinced that the European officials who had been appointed to rule the Samoans were incompetent, and he published A Footnote to History after many futile attempts to resolve the matter. This was such a stinging protest against existing conditions that it resulted in the recall of two officials, and Stevenson feared for a time that it would result in his own deportation. He wrote to Colvin, "I used to think meanly of the plumber; but how he shines beside the politician!"

He also found time to work at his writing, although he felt that "there was never any man had so many irons in the fire". He wrote The Beach of Falesa, Catriona (titled David Balfour in the US), The Ebb-Tide, and the Vailima Letters during this period.

Stevenson grew depressed and wondered if he had exhausted his creative vein, as he had been "overworked bitterly" and that the best he could write was "ditch-water". He even feared that he might again become a helpless invalid. He rebelled against this idea: "I wish to die in my boots; no more Land of Counterpane for me. To be drowned, to be shot, to be thrown from a horse — ay, to be hanged, rather than pass again through that slow dissolution." He then suddenly had a return of energy and he began work on Weir of Hermiston. "It's so good that it frightens me," he is reported to have exclaimed. He felt that this was the best work he had done.

On 3 December 1894, Stevenson was talking to his wife and straining to open a bottle of wine when he suddenly exclaimed, "What's that?", asked his wife "does my face look strange?", and collapsed. He died within a few hours, probably of a cerebral haemorrhage. He was 44 years old. The Samoans insisted on surrounding his body with a watch-guard during the night and on bearing him on their shoulders to nearby Mount Vaea, where they buried him on a spot overlooking the sea on land donated by British Acting Vice Consul Thomas Trood. Stevenson had always wanted his Requiem inscribed on his tomb:

Under the wide and starry sky,

Dig the grave and let me lie.

Glad did I live and gladly die,

And I laid me down with a will.

This be the verse you grave for me:

Here he lies where he longed to be;

Home is the sailor, home from sea,

And the hunter home from the hill.

Stevenson was loved by the Samoans, and his tombstone epigraph was translated to a Samoan song of grief. (Source: Wikipedia)